MW00833862

VALLEY OF SECRETS

THE LAST HEIRESS ~ BOOK 1

Morgan Knight

GREEN RHINO
MEDIA

www.greenrhinomedia.com

Valley Of Secrets

First Edition

Green Rhino Media LLC
228 Park Ave S, Suite 15958
New York, NY 10003-1502
United States of America

www.greenrhinomedia.com/valley-of-secrets

ISBN 978-1-949247-14-5 (hardcover)
ISBN 978-1-949247-13-8 (paperback)
ISBN 978-1-949247-12-1 (eBook)

Library of Congress Control Number: 2019914712

ACKNOWLEDGMENTS

The journey of a debut author is rife with unknowns and self-doubt. To that end I wish to acknowledge those who believed in me, helped me stay the course, kept the faith and cheered me on. Their dedication has enabled this book to come to life.

Diana—I still remember the beginning of this journey; having never done anything like this before I think there was some due skepticism about heading down this path. Your incredibly surprised and genuinely encouraging reaction after reading the first draft of the first chapter was all I needed to find the energy to finish it. Now here we are, published! So many readthroughs, so many additions, changes, deletions…there's no way I could have done this without you…thank-you!

Nikki—for editing up a storm on this project and helping to breathe even more gusto into every word.

Toni—for proofreading like a legend, despite getting tongue-twisted over our hate-to-love villain, Massimino.

Jessi—for your tireless iterations of the cover and putting up with the idea changes and the back-and-forthing until we got it *just* right!

My reading team—thank-you for your input and considerations.

My family—you guys rock—I missed out on so much as you went off to entertain yourselves while I sat at home and typed out chapters. I appreciate your patience, your understanding, and the significantly reduced level of mayhem that remained as the house sat quiet in your absence. This is all for you.

CONTENTS

Chapter One

T he warm glow of candles, too many to count, evoked
cautious comfort as their light flickered against the gray
stone walls.

It's a church, a small church—no, a chapel.

Ahead of her was an imposing stone altar set below three tall, lancet
windows, and even from the back of the building, it commanded her
attention. Heavy wooden beams, blackened and charred, supported
the high, steeply-pitched roof above. The pews were arranged in
perfect, even rows on either side of the central aisle. The floor was
marble; its surface cool and smooth beneath her bare feet.

The air felt stagnant and smelled musky, as though the doors had been
closed for a long time, starving the space of fresh air.

She peered over her shoulder; the motion alerted her to a hood
shrouding her head. She reached up with both hands to gently push it
back; freeing her long, dark brown hair, she stared down at a shapeless,
kaftan-style linen cloak.

A white robe? This isn't mine.

Wait, someone has dressed me!

There was no opening in the front or back—only at the top, and it
hung loosely around her neck and shoulders. It was full-length,
reaching her ankles. Raising a hand to her chest revealed that she was
naked beneath the robe, her skin tingled at the sensation as her fingers
grazed her left breast and continued down toward her belly.

The strangeness of the situation raised alarm bells, though nothing
appeared overtly threatening. The place and her clothes were
unfamiliar, and how or why she came to be here was unknown.

Individually, these elements might have aroused curiosity, but combined, they led to a sense of uneasiness. Danger. *Fear.*

Run! screamed her rational thoughts.

Her eyes darted around the rear of the chapel before focusing on the entrance. Beyond the wooden, double doors, two roaring fire pits burned, and between them a rocky path wound its way from the chapel. Farther in the distance, she marveled at the rugged beauty of the mountains, their peaks soaring above the scattered clouds; the entire shadowy scene was bathed in a pale white glow from the hidden moon overhead.

Where am I?

A light gust blew through the entrance, carrying with it the earthy smell of pine and sending another tingle through her body as the robe fluttered against her bare skin. The breeze diminished and seemed to dissolve her confusion and uncertainty—somehow the fear no longer disturbed her. It had been replaced with a sense of calm, and a desire to venture deeper.

The candles swayed feverishly, disrupted by the wind. She drew her gaze from the mountains, past the glowing fire pits, through the arched doorway, and back toward the front of the chapel. She took a few measured steps forward, the faint padding of her feet against the floor breaking the silence.

The sultry radiance of candlelight stirred feelings of intimacy in a place otherwise regarded as sacred—safe; a space to be revered and to seek salvation, or even refuge, if needed.

Decapitated saintly statues lined the walls, positioned on shelves that were recessed into the stone. Despite their circumstance, each was neatly in its place, indicating an obvious sense that the chapel had been maintained, just infrequently occupied.

Who lit all these candles?

"Hello?" she asked softly, not intending to sound so timid. There was no answer as she cautiously continued on.

"Hello? Is anyone here?" she called again; more poised this time. The faint echo of her words reverberated in response.

Her attention was drawn to the three tall windows beyond the altar; through the clear glass, a brilliant full moon came into view. It rested above the mountains in the distance, nestled between wispy clouds as they drifted across the sky.

Halfway up the aisle, she shifted her focus to the headless statues as another flurry of wind swept in from the entrance, this time causing a goose bump-filled shudder to envelop her.

"The altar." The words pierced the whirling frenzy of air in a loud whisper, as if the wind itself spoke them, the candles flickering their discontent at the disturbance.

Who was that?

She snapped her head around to the chapel entrance, eyes wide and hair whipping her face as she searched for the source of the voice. She was still alone, as far as she could tell.

"Please answer me. Is anyone here?" She spoke firmly, attempting to sound in control of the situation while feeling quite the opposite.

Okay, her common sense interjected, again trying to be heard over her wayward emotions. *It's time to get out of here! Nothing about this feels right; let's go—now!*

Before she could react, another breeze swirled through the air, sending a prickly chill through her body. Once again, the eerily whispered words floated through the space, spoken clearer and more like a command: "The altar."

The blaring alarm in her mind instructed her to turn and run, but something held her there, in a trance-like state—she was unable to respond to her rational self, yet she was completely aware of everything.

She started making her way toward the altar.

Or maybe I'm doing exactly what I want to be doing, enticed another—perhaps deeper—part of her mind.

Her inner battle of sensible versus emotional was cut short as she neared the altar. Something unknown, unnatural—far more powerful than curiosity—continued to compel her forward.

The sanctuary was two steps above the rest of the chapel. The impressive altar lay dormant, with heavy sandstones forming a solid base. The top was made of the same material; a single slab, unpolished and roughly textured in its natural form. Something seemed amiss, but she could not fathom what.

Her attention wandered across the details in the masonry work as she ascended; the stone surface tainted by dark stains.

Did someone spill the communion wine? she wondered, noting that the moon was nearly directly in line with the central window; its light was blushed now with a reddish tinge.

Wait, is this just a dream?

The idea made sense to her as she raked a hand across the altar, almost caressing—connecting—with the stone and the stains; its solid ruggedness felt inviting and comforting, as if somehow bridging a pathway to something—to some*one*.

If this is a dream, it's unlike any I've had before. But it can't be, it's too clear...the sensations are too real, too vivid.

A glint of reflected candlelight caught her attention. *Metal, a dagger? Two daggers!*

Beneath the windows and, until now, hidden from view by the altar, hung a pair of daggers in the center of the wall. They were mounted diagonally, one above the other, each tip pointing in opposite directions. They appeared old, though expertly crafted and meticulously polished.

There's no crucifix here?

This was what seemed off earlier; an altar with no crucifix! In fact, there were no crosses *anywhere* in the chapel.

Decapitated saints, no crucifix, daggers. This doesn't seem like a place where good things happen.

Another rush of wind, gentler this time, broke her thoughts, and she found herself listening for the ominous whisper once more.

"Emilia..."

From the front of the altar, she spun toward the entrance.

Who said that?

Standing in the center of the double doors was a figure. Judging by the build, it appeared to be a man. He wore a dark brown or perhaps black robe, his face concealed by a hood.

"H-Hello?" she stammered.

He started down the aisle, saying nothing.

"Who are you? Where is this place—how did I get here?" she demanded.

There was still no response as he proceeded at an unrushed, measured pace toward her. As he neared, the details became clearer: his monk-style robe was black, and a simple, frayed beige rope pulled it in at the waist. The top of his hood hung over his head, preventing Emilia from seeing his eyes. Candlelight glistened off his chin, hinting that perhaps he had a short beard, though it was difficult to tell. In the low light, she noticed his hands were behind his back.

What's he holding? He's almost here. Should I run? Get one of those daggers? Get both *of those daggers? Oh my God, what do I do? Get me out of here!*

The logical part of her mind raced as it cast all the knowns and unknowns of the situation in a dangerous light, searching for a way out. But she remained fixed there, watching him approach. The mysterious stranger stopped a short distance from her. He brought his hands in front of him.

He's not holding anything.

Pushing the hood off his head, the glow of candles illuminated the stranger's features. Yes, it was a man; tousled dark hair, olive complexion, chiseled jawline, and a scar beginning high on his left cheek and disappearing beneath his short, well-groomed beard.

He appeared older than her, and his liquid, sea-blue eyes were striking, filled with intensity and raw, untamed emotion.

I don't know this man, but he seems familiar. That look in his eyes— on his face...what is that? Longing? Excitement? Desire? Love?

"Who are you? Where are we?" Emilia asked, painstakingly working to hide the panic and fear she was sure were present in her words.

"Be calm." His voice was deep and rugged as the wind blew again, cueing the candles to frolic and her skin to tingle.

The wind passed and this time left her feeling as if she were in a loving embrace, protected from harm.

He continued down the aisle and up the stairs of the sanctuary. He was tall, and as he stood before her, Emilia inhaled, overcome by his divine earthy scent. It felt comfortable, like a good memory.

Sandalwood? Cedarwood?

She offered no resistance as he leaned into her, turning her face to his and closing her eyes, awaiting his kiss.

Instead, he pressed his forehead to hers. "I've found you."

Found me? Emilia's eyes popped open.

"Are you ready?" He stepped back and looked toward the windows; she followed his eyes and saw the moon was now looming in almost perfect alignment with the middle window, strikingly red and sinister.

"Ready for what? I don't know who you are. You must be thinking of someone else," Emilia replied, knowing the words to be true yet allowing herself to nurture the inexplicable longing to indeed be the one he was searching for.

Her thoughts were suddenly interrupted by a shuffling sound coming from behind her. She watched as a group of people entered, all shrouded in identical hooded robes, and proceeded single file toward the altar. The last of the group pulled both doors closed with a solid thud, sealing them all inside.

Ignoring the commotion, the enchanting stranger gazed deeply into Emilia's eyes, caressing her cheek. His hand was soft yet reassuring. "All will be as you want it to be," he whispered before circling the altar as he headed for the window.

The daggers!

Her mind raced but she felt no fear, only a composed state of calm; this extraordinary situation was exactly the way things were supposed to be.

She stared at the figures entering the chapel—a dozen of them had now formed an arc below the steps to the altar, blocking the aisle. All still cloaked in hoods, they faced her with their hands clasped in front of them.

Perhaps one of these people will tell me what's going on?

Before Emilia had a chance to speak, her mysterious stranger returned with one of the daggers. He held it in his right hand, fingers gripping the handle against his upper chest, with the tip of its blade pointing to his stomach. "Finally, it is time. Ready?"

Time for what? No, I'm not ready!

"Yes," she exhaled in a whisper, her own voice betraying her.

Reaching out, he took the neck of her robe in his left hand, pulling it away from her body. The gathered crowd began chanting a solemn verse in a language she didn't recognize.

Staring intently into her eyes, the stranger touched the blade to her robe. Its razor sharpness effortlessly sliced through the taut fabric, the sound barely reaching her ears over the chanting.

Emilia's common sense mounted a fresh protest: *Stop this! Get out of here!*

She said nothing, standing completely motionless as the dagger split the robe before he set it on the altar; a metallic *clink* and the harsh scrape of metal on stone rang in her ears as her pulse quickened. The cool evening air sent a tingle across her exposed skin as he tore the rest of the robe apart and pushed it over her shoulders, letting it fall into a crumpled pile at her feet. She stood naked before an altar, in a foreign chapel, facing an unusual congregation—yet even so, an eerie sensation of calm and familiarity remained. It was as though this was the most normal thing in the world, her usual modesty replaced with a serene comfort.

The stranger scooped her into his arms, the roughness of his robe prickling against her as their eyes locked; his seeming to reveal many lifetimes of experience. "I love you always. I will forever be grateful to you for this," he whispered, sending an explosion of heat through every fiber within as he softly kissed her lips.

She offered no resistance as he laid her on the altar; Emilia's silky hair settled around her face as she felt the coarse stone against her bare skin.

The chanting heightened; beauty to her ears despite the unsettling screech of the dagger as it was retrieved from the altar.

He's going to hurt me, maybe even kill me—get out of here now!

"This is where I'm supposed to be." Her voice was assured, her breathing shallow.

Whoa, where did that come from?

Emilia looked on as the stranger took the dagger to his own robe. Cutting first at the neck, then downward, he stopped when he reached the worn rope serving as a belt. Placing the dagger on the altar, he fluidly shrugged out of it, allowing the top half to hang behind him while the rest of the robe was held by the braided rope around his waist. Emilia's eyes were drawn to his chest where a scar, long-since healed and overgrown with hair, cut a line across his torso.

He spoke no words as he picked up the dagger once more, catching Emilia's eyes with his intense gaze. She felt her heart pounding as the handsome stranger deftly moved the blade to his chest, watching him wince, almost imperceptibly as he followed the same line as the scar, reopening the old wound and causing blood to seep slowly from it. Emilia gulped before nodding, each movement of her head slow and deliberate as though she understood why this was happening.

His eyes pierced hers as he touched the blade to her chest, just above her left breast. Emilia inhaled sharply but could not seem to summon the will for any action to stop it. She felt the cool metal break her skin and every hair stood on end as it glided, slowly—sensually across her body, almost reaching her thigh.

Lifting the dagger, he held it high above his head, fists clasped tightly around the handle. The blade was pointed directly downward, revealing a trace of red liquid along it.

His blood, my blood.

Her breath quickened further as she noticed tears welling in his eyes, the candlelight shimmering in them.

"I know this is how it must be, I *do* want this too," she offered, trying to relieve his pain, fighting back tears of her own.

Why am I trying to comfort him? Her rational side fought to be heard. *He just cut me! He's going to stab me with that dagger—get up and run!*

The crowd's chanting increased in both volume and intensity, building to a crescendo.

"I promise, this will not be like the last time," he murmured, directing the dagger's blade over Emilia, the tip hovering high above her heart. He glanced out the window; her eyes followed his and she gasped at the sight of the moon—it was the color of red rust.

A howling gust stormed through the chapel and the chanting persisted even louder than before. Over the noise, a foreboding, raspy voice uttered one word: "Now."

No, definitely not now! Stop!

"Yessss," she whispered. With blood seeping from her fresh wound, Emilia thrust her bare chest upward, surrendering to her fate as the candles swayed wildly, each mounting its own final protest before every last one extinguished, plunging the chapel into darkness.

Chapter Two

With a gasp, Emilia's brilliant green eyes burst open. She sat bolt upright in bed, disoriented and breathing heavily as her gaze darted uncontrollably around the room. There was a quick knock at her door before the handle clicked and it was pushed open.

"Hey sleepyhead, want some breakfast?" Amanda asked, barging in, her long, wavy blonde hair streaming behind her. "Whoa—are you all right?" Amanda's brown eyes widened as they scanned the room.

"Um, yeah…I mean, I guess so…sorry, I just had the wildest dream…I think…" Emilia trailed off as she fell back onto her pillows, closing her eyes for a moment.

"Well it must have been an interesting one—what have you done in here? It looks like a tornado sprung up during the night!"

"Interesting doesn't begin to describe it." Emilia opened her eyes once more and looked around. There was clothing strewn everywhere, an overturned lamp in the corner, and practically every object atop her dressing table was askew in some fashion. "What the…? I…it wasn't like this when I went to bed last night. Did you do this?"

She propped herself back up and touched her face, scrunching her eyes shut then opening them again to make sure she was conscious.

"Wasn't me! Unless you had a visitor last night, this mess is all on you. Like, literally." Amanda picked up a couple of sweaters scattered across the covers before bending down to collect another top from the floor.

Emilia's thoughts flashed back to the swirling wind in her dream as she surveyed the chaos that was her bedroom.

"Sleepwalking maybe? You said you had a wacky dream; want to talk about it?" Amanda asked, settling herself down onto the bed, folding one leg under her.

"No," sighed Emilia. "Maybe later though. Let me think about it a little. It was so weird…so real, so…" She struggled to find the right words in her groggy state.

"All right, I'm here if you want to chat," Amanda said. "How did things go with Brandon last night anyway? Did you two work things out?"

Emilia sighed and rolled over. "No, he broke up with me. Or how'd he put it? We're going to 'take a break for a while and see what happens'."

"What? Emmi, I'm so sorry…" Amanda's shoulders slumped. She reached across and patted Emilia's leg through the heavy covers. "What happened?" Amanda scooted closer, rubbing Emilia's back.

Emilia forced a smile though her eyes were mournful. "Oh, you know…same old story. He said I was being too distant and thought I wasn't interested in being together. But it's not true, I really like him. It's like all the others, they all say the same thing. I just don't get it, what do they want—"

"Whoa, whoa, slow down…don't make this something it isn't…you haven't even had that many boyfriends, I mean, I've had *way* more." Amanda winked.

"What does *that* mean?" Emilia countered defensively, "Is it supposed to make me feel better that you've had more boyfriends than me?"

"No—no, no, no…that's not what I meant at all." Amanda looked down at some of the clothes scattered on the floor as she raked her fingers through her hair and clutched the back of her neck.

"Well, what *do* you mean then, Miss I've-Had-So-Many-Boyfriends? Because it kind of seems like you're being a bit of a jerk…I just got dumped!"

"Emmi! All I meant was, it's not like you've been dumped *that* many times."

Emilia sighed and fell back against her pillows again. "I'm sorry, I know, I'm just..."

"Hey, it's all right." Amanda lay down next to Emilia and gave her sister a hug.

"Thanks." Emilia said quietly as she squeezed Amanda, a smile reluctantly creeping across her face and a quick laugh escaping her lips.

"Okay, that's better. Now, want to start over?" Amanda giggled as she sat up, extending her arms toward Emilia.

Emilia took hold of Amanda's hands, pulling herself up.

"So...Brandon. I know you felt like something was up with him, but you weren't expecting this—*right?*"

Emilia paused in thought, gazing out her window then back to Amanda.

"I don't know...I mean, yeah, I kind of knew this was coming—I told you about the talks we'd been having lately and how he was getting frustrated with me. I could kind of *feel* it too. I just didn't know what to do about it. I mean, I get what you're saying about it only being a handful of guys but it's kind of a pattern for me, you know? It's definitely not the first time I've heard this, or something a lot like it— why do I put up these walls, why am I so afraid of letting people get close to me?"

"Hey...don't beat yourself up—you know *we're* close, and there's Chelsea, Mom and Dad; you're totally capable of opening up...just really selective or something. As for the guys, I mean, who's to say you just haven't found the right one yet—"

"That's not it! I mean, Brandon's a *great* guy; he's sweet, funny, works hard, plus he's really hot." Emilia looked at Amanda who was nodding in agreement. "Jake, Chase, Luke...yeah, my list might not be that long, but they were all really cool guys...and for whatever reason I just couldn't ever open up to them. I'm not a robot, I have feelings, but...I don't know."

"Well, you still keep in touch with Chase, you two are friends and you still hang out." Amanda's expression seemed hopeful—like she'd found a possible silver lining in the dark clouds which seemed to be circling her sister.

"I guess, but we're just friends—most of the time anyway...I guess the occasional benefits are a good thing." Emilia managed a smile. "But he's up at MIT, I'm here...and you know I don't really think we'll be more than that—even if we did live in the same city."

"All right, look...I've known you almost your whole life and I really don't think there's anything wrong with you. Okay, so you're kind of guarded. Maybe it's something to do with what you went through—you know, with your parents and everything, or maybe it's just your personality...but Emmi, you're awesome."

Emilia nudged Amanda affectionately.

"As for guys, you're the picky one! There are a bunch of great guys out there. Like, really good guys who are totally into you. You just keep your guard up for a long time and I think that maybe comes off as being a little...unavailable, or something. But now you *are* available, hmm..." Amanda raised her eyebrows.

"Whoa...slow down." Emilia rubbed her eyes. "I don't even want to *talk* about other guys right now, so put your arrows away, Cupid. Okay?" Emilia wore a stern expression as she stretched.

"Okay, okay...fine, I was just—so it was a wild one, hey?" Amanda glanced around the room.

"Not really, we just went out to dinner and he said his piece. He even took me to my favorite restaurant, which was nice of him. I guess he wanted to let me down gently."

"Spice? That's nice...I mean, nice restaurant, I like...ugh." Amanda smiled apologetically, "But I was asking about your dream; it sounded—and looks—like *it* was wild."

"Oh, right." Emilia blushed at her misunderstanding.

Amanda chuckled, snuggling under the covers and giving Emilia a loving squeeze. "I'm going to take full advantage of your new relationship status and get your mind off him; we're going out tonight! Wait, what's the rest of your mid-term schedule look like again? I've got my last one today." Amanda's eyes lit up at the prospect of planning an impromptu night out.

"I've just got one more on Thursday: *online journalism and click throughs, cracking the algorithm*. And then I'm done. I've got a little more prep to do for it, but the course is pretty easy, and the professor likes me."

"Oh, I know the answer!" Amanda's eyes widened. "Just put a Kardashian's name in the headline and everyone clicks on it and they message you a Pulitzer, right?"

"Ahh, that economics wit, quit beating on this lowly journalist."

"Correction," Amanda held up a finger. "I believe that's lowly journalist wannabe, isn't it?"

Emilia tossed a pillow at her. "Get out of here!"

"Fine then, you can clean all this up by yourself. Just doing my part to help you feel better." Amanda winked.

As Amanda neared the door, Emilia called, "Wait! What time is it?"

"It's a little after ten."

"Ten?" groaned Emilia. "I can't believe I slept this late."

"Yeah, I knocked earlier, kind of loudly, to see if you wanted some eggs—but you didn't answer...must have been dead asleep."

Emilia's mind flashed back to the altar, lying naked upon it and the dagger plunging toward her chest. She could almost feel the wind rushing across her skin.

"Whoa, are you really okay?" Amanda asked. "You look like you've just seen a ghost."

"Yeah...yeah...I'm fine." Emilia came back to the present moment. "I almost feel like I *am* a ghost."

Amanda reached out, playfully pinching Emilia's arm.

"Ouch!" Emilia shrieked.

Amanda giggled. "You're not." Crossing her arms over her chest, she added, "But you've got to fill me in on this dream...you seem a little freaked out by it—and I'm a little freaked out by this." Amanda gestured to the mess.

"All right," Emilia relented. "Later though. Let me wake up and...get my thoughts together."

"I was getting ready to head out to campus anyway—unless you want me to make you some breakfast?"

Emilia shook her head.

"Well then, you've got the place to yourself until this afternoon." She hesitated by the bed. "I've got my macro exam, but if you're not feeling right call me, okay? I'm here for you, anytime, anything you need."

"Thanks. I'm fine." Emilia appreciated Amanda's concern, but she couldn't talk about this just yet. She still hadn't fully processed it herself. *How would I even start to explain this dream to Amanda? It's just too strange.* "Good luck on your exam, and thanks again for caring."

"Sure thing. I'll see you later." Amanda kissed her on the cheek. "I love you. Stay safe, okay?"

"Love you too, and of course I will."

Emilia and Amanda were sisters in all but the biological sense, after Emilia's mother and father passed away, they had been raised together by Amanda's parents. Their two families had been very close prior, and Emilia, having no other known relatives, was taken in by the Campbells. Amanda's father, Brian, was a partner at a successful wealth management company and her mother, Pamela, chaired a non-profit organization advocating for better access to education for inner-city neighborhoods. Both found their work intellectually fulfilling, and Brian's hard work and success provided a comfortable lifestyle for their family in Short Hills, New Jersey. After adopting Emilia, they had no more children and raised Amanda and Emilia in a happy home filled with love.

Best friends and sisters, after completing their schooling together, Emilia and Amanda moved to Philadelphia to study at the University of Pennsylvania. Now in their senior years, Emilia chose to major in communications, while Amanda pursued an economics program.

Their parents had purchased an apartment for the girls in the Rittenhouse neighborhood, across the river but close to their school in University City. Brian had joked that he believed it would be a good investment and he hoped to sell it at the end of their degrees with enough gain in value to cover their tuition costs. He cherished both girls dearly and made it a personal mission to help set them up for professional success. He was also a practical, business-minded man, too; Emilia and Amanda would be able to focus on their studies if the financial burden of their education wasn't a concern.

After a few minutes of shuffling around, Amanda left the apartment, the door closing with a solid click. Emilia stayed in bed a little longer, checking her phone and sorting through a few messages and posts.

Oh, nice one, Brandon. Don't waste any time letting the world know you're single again. I just finished telling Amanda how great you are— now you kind of seem like an asshole!

Emilia let her phone drop with a light thump on top of her feathery quilt. She did her best to push the breakup out of her mind as she enjoyed a satisfying stretch before getting up and heading to the kitchen.

The apartment was quiet and still; the morning sun of a fall day in October shone through the floor-to-ceiling windows. Emilia noticed the warm light reflecting off the tiny flecks of dust floating through the air, and the aroma of bacon lingered from what must have been Amanda's breakfast.

Out the windows, the sky was a clear, striking blue without a cloud to be seen. She gazed across the skyline and contemplated how to best start the day. Below, the city bustled with mid-morning activity; cars, trucks, and buses stopped and started their ways through the grind of traffic while pedestrians paced along the crowded streets. Just another day to most people.

16

For Emilia, it felt anything but routine. Her mind still replayed her dream—the emotions, the images, all burned with intensity.

I need to clear my head. I need a run.

Changing into her black running tights and a long sleeve shirt, Emilia laced up her running shoes, pulled her silky brown hair into a ponytail, then headed downstairs.

The elevator pinged as the doors opened to the lobby. Alfred, the building's bellman, glanced up from his desk by the entrance.

"Good morning, Miss Campbell." His friendly and familiar grin matched his kind brown eyes, and his hair was neatly styled; its silver color complementing the manor house gray of his uniform.

"Good morning, Alfred," she replied. "How are you today?"

Alfred had worked the day shift since the building opened a few years earlier—the perfect way to ease into retirement, as he described. It suited him to be on his feet and active, and he kept the building ticking like a well-made clock.

"Oh, just wonderful, Miss Campbell. A fine morning, another splendid day to be alive."

"You're right, I love this time of year!" she agreed. "I'm heading out for a run, so I'll see you soon."

"Enjoy. I'll be here."

Emilia opened the main lobby doors before jogging down the steps. Her usual route brought her a few blocks through the city before leaving the grid and intersections in favor of the trail skirting the Schuylkill River. She ran north, toward Fairmont Park; at this time of morning, it was void of the typical weekday exercise enthusiasts. Emilia became lost in the motions, allowing her legs to direct her course while she took in the scenery. The river to her left was the smaller of the two framing the center city area. It flowed into its bigger brother, the Delaware River, which then became the Delaware Bay before completing its journey out to sea. On the other side towered the commanding 30th Street Station, and several bridges drew her attention along the trail.

As Emilia approached the Philadelphia Museum of Art, the crazy events of her dream continued to appear in her mind. The impressive building was perched upon a hill, constructed from tan stone and complete with soaring columns borrowed from Greek temple design. Emilia's legs led her in front of the museum, though not up the "Rocky" stairs made famous by Sylvester Stallone's character—more than a few tourists were already following his footsteps. A short distance past them, another small group took turns posing with his bronze likeness, all with hands held in victorious gestures above their heads.

She continued around the path and onward toward Boathouse Row, where rowing clubhouses lined the eastern shore of the river. The northernmost was the Sedgeley Club, distinct with its red hues and incorporation of the city's only operating lighthouse.

At the central terrace sculpture garden, Emilia took some deliberate, deep breaths as she marveled at The Spirit of Enterprise monument; the curving and twisting bronze behemoth of a man and eagle seized her attention as her heart thrashed in her chest, and heat radiated from her body. A solo rower headed upriver in a red boat. Beyond that was the busy interstate and closer by, cars whizzed along Kelly Drive. The earthy smell of fall lingered as she inhaled; Emilia heard the rustling and felt the slippery sensation of freshly fallen leaves on the path beneath her feet. Feeling aware of—and in tune with—the present moment, Emilia smiled.

It was just a dream. Must have been in some sort of sleep-walking rage last night and messed up my room. A crazy dream; that's all. Guess I took the break-up a little harder than I thought.

Refreshed and mind clear once more, Emilia picked up her pace, this time homeward bound. The sun, now a little higher in the sky, warmed the world around her. The reflections from small ripples off the river caught her eye from time to time as a slight breeze gently swept over her. It was a welcome relief toward the end of a good run, and so was the realization that her wild dream had been nothing more than that.

Chapter Three

Alfred was near the door as Emilia approached the entrance to her building.

"Welcome back, Miss Campbell. I trust you enjoyed your run?" he greeted, his long arm closing the door behind her.

"Yes, absolutely," she answered. "It was just what I needed—thanks for asking; and I know I've said it before, but please call me Emilia—or Emmi."

Alfred chuckled. "No can-do, I'm afraid. Call me old-fashioned that way, but you'll always be Miss Campbell to me. Also, before you go upstairs, I have a delivery for you—hold on, it's at my desk."

"Oh great. Has Amanda been shopping on Amazon again?"

"I don't think so. Not this time at least," Alfred replied a little more seriously. He collected a large envelope and handed it to Emilia who was tapping an upbeat tune with her fingers on the reception desk. "This was delivered by a local courier about ten minutes ago; it's addressed to you."

Emilia took the envelope from Alfred. "From the Law Offices of Rothman, Goldberg, and Holland," said Emilia out loud. "I haven't heard of that firm before."

"Well, I'm sure it's a mystery easily solved by opening it and seeing what's inside, Miss Campbell," Alfred winked.

"That's true," agreed Emilia. "It shouldn't require too many of my investigative journalistic skills to crack this case! I'll see you later." She tore open the envelope as she headed toward the elevators, pushing the call button when she reached them.

As the elevator whisked her toward their apartment on the twenty-first floor, Emilia removed a single page letter from the envelope; it was printed on the firm's letterhead and she quickly headed inside to read it.

Dear Miss Campbell,

Our firm has been engaged by a European law firm, Martin H. Thiess and Associates, who is seeking to contact an Emilia Meyer, born to an Anton and Genevieve Meyer, in relation to an estate matter in Slovakia. Through our collective research, we believe this may have been your name prior to being adopted by Brian and Pamela Campbell.

I do hope you will excuse the brevity of this letter; however, our objective here is twofold. Firstly, to locate Emilia Meyer, and then verify certain identifying information to ensure she is the correct individual being sought. Please understand that disclosure of any further details at this stage may work contrary to the latter part of our task.

There is some time sensitivity to this search and if, based on the cursory information provided here, you believe you may be the person whom we are seeking, I request that you contact me at your earliest convenience to discuss the matter further.

Yours Sincerely,

Jonathan Rothman
Partner

Emilia leaned back against the door, a look of disbelief on her face. Hope washed over her.

My parents! They know something about my parents!

That *was* her family name, and those *were* her parents' names, so could this be true? She needed to call this guy.

Emilia's heart raced. Her mouth was dry as she retrieved her phone, tucked snugly into the back pocket of her tights, and with a nervous anticipation dialed the number on the letterhead. After two rings, a friendly but professional voice answered.

"Rothman, Goldberg, and Holland. How may I assist you?"

"Hi…uh, my name is Emilia Campbell—Emilia Meyer…I received a letter from Jonathan Rothman…"

"Ah, yes, Miss Campbell. My name is Bridget. I organized the courier for your letter this morning. Mr. Rothman is eager to meet with you and asked me to schedule an appointment as a matter of priority when you called."

"Great, can you put me through to him now?"

"I'm sorry, but he's currently with a client."

Emilia fell silent. She felt she might burst having to delay her curiosity about something this important to her.

"Would you be able to come in this afternoon? Let's see…at four o'clock? I do know he'd like to meet you in person, and as soon as possible."

Emilia's spirits lifted. "All right, sure. That can work. Do you know what this is about at all?"

"I'm afraid I don't really know any more details—only that I need to ask you to bring as much identifying information as you can about yourself and your parents."

"Okay, I have my driver's license and passport, oh, and my birth certificate. But I really don't have much for my parents. I'm kind of hoping Mr. Rothman may know some more about them. There were a few papers we had, um…nothing that was all that useful—but it's all in a box at my parents'—my adopted parents'—house in New Jersey though." Emilia's hand shook, causing her phone to slip down slightly.

"No problem. I think the most important thing at this stage is meeting with Mr. Rothman. Come in this afternoon, bring what you have with you, and we'll start there."

"Okay, see you then." Emilia felt her chest pound as she placed her phone on the kitchen counter and set the letter beside it. She read it again, just to be sure she hadn't missed any information that might be helpful.

Is it really possible this could be a lead to learning more about my parents?

It was now almost noon. Emilia prepared some fresh fruit and yogurt before showering, dressing comfortably in sweatpants and a T-shirt, and getting ready to study.

Over the next few hours, she worked hard to stay focused on preparing for her last mid-term exam. It was difficult, her mind frequently wandering to her parents and what new information she might soon learn about them—yet at the same time, she told herself not to get her hopes up.

Shortly after three, Amanda returned home and saw Emilia with her books and notes spread out over their dining table.

"Hey, Emmi. Good to see you up and about—and even working hard by the looks of things. How are you feeling?" Amanda set her bag down on one of the chairs.

"Hey! Yeah, I went running earlier and feel so much better—and I got some good studying in, too. So how was your exam?" Emilia asked as she neared the kitchen counter and picked up the letter.

"It was fine; no real surprises, and I think I did well. Are you up for some yoga this afternoon? I think Jude has a class."

"Um…yoga would be great, even though your motivations may be a little different than mine—" Emilia grinned, raising her eyebrows suggestively.

Amanda smirked and bit her lip.

"But, I can't this afternoon. I've got some news."

"What news?"

"*This* news." Emilia handed the letter to Amanda, watching intently as she looked it over.

Amanda remained silent as she read; upon reaching the end, she looked up at Emilia with an expression somewhere between confused and surprised. She attempted a little humor. "Well…I guess this is far too specific to be one of those African email scams. Did you call them yet?"

Emilia chuckled. "Yeah, I sure hope that's not what I'm walking into! I'm meeting him at his office at four today. I need to leave soon, actually."

"Oooh, can I come too?"

"Sure, that would be great! Honestly, I'm feeling nervous—probably just anticipation. Their office is at Eighteenth and Market, so we can walk. You're sure you can handle missing Jude's class?"

"Well…I was looking forward to seeing that hunky yogi-god, but this is *way* cooler—he'll understand. That letter is kind of intriguing—a family estate matter in Slovakia? How exciting! Who knows? Perhaps you're some sort of long-lost princess!"

Emilia laughed. "Perhaps not. I think if I was royalty, I would have been able to find out a lot more about my family, you know, at least *some* path to follow."

"You never know." Amanda raised her eyebrows. "Maybe that's *why* you can't find anything about them; your family could have been forced to flee and go into hiding after some sort of revolution, or—"

"Yeah, or perhaps some great aunt left me a set of pearls."

"Oh, there's no way they'd go to *this* much trouble to find you all the way over here for that." Amanda waved a dismissive hand. "This is going to be awesome!"

"On that note, I'm going to get changed while you calm your imagination—a *lot!*"

Emilia headed to her bedroom and dressed in a navy ruffled lace sleeveless top and beige pencil skirt, then threw on a preppy tailored navy blazer before returning to the living room where Amanda was snacking on some trail mix, reading the letter again.

She looked up when Emilia entered the room. "Well, you look good of course, but not necessarily like a princess."

"Very funny," Emilia deadpanned. "That's enough with the whole princess thing. Do they even have princesses there?"

"Hmmm, good question. I'll have to look that up!" Amanda joked back. "I'll stop now. Just having some fun…seriously though, this is super interesting—even if you're not royalty. I know how much time you spent looking for answers when we were growing up."

Emilia sighed at the floor. "I still wonder about them at least once every day. Brian and Pam are incredible, and they really are Mom and Dad to me, but to know something about where I come from and where my parents grew up would be amazing. It's like there's a missing piece to me or something." Embarrassed by the cliché words, a goofy grin crept across her face.

"Oh, Emmi, it's ok," Amanda giggled at her sister's awkward expression, "I get it…well, I understand where you're coming from anyway," Amanda encouraged. "Let's get going—I want to say don't get your hopes up, but mine are kind of right up there for you, too. Come on, let's find out what this Mr. Rothman knows."

There was a slight chill in the air as Emilia and Amanda walked the few blocks to the law office, but it was a pleasant fall afternoon, nonetheless. The smell of roasted peanuts warming on a street cart hotplate wafted enticingly past Emilia's nose, and as they wove around other pedestrians and stopped at intersections, the two women talked over the noisy afternoon traffic as they strolled side by side.

"You know," Amanda said, "we're on break in a couple of days and we don't have any plans."

"I was thinking we'd probably go home for a few days at least."

"Yeah, but Mom and Dad will be away for another couple of weeks, so it would just be the two of us. We might as well just stay here."

"Gosh, they travel so much these days," Emilia said. "I think they've been away even more this year than last—they've definitely been making the most of their empty nester status since we came here for college."

"Yeah, the photos they've been posting of Argentina are pretty amazing though. Dad says 'hi' by the way—we spoke last week. They're having a great time and were getting ready to board their Antarctic cruise, so they'll be out of contact for a few more days. Anyway, I feel like *I* want to go away somewhere—maybe Mexico or somewhere else hot with a beach?"

"Well that could be fun I suppose," Emilia answered. "But what are the odds that Mom and Dad will fund another vacation for us right now?"

"Hmmm…you think Dad's still mad about Spring Break?"

"I think he may remember that one for a while—and he'll make sure we do, too."

"All I remember is he told us that since we'd both done *so* well the semester before, we could do something to celebrate, because they were going to be away themselves anyway."

"Yeah, but I don't think he was expecting that our girls' night out would end in us all drinking too much and booking a trip to the Bahamas leaving the next morning—then charging it to his credit card! And, might I add, *you* hatched the whole plan with Chelsea, I didn't even know you'd done it, but he was just as angry with *me*!"

Amanda chuckled mischievously, "Yeah, but wasn't it an awesome trip though?"

"Right up until we tried to check-out and they told us the card had been reported stolen, I thought we were going to end up in jail down there or something."

"Yeah, he wasn't in such a good mood when we called him to ask for help."

"That's the understatement of the year, I'd never even heard him say some of those words before." Emilia shook her head.

"Look, the girls came up with their shares—"

"Eventually," Emilia interjected.

"True—and we had an incredible vacay, I mean, it was wild right? I say all's well that ends well…"

"Maybe, but I think we're permanently cut-off from ever planning our own trips again, at least until our own paychecks can support it."

"Or…" Amanda raised her pointer finger dramatically, "we find your long-lost kingdom and can travel like royalty wherever we want to go!"

Emilia rolled her eyes.

Suddenly an excited yapping sound rose above the street noise; Emilia and Amanda turned to seek out the source.

"Coco! Coco! Come back here!" called an elderly, frazzled voice.

A pure white Bichon Frise puppy came into view further down the street, heading toward Emilia and Amanda as it darted in between and around the legs of several pedestrians; a red lead tinkering along the pavement behind it.

"Oh, no!" Emilia exclaimed, kneeling and clicking her fingers toward the wayward pup. "She must have gotten away."

"I guess so." Amanda chuckled at the commotion.

"Coco! Coco! Is that your name? Here, girl," Emilia called, motioning to the rebellious canine with open arms.

The puppy seemed spooked by a bike messenger who'd ridden up onto the sidewalk; she yapped at the rider before bolting away, toward the busy street.

"Please! Someone stop her!" The elderly woman panted.

"Coco, stop," Emilia's command was but a whisper, goose bumps prickling her skin at the thought of what was about to happen.

The puppy stopped in her tracks, turning to look directly at Emilia before switching direction again and bounding toward her.

"That-a-girl. Come on, come here cutie!"

"Geez Emmi, what is it with you and animals?" Amanda joked, shaking her head as she watched Coco yelp playfully and lick Emilia's face as if she were her long-lost owner.

"Oh, don't listen to her...you've got such a fluffy coat, don't you? Who's got a fluffy coat?" Emilia cooed as she ruffled the soft fur.

Coco was lapping up the attention when her owner arrived.

"Oh, thank you so very much. I was just rearranging my grocery bags and I guess the lead must have slipped out of my hands, next thing I know she's dashing off down the street. She's just a puppy."

"Awww, were you being a naughty puppy?" Emilia playfully goaded the dog as she retrieved the lead and stood to hand it back to the elderly lady who looked relieved.

"Here you go, puppies will be puppies!" Emilia shrugged.

"Thank goodness you were here, and she took to you so easily; she hasn't been very friendly with strangers—or anyone except for me, really—I was so worried I'd lose her. When I saw her running toward the cars..." The lady shuddered as if shaking off an unpleasant thought.

"Well, she's safely back with you now," Emilia smiled reassuringly. "Can we help you home? We can carry your bags—do you live far?"

The lady smiled appreciatively. "You're too kind dear, the world needs more like you! But no, I live on the next block, Coco and I will be fine from here."

"Come on Emmi, we're going to be late..." Amanda prompted.

"Well then, if you're sure you'll both be okay." Emilia smiled before turning her attention down to Coco and playfully wagging her finger, "Now you behave, and no more running away!"

"Thank you again dear, good-afternoon." The elderly lady smiled and continued on her way.

"You too." Emilia turned back to Amanda who seemed impatient as they resumed their walk.

"Oh, come on, Amanda—how can you not have a soft spot for an adorable furry little creature like that?" Emilia made her own puppy dog eyes at her sister.

"*Meh*, dogs…I don't love 'em, I don't hate 'em—nothing's changed. If I had to choose, I'd pick a cat—if I *had* to choose. Here's the building!" Amanda announced. She moved swiftly up the stairs and opened the door for Emilia to enter, "After you…Your Highness."

Emilia gave her a disapproving look.

"Sorry, couldn't resist! Ah…what floor are we going to?" Amanda quickly worked to change the subject. "Looks like the elevators are over here."

Emilia's reply was curt. "Eighth floor—let's go."

Chapter Four

Emilia and Amanda rode the elevator in silence; Emilia anticipating what new information she might discover about her family's history, and Amanda thinking better of any more kidding around for the moment.

After the elevator slowed to a stop, the doors rattled open followed by a *bing* announcing their arrival. Ahead of them were two large doors with *The Law Offices of Rothman, Goldberg and Holland* frosted onto the glass.

"Well that was easy to find. How are you feeling?" Amanda asked.

"Still a little nervous, but really I'm fine," Emilia smiled back and stepped ahead to pull the door open. "I'll get it," she joked, winking at Amanda.

The office was contemporary-classic in design. The entrance and waiting area had a high ceiling with intricate crown molding work, wooden walls, and polished tile floors along with some tasteful yet modern artwork and sculptures arranged thoughtfully throughout.

Behind the reception desk, a middle-aged woman with black hair tied in a bun and wearing glasses looked up from her screen and smiled politely. "Good afternoon, ladies. How may I help you?"

"Hi, I'm Emilia Campbell. I'm here to see Mr. Rothman."

"Of course!" Her grin widened into something more genuine. "I'm Bridget; we spoke earlier on the phone. It's nice to meet you."

"It's nice to meet you, too. This is my sister, Amanda," Emilia replied, feeling some of her anxiety fading.

"Hi," Amanda piped in with a wave.

"Lovely to meet you." The receptionist nodded in her direction. "Please take a seat while I let Mr. Rothman know you're here."

Emilia and Amanda started toward the waiting room chairs as Bridget tapped some buttons on her phone and announced their arrival.

"Of course. I'll bring them through now." Bridget rose from her desk just as Emilia and Amanda took their seats. "No time to sit after all," she explained with a smile. "Mr. Rothman is ready to see you; please follow me this way."

The pair returned her smile and followed Bridget down the hallway that led beyond the entrance.

"Here we go," Amanda whispered, squeezing Emilia's hand.

Emilia glanced over her shoulder and could only offer a half-smile in response before she faced forward once again. Taking in Bridget, Emilia noted her attire was professional but stylish; pencil skirt, floral print blouse, and shoes with a modest heel.

Off the central hallway were offices on both sides, and further down was what appeared to be a conference room. The doors were open, and the windows beyond the large oval table formed the perfect backdrop as the sun sank on the horizon. Stopping short of the entryway, Bridget stood at an open door to the left and motioned for them to enter. "Here we are," she announced, before offering the girls a beverage; Emilia and Amanda declined. Bridget gave a brief nod as she closed the door behind her and headed back down the hallway.

Jonathan Rothman was neatly presented and showed some physical signs of being beyond middle age: a receding hair line of mostly gray hair with a matching gray beard and mustache that was kept neatly trimmed. He wore glasses and was dressed in a light blue shirt with a red tie and navy suit pants, the matching jacket hanging from a coat hook in the rear corner of his office, closest to the entrance. His demeanor personified the essence of a well-heeled attorney as he rose from his desk to greet them.

"Miss Campbell, it's a pleasure to meet you," he said, reaching to shake her hand with a smile.

"Likewise, and please call me Emilia." She managed a tight nod as her nervous anticipation gathered once more.

"Of course, Emilia. And please, call me Jonathan. Thank you for coming today."

Perhaps sensing her sister's anxiety, Amanda stepped forward and introduced herself.

"It's nice to meet you, Amanda," said Jonathan as the two shook hands.

"And you too, Mr. Roth—Jonathan."

The office was spacious and blended old and new style. A dark, vintage wooden desk featured prominently, and an antique oak swivel armchair provided its own point of interest. Matching wood shelves containing legal reference books as well as photos of Jonathan's family and friends—she assumed—sat adjacent to the tall windows, which framed a fantastic view to the city beyond them. A degree from Yale Law drew attention on the wall opposite the windows.

The space conveyed a sense of the busy yet efficient accomplishment of a hard-working person. There were two guest chairs at the main desk, however Jonathan motioned toward a set of tan leather sofas arranged around a coffee table at the opposite end of his office. "Please, let's sit down and talk."

Collecting a folder from his desk, Jonathan joined the women at the sitting area, choosing the single seat next to them: Emilia and Amanda sat together on the sofa which faced toward the windows. Laying the folder on the coffee table between them, Emilia stared at it, anticipation filling her.

Jonathan noticed Emilia's gaze. He raised his eyebrows slightly and tilted his head. "I'm sure you have some questions for me, and I have some for you, too."

Exhaling, Emilia glanced at him and then back down toward the table before responding in a flat tone, "That would be an understatement."

Jonathan regarded her with a curious expression, but it seemed he understood where she was coming from.

Shaking her head and swallowing the lump in her throat, Emilia started over. "I've tried so many times over the years to find out more about my parents and where I came from. It's not as though the trails don't lead anywhere; I've just been unable to find *any* trails to follow. It's as if they didn't even exist before they came to America—before I was born."

Amanda looked at Jonathan. "Your letter today is the first hint at any new information. Ever." She reached out and held Emilia's hand, doing her part to be a supportive sister.

"I'm sorry. That must have been very difficult," Jonathan replied sympathetically. "You don't know anything *at all* about them?"

"Well, some details, sure—based on things Brian and Pam knew and some paperwork that was found in our house. Their names were Anton and Genevieve Meyer; they moved to the United States—to New York—the same year I was born. Then a few years later they moved to Northern New Jersey.

"That's when we met and became friends," Amanda chimed in, smiling at her sister.

Emilia returned the gesture and squeezed Amanda's hand. "That's right; my parents had moved to the same neighborhood as Amanda and we used to play together all the time. I guess our parents had become friends as well. I was young, but I remember we'd sometimes all spend time together. You know, like meeting up for dinner. Pam has some photos of a trip we all took to the shore one summer.

"I mean, it's not like I was a baby when they died, I was seven. I remember a lot about them. My father would read me a story every night and he never said no when I asked for a second book, or an extra chapter. My mother was kind and loving, she doted on me. The two of them were affectionate; even though I was young I could tell they adored each other. Thinking back, I remember asking them questions…you know, my friends and other kids at school all had grandparents, aunts and uncles. They would just clam up and tell me that the three of us were a family and that's all that mattered."

Jonathan nodded.

"I got the same vague answers when I asked about what things were like when they were children, where they grew up and who their families were. I was curious and persistent, especially since they were so normal in every other way but strangely guarded about their upbringing. But they either changed the subject or said they would tell me about it when I was older, never any more than that."

"I see," said Jonathan.

"One day, I didn't know it at the time, but it couldn't have been too long before they left on their trip, *the* trip…I was asking my mother about her childhood again, we were in the kitchen, she was cooking meatloaf…I still remember the smell." Emilia smiled and let out a thoughtful sigh at the memory.

Amanda reached across and patted Emilia's hand.

Jonathan smiled warmly, "For me it was my mother's apple pie."

Emilia grinned. "It's funny the things you remember sometimes—this one just stuck with me."

"Anyway," Emilia continued, "I said I didn't understand why they wouldn't tell me things. In all of my seven-year-old wisdom I yelled something at her about keeping secrets from me. She got really upset, she yelled at me and she was crying. I ran away to my room."

"That evening, my father got home from work and came to speak to me. He explained that my mother was upset because of the unpleasant memories my questions triggered for her—for them both. I could see, no, more than that…I could *feel* how hurt he was, and I promised I wouldn't ask again—and I never did."

Emilia allowed a single tear to stream down her cheek, the soft tick of it landing on her skirt broke the silence that followed the recollection.

Jonathan stood from his chair and made his way to a cabinet on the other side of his office where he retrieved a box of tissues, Emilia pulled one out with a swish.

"Thank you." Emilia dabbed the tissue against her cheek, drying up the liquid as she recomposed herself.

"I'm sorry to have to ask you to recount any of this—"

"It's fine," Emilia assured him. "I've had a lot of time to get used to it, and Brian and Pam—and Amanda, of course—are my family now. They're amazing, and I know they love me as if I were their own. It's the mystery of where my birth parents came from, and why they moved here, that I wonder about more than anything."

"I see. Well, there are a few specific things I do need to know…"

"Of course, ask away." Emilia smiled reassuringly at Jonathan.

"Thank-you, okay, let's start with what happened to them? When did they pass away? Take as much time as you need and please don't feel any pressure here if anything is uncomfortable for you." Jonathan remained sensitive while continuing to move the conversation forward.

Emilia paused and looked out the window, staring into space to collect her thoughts.

"It was fifteen years ago now, no one really seems to know why, but they had to go away on a trip to Upstate New York and they were in a car accident there. My birth parents were both killed instantly…apparently there wasn't even another car involved; they just went off the road and the car flipped over, hit a tree, and caught fire. There weren't many details, but the police report said it was likely the car slipped on ice or they swerved to avoid colliding with an animal. We had to have closed caskets at their funeral because they were so severely burned. I never saw—"

As tears flowed, Amanda wrapped an arm around her sister, resting her head on Emilia's shoulder briefly before pulling another tissue from the box. Emilia smiled weakly in gratitude and dried her cheeks. She took a few deep breaths and looked at Jonathan.

"Brian and Pam have a friend—Dan Palmer, who's a police officer. He liaised with the local police for us and I believe investigated it to some extent, too. His opinion was the same as the official report: it was just a terrible accident. When I was sixteen, I went up to the area to see if I could find out anything else about them, but there were no clues as to where they had stayed or what they were doing there. Asking around didn't seem to jog anyone's memory, and there were no hints at all on the road where the accident happened either—though none of that was too surprising considering so many years had passed. So, I returned empty-handed." Emilia shrugged.

Jonathan nodded. "And you mentioned files. You weren't able to find anything useful there?"

Emilia shook her head. "No, only day to day paperwork, a few bills and things like that...nothing at all about their lives prior to moving to America—not even passports to show where they were from. We assumed they must have traveled with them and they were destroyed in the fire."

"And your adoptive parents," Jonathan glanced at his notes, "Brian and Pamela Campbell. You said they were friends—they didn't know any more?"

"Believe me, I asked and asked, and then asked again. They told me they were wonderful people who cared about me deeply. They were good friends, but they had always avoided talking about their past. Brian and Pam did sense an unease when that topic came up, so they didn't pursue it. As far as their trip goes, it was all very last-minute apparently. My birth parents asked Brian and Pam if I could stay with them for a few days—that there was something they had to take care of urgently—but they didn't share any details. I think Brian and Pam assumed they would fill them in when they returned, but they never did."

Emilia paused to take a breath, looking to Amanda for strength. "Brian and Pam knew there were no relatives and didn't want to see me end up an orphan. They took the steps to adopt me, and my best friend became my sister."

"It sounds as though—given the tragic circumstances of course, that it all worked out as well as it possibly could—which is very nice to hear," Jonathan added. "How about work? Do you know what your parents did?"

"I know, I am incredibly fortunate—the Campbells are saints as far as I'm concerned. As for work, my mother was raising me, and my father was a floor manager in a clothing factory, I went to visit and the people there who remembered my father all spoke very highly of him and his talents. But it seems he never spoke about his past at work either. No one knew any more information than I already did; they were just shocked and saddened by his passing."

Emilia looked out the window again. Daylight was fading, and a pink-orange glow filled the sky.

Amanda followed her gaze for a moment before turning her attention back to Jonathan. "Please excuse my impatience, but where is this all going, anyway? Do you know about Emilia's parents? Do you have some new information you can share?"

Jonathan gave a half-smile and nodded slowly. "Of course—perhaps I should have started with some explanation. I will certainly give you all the answers I can, but before I go on, may I see your birth certificate please?"

Emilia retrieved the birth certificate from her bag and handed it to Jonathan.

He studied the paperwork, scanning back and forth between the birth certificate and a separate document in his hand until he appeared satisfied. "Miss Campbell, I will share all that I do know," Jonathan cleared his throat, "I was contacted early last week by a lawyer based in Austria—well, Vienna, specifically."

"Vienna?" Emilia practically gasped.

"Yes, though it seems he is working on behalf of a client—or an estate by the sound of it—in Slovakia."

Satisfied Emilia's birth certificate matched his expectations, Jonathan placed the document on the coffee table. "Do you mind if I make a copy of this?"

"That's fine. Um…Slovakia? What does that have to do with my parents? Is that where they are—were, from?"

"It is possible. I'm sorry, but I can't say for sure. Martin Thiess is the lawyer who contacted me. Apparently, they have been investigating Genevieve Blagden—or more specifically, any heirs she may have had."

Emilia's eyes widened as she leaned in closer. "Blagden? That's not a name I've heard before."

"Based on what you've told me today, I'm not surprised."

Jonathan leaned forward in his seat, collected the folder from the coffee table, and opened it. A short stack of pages lay beneath a letter which he began to reference.

"As I understand it, with a reasonable degree of certainty, they have concluded that Genevieve Blagden married an Anton Meyer. She took his name at that time and emigrated here to the United States, where she gave birth to a daughter named Emilia. I believe you know the rest of the story from there: when Emilia was orphaned at a young age, Brian and Pamela Campbell adopted her. At which point, her name became Emilia Campbell."

"Emmi, that's you!" Amanda blurted excitedly, giving Emilia's arm another squeeze.

Emilia stared down at the table, contemplating what she had just heard. "I'm sorry. I just need a moment to process this." A shaky breath escaped her lungs before she began firing questions. "Okay, wow...so, what else do you know? You mentioned a lawyer was trying to find me?"

"I can certainly appreciate your situation and the need for answers, but I'm sorry, there really isn't any more background that I've been made privy to. The scope of my involvement in this matter is fairly limited."

"What do you mean by that?" Amanda queried.

"Well, this firm was engaged to make contact with you specifically, Emilia, and to do some investigating and verification of your identity in an effort to determine whether you're the individual being sought. As you can imagine, many people share the same name—in some cases the parents' names can also match. All the research into the lineage and who they have been seeking was evidently completed prior to my involvement, so I can't speak as to that process. Our task has been specific to you."

"Uh…what sort of investigating?" Emilia asked warily.

Jonathan raised his hands from the armrests in a disarming manner. "Nothing too intrusive or cloak-and-dagger," he said with assurance, "though we had to be sure your name wasn't simply a coincidence. For all I know there may have been other firms in other places looking into the lives of other women named Emilia Campbell."

"All right, I understand. So, it's possible these may not be my parents at all?" Emilia did her best to avoid sounding too deflated, but she felt herself slumping back into the sofa.

Jonathan paused briefly, considering his response. "Yes, that is a possibility, but I think it is unlikely. Based on the information provided by Mr. Thiess, the research we have completed on you, and the information you've shared with me today, I believe there is a very high probability that you are *the* Emilia Campbell they want to locate and meet. There are far too many similarities between their research and your life—and I must admit, yours isn't a typical story at all. Pardon the oversimplification, but if it looks like a duck and quacks like a duck as they say…"

Emilia couldn't help but chuckle. "Well that's encouraging for sure! You mentioned they want to meet me? Perhaps they have more information? When can I talk to them?"

"I can't speak about how much more they know of your past, but my sense is that they've researched your lineage in some detail prior to contacting me so it is quite possible they will be able to provide you with some more information when you get over there."

"When she gets over to where?" Amanda questioned impatiently. "Slovakia?"

Jonathan cleared his throat quietly. "I spoke with Martin Thiess this morning, and he advised that following a successful in-person meeting today, he wanted to arrange for Emilia to travel there to meet with him as soon as possible." Jonathan shuffled through a couple of pages in the folder. "A village called Zillah in Slovakia. He was quite emphatic that time was of the essence, though he didn't elaborate on why. Mr. Thiess also offered funding for travel expenses if necessary."

Amanda's eyes sparkled as she looked to Emilia. "A trip to Europe? Wait, make that a trip to Europe *and* finding out where you're from?" Amanda could barely contain her excitement. She managed to refrain from leaping off the couch and fist-pumping the air, instead doing a little dance number from her seat. Both Jonathan and Emilia couldn't help but smile at her reaction.

Amanda did her best to compose herself before turning her attention back to Jonathan. "And I assume that includes her sister as a vital and necessary traveling companion—as well as a stop-over in…Paris, yes, Paris, for a couple of days?" she asked in the most serious tone she could muster.

"Amanda!" Emilia rejoined the conversation, slapping Amanda lightly on the leg.

Jonathan smiled. "There hasn't been any discussion about traveling companions or turning this into a European vacation, though I can certainly relay your request."

"Thank you very much, Mr. Rothman," Amanda replied smugly as she shot Emilia an unapologetic smile.

Emilia tried to take back control of the discussion, returning to more practical details. "So, you're serious about this? This Martin Thiess wants me to travel to this place, Zill…?"

"Yes, Zillah. Z-I-L-L-A-H," confirmed Jonathan.

"Right, Zillah. About an estate matter?"

Jonathan nodded. "Yes, essentially, and as soon as possible at that. I don't know much more about the estate matter I'm afraid, but it seems you're involved in it and they have gone to quite some effort to be certain that you are in fact *the* Emilia Campbell they seek."

Emilia's chest fluttered with optimism. Perhaps the mystery that had plagued her almost her entire life might finally be solved. "So…what do we do next then?"

"Right. I'll reach out to Mr. Thiess to relay the details from our meeting today. It is late in Vienna now, so we may not connect until tomorrow. As soon as I have some more information, I will contact you."

"And don't forget to talk about her traveling companion," Amanda added. "I am an indispensable addition; it is a big trip to a strange place after all." She was determined to build her case for joining her sister in Europe.

Emilia laughed this time. "You're incorrigible! This isn't some sort of vacation; someone has probably died, and this is to learn about my family."

"Well we can sort all of that out, too…I suppose," Amanda joked back.

Jonathan smiled. "Unless you have any more questions, that's about all we can go over right now. I'll be in touch with you, Emilia. Thank you both for coming in."

"Thank *you*, Jonathan," Emilia replied. "This is such huge news to me—I can't tell you how incredible it will be if this helps fill in the gaps and answers some of the unknowns about my parents. I'll wait to hear from you."

Emilia and Amanda confirmed their contact details and waited while Bridget took a copy of Emilia's identity documents.

Neither spoke as they waited for the elevator to arrive, Emilia lost in her thoughts as she took a few moments to think through the events of the past hour or so.

The elevator pinged and the doors rolled open.

Amanda broke the silence. "So…how are you doing? Still feel like going out tonight? I totally get it if you don't want to do anything too crazy…"

"Um, yeah…maybe not."

Amanda's disappointment shone in her eyes and Emilia felt bad. "Uh…all right—nothing too wild though. I kind of feel like I want an early one tonight."

Amanda's face broke out in a grin. "Great! I guarantee I'll get you feeling like your normal self again! How about Havana? It's not that far from here and shouldn't be too busy tonight. Plus, we can get some of that delicious ceviche for dinner, too!"

Emilia settled into this odd development; at least going out with Amanda was a common occurrence. Being informed someone had information on her past—that they wanted her to travel to Slovakia—didn't happen every day.

"Yeah," she answered. "That's perfect."

It was dark outside as the two women descended the building's stairs back down to Market Street. Cars hummed along in the steady traffic and a loud truck with an offensive exhaust odor rattled past as they reached the sidewalk. Just then, a gust of unseasonably cold wind rushed over the pair. Emilia was momentarily transported back to her dream from the night before. The past few hours had kept her from thinking about it, and the sudden intensity of the memories and images flooded back into her mind, causing her to gasp.

Amanda was slightly ahead and shivered when the cold sensation engulphed her. "Where did that come from? Let's get a cab."

Hands clenched in her pockets, Emilia closed her eyes and absorbed the cool caress across her face.

"Emmi, are you all right?"

She opened her eyes. "Yeah…yeah, I'm fine. A cab…great idea."

Amanda hailed a passing cab and it pulled to a stop. "Are you sure you're all right?" Amanda asked, following Emilia into the car as she shimmied across the backseat.

"Yup, all good. It's just been a big day and I think I'm feeling a little tired."

"Where to, ladies?" called the driver.

"Havana please," Amanda answered.

"Sure thing."

Amanda pulled out her phone, aimlessly scrolling through her notifications. "I was thinking about inviting a few of the girls along. Are you up for that? Never know, you might meet your dream guy tonight...or at least a fun rebound."

Emilia slowly inhaled, her sister's words prompted visions of the mysterious man from her dream to flash across her mind as she rested her head against the back seat. "You know, I'm exhausted and drained in so many ways...but I sure could use the distraction—no dream guys and no rebounds though, just friends—okay?"

"That's my girl! What about *male* friends?" came Amanda's cheeky reply.

"I wonder if Oliver will be there? Ugh, no! What am I saying...so don't want to even *think* about men right now—and not too late," Emilia insisted.

"No promises..." And Amanda began messaging some of their friends to coordinate.

Chapter Five

Emilia relished a few moments of quiet, thoughts swirling and her fingers tapping gently on the worn vinyl armrest as she watched the lights zip by out the cab window; Amanda's eyes were glued to her screen, organizing their evening.

"Here we are, ladies," the driver announced. He stopped the cab on Walnut Street flicking the hazard lights on; Emilia looked at the meter and handed him a ten-dollar bill.

"Keep it," she said as they stepped out of the car.

The distinctive yellow building with white fittings and red neon signage on the portico above the door welcomed them back. Since moving to Philadelphia for college, Havana had been one of their favorite night spots.

Emilia and Amanda headed inside and followed the stairs down to the bar and lounge area.

It was still early, and a weeknight, so it was quite empty save for a small group of executives in suits and loosened ties unwinding with a beer after a long day at the office. Emilia also noticed a couple sitting in the lounge area deep in conversation, smiling way too much it seemed; perhaps a first date?

The girls made their way toward the lounge and spotted Oliver sitting at the bar, sipping a gin and tonic.

Amanda punched Emilia playfully in the arm. "How do you always seem to know...?"

Emilia just shrugged.

Catching the girls' reflections in the mirror lining the back wall, he swung around to greet them. Oliver wore a simple black T-shirt and jeans, and his toned muscles—from years of being on the rowing team—moved under the skin of his tanned arms to lift the glass to his mouth. His hair was blond, and he always met Emilia and Amanda with a kind smile.

His intention to downplay his enthusiasm failed miserably; it was obvious he enjoyed seeing Emilia. "Emilia, Amanda, hey! Well, now I'm glad I let the guys talk me into coming out tonight. How are you?"

"Hey, Olly," Amanda replied. "We're great! We're celebrating tonight!"

"Hi, Oliver," said Emilia politely.

"Celebrating?" he asked, gesturing to the empty seats beside him. "What's the occasion?"

Sitting down, Emilia attempted to correct him. "We're not—"

"Oh, big news!" Amanda interrupted. "Emilia's single again—" She winked at Oliver. "Yup, though it's still a little sensitive." Amanda lowered her voice, looking apologetically to Emilia at the disclosure before turning back to Oliver. "But wait, there's more..." Amanda was in her element dominating the conversation, "it's possible she's a European princess, though we're waiting to find out more about that."

"Oh my gosh, Amanda!" Emilia quickly switched from exasperation to laughter, appreciating her sister's playful nature. "Ignore her, Oliver. I don't know what's gotten into her today."

Oliver chuckled and winked at Amanda. "Say no more. I think we both know she can get a little carried away sometimes." Turning his attention back to Emilia, he smiled affectionately and added, "Seriously though, I don't know the details, but that guy must be a fool if he let you get away."

His eyes were deep-blue, and his sand-colored, ivy-league-styled hair against his sun-kissed skin made them stand out more.

"Thanks, Oliver. Yeah, actually we're...kind of just on a break for now—who knows how it'll work out."

He leaned in further. "You know, I think it will work out just fine." He paused for a moment; his eyes locked with Emilia's before he settled back against his barstool. "Now, what's this about you being a princess?"

Amanda chuckled; Emilia sighed.

"No," Emilia said. "I'm not a princess—it's nothing. I just got some information about my parents today and Amanda's taken it way out of context. Really, I don't want to talk about it right now."

The bartender passed and they ordered their Havana usual: mojitos.

Amanda took the lull in conversation as an opportunity to change the subject. "The girls will be here soon—we're going to get a seat in the lounge before they're all taken. Any chance you can bring them over to us?" She batted her eyelashes.

"For you two?" He stroked his five o'clock shadow; it was obvious he saw through her blatant flirting, but he humored her anyway. He was too nice of a guy not to. "Anything."

Only Amanda could flirt her way into getting service from someone who didn't even work there—didn't need to work *anywhere*. Oliver was from a well-off family who owned one of the largest construction entities on the eastern seaboard; he only needed to concern himself with school.

Havana was one of their favorite places; it had a certain charm other night spots didn't offer. The exposed red brick walls in the bar area formed the backdrop to high shelves lined with bottles, while louvered windows and black and white photographs projected onto the lemon walls in the lounge area added interest and atmosphere. Table lamps with cream-colored shades and dark-wood stands complemented the pastel-yellow couches and transported patrons to their very own slice of Cuba, adding warmth and a stay-a-while hangout vibe.

Emilia and Amanda made their way to the corner set of sofas and sat down. Tucked away beneath the staircase that led up to the dining area, the alcove provided a little more privacy amongst the slowly growing crowd.

"Please don't try to set me up with Oliver, or anyone right now, okay?" Emilia pleaded, glancing to the bar and watching as their drinks were delivered to him. "I've barely been single for a day! And stop telling people I'm a princess."

Amanda smirked. "You know, he's a pretty good catch, the perfect rebound—or longer. And he's totally into you. Think about it: I tell him you're not with Brandon anymore and that you could be a *princess*, and the first thing he's focused on is you being single!"

Oliver had picked up their drinks. He would join them in seconds. "Look, I don't disagree with you necessarily. Just not tonight, all right?"

Satisfied for the moment, Amanda grinned. "All right. Whatever you say then. I'll back off...for now."

"Thank you."

Oliver approached with their drinks. "Here you go." He placed the mojitos down on a coaster in front of Amanda and then Emilia, flashing a sexy smile at her while doing so.

Without thinking, Emilia bit her lip, flirting a little without even realizing it. "Thanks, Oliver."

Oliver glanced back toward the bar, where similarly tanned, muscled college-aged men had arrived. "I need to go and say hi to the guys," he explained. "Otherwise," he added, leaning closer to Emilia so it felt like he was only speaking to her, "I'd love to spend my evening with you."

The tone of his voice sent all kinds of butterflies through her stomach—Oliver seemed to have a way to make her smile—really smile—from the inside out.

Before she could reply, he was already sauntering off to meet his buddies at the bar.

"Are you sure you're not in the mood tonight?" Amanda asked, at least having the sense to pick up her jaw from the floor. "From where I'm sitting it looks like you both might be."

"I'm not even going to answer that," Emilia said evenly. "Cheers." They raised their glasses and sealed the end of the conversation with a soft *clink*.

Or at least Emilia had *thought* it had been the end; Amanda remained relentless. "Oh, go on, have some fun! You deserve it!"

"I could use some fun I suppose," Emilia admitted, glancing at Oliver, who had been all but swallowed up by the group of men, discussing some sport or another she was sure.

As the crowd grew, the ambient noise intensified with conversations humming amongst the rhythm of Cuban music playing in the background. Sitting at the far end of the lounge area still afforded Emilia and Amanda the ability to talk without yelling—at least for a little longer.

"I know I've been making a lot of jokes today," Amanda finally said. "I'm sorry if I went too far; you know me, I just like to try and lighten the mood when things get a little serious."

Emilia nodded lovingly. "I know. Thanks for saying that, but really it's fine."

Seemingly relieved, Amanda sipped her mojito. "So how are you anyway? This kind of turned out to be a pretty crazy day."

"Right?" Emilia agreed. "Honestly, I'm still trying to wrap my head around it all. What if everything Jonathan said is true and my parents came from Slovakia? Could there really be someone over there who knows all about them? What about this whole estate situation? Does that mean that there's nobody left in my family—just a lawyer looking for someone to give some old books and trinkets to?" Her head was already spinning, and it was too soon to be from the alcohol. She groaned. "I don't know what to think about it all right now."

Amanda regarded her. "I definitely understand. I'm your sister and I promise that anything you need, I'm here for you. I love you, Emmi."

"Thanks." She patted her arm across the table. "I really appreciate it. And I love you, too."

"So," Amanda's expression brightened, "are you at least a *little* excited about possibly going to Europe—if it turns out you're who they're looking for?"

Now feeling a little more relaxed, Emilia couldn't help but smile and even laugh a bit. "Oh, totally! Excited doesn't even begin to describe it," Emilia looked thoughtful, "and of course they'd have to let you come with me," she winked as she took another sip of her mojito.

"For sure!" Amanda said. "I wouldn't let you go off alone to some random place no one has ever heard of. That would be crazy! But the two of us traveling to Europe to learn all about your past? Well, that sounds like the perfect way to spend our break—and we were just complaining that we didn't have any plans, or a way to pay for some," she added. "Life sure has a way of working out."

"You're right." Emilia's sister would also be an enormous comfort in a foreign place. "I don't know much about Slovakia at all, let alone this village, Zillah."

Amanda pulled out her phone and searched *Zillah, Slovakia.*

"Hmmm…let's see." Scrolling past a few ads for places to stay while in Slovakia, she zeroed in on the information she was looking for. "'Zillah is a small, remote medieval village located along the Belá River in the Tatra Mountain region of Slovakia', da-de-da…"

Amanda skimmed over some of the less interesting demographic data before reaching a section on the history of the village.

"'…Was first established in the thirteenth century by a wealthy German family, the Blagdens, who continued farming and agriculture, as well as began mining operations in the area. Over time, they constructed the castle residence and expanded their realm. Successive generations worked to grow and diversify economic interests to include smelting of the minerals mined and production of high-quality metal products and jewelry, which was traded well beyond their borders.'"

Amanda looked up at Emilia, who had been listening intently. "Wasn't 'Blagden' the name Jonathan mentioned? Maybe I was wrong. You're not a princess, you're a baroness or something!"

Emilia laughed and bit her bottom lip, shrugging with disbelief. She took another sip and encouraged Amanda to continue, "Well, come on. What else does it say?"

Amanda smiled, relieved that Emilia was relaxing a little. She took a gulp of mojito and focused on her phone once again. "All right, where was I? 'The ruling family did a better job than many over the ensuing centuries of either negotiating and collaborating with—or defending against—the series of invasions and occupations that affected the greater region. The town's natural isolation and limited access also contributed to their insulation from difficulties experienced elsewhere. This relative stability combined with the success of their mining, agriculture, and production allowed the population to peak at over ten thousand inhabitants.'"

Amanda looked slyly at Emilia "Well, this is certainly sounding good!"

"Sure is!" Emilia nodded, anxious to learn more.

"'Many generations of growth and prosperity ended abruptly in the late eighteenth century,'" Amanda read on. "'The town entered a steep decline, primarily attributed to a complete drop in production from the mines and a series of personal tragedies that befell the Blagden family. Many residents moved away and left the area during this period. Once the economic prosperity had ended, there was little interest by many to justify the journey to this remote area and the village decreased significantly in both size and influence. Much of the core fortified village does remain today, albeit with far fewer inhabitants—as does the castle, still occupied by descendants of the village's founders. At present, the once prosperous mines remain shuttered, and much of the village as well as the castle are in various states of disrepair.'"

Amanda appeared equal parts bewildered and aghast. "Well...this is a bummer. Sounds like you're a few centuries too late."

"Um, yeah—"

"Though it does also say here that 'the village receives a limited number of tourists and sightseers each year who have described Zillah as a place frozen in time, and several have mentioned they were made to feel unwelcome by the locals—'" Amanda went on, reading more information from her phone. "'Those who do make the journey are rewarded with spectacular natural scenery and the interesting, though deteriorating, medieval architecture of the village and castle'. Hmmm…it sounds like the surrounding Tatra Mountains area is beautiful, though visitors tend to stay in the larger towns because they're more easily accessible and developed."

"I wonder how closely related I am to the family still living there," Emilia thought out loud.

Before Amanda had a chance to respond, a call from across the lounge drew their attention. "Emilia! Amanda! Hey!" The girls looked up and saw three of their best friends, Jasmine, Chelsea, and Megan, walking toward them. Emilia had met Chelsea during her sophomore year at college when they'd both taken part in a volunteer mission to an orphanage in Peru. They bonded instantly, sharing a passion for assisting children's charities, as well as a mutual obsession with spicy foods; regularly combing the city in search of the best buffalo wings.

Jasmine and Megan studied economics with Amanda, and together the five formed a fabulous group of smart and sassy young women.

By now the lounge and bar had filled in; one of the waitresses came over and took a drinks order while everyone settled into the couches. Wasting no time, Chelsea looked curiously between Emilia and Amanda, her almond-shaped eyes inquisitive like a bird. "So, Amanda mentioned some exciting news. What's going on?"

Amanda raised her eyebrows, gazing excitedly at Emilia. "Can I tell them?"

Emilia giggled and took to her mojito once more. "Go right ahead, but no princess stuff—for all we know, my grandparents were the bakers or something in this sleepy village."

"Of course, baroness!" Amanda retorted.

Pressing her hand to her forehead, Emilia sighed. While the newcomers looked at her with confusion and intrigue, Amanda began to recount the day's events. At the bar, Emilia watched the people moving about; amongst them was Oliver who appeared engaged in lively conversation with his friends, though on more than one occasion she noticed him glancing back at her.

Chapter Six

Martin Thiess was sitting in the small library located on the ground floor of his home. The late evening darkness was brightened by his desk lamp and a warm glow spilling in from the hallway beyond the open French doors at the room's entrance.

Even in the low light, Martin's fatigue could not be concealed. He was balding, though short gray hair remained on the sides of his head; his bushy dark eyebrows were flecked with gray and he kept the patchy stubble around his chin and mustache styled in a goatee. His stature was short and pudgy; he had been ready to retire for the evening and thusly was dressed in long, pale blue pajamas covered by a full-length brown robe with matching slippers.

The email he'd just received from the American lawyer prompted Martin to immediately pick up the phone—time was of the essence. As he leaned back in his chair waiting for the conversation to start, he removed his spectacles and looked around the room. Dark wood shelves lined the walls from floor to ceiling; they were filled with a collection of books and journals, as well as pieces of art and collectables. A thin layer of dust covered most of the surfaces; they were seldom moved or used for any function other than decoration.

One set of objects drew his attention: a pair of medieval daggers on a stone stand—a gift, many years earlier, from the client he was presently working for. He had kept them as a reminder to never involve himself in such things again; the memory they stirred began to rouse a feeling of remorse which quickly turned into dread. Involuntarily, Martin grimaced as he inhaled and closed his eyes. He was brought back to the present moment upon hearing Jonathan Rothman's voice.

"Martin, you must be working late this evening," he said. "I wasn't expecting to speak with you until tomorrow."

After a brief pause, Martin collected his thoughts and responded in perfect English, though with a strong Austrian accent. "Hello, Jonathan. Yes, well, this is a matter of extreme importance. When I received your earlier update that you expected to meet with her today, I waited up to ensure we could speak as soon as possible."

"Of course. I did meet with Miss Campbell this afternoon along with her sister, Amanda. Both of whom were delightful young ladies."

"Sister?" Martin interrupted.

"Yes, Amanda Campbell, her adopted parents' daughter."

He relaxed. They weren't related by blood. "Yes, yes, forgive me; it is late. Please go on."

"I understand. I'll do my best to be brief. We talked specifically about her upbringing and her parents and, based on the identifying information you provided—names, dates, and so forth—everything she knows, the details she was able to provide…it all matches. As I noted in my email to you from a few moments ago, I am very confident this Emilia Campbell is the person you have been searching for."

Martin remained composed. "This is very good news."

"I can share with you also," Jonathan went on, "that she has a lot of questions. Miss Campbell was very young when her parents passed away and has been looking for more information about where they were from but with no success. She'd gone to some effort by the sounds of things, but unfortunately those efforts yielded virtually no results."

"I'm not necessarily surprised. It is possible—perhaps even likely—that steps had been taken to conceal this information from her. This is helpful. A curiosity such as this can be a powerful motivation."

"I don't follow," Jonathan replied. "Who…why would someone take such steps?"

Martin sensed concern lacing the American lawyer's voice. He paused, feeling he might have spoken a little too candidly. "I cannot be certain. In any event, it is of little relevance at this point. The important thing is that we've located her. Please provide her passport details and I will organize her flight to Vienna. I can then drive with her to the village—we need to get her to Zillah as soon as possible."

"I'm curious about the urgency. This is an estate matter, correct?"

Martin did his best to curb his frustration at such irrelevant questions. "Yes, this is an estate matter. It appears Miss Campbell may be the last in her family line and as such, she is quite possibly the only heir to certain family assets and property in Zillah. We have been working to locate her for some time now, and the law and local customs dictate that certain processes need to happen within predetermined time frames which are now close to expiring. I'm sure you understand."

There. It was a plausible explanation, and in essence, the truth.

"Very well, I understand," Jonathan finally relented. "I did speak with Miss Campbell about traveling to Zillah; she was open to the idea and would like for her sister to accompany her on the trip."

"We do not need the sister," Martin retorted, "we need the Blagden girl—as soon as possible." He was unable to conceal his frustration now, though immediately realized his response was brash and inappropriate. He worked to mitigate the concern he had likely raised from the American lawyer. "Please, again, you'll need to forgive me...it has been a long day."

The silence was deafening for Martin. The last thing he needed was to arouse any suspicion from Jonathan—he already had enough to deal with. "Jonathan?" he queried.

"Yes, yes...I am here," the lawyer answered. "When I met with both young women this afternoon, I got the sense that for a trip such as this—big in many ways—there would be a much higher comfort level for Miss Campbell if they traveled together. I also think that perhaps for practical reasons as much as any, that it would be best for travel to be arranged from this end. I can have our corporate travel agency take care of the details. When do you need her there specifically, and on what date shall I arrange their return?"

Martin looked at his calendar briefly, reminding himself that less than a week remained until the full moon. Sensing that failure to oblige might lead to more probing, or worse, delays, Martin took a deep breath and replied in his most cordial tone, "Yes, I understand the concerns, and whatever arrangements you make will be fine, though she must arrive before the weekend.

"Please advise the costs once everything is taken care of and I'll wire you the funds. It is important that they arrive as soon as possible—and, if you must…uh, I mean, yes, you can book their return travel for any time after this coming Monday. The matter will be concluded by then." Feeling the need to once more convey the time sensitivity, Martin added, "The estate will cover any costs, this is not a concern. Again, it is very important that Emilia Blagden be in Zillah as soon as possible."

"Understood. I can work to arrange this with the utmost urgency."

"Thank you, Jonathan. Please do your best to ensure all goes smoothly."

"Certainly. In the meantime, I'm curious about this matter; is there anything else you can share with me?"

Martin closed his eyes, leaned back in his chair, and pinched the bridge of his nose with his thumb and middle finger. "I'm sorry, that is not possible. Unless there is anything else, I wish you goodnight."

"Very well. I'll be touch; goodnight."

Calm down, Martin told himself, sighing deeply. *This will be over soon.* After a few breaths, he slowly opened his eyes and reached for his phone once more. Martin stood from his desk, selected the number he needed and paced across the room toward the library window. The curtains were drawn to each side, held open with decorative rope sashes. The window faced the street; it was quiet at this time of night. The orange hue of the ornate streetlamps lit wide arcs beneath each, a small car drove by, breaking the stillness. The sound was barely audible through the thick glass. The phone had rung three times now, but Martin had tuned it out, distracted by the remaining steps he'd need to take over the coming days.

Halfway through the fourth ring, it stopped. There was a brief silence before a man's voice, deep and familiar, answered calmly, "Hello, Martin."

"Massimino," Martin said. "I would apologize for calling you so late, but you never seem to sleep."

Massimino laughed once. It was more like a snicker. "What news do you have for me, my friend?"

"I have confirmed the identity of the Blagden girl, Emilia. Preparations are being made for her to travel to the village as soon as possible."

"I am relieved to hear this. I sense also that she is the one we have been seeking. I am heartened to know she will arrive soon; the time draws near—the culmination as it were."

"Yes, I am very aware. Everything is in order; I will make sure."

"I believe you will. You sound tired, my friend. Get some rest."

Martin paused, considering his response. "I do feel weary. This task is…an unpleasant one. It seems to be weighing on me more than I expected."

"Perhaps, but it must be done. Should you need additional…motivation, set your thoughts on the vast wealth that will be yours once your work here is complete."

"Of course. It is just the late hour. This is not the first time, after all, I will keep you apprised should anything change. Otherwise I will see you in a few days. Goodnight."

"Goodnight, Martin."

Martin glanced at the 'Call Ended' display on his phone before looking back out the window, his mind cloudy though his mission clear. He turned off the desk lamp before retiring upstairs to his bedroom where he joined his wife, who was already sleeping soundly.

Jonathan Rothman sat at his desk, contemplating how best to proceed. What had begun as a rather straightforward matter had now left him with a feeling that he was involved in something more complicated. After a minute or so of contemplation, he decided that much of his concern could be a simple cultural difference mixed with a tired man, late in the evening. If that was the case, there was really no cause for alarm—though he still felt better that Miss Campbell's sister would join the journey. Handling their travel arrangements provided some protection and reassurance that Emilia wouldn't be completely dependent on someone he wasn't sure was trustworthy.

Given the apparent time sensitivity, Jonathan looked up Emilia's phone number and dialed.

Chapter Seven

Amanda was retelling the day's events in her animated way—taking some liberties and embellishing here and there—as their friends listened intently, completely intrigued.

Emilia's bag rested against her leg on the lounge seat and she suddenly felt pressed to retrieve her phone and keep it handy, as if anticipating a call. Just then, it lit up and began to ring over the hum of the bar. She immediately recognized the number on the screen.

"I think this is the lawyer," she gasped, her excitement surprising her; Emilia sounded more like she was about to win a prize, not answer the phone.

"Well go on, answer it!" urged Amanda, eyes wide.

"I'll never hear him in here," Emilia explained. "I'm going outside—be right back." She slipped through the crowd and disappeared up the stairs.

"Hello?" she answered on her way to the entrance. "Just a minute; I'm going somewhere a little quieter."

"No problem, Miss Campbell." Emilia barely made out his reply, but she heard enough of Jonathan Rothman's voice to confirm it was him.

As Emilia reached the entrance, a man holding the door open for his wife signaled for her to walk through as well.

"Thank you." Emilia smiled as she held the phone to her ear, hardly noticing the chill in the night air as she stepped onto the street. The noises of the city—cars braking, trucks clattering by, horns sounding, music playing, people talking—all fell into the background. Emilia could only focus on what Jonathan had to say.

"Hello, Jonathan?" she asked after a short breath. "I'm sorry, I was in a bar and it was too noisy to talk."

"That is fine, Miss Campbell," Jonathan's voice was calm and to the point; Emilia was envious of his composure. "Please pardon the intrusion. Ordinarily, I wouldn't call after-hours like this, but I had some news I thought you might be interested to hear."

"Yes, of course," Emilia choked out.

"Well, I've spoken with Martin Thiess, the lawyer who contacted me from Vienna."

Emilia found herself nodding slightly. "Yes, I remember."

"In short, he would like for you to travel to Zillah to meet him. He has also conveyed that this needs to happen with the utmost urgency. He'd ideally like you there by end of week if that is possible."

An enormous sense of relief swept over her; Emilia was eager to put all the missing pieces together. "So, I'm Emilia Blagden then, and my parents were from Slovakia…" She beamed as she placed her hand over her heart. "Does he know much more about my family there?"

"Yes, ah…it would seem so," Jonathan said. "He hasn't shared any additional information about your family with me. It was late there when we spoke, and he was mainly concerned about the timing of your visit. I would expect more information about your ancestry and any relations will be available when you meet with Mr. Thiess."

"All right, I understand." Emilia tried not to sound as deflated as she felt. She would have answers soon enough. "Amanda and I did a little research on Zillah earlier, but I don't even know where it is on a map to see how long it will take to get there."

Jonathan chuckled politely. "Yes, I have to admit I'm not terribly sure of the location or logistics myself. We work with a very good agency and I can have them make the travel arrangements. With a little insistence, Mr. Thiess agreed that Amanda could accompany you— and reiterated that all costs would be covered by the estate."

Emilia couldn't stop grinning, looking forward to the adventure that lay ahead during fall break. "Thank you. That sounds…perfect!"

"Okay," Jonathan said, professional as ever. "It sounds like time is of the essence here, and he indicated you'd need to stay in Zillah at least through Monday, so when would you be able to leave?"

"I have my last exam on Thursday morning and Amanda is done already. I guess we can leave any time after that. As for a return date, we can probably come back right after..." Emilia smiled again; she always loved spending time in Europe, everything about it sparked joy—the people, the history, the architecture, the food...why hurry home? "Or," she added, "maybe we can spend a few extra days and Amanda and I can hop across to...Paris, after we're finished in Zillah? We don't need to be back until the following week anyway."

"I can't see any problem with that. Making the most of it while you're over there sounds sensible to me." This man had the ability to make a vacation of a lifetime sound as dull as taking an exam. "All right, leave this with me and look out for an update tomorrow."

"Jonathan, thank you so much," Emilia said, hoping he could feel her happiness through the phone.

"You're most welcome." He sounded proud, pleased with a job well done. "You have a good evening, Emilia."

Once she'd hung up, Emilia clapped her hands together and did a quick dance on the spot before hurrying back inside. She emerged from the crowd grinning with excitement as she joined the others.

"Well?" Amanda prompted, jumping out of her seat and practically dragging Emilia to the table. "Tell us! What happened? What did he say? You look like you're about to burst!"

"It's me!" Saying it out loud filled her with a surge of relief. "I'm the Emilia Blagden they've been looking for! Can you believe it? I might finally find out something about where I came from!"

Amanda wrapped her arms around her sister. "Oh my God, Emmi! I'm so happy for you!"

"But wait, there's more," Emilia said once she was able to breathe again. "They want to meet with me in Zillah as soon as possible— and you can come, too!"

Emilia and Amanda squealed and hugged again. "See?" Amanda said. "*Now* aren't you glad I kept asking about that?"

"Yes!" Emilia conceded. "Yes, I am!"

Once the group had settled down, Amanda asked, "So, when do we go?"

"Well, I said we could leave after my last exam on Thursday. And get this—the estate business should only take a few days and he was fine with us going to Paris afterwards."

Amanda's eyes lit up like she was about to giggle, but she held it in. "Emmi, we're going to have so much fun!"

"This whole sister trip sounds great and all, but any chance you can bring a few friends too?" Chelsea winked cheekily.

Emilia laughed. "Oh, how great would that be? The lawyer said the estate is paying for the two of us, and that took a little arm-twisting by the sound of it. I don't know that they'll spring for three more tag-alongs."

"Bummer," Megan replied. "That counts me out—at least for this semester."

"Yeah, me too." Jasmine frowned and took a sympathy sip of her cocktail.

"Although..." Megan added, narrowing her perfectly-lined eyes. "If it turns out that you *are* a long-lost princess, you'd better bring us all along next time!"

"Deal!" Laughing, Emilia clinked her drink against Megan's, and the others joined them.

The waitress brought over another round of drinks, which she informed them were sent by the blond-haired rower at the bar. Emilia felt the heat flooding her cheeks and covered it by taking a sip of her mojito. Another round was quickly consumed after that, and the impromptu, low-key mid-week catch-up began to morph into a somewhat less tame evening.

Chapter Eight

Perched high in the hills above a remote Slovakian village, the Blagden castle stood mostly darkened, its imposing walls and steep rooftops striking a foreboding silhouette against the night sky.

The southern end of the complex was closest to the village and from its elevated location, the top floor of the south tower offered an incredible view of the town and river below. Mountainous scenery spread in all directions, and tall windows framed the magnificent landscape.

Inside, the staircase snaked its way through the preceding four levels before reaching the top; a sweeping space capped by a vaulted ceiling. The room's heart was a stone fireplace, open on all four sides, separating the vast loft into as many distinct areas: a landing followed by the den, boudoir, and lounge.

The wooden floor was worn from years of use and a crackling fire burned in the hearth, filling the air with the scent of pine. It warmed the room to an almost uncomfortable level; the radiating heat was a stark contrast to the cold evening.

Decorating the stone walls were intricate tapestries, woven long ago by women from the village. The den's prominent feature was a redwood desk flanked by tall shelves filled with rare books, manuscripts, and scrolls. They were all original editions, and in some cases the only surviving copies. The collection spanned hundreds of years of recorded knowledge, notes, and experiments on the darker forces of the universe.

The other levels of the tower were unremarkable. Mostly utilized for storage, they had become a virtual graveyard of items long forgotten, layered in dust and cobwebs. Of course, this was intentional; the tower's single occupant preferred privacy much of the time.

The phone was heavy, an early model Massimino hadn't bothered to update. He placed the handset in the cradle and leaned back in his ornate vintage chair, a small squeak escaping from below as he reclined. Placing one hand on each armrest, he felt the soft, well-worn leather beneath his palms and fingertips as he focused on the surface of his desk. In many ways it was a work of art: sturdy and functional, built by a master craftsman with silver sculptures of serpent pairs set into each corner. A green marble work surface was recessed into the top of the desk and featured a diamond inlay of stars. A couple of piles of recent newspapers from around the world sat in the upper right corner. A simple wood and gold desk clock ticked on the other side, and a brown leather folio which had arrived a few days prior sat close at the lower right corner.

As the fireplace blazed, flecks of light reflected off the stars and danced in Massimino's eyes. A small yet contented smile formed on his lips.

The moment is almost at hand. At last, after all this time, no longer must I remain banished in this place, I will be able to free myself of this curse.

Massimino opened the leather folio, separating several pages of typed notes and information across his desk. He carefully viewed several photographs, placing each one down as he focused his attention on the next, and the next.

The photos were of a beautiful young woman. Her silky dark brown hair framed an oval face with high cheekbones. Her lustrous green eyes were filled with fervor, and she had perfect, full pink lips. She was dangerously desirable, her smile warm. The pictures had been taken discreetly and without her consent as she went about her daily activities over the past week or so. As Massimino stared at a close-up photo of her face, he paused. Without shifting his gaze from the photograph, he placed the others upon his desk, and to the tune of brass wheels rolling along the wooden floor, he pushed his chair back and stood up.

Emilia, where are you now?

The old floorboards creaked ever so slightly as Massimino strode to the windows behind his desk, peering down in the direction of the village below. It was a clear night, and given the late hour, all was quiet and still. The streetlamps outlined the roads through the village while an occasional house light shone from a window; its inhabitants yet to settle for the evening.

Massimino turned his attention back to the photo of Emilia.

Is it too early to say hello? he mused while tracing his fingers along her face. Breaking his gaze, he looked across to the clock. *Yes, still too early. I don't want to risk a visit if she is awake—not yet anyway.* He sauntered to his desk, placed the photo on top of the others, and sat back in his chair once more. *There won't be much time once she arrives; I need to make sure she is willing and compliant very quickly. Last night was a good start, but this must go well. She is the last of her line...my last chance.*

His focus was broken by a soft muffled murmuring from across the room. The bed—an elaborate and impressive structure in its own right—took up the boudoir area. Constructed from heavy wood and painted black, it had worn over the ages with some flecks of the natural timber exposed. The bedframe featured a spectacular arched canopy that soared into the open space above, pointed turrets marking each corner. The bed was wide enough for five people and was donned with plush and luxurious linens; black, gold and red tapestry-style velvet blankets sat atop smooth, black silk sheets.

On the bed was a young woman from the village: Luna. She was naked, lying on her side and facing toward the edge. Her straight reddish-brown hair was tangled around her as a black silk sheet rested across her derriere, working its way lower as she moved about in her deep and restful sleep. She subconsciously exposed more of her freckled white skin as her legs stirred in an attempt to cool her body in the warm room.

As Massimino looked on, she shifted again, letting out a series of soft murmurs as she nuzzled her head into the pillow.

Perhaps a distraction is the best thing right now.

"Wake," he whispered, moving his right hand and forearm in a gentle clockwise wave through the air. A breeze swirled around Luna, tickling her fair skin and causing goose bumps to form. Responding to the sensation, she rolled onto her back and stretched her arms above her head, entwining her hands and arching her back, which pushed her pert breasts upward as she sighed. Then her body relaxed, and her eyes opened. They were drawn immediately toward Massimino, sitting at his desk with an amused grin. Luna smiled back and gathered some pillows to comfortably prop herself up, making no effort to conceal her naked curves.

"Have you been watching me sleep?" she inquired.

Massimino's eyes wandered over her: the disheveled fine red hair, fair, freckled skin, feisty hazel eyes, and teeth that were perhaps a little too big for her face. It gave her an appearance of innocence. An innocence he'd recently taken great pleasure in corrupting.

"I was," Massimino replied, his voice deep and sultry. "Were you having a...pleasant dream?" He already knew the answer.

Luna giggled, stretching and sighing again as she crossed her arms behind her head. "I *was* having the most incredible dream. I was whisked away from my lowly life as a waitress and maid in the village to a castle tower where a charming—but maybe *dangerous*—man seemed to take over my mind and body. I used to be such a good girl...well mostly anyway, and now, when I think about the things we've done..."

She locked eyes with Massimino.

"But maybe it isn't a dream at all," she said with a soft smile. "It's strange because I actually *do* remember dreaming something like this, even before I first came here."

He felt himself becoming aroused as he relished her youth and natural beauty. Her floral scent was alluring, her words stirring memories of their intimacy. "No, this is certainly not a dream."

Luna looked toward the fire, Massimino fully aware of the warmth surging in and outside of her body. "It's so hot in here." She stared back at Massimino, suggestively spreading her legs.

The fire danced in Massimino's eyes. "Come to me," he commanded.

He engulfed Luna's body with a wave of heat, the sensation coursing through her from head to toe as she rose from the bed, almost in a trance. His influence heightened all her senses.

"Oh my God, what are you? How do you do this to me? I feel so powerless." She spoke almost breathlessly as step by step, without inhibition or modesty, she strode over to Massimino's desk.

"Shh," he cooed. "Be calm."

Biting her lip, she stared at him with quickened breaths. "How can I be calm when...when I feel like I'm about to explode?"

Luna untied the braided belt from around Massimino's waist, allowing it to fall to the floor with a faint thud. He pulled the robe over his head, purposefully grazing her nipples with the coarse fabric as he removed it. She inhaled sharply. Luna stood on her toes, pressing her naked body to his as they embraced, her mouth seeking his with the urgency of someone drowning, desperately needing air.

Massimino's tongue explored Luna's mouth with insatiable hunger while their hands roamed one another's bodies. Massimino pressed his hardness against her.

"How...can I please you?" she panted, licking her lips. "I'll do anything...for you."

He glared down at her the way a wild beast looked upon its prey. Lifting her as if she were a toy doll, he placed her on his desk. She steadied herself quickly with her arms before arching, chest pushed out, her head coming to rest almost upside-down as she gazed toward the fire. Massimino's large hands roved across the soft flesh of her breasts and stomach as he moved them down her body toward her thighs, which he spread apart forcefully before entering her.

Luna let out a deep, long moan as Massimino worked himself inside. "Oh my God, Master. Yes!" Her intense longing welcomed him easily as he began to move back and forth. Her body writhed and bucked on the hard marble, scattering the photographs onto the floor. She only gave them a glance, her expression curious for a moment before Massimino reclaimed her attention.

Massimino's energy levels rose as their encounter continued, a layer of sweat visible on both their bodies as he penetrated deeper, the waves of pleasure growing within them before ending in a dramatic climax. Luna slumped against the desk, staring up at him. She opened her mouth to speak but couldn't form words.

Massimino looked down at her; she was exhausted. "You need not speak," he reassured her. "Rest now." With a wave of his hand, a breeze encircled Luna, lifting her carefully into the air. As she rose, he gestured toward the bed and she was carried and placed down gently on the mattress. Barely conscious, Luna would not be fully aware; upon feeling the softness of the sheets and pillows, she rolled to one side and curled up with a sigh, drifting into a deep sleep.

Massimino watched, feeling completely revitalized. As she slept, he whispered, "Thank you, my beautiful thing. What you've given me these past weeks has been just what I've needed to ready myself for the task ahead."

Now, I must prepare to visit the heiress.

Massimino closed his eyes and consciously slowed his breathing to a deliberate, well-practiced rhythm as he focused solely on the image of Emilia in his mind. Around the tower, wind began to swirl on what had until now been an eerily calm evening. Massimino's eyelids remained closed, the rapid movement of his eyes beneath them pronounced. Visions of stars and light flashed by as if he were crossing the universe into a sudden stillness.

The silence was broken by voices; conversation, laughter, music. Then images began to appear, hazy at first, then more defined. It was an unfamiliar place.

Darkened, women around, young women—a man also. The laughter and conversation stopped abruptly, faces turning toward me, concern in their expressions.

"Emilia, are you okay?"

Massimino let out a deep sigh as the images flickered before him as if Emilia's eyes were his own.

"Emmi, what's wrong?"

She's awake, he realized. *And worse, she's not alone. I need to leave, but first...*

"Sleep, Emilia," Massimino whispered in this state, sending the instructions echoing through her mind. *"Sleep."*

Massimino felt his anger ignite as the lights, colors, and stars tore past him in reverse. He opened his eyes and looked out the windows of his tower once more.

I must be patient, he told himself. *But there is so little time.*

Chapter Nine

*I*t *must be getting late,* Emilia thought as she looked around the lounge at Havana. They were the last patrons there except for Oliver and two of his friends at the bar. Her head starting to swim as she felt the buzz brought on by the many drinks she'd been enjoying.

"Well, looks like we've closed this place out for the night," Amanda said, "So...where to next?"

"How about we go around the corner to Maison and chill a little?" suggested Chelsea.

"I want to dance," Jasmine replied, throwing her auburn hair into a messy bun. "You know, since we're out already and all."

"I think it's time to..." Emilia stopped her protest as Oliver approached. She couldn't help but be taken in by his smile and found herself beaming back at him.

"Ladies," he said in that deep, charming voice of his, "the bartender said it's last call. Can I get any of you another drink before they close up?"

Seemingly catching Emilia's goofy smile, Amanda nudged her sister. "Olly, Emmi here was just about to tell us all how she'd like to call it a night and go home."

Emilia shot her a hard stare, her jaw dropping a little in shock. *Am I that predictable?*

Amanda tilted her head, pulling out her batting-the-eyelashes move. "So...since you're about to leave too, do you feel like joining us and convincing her to stay out just a little longer? Your friends are welcome to come along."

Oliver's face lit up, though he did his best not to seem too eager. He glanced at his watch before raising an eyebrow toward Emilia, who found herself expectantly staring back at him, hoping he'd say yes.

"What do you say, Emmi?" Her nickname on his lips made her face heat. "Are you in?"

"All right," Emilia said, adding a dramatic sigh. "I'm in." She winked at Oliver.

The girls burst into spontaneous applause and Emilia couldn't help but blush at the attention.

"What *have* I gotten myself into?" Oliver joked. "I know the guys need to head home—they've got exams first thing tomorrow—so I'll wrap up with them and meet you outside." He returned Emilia's secret wink before joining his waiting friends back at the bar.

Taking their last sips and picking over what was left of the snacks, the girls decided that Maison was the best choice to settle in for a night cap. They'd save the dancing for another night; it was only Tuesday.

They made their way out of the bar and back onto the street. The air was brisk now, though no one seemed bothered by it; they were all engrossed in conversation about Emilia and Amanda's upcoming trip. The earlier hustle of the city had slowed to a hum. Walnut Street congestion had eased to a steadier pace while occasional pedestrians made their way along the sidewalks.

Oliver appeared further behind them, and he had slipped on a black leather jacket over his shirt. He smiled as he heard a collective murmur of approval upon joining the group at the crosswalk, and Emilia returned the gesture. Then the light changed, and they crossed.

Maison was a cozy, Parisian-style bistro that offered the perfect people-watching opportunity with its outdoor seating that spilled onto the street across from the tree-lined, picturesque Rittenhouse Square. As they approached the entrance, Emilia saw the park was mostly dark save for a few tall lamps illuminating the walkways. Nudged by the cool wind, the trees produced swaying silhouettes against the buildings surrounding the square. Although quite different, the scene was enough to draw Emilia's mind briefly back to the darkened forest beyond the chapel in her dream. Before the thought had a chance to develop further, Oliver's voice called to her.

"After you, ladies." He was holding the door open, waiting for them to walk through.

"Thank you, Oliver," she said quietly.

"Sure thing, Emmi." He winked and flashed her a flirty smile.

The space inside had an old-world feel about it, with dark wood, velvet curtains and chairs, and heavy drapery adorning the walls. The low lighting and soft jazz music always created an inviting vibe for those evenings when it wasn't quite time to head home. The central bar was about half occupied, while the tables were mostly empty; the diners had left hours ago.

Amanda led the way to the corner by the front window and they all removed their coats and sat down, shuffling to ensure Emilia and Oliver sat side by side on the couch-style booth seat.

"You two need to…talk," Amanda insisted to a shared laugh by all. A friendly waitress stopped by and they all ordered drinks as Emilia began to fill Oliver in on the unexpected developments of her day.

She was in the middle of describing the medieval town when a sudden wave of dizziness swept over her. Attributing it to the drinks, she closed her eyes and waited for the waitress to return so she could order water; she'd had enough alcohol. It was as if a strobe light was blinking behind her eyelids. She couldn't make it stop.

"Emilia, are you okay?" Amanda demanded. Emilia's tongue didn't seem to work. She was exhausted now that her eyes were shut, but she didn't think sleeping at a bar with her friends watching was a good idea.

Slowly opening her eyes, she blinked again a few times before glancing up.

Whoa, what was that?

"Emmi, what's wrong?" Amanda clamped a hand around her arm. "What was that about?"

"I...I don't know." She gulped. "There were bright lights...like stars flashing, or something... it's gone now." Amanda carefully shook her, trying to make sense of what just happened.

Oliver placed his hand on her shoulder. "Do you need a doctor?" he asked. "That doesn't sound so good."

Emilia paused. "No, I'll be okay," she assured him. "Just exhausted. Maybe I need to go home and get some rest."

Amanda nodded and studied Emilia for a few moments. "You're right—it's been a long day; let's get you home."

Emilia started to stand up but felt unsteady, her knees threatening to buckle.

Oliver stood to catch her just as she lost her balance. "Here, lean on me," he offered, gliding her arm over his shoulder as he held her waist and began walking her toward the door.

"Goodnight, Emmi!" the rest of her friends called after them in unison. "Hope you're feeling better in the morning," added Megan.

Emilia turned back and smiled. "Thanks, girls. I'm sorry I'm...flaking like this; I'll be fine tomorrow. I just...need a...good night's sleep."

Amanda told them she was saying goodbye and leaving some money; Emilia and Oliver would wait for her outside.

Emilia rested her head against Oliver's chest as they stood at the curb. The evening was quiet, and she watched the trees undulating back and forth in the park across the street. As she listened to Oliver's heart beating against her ear, she enjoyed the smell of his cologne and the soft leather of his jacket against her cheek. A cool breeze blew past them and Oliver wrapped both arms around Emilia, turning so he shielded her.

Emilia looked up at Oliver and smiled at him through sleepy eyes. "Thanks Oliver. You're the best."

Amanda came up behind them and all Emilia could see was her smirk. "If I didn't know any better, I'd say you two were lovers."

Before Emilia had a chance to reply, her knees felt weak and she gripped Oliver to steady herself.

"How are you feeling, Emmi?" Amanda asked as she wrapped her arm around Emilia to help support her.

"I'm feeling all right," she said, "A little dizzy or something, but not as bad as before. Tired," she sighed, almost breathless. "I feel tired."

"Olly, do you mind coming with us?" Amanda asked as she pressed the button at the crosswalk light. "Emmi's definitely not feeling so great and I might need your help to get her upstairs."

Oliver nodded, focused on Emilia while he held her waist ready to help her across the street. "Sure, whatever you need."

Emilia was sandwiched between the caring arms of Oliver and Amanda as they guided her home. After a stretch of time she wasn't aware of, strong arms lifted her. She was in her apartment, then in her bed. Emilia's groggy eyes cracked open just long enough to see Amanda fluff her pillows and tuck her in.

Chapter Ten

T he stony structure seemed to hover in the distance amongst the fog.

The chapel again, Emilia thought. *Another wild dream?*

Emilia closed her eyes, rubbing them gently with her fingers as if doing so would erase her vision.

This feels so real. How can this feel so real? I know I need to wake up.

But the same musty smell filled her nostrils once more and she felt the sensation of the cold marble beneath her feet. She was inside the same mysterious place she'd visited in her sleep the night before.

I really need to wake up now.

With her eyes still closed, Emilia became more present in her current circumstance; she pushed back the hood, so it pooled around her shoulders. The tips of her fingers stroked her cheeks, neck, breasts, stomach, and front of her thighs. The subtle sensation of the fabric against her bare skin tingled through her body.

A gentle breeze whispered against her back, circling her and causing goose bumps on her soft skin.

"Emilia…" a voice reached her ears and her eyes popped open, urgently seeking the source.

Candlelight danced off the walls, ceiling, and pews, the beheaded statues lined up along the sides. But this time, she wasn't alone. Ahead of her, standing patiently in front of the altar was the same mysterious robed figure she'd encountered in her last visit to this strange place. Even though she could not see his face, Emilia *felt* it was him.

Much of his expression was obscured by the hood of his robe, but candlelight bathed his exposed lips and chin in a warm orange glow, shadows swaying over him as she watched his mouth move.

"Emilia, come to me." His whispered words seemed to compel her with a need to move toward him more than any shouted command ever could.

Emilia found herself walking down the aisle of the chapel toward the robed stranger at the altar.

No, not again, she wanted to scream. *I remember what happened last time!*

She dismissed the thoughts of caution urging her to turn back, driven instead by some deep emotional connection taking precedence over fear—or even self-preservation.

Where is this feeling coming from?

As Emilia reached the steps of the sanctuary, the figure reached both hands upward, slowly pushing the hood away from his head, the rough black cloth crumpling around the back of his neck and shoulders. Emilia inhaled sharply, holding her breath as her eyes met his—blue and set alight by the orange and yellow flames reflecting within them.

His eyes softened, a sense of longing flooding his expression. The corners of his mouth formed the faintest smile. The mysterious man uttered a single word, tenderly and confidently: "Emilia."

His voice was deep, his gaze relentless. She was captivated. "Yes, I am Emilia. Who are you?"

"I am Massimino." He did not blink or break eye contact.

Emilia began a rapid fire of questions. "Massimino? Do we know each other? Where are we?"

"I am sure you have many questions," he murmured. "Maybe you do not even know who or *what* you are, since your parents were…taken from you, and you were raised as an ordinary person in a faraway land."

Emilia frowned with confusion. "I don't understand, of course I'm...ordinary. What do you mean? Who do *you* think I am? And what do you know about my parents?"

"Emilia," he smiled, "you are far from ordinary. I am sure there is much you want to know and many answers that you seek. I have searched for so long, and now I have found you."

Frustrated, Emilia's confusion only grew. "None of this makes sense; the more you say, the more questions I have."

Massimino gazed at her sympathetically. "First, you need to trust me...surrender yourself to me."

Emilia averted her eyes and stared at the ground. "I don't even know you."

"You will." When Emilia looked back at him, Massimino's eyes locked on her. She wanted to respond, to ask the hundreds of questions that had been running through her mind only a few moments earlier, but his stare triggered something within her. A warmth spread through her body, her thoughts cloudy and her confusion replaced with intense desire.

A breeze blew gently through the chapel, causing the soft fabric of Emilia's robe to flutter against her fair skin. As the coolness of the air washed over her, it highlighted the warmth burning within.

Emilia felt her lips part and from somewhere deep inside, a moan escaped—a moan of sensual pleasure as she began to surrender to the ever-intensifying sensations filling her.

Massimino cocked his head to one side, his smile morphing into a mischievous grin as if he knew what she was feeling and was somehow responsible for it, despite never having laid so much as a finger upon her.

He knows! How?

Before she could find the words, Massimino waved his right hand to gesture her closer. A swirl of wind encircled Emilia again, compelling her forward.

"Come to me."

The flaming sensation enveloped Emilia's body and forced her to gasp and moan again as her desire for this man—this *stranger*—continued to grow. Their eyes locked, Emilia eagerly succumbed to Massimino, the man who had sacrificed her on the very altar he stood in front of only the night before.

The candlelight continued to shift across the stone walls of the chapel and became even more wild as wind swept through the space. The moon, bright in the sky, shone through the windows behind the altar.

Driven by a craving and lust like no other, Emilia found herself striding up the steps to Massimino. A brief, uncomfortable realization entered her consciousness: at this moment, standing before him, she would do anything to satisfy the burning hunger within her.

"Do you trust me?" Massimino whispered. He ran his hands through her hair, drawing her into a passionate kiss which seemed everlasting as their tongues twirled harmoniously, furiously, insatiably.

Lips parting, a breathless Emilia looked beseechingly into Massimino's eyes. "Yes," she replied.

Taking a step back, Massimino created an opening between the two, but before Emilia could move closer to him again, Massimino's hands reached out and tore at the fabric of her robe; the sound registered in her mind as it fell to the floor.

Emilia's excitement overpowered her usual modesty, instead, longing for his gaze and hands to roam her body had taken over. Massimino scooped her up in his arms, his rough robe grazing her skin as he placed her on the coarse stone altar.

Emilia looked toward Massimino before her eyes were drawn to the daggers on the back wall, their shiny surfaces reflecting the candlelight like mirrors.

Massimino followed her gaze. "You remember. Good," he said. "Not tonight, but you know that time must come?"

Still overwhelmed by the sensations racing through her, Emilia could only nod, indicating acceptance of her eventual fate while reaching to untie the rope holding Massimino's robe around his center.

"Good," he said again. His flat response came with an unusual smile that disappeared behind his robe as, in one fluid motion, he lifted it over his head and flung it to the floor.

Now it was Emilia's turn to grin as she allowed her eyes to roam his body. As she marveled at his towering frame; his sculpted chest sprinkled with black hair, he appeared to levitate before her very eyes as if carried by the wind. He landed gently above Emilia, between her splayed legs.

She moaned shamelessly as he entered her, arching her back as she caressed his body. She squirmed, gripping him tightly as she thrusted in a determined effort to feel him inside her.

Chapter Eleven

"**E**mmi! Emmi! Emilia!"

Amanda?

She searched for her sister, but the lovers were still alone. Still, the scenery around them shimmered as if about to dissolve, and a pained look flashed across Massimino's face. Emilia tried to reach out to him but found she could not move. Then all at once, he was gone.

Emilia squeezed her eyes closed. "No!"

"Emmi!" Amanda's voice sounded less far away. "Are you all right? Wake up!"

Emilia felt disoriented as she opened her eyes, blinking to see her sister's concerned expression. A quick glance snapped her back to reality; she was in her room, comfortable bed beneath her. The lamp on her nightstand had been switched on.

"Emmi, please say something." Amanda spoke softly as she stroked her cheek.

Emilia felt breathless, her chest rising and falling rapidly beneath the sheets. Her mouth was dry, and she had to clear her throat to speak. "I'm...fine. Another dream."

"I came to check on you and heard you making noises," Amanda explained, sitting herself on the mattress beside her. "It sounded like something was wrong." She frowned, the back of her hand against Emilia's forehead. "You feel hot, and you're all flushed. What were you dreaming about?"

Emilia closed her eyes and lay still for a few moments, understanding she was awake but yearning to return to her dream. Return to Massimino.

That made her pause. What was wrong with her?

This is messed up.

Forcing a half smile, Emilia sat up against the headboard. She quickly realized she was naked under the sheets except for a pair of lace panties and rushed to cover her chest.

Amanda smiled and shrugged. "Sorry. You were out of it when we got home last night. I got you undressed so you'd be more comfortable, but I couldn't get these on you." She gestured to her pajamas sitting on the nightstand.

Emilia giggled. "I'll be fine. I *am* fine—just a crazy dream, but I'm okay. Thanks for checking on me."

Her sister didn't seem convinced. "Are you sure? Do you need anything?"

Emilia shook her head. "No...no, thanks. I'm all right, really. You look tired; go get some sleep. We can talk in the morning."

"Okay. But just call me if you need anything..." Pressing a kiss to her cheek, Amanda rose from the bed. "Love you, Emmi."

"Love you, too," she offered Amanda a smile and tucked herself back in. "Night-night."

The longer Emilia lay in bed, the more the same warmth and intense urge from the dream continued to pulse within her. She heard the soft thud and click down the hallway of Amanda's door closing and let the sheet fall away from her chest.

Tossing her head back, Emilia cupped her breasts, tugging lightly on each hard nipple. The tingling sensation was more heightened than anything she'd experienced before. Emilia released a moan as the sensitivity carried down to her throbbing sex. Toying with her nipples, one hand slowly trailed down her abdomen in search of her pulsing need.

Her fingers found that magical spot and she felt her smooth wetness, igniting an explosive sensation within her as she gasped and quieted her cries.

Quiet, what if Amanda hears me and comes back?

No...I need more...

Emilia continued to pleasure herself, whispering, *"Massimino,"* as she recalled her fiery dream.

She could almost feel the robe as he tore it from her skin; his complete power over her. She could hear his voice and the wind around them as he hovered above her. As he entered her.

Emilia stopped herself before things could go too far.

This is ridiculous; I'm getting off to some imaginary guy I dreamed up.

With all the willpower she could gather, Emilia broke the spell of lust, at least enough to force her eyes to open. Her heart pounded and desire still coursed through her as tiny beads of sweat dotted her body like she was on fire from the inside out.

She got up and caught sight of her pajamas waiting on the nightstand.

No, I'm too...hot for those right now.

Opening her bedroom door, Emilia quietly traipsed along the hallway toward the kitchen.

I'm going to have to do something about this...desire, she thought, unashamed of her near nakedness—it was so late that there was little risk of Amanda spotting her. *I don't remember ever feeling this way before—not even with Brandon. What is going on with my body?*

Emilia fetched a glass from the cupboard before heading to the freezer. The cold air billowed out against her naked skin, sending a pleasing shiver through her body and causing her nipples to stand at attention. She grabbed a handful of ice cubes and listened as they clinked against the sides of the glass before filling it up with water.

From the kitchen, Emilia looked through the living room to the city lights beyond the glass; she would never tire of the sight. She took a long drink and felt the cool liquid attempting to soothe the heat smoldering within her as she wandered through the living room to the windows and gazed out.

What a dream, she mused. *I wish I really did have a Massimino in my life. I can't believe how worked up I am right now.*

Without a second thought, Emilia's hand wove intricate lines over her body, uninhibited by the potential exposure from outside.

God, I'm a shy, good girl. I don't touch myself while standing in front of a window. Oh…but it feels so—

"Emilia?" came a sleepy voice from behind her.

The shock almost caused her to drop her glass—she'd been too caught-up with whatever had taken over her body.

But she recognized the voice.

"Oliver?" she blurted, suddenly very aware of her near nakedness as she looked back over her shoulder to see his silhouetted frame on the sofa.

"Are you all right?" he asked, sounding tired and concerned.

Arms over her chest, she didn't quite face him. "What are you doing here?"

"Uh…I helped you home last night. It was late…Amanda let me crash here."

Her heart swelled at his sweetness. *Oh, Oliver. You're such a great guy.*

Emilia felt her libido racing into overdrive, taking control as she contemplated her friend—her *sexy male friend*—Oliver. He sat mere feet away in a tight T-shirt and underwear; she could see the outlines of his muscles and curves in the dim light. A duel raged inside her mind as if two competing parts of herself were locked in conflict.

He's my friend, it's not like that with him.

But it could be.

I need to cover up and go back to bed. I don't do things like this.

The need would not be ignored, greedily clawing at her. Driven by a lust she couldn't understand or control, she turned toward Oliver,

82

exposing her naked breasts to him as she moved closer. Setting down her glass on the coffee table, Emilia purposefully leaned over Oliver as if he were her prey.

"Whoa...Emilia?" Though he was still a little groggy, the city lights in his eyes shone back at her with yearning.

"Oliver..." she wasn't sure what to say at first, but then the words flowed freely. "I...need your help with something." Emilia's voice was as seductive as any temptress as she straddled his lap, resting her knees on the sofa. Before Oliver had a chance to reply, she tossed her hair from her face and sought out his lips.

The taste of alcohol and the warmth of Oliver's tongue made it impossible for Emilia to contain a series of moans as she ran her hands wildly through his hair.

Breaking the contact, Oliver didn't go far. "Emilia, are you sure about this?"

Emilia stared deeply into his eyes as she breathed heavily, the hunger threatening to devour her if she didn't do something about it. "I don't know what's come over me, but I do know there's nothing else I want more than this right now."

She felt his hardness between her legs as she ground her sex against him, sending waves of pleasure through them both. She bit her bottom lip and fixed him with a wicked grin. "It feels like you want this, too."

Oliver abandoned his restraint and their mouths crashed into each other again, hands roaming where they had been too shy to venture until now. He was in a trance, as if working to memorize every curve of her body, every freckle on her skin like his first time with her would be his last. He nurtured her breasts, rolling his fingers over her sensitive nipples, and delicately pinching them.

It sent Emilia into a frenzy. She broke their kiss and leaned back, grabbing at the collar of Oliver's T-shirt. With strength she didn't know she possessed, she tore it open, eliciting a gasp from him that indicated he desired more.

The action briefly transported Emilia back to the chapel with Massimino when he'd ripped open her robe before placing her on the altar. The memory only seemed to fuel her arousal.

Oliver inhaled sharply, "Should we...go to your room?"

"No..." Her breaths were deep and rapid. "Here is...fine. I need this...*now.*"

Not bothering to undress him, Emilia popped open the fly of his boxers. He panted as she sank down on him, then chuckled into her mouth, which she met with a quiet moan. Emilia let her body take over as she moved against Oliver who nipped at her neck, heightening the sensation even more. The pair found a shared rhythm that intensified their longing for each other, the lines between them became blurred with desire. Oliver sought out Emilia's mouth once more, drawing her into a passionate kiss that further stoked her arousal. Gripping his head to her chest, Emilia fully surrendered to the heat consuming her as the world around them faded away.

With a flash of light, Massimino's eyes opened, his breathing calm and steady as it was when he began his journey across time and space that evening. Daylight had begun to stream through the tower windows as he lounged upon an enormous plush rug and a pile of cushions; the fire still burning in the hearth.

Somebody must have woken her. Perhaps the power of our connection is weakened over such a long distance? No matter. She is succumbing to me and is accepting the idea of offering herself in sacrifice when the time comes.

A sly grin crept across his face. *So much progress in such little time.*

"What were you doing?" Luna's voice drew Massimino's attention away from his musings.

She stood beside his desk, naked and unabashed. The light in her red hair made her appear almost mystical as she intently watched Massimino. He had no idea how long she had been there.

"Visiting the heiress," he replied as if the answer should make sense to her.

Rather than displaying confusion—after all, he hadn't been anywhere; she was with him the entire time—Luna picked up one of the photos of Emilia from Massimino's desk. "Is it her, the heiress?"

He replied matter-of-factly, "Yes, that is her."

There was another pause as Luna spread out several of the photographs, eyes gliding from one to the next. "Will she come here?"

"Yes, plans are being made for her arrival, she comes from far away."

"She's beautiful."

"She is very beautiful," Massimino agreed, fighting a smirk.

"Will you be...close with her?"

Massimino stifled the urge to laugh as he sensed Luna's jealousy. "I believe we will be more than *close.*"

Her troubled brow was endearing. He chuckled again. "My dear Luna. Do not be jealous..."

"I am not jealous," she lied.

Massimino ignored her defiance. "It is not my destiny to be constrained by these mortal ideas," he explained. "We will always be connected now—and of course I will summon you from time to time and you will always come, as with others in the village. This is the way of things, or at least it has been, but change is in the air my dear Luna, and I am about to break my dependence on this cycle."

He studied Luna's face as shock and confusion overcame her. "I don't understand what you say—what will change?"

Massimino shrugged off her distress. "You will come to understand...when the time is right."

Luna looked out the window, seemingly unsure what to say next.

"All is as it should be. This is how it is *meant* to be," he whispered, slowly turning his hand to form a gust of wind around Luna, filling her body with a tingling sensation.

Suddenly, her demeanor changed to an eerie compliance as Massimino beckoned her with a gesture. "My dear Luna, come to me."

Her longing for Massimino grew as she tiptoed toward him.

Chapter Twelve

W hen Emilia had first entered the darkened kitchen, it had been during the early hours of the morning. Now, the sun had begun to rise, and warm light filled the room with a golden glow as they lay on the sofa, Oliver holding her in his arms as they gazed out the window. Their breathing was only now returning to a regular rhythm.

"Well, that was amazing," Oliver finally split the silence. "Unexpected—don't get me wrong." He ran a thoughtful hand through his mussed hair. "I'm not sure how to say this, but...I never expected you would be so...intense." Oliver's fingertips traced down her arm, his nose in her hair.

Emilia thought for a moment. "I don't know what came over me," she admitted. "I've never been like that before. I-I...had this dream and...I'm sorry."

He kissed her shoulder. "Sorry? Are you kidding me? It was incredible—*you're* incredible."

Emilia snuggled, wrapping his arm a little tighter around herself. "Thanks, Olly."

"You've got to promise to tell me more about this dream," he joked. "If it had an effect like *that,* I want to know everything."

Emilia laughed and playfully elbowed Oliver in the chest "Hey, don't go being a jerk."

He grinned and kissed her again.

"The dreams are pretty crazy," she said, settling against him and closing her eyes. "And the sex, of course...I'll tell you about them another time. Right now, I need to sleep."

"*Them?*" Oliver teased. "You mean there's been more than *one?*"

"Yeah," she said through a yawn. "This one was the second; the first one was…different, but similar. I think I've got a lot going on in my head right now."

"Okay," he relented, tucking her hair behind her ear. "If you'd like to talk about it, I'll listen."

"Thanks, I appreciate that." Emilia turned and smiled up at him. "I hope things aren't going to be weird between us or anything. Really, I'm not normally like this."

Oliver smiled. "Hey, let's not get too hung up on anything—you've got your trip coming up and a lot happening; everything will work out the way it's supposed to. And, well, I don't see any of this as a bad thing, far from it—seriously, Emmi—that was…wow—like nothing else.

Emilia smiled back.

"Hey," he said, cupping her cheek, "I don't want you to think I'm just trying to get out of here or anything—honestly, I'd love to stay all day—but I've got a breakfast meeting with one of my uncle's friends. We scheduled it weeks ago and missing it would be a huge deal. I need to get home and cleaned up and…I need to track down a new shirt."

Emilia bit her lip as she gave him an innocent smirk. "Oh…yeah, that. You'd better leave then—and don't worry, I totally get it."

Emilia walked Oliver to the door, where they shared one last intimate kiss.

"Good luck with your meeting," Emilia said when they'd surfaced. "And you haven't even slept!"

"I'll be fine," Oliver assured her. "Good luck with your studying. Will I get to see you again before you leave?"

"I don't know." She fought the urge to frown. "I'll find out today and let you know."

"All right." He pecked her cheek. "See you…soon I hope."

Emilia's lips spread into a wide grin. "Me too."

Once she had closed the door behind him, feeling a mixture of confusion, joy, and exhaustion, Emilia made her way to her room. Falling into bed, she drifted off into a deep, contented sleep.

A few hours later, her phone rang, waking her from a refreshingly dreamless slumber. It was the travel agent calling to confirm the arrangements. Emilia went over the details then hung up and contemplated the day ahead.

I could really use a run, but I've slept too long. I need to study for my final tomorrow.

She rolled out of bed and strolled into the kitchen hoping to see Amanda, but Emilia was alone in the apartment. She found a series of fluorescent pink sticky notes tacked to the refrigerator door.

I know what you did last night—I think most of the building does!

We need to talk! We may need a new sofa! Be back this afternoon.

Love, Amanda.

Emilia's cheeks flushed with embarrassment as she recalled the early morning hours.

It couldn't have been that bad, could it?

She glanced toward the sofa, the memories flooding back in vivid detail. How she'd torn his shirt from him, his moans as he moved inside her...

Oh, God, it was crazy!

She inhaled a bowl of muesli, took a long, hot shower, arranged her study notes—all meticulously organized—and got her mind into online journalism mode. She set her phone to silent to avoid any interruptions and soon found herself lost in the material. She began to feel like herself again and the academics provided a welcome distraction from the emotional ups and downs of the past few days.

Late in the afternoon, Emilia heard the clicking of a key in the lock. Amanda was home.

Looking up from her study space at the dining table, Emilia remembered the note and smiled apologetically at her sister.

Amanda made an exaggerated show of looking around the apartment as if searching for someone. "Sooo...are you alone? Is it safe for me to come in?"

So, she's going to play it this way, huh? Fine, I'll go along.

"Yes, for now," she replied. "You know me: diligent, mild-mannered student by day and wild sex goddess *after* midnight."

Amanda burst out laughing, obviously impressed by her sister's confident and sassy reply.

"Speaking of which, can I tell you something super embarrassing?" Emilia asked.

"Oooh, I sure hope so!" Amanda exclaimed, clearly excited to learn whatever gossip Emilia was about to reveal.

Emilia chuckled "I went next door to see Mrs. Davis earlier."

"That's nice—how is she?"

"You know, she wasn't looking that great today...she was trying to be her usual perky self, but something felt a bit off—I hope she's not coming down with anything."

"Aww, sorry to hear, she's such a sweetheart and I think she gets lonely—her family lives in California, right?"

"Yup. That's why I like to keep her company, you know?"

"Sure, we rode the elevator together a while back and she told me how much she enjoys your visits. But skip to the good bit, will you?"

Emilia blushed, her eyes finding the floor. "Well, I thought it was bad enough that *you* heard Olly and me."

"Oh my God, *no way!*" Amanda blurted, bursting into laughter.

"*Shhhh!*" Emilia raised her pointer finger to her lips and tried to hide her embarrassment.

"So, what did she say?"

Emilia paused, contemplating whether she'd said too much already.

"Come on, you've gone this far, don't get coy with the details now," Amanda encouraged.

"She asked if my—*friend*—has a grandfather in the area."

Amanda's eyes widened and she covered her mouth with both hands as she and Emilia chuckled uncontrollably.

"Feisty Mrs. Davis…sounds like she's just fine to me. That's priceless!" Amanda replied once the laughter had settled down.

"By the way, I got my lime and pomegranate bodywash back from your shower—again. You've *so* got to get your own! At least I noticed it was missing before I got in this time." Emilia loved living with her sister, but she drew the line at not returning her bath products.

"I *did* get some of my own, but it ran out, and…" Amanda shrugged with a cheeky grin.

Emilia shook her head and giggled, packing up her notes; she was as prepared as she could be for her final.

"Have you heard from Olly today?" Amanda wouldn't let her off that easily. "Is he still able to walk?"

"Oh, *ha-ha*. I had my phone off while I was studying, let me check."

Emilia found two messages from Oliver; he'd let her know that he had a good meeting and hoped her studying was going well. He also wanted to find out more about her trip to Europe and when they could meet up again.

"He wants to see me before we leave."

"I'm not surprised after your performance last night," Amanda winked. "Speaking of leaving, any news about the trip?"

She ignored the first part of Amanda's reply. "Actually, yes. I spoke to the travel agent this morning: we're leaving for Zillah tomorrow!"

Amanda's eyes grew wide. "No way! Why so soon? What about your exam?"

"Apparently it's *really* important that I be there ASAP. Jonathan didn't know all the details. My exam is in the morning and we don't leave until the afternoon," she explained. "The travel agent was going to send over an itinerary—" Emilia scrolled through several unread emails before finding the correct one from Nancy—the agent Jonathan had set them up with—and opening it. "Here it is…"

Emilia looked over the details. "Okay, so it looks like we're on an overnight flight to Vienna, I guess it's the closest city to fly into from here. Then we take a train into Slovakia, it takes us most of the way, then we collect a rental car and drive to Zillah from there."

"Yikes. We'll be exhausted by the end of that!" Amanda commented. "I sure hope this village of yours is a nicer place than it sounded on that web page last night."

"Ooooh," Emilia said, reading further. "It looks like the flights are in business class and they've arranged for us to stay at an inn in the village—that's the only place there. We have a reservation until Monday—then it looks like we'll take another train and a flight to Paris and on Friday we fly back here."

"Nice! A few bonus days to traipse around Paris? How fab! I don't think they'd fly both of us over there in business class just to give you a set of pearls, Emmi," Amanda pointed out. "Remember us ordinary folk at your coronation or whatever it is they do over there!"

Ordinary. The word struck Emilia like a lightning bolt, transporting her back to her dream and the conversation with Massimino about how she was anything but.

"Hello?" Amanda waved a hand in front of her face. "Earth to Emilia. Where are you?"

Emilia blinked the images away. "Sorry. What was that?"

"You totally spaced out on me. Is everything all right with you?" Amanda crossed her arms over her chest, studying her sister. "I'm kind of starting to worry. First you almost pass out at Maison last night, then you wake up and get all carnal with Olly, and you're spacing out now. You've got to tell me: what's going on?"

92

Caught, Emilia sighed. "It's nothing…really. I just had another one of those dreams last night. It was different than the first one but totally weird. It's kind of what caused me to lose control and ravage Olly."

"Wait a minute." Amanda's eyes narrowed. "You're telling me a *dream* got you all worked up like that? No exaggerating, but you sounded like an animal—in heat!"

Emilia raised her eyebrows and shot a look of disbelief toward Amanda.

"Well, maybe not *that* wild," she amended, "but we've been roommates for a long time and sisters forever before that. We don't really have any secrets and you've *never* been like that before—that's for sure."

"No, never," Emilia was inclined to agree. "It was like I wasn't myself or something. What am I supposed to do if Olly wants a repeat performance?" Emilia tried to lighten things.

Amanda didn't bother holding back a laugh. "You and Olly have been ignoring your attraction to each other for a long time; if it wasn't for Brandon, you'd probably already be together." She shrugged as if it was obvious. "I wouldn't get too hung up on last night."

"I guess so…geez, it was great though. Better than great," Emilia corrected herself. "But it's never been like that before. *I've* never been like that before." Her face reddened.

"Dream or no dream, that *was* you," Amanda said. "He's wanted you for*ever*, Emmi. Now you just need to decide what you want—or don't want—and work it out from there."

"I have no idea what I want," Emilia grumbled. "And these dreams aren't exactly helping me think more clearly. I like him for sure, but I don't know if I'm ready for another relationship so soon after Brandon. Besides, we're going away tomorrow and—"

"Hey, calm down, everything will be all right. He'll understand. And from what I heard, it sounded like you *both* really enjoyed yourselves. He's messaged you, right?"

Emilia nodded.

"So definitely get back to him. I'd say let him know there's not much time before we go away, and you guys can catch up when we get back."

"You know, that's a good idea. As much as I'd really like to see Olly again, what would I even say to him right now? He's an amazing guy, I'm just not sure either of us want anything more than...what we did." She blushed. "Or maybe I do, I don't know...I just couldn't control myself. I hope I haven't messed things up with him."

"Nah," Amanda shrugged it off, "Olly is perfectly capable of looking after himself, you don't have to worry about him. Anyway, this trip is probably causing a whole lot of stress you aren't even realizing, and this news about your parents has got to be weighing on your mind too. When we get back it will all be sorted—and you might have a better idea of what you want."

Emilia gave Amanda a big squeeze. "Thanks, sis."

"Of course! I'm always here for you, Emmi."

Emilia grinned; her sister always knew the right words to say to put her at ease.

"So, we've got packing to do and you need to get a good night's sleep tonight. Let's just stay in and we can have a quiet one." Amanda stood at the kitchen counter with Emilia. "We'll figure it all out, okay?"

Emilia nodded, "Okay."

"Great! Now, pour us a glass of wine and tell me about these dreams—you owe me *all* the details," Amanda joked, playfully nudging Emilia's arm.

They talked while they whipped up a chicken noodle stir-fry, and Emilia surprised even herself at the vivid details she remembered. Most of her dreams faded with time, but these seemed to intensify. She didn't understand how or why, nor could she fully comprehend the magnitude of the emotions racing through her as she relived her encounters with Massimino—and the sleepwalking episode she must have had; the only logical explanation for how her room was all messed up.

Emilia looked to Amanda for reassurance. "Please tell me I'm not going crazy."

Amanda gave her a comforting smile, arm around her sister's shoulder. "No, I don't think you're going crazy. I think you've got a lot on your mind right now—especially emotionally—and your imagination is going wild with it all. The sleepwalking thing is a little weird I agree, I don't remember you ever doing that before, but really, no harm done, right?"

Emilia nodded. "I know, and I keep telling myself that too. I've never experienced anything quite like this—I don't think I even realized how much this has affected me until I started talking to you about it."

Amanda squeezed a little tighter. "Look, I can see why you're a bit weirded out by all this, but I'm more concerned about you getting some rest than I am about this Mass...?"

"Massimino. He says it with this incredible accent, like *Mass-e-me-no.*"

"Right."

Emilia could tell Amanda was doing her best not to laugh.

"Your subconscious has conjured up an...*interesting* character. I'll bet any therapist would love to get their hands on this one!" When Emilia's face fell, Amanda nudged her; she was joking. "At the end of the day, it's just two bad dreams—or, I guess one bad dream and one wild, sexy sort of dream. Or something."

Emilia giggled, feeling more at ease; her sister's efforts to rationalize and lighten the mood had been helpful. "Yeah, I agree with you—at least the logical part of me does. Thanks for listening."

They'd since moved to the sofa, Amanda tucking her legs under her and setting her wineglass on the coffee table. Emilia began to feel the effects of her one very full glass of wine as she rested against the cushions, looking out the windows at the city lights beyond.

"So...are you as excited as I am about this trip?" Amanda asked eagerly.

"You know," Emilia said, relaxing a fraction, "between studying, Olly, and these crazy dreams, I don't think it's really sunk in that we're leaving tomorrow—for *Europe!*" she beamed, loving how it sounded.

Amanda smiled back. "Yes! That's what I've been looking for, there's the Emmi I know! I think this trip is exactly what you need right now." She did a little shimmy in her seat. "Boy, are we going to have a blast!"

"For sure," Emilia agreed. "I don't know what to expect from Zillah, though; it's all so mysterious. I feel like I have a thousand more questions after meeting with Jonathan yesterday." She sighed then perked up again. "I definitely like the idea of a few days to just relax after that's all over."

"I know! *Oui, oui,* Paris here we come." Amanda checked her watch and stood, realizing they had a big day ahead the next day. "I think the most important thing right now is for you to get a good night's sleep. Then get up and ace that exam tomorrow so we can fly away on our European adventure!"

"You're right." Emilia gave Amanda a bear hug. "I feel so much better, I just hope I don't dream about—"

"Don't even say his name!" shrieked Amanda. A good laugh before heading to bed was just what the doctor ordered.

Chapter Thirteen

Emilia sat on the living room sofa, staring out the window as the sun rose over the city. She sighed and tucked her legs beneath her as her sister's footsteps padded along the soft carpet in the hallway, becoming louder as Amanda approached.

"Morning," Amanda greeted as cheerfully as possible while warming up the coffee machine. "Your room is all messed up again—been up long?"

"Hey," Emilia answered without looking at her. "A few hours, I guess. I had another dream."

Amanda paused. "What, Massimino again? I'm sorry, Emmi. Would you like a coffee?"

"Yes—to both, and how could I not remember doing that to my room?"

Amanda handed Emilia a mug and joined her on the sofa. Not even the soothing aroma of freshly ground beans was able to perk her up. Her spunky, vibrant glow had faded, replaced instead with dark circles under her eyes, a nervous twitching of her bottom lip.

"Thanks." Emilia gave her a half-smile as she took a sip of the hot coffee.

"So, what happened this time," Amanda said as she did the same. "Were you an insatiable vixen again?"

Emilia shook her head as she stared blankly at the dark brown liquid in the cup, swirling it slightly. "Not at all. It was like the first dream again. He killed me on the altar...and I wanted it to happen."

Amanda sighed. "What can I do to help you get past these nightmares? This just started a few days ago, right? I don't remember you ever mentioning anything like this before."

Emilia glanced at her and nodded. "Yeah, just three times—feels like three hundred somehow." Stretching her neck, she took another drink. "I've never had recurring dreams like this before. What do you suppose it means? Who is he, and why do I want him to...to *kill* me?"

Emilia's hand trembled as she set down her mug.

"Emmi, this doesn't seem right. It's not like you to be this shaken up. I know they're pretty freaky, but they are just dreams—they can't actually hurt you."

"I know...the strange stuff going on freaks me out a little for sure, but it's more than that." Emilia stared at the lightening cityscape beyond the glass. "They don't feel like normal dreams; they're *so* vivid, *so* real—it feels like it's actually happening. My body responds as if it's really happening. Even worse: my *mind* responds as if it wants it all to happen. It doesn't make any sense. It's me and I'm feeling and doing all these things even though I know I shouldn't be...but I want to...?" Emilia was becoming exasperated. "I don't know."

"Emmi, you've got *so* much going on right now," Amanda reasoned. "You're exhausted from not sleeping well on top of it all, which is only making things worse. I mean, you'd never really want any of this to happen, would you?"

Emilia paused for a few moments.

"That wasn't supposed to be a difficult question." Amanda raised her eyebrows, she sounded alarmed.

"No, no." Emilia shook her head. "I wouldn't...I don't think that would be good." Not even Emilia seemed to believe her words as she uttered them.

"Okay, that sounded about as convincing as a politician making an election promise."

Emilia sighed and bit her lip, her shoulders lowering in resignation. "What if it *has* to happen?"

Amanda's eyebrows drew together. "Um, Emmi, listen to yourself! Snap out of it. You've had a few bad dreams—that's all. None of this is real and none of it will *ever* happen!"

"You're right," Emilia said quietly. "I know you are. I just want this all out of my head—it's definitely not real, is it?"

"Absolutely not!" Amanda confirmed. "Seriously, whatever this is, it will pass."

Emilia nodded, feeling better. "Thanks. You're right." She smiled and took another sip of her coffee.

"I love you, Emmi. They're just dreams, okay?"

Emilia hugged her sister. "Okay," she agreed. "I love you, too."

Standing, she felt lighter after speaking to Amanda. "Time to get this day started, right? I'm going for a run."

Some exercise was a good idea. The early morning sounds along the Schuylkill River helped clear Emilia's mind, and the more she ran, the less exhausted she felt. She breathed in the crisp fall air and the farther she went, the more distance she was able to put between herself and the seductive figure of Massimino. By the time she returned home, Emilia was invigorated and renewed.

After a nourishing bowl of granola—and some envious comments from Amanda about Emilia's brilliant ability to retain all the content necessary to excel in her exams—Amanda asked again about Oliver.

"Yeah, we messaged a bit then talked on the phone last night..." Emilia recalled their mostly innocent conversations. "He's really sweet. It won't work out to get together today, so he wants to drive us to the airport. That way we get a chance to say goodbye."

"Well that sure sounds nice of him."

"Yeah, I thought so."

Amanda raised her eyebrows. "Perhaps there could be something to this then?"

Emilia didn't want to give anything away. She didn't quite know where they stood herself. "Maybe..."

"Just don't go and jump him in the car," Amanda joked. "We could have an accident!"

Emilia laughed and felt her cheeks flush with embarrassment. "Amanda!"

"I'm kidding!"

Just then, Emilia's phone rang. It was Jonathan Rothman.

"Good morning, Miss Campbell," he greeted. "Is now a convenient time to talk?"

"Absolutely, now is fine," she answered. "And please call me Emilia."

"All right." His tone was businesslike as usual. "Emilia, I wanted to check in with you to ensure you were satisfied with the arrangements that have been made for your trip."

"Yes, absolutely—oh, and thank you for booking us Business Class by the way. That was a neat surprise!"

"Certainly, and you can thank Mr. Thiess when you meet him. It's the least they can do given all the pressure they have placed upon you in this matter."

Emilia smiled. "Well, we're both really excited to be going; I'm curious to learn more about my parents, and what's *not* to like about a free trip to Europe?"

"I'm very glad to hear." There was an actual hint of emotion in his voice. "I really do hope you find the answers you seek. If you wouldn't mind contacting me when you return, I'd be grateful to know how this all concluded."

"Of course, I will," Emilia said. "I can't tell you how much I appreciate all your help."

"I know you have an exam today, so I won't keep you any longer— please don't hesitate to call if there is anything I can assist with while you're away."

"Thanks again, Jonathan. I'll keep in touch."

Jonathan Rothman took a few moments to reflect on the call with Emilia before moving on to his next task. He found himself walking a thin line between wanting to ensure her safety in a situation he wasn't quite certain he trusted, while at the same time maintaining an appropriate level of professionalism between all parties involved.

Ultimately, there was little he could do—likely he didn't need to do anything. He dialed the number for Martin Thiess; after a few rings he answered.

"Martin, this is Jonathan Rothman. How are you today?"

"Jonathan," he said. "Very well, thank you. What news do you have for me?"

He's certainly not one for pleasantries, Jonathan thought. "I wanted to let you know that everything is arranged and confirmed. I've just spoken with Emili—Miss Campbell. She is looking forward to traveling this evening. I will have the details of their trip sent to you, but they should be in Zillah by tomorrow afternoon."

"Thank you, Jonathan. This is good news. You have done well."

"Pleased to be of service. I appreciate you selecting our firm." He took a breath. "One request if I may: would you be so kind as to keep me updated on how things go with Miss Campbell and her sister once they arrive? If I can provide any support from this end regarding the estate matter, please don't hesitate to reach out."

Jonathan heard a faint sigh. "Yes, yes…of course. I must be going now. I am on my way to Zillah ahead of the Blagden girl's arrival. Good day to you."

"Good—" The line went dead before Jonathan could finish.

The call did not help the uneasiness growing within him.

Chapter Fourteen

Martin Thiess left his home shortly after breakfast. His black Audi sedan sped along the E50 Motorway through Northern Central Slovakia, the rugged mountain ranges looming against a cool, bleak day. This all faded into the background for Thiess—his attention was elsewhere.

Pressing the voice command button on his steering wheel, Thiess said, "Call Massimino."

A few seconds later, ringing could be heard through the car's speakers. Thiess was accustomed to the extended time it often took Massimino to answer a call and his mind wandered to the tasks he would have to complete over the coming days. Worry weighed heavily in his gut. He reminded himself of what he stood to gain; the difficulties and tribulations would ultimately be more than worth his while.

"Martin, my friend," Massimino's voice broke Thiess from his thoughts. "How are you this day?"

"Massimino, I have news on the Blagden girl."

Massimino must have sensed how torn he felt about the matter. "Calm yourself, my friend. The anticipation of an unpleasant task is often far worse than the task itself, no?"

"This may often be the case, I agree," Martin changed his tone. "However, I fear my experience is telling me this task may be an exception, Massimino."

"True as this may be, try to keep a calm mind so we may stay the course."

A moment of relief at Massimino's demeanor was short-lived as Martin slammed on his brakes to avoid a collision with a car cutting him off to make its way to an exit.

Catching his breath, he resumed a normal speed. "I was calling to let you know that the Blagden girl will be arriving tomorrow. She flies tonight and then will take a train and a car to Zillah."

"She is not traveling here with you?"

Thiess sighed unapologetically. "No. The plans had to change—it is inconsequential; she will be there tomorrow afternoon, and there are still three more days before your...ritual. All will be fine."

"All right," he sounded a tad skeptical. "As long as there are no problems. You must be certain of that."

"She *wants* to come, Massimino. She does not know about her parents—or what happened to them. She believes she may find some answers in Zillah, so she is motivated."

"Good...good." This appeared to please him more. "When do you arrive then?"

"Later this morning. I have some experts coming to assess the mine conditions; I want to restart operations as soon as possible once she signs the paperwork."

"So soon?" Massimino asked. "Perhaps you should wait until everything is finalized before taking such steps."

Thiess felt the pang of worry growing within him. "You've assured me, Massimino. What need is there to wait? As I understand it, reopening these mines may not be easy. I don't want to lose any time."

"Please, have patience." Massimino's voice was smooth and warm. "I will do all I can to influence things to be as you wish. With the mines, do what you believe is best; what I seek from this arrangement is far more precious than anything buried in the ground."

"All right, I will be there in a few hours, and we will get underway."

"Very good. I look forward to seeing you—it has been some time."

"Goodbye."

In a heavily forested area of the mountain range, Thiess drove slowly across the rickety wooden bridge. The groans and creaks caused him to grip the steering wheel with both hands as he crept forward. Not realizing he'd been holding his breath, Thiess exhaled when the welcome sound of gravel crunching beneath his tires could be heard once again as he reached the other side.

That bridge was in poor condition last time I was here; now it is barely standing. Why haven't they done anything to fix it? Thiess wondered as he accelerated up the winding mountain road toward the village, the car's traction control struggling against wet leaves and mud.

After an extended stretch of twisting up the mountain, Thiess reached the first houses on the edge of the village—several appeared abandoned and in disrepair. Then he felt the bumps of the cobblestone street, the car's suspension fighting a losing battle to provide a comfortable ride for its occupant.

Massimino had better be right about there still being gold buried under this forsaken place.

An elderly woman began to cross in front of him without warning and Thiess jammed his foot on the brakes, jolting to an abrupt stop on the slippery stones. She was hunched over, and despite being shadowed beneath a ragged shawl, her expression appeared startled. She raised her shaking hand, pointing an arthritic finger at Thiess and mumbling something indecipherable in his direction as she hobbled on her way.

"Hurry up and cross the street!" called Thiess, tersely waving his hand.

Once his path was clear again, he continued along, paying a little more caution to the narrow side-streets until he reached the central square.

Thiess recognized Massimino instantly. He wore a long coat over a black buttoned shirt and dark pants. Massimino's hair was salt and pepper—still thick—and matched the neatly trimmed beard along his jaw. He stood in the middle of town, talking with two local men next to a large, poorly maintained fountain. It hadn't been operational for years, and the small park surrounding it was equally unkept.

He doesn't look a day older than the last time I saw him, and that was fifteen years ago.

Thiess glanced at his reflection in the rearview mirror as he stopped the engine. In contrast, he had become a tired-looking, old man. His wardrobe stuck to neutral colors that didn't draw attention to his age.

I wish I could say the same. This is the face of a weary old man. Business like this does nothing to help.

Thiess subtly shook his head and stepped out of his car—the fresh mountain air left no doubt he'd traveled far from the city. It felt good to move about and stretch his limbs after several hours of driving. Rolling his head in a circular motion, he eased the stiffness in his neck.

Massimino gestured for the two villagers to leave. They glared disapprovingly at the outsider before walking off toward the other side of town.

"Martin, welcome back to my quiet corner of the world," called Massimino as he strolled up to meet him.

"Massimino, I see the weather here is much as I remember it," Thiess replied, looking to the heavily misted, gloomy air surrounding the village.

They customarily shook hands, Thiess almost wincing at Massimino's grasp and the intent stare that came with it. Massimino forced a half smile. "Too much sun would only make this village more attractive to outsiders. I prefer this place to be more secluded; less accessible."

"That would explain the bridge, then," replied Thiess, quickly composing himself.

"Yes, I've heard the condition has been…better," Massimino acknowledged. "It does the job though, no?"

"It may not be suitable for large trucks to come in and out of here, once the mines have been reopened again."

"Well, I'm sure you will resolve any such obstacles." A smirk appeared at the corner of his mouth. "In due time, of course."

"Why do you say such things?" Thiess kept his temper under wraps, not giving anything away. "I want to be able to trust that all will be as you've promised…"

Chapter Fifteen

*T**he greedy old wolf is too impatient to wait for his feast.*

Massimino felt a pang of rage but stifled it, sensing he must tread carefully with Thiess, at least for the moment.

"I will certainly do what I can to influence the outcome in the direction you wish, but I urge patience. It is a sensitive process and there is much ground to cover in a very short time. As for me, once the ritual is complete, I will have no need to seek refuge in this place and can set about correcting wrongs of the past." Massimino frowned in reflection. "This place can be yours to do with as you please."

Thiess stared blankly at one of the discolored, aging dragons sculpted into the fountain behind Massimino. Before either could speak again, their attention turned toward the road leading into the square and the rumble of a truck's diesel engine.

Massimino smiled wryly at Martin. "My, my. So many outsiders in one day. The villagers will be quite curious."

"These are the mining consultants," Thiess explained. "They will be here today and tomorrow to assess the conditions and start working on a plan to restart production—a silver lining to the Blagden girl's delayed arrival as it is less time I will need to keep the two separated..."

"Do what you must. I've had a room prepared for you at the castle. Should I make arrangements for your men?"

Thiess looked up the mountain toward the castle and Massimino did as well, the dark stones barely contrasting against the gloomy sky. "Thank you, but I'm sure their company will have booked them lodging at the inn. I will let you know if there is a need."

"Very good. Then I shall leave you to your tasks and return to my own. I will send Jakub to assist you. The entrances are secured, he will be able to provide access and show you where everything is. Do not enter shaft-D—it is...unsafe. Best to leave it permanently sealed. We will dine together this evening."

Thiess nodded. "All right. Thank you, Massimino."

Massimino grinned as they parted in different directions, he had several tasks of his own that needed tending to while in the village.

Above the Italian trattoria was an apartment occupied by the restaurant's owners. The dwelling's entrance was located to the side of the eatery, and Massimino rapped the tarnished brass knocker on the green door before stepping back and clasping his hands at his waist; his expression impassive as he waited.

After a few moments, the sound of footsteps descending the staircase beyond the door could be heard, and with a scrape, it opened inward. The woman's eyes widened; Massimino could sense shock and even a small amount of fear in her.

"My beautiful Rose, I do hope I am not disturbing you." His brazen demeanor was unapologetic, as the corners of his mouth curved up slightly.

"Massimino...no, not at all, I—"

Massimino raised his hand, gesturing for her to stop.

"It matters not; the reason for my visit is simple and I shall not detain you for long."

"All right, uh—" Rose began to fidget with the sleeve of her shirt; squinting as if anticipating something unpleasant.

"Genevieve and Anton, it seems they had a daughter together—an heiress."

Rose nodded, dropping her gaze. Massimino could feel tension mounting within her though Rose did not appear surprised at the

108

revelation; he cocked his head to the side, regarding her for a few long moments, neither speaking.

"She has been located, and plans are being made for her to return home, here to our village."

Tears began to well in Rose's eyes and she swallowed heavily before looking back to Massimino.

"What is it that you...need from me?"

"You would weep for a stranger...one you have never known? I urge you to see things practically, my dear Rose."

Rose gazed across the square.

"Enzo will arrange the congregation once more; I have no doubt that you will set aside any conflicted thoughts and do what must be done."

There was an extended pause before Rose managed a meek response. "As you say, she is a stranger to me, I understand that you require my obedience."

"Good." Massimino's tone was curt, his expression even.

Rose placed her hand on the knob and began to close the door. A gust of wind pushed it open again, sending it banging against the wall.

"There is one more thing," he calmly stroked his trimmed beard, "the reason I came to visit you, specifically."

Rose met Massimino's stare with a curious expression. "Oh? What is it?"

"In order to ensure that the ritual is...successful this time, I must carefully orchestrate my...relationship with her. I do not want the girl's thoughts to be complicated by unnecessary details from the past, nor do I wish for my existence to be revealed to her until *I* decide it is time."

"But what—"

"Should you encounter her, you are not to speak of her parents, or your...connection in any way—and do not speak of me either. If I even so much as sense—"

"Yes, I understand, I will not tell her anything about...what happened, nor about you."

"Very good, it has been a pleasure, my beautiful Rose. That is all." Massimino smirked as he turned and left, he heard the door close and the sound of the latch clicking as he made his way back across the square.

A brass bell clanged overhead as Massimino opened the door to the butcher shop, drawing the attention of those present and cutting short their conversation mid-sentence as he strode in.

The owners Enzo and Sofia stood behind the counter and exchanged uneasy glances as Massimino entered. Enzo wore a dirty, bloodied apron over worn clothes and a taut belly. His graying curly hair stuck to a fine sheen of sweat across his forehead as he worked. Sofia was dressed in a dark, hand-sewn dress she'd made from what looked like an old set of curtains. However, they hugged the ample curves of her body and the color went well with her black hair, which framed a round, pretty face. The only customer in the store quickly decided to make herself scarce—she was not the one Massimino had come to see.

Grabbing her paper-wrapped meat on the counter, the woman smiled nervously at Enzo and Sofia before scurrying out the door, avoiding eye-contact with Massimino.

The store consisted of a small, half-filled refrigerated display case as well as an assortment of dust-covered condiments arranged haphazardly on shelves. To the rear was a partially processed goat's carcass sitting atop a large, blood-stained wooden table. A selection of knives and cleavers were neatly arranged across the back wall.

"Massimino, I thought we might see you, sir," said Enzo politely as he deposited some coins into the antiquated cash register, but Massimino spotted his trembling fingers.

"Oh? And why is that?" Massimino replied, amused by their apparent discomfort at his presence.

"We heard the rumor," replied Sofia, fidgeting slightly. "Is it true?"

"Please enlighten me, what rumor is that?" Massimino feigned interest, tormenting the pair.

Sofia's brown eyes widened in disbelief. "Well, the heiress of course," she said quietly. "They say there is another Blagden girl...and that she's coming here; that you're gonna...try again."

"Ah, well, in that case, you do already know why I'm here." Massimino smiled.

Sofia turned to her husband and watched as the color drained from his face. Massimino had no doubt the man's mind wandered back to horrendous memories.

"I don't know if I can do that again, Massimino. It was just too...awful," Enzo muttered, staring at the counter and wiping his hands on his apron.

Sofia reassuringly rubbed his bulky arm.

"You can, Enzo, and you must." Massimino's tone was firm though still cordial. "It will be different this time, I assure you. But you must play your part for it to work."

Enzo shook his head. "I don't know..."

"Perhaps I am being unclear." Massimino spoke forcefully now, his anger building. "This is not a choice—if I must replace you for the ritual, I will see to it that you *both* suffer for the...inconvenience this will cause me. You *will* do this."

Enzo and Sofia recoiled, their expressions shifting to a mixture of concern and fear.

"Massimino, it will be all right," his wife reasoned, leaning over the counter slightly. "I'll talk to Enzo and we'll work it out."

"Good." He was pleasant toward Sofia before he pointed at her husband. "You must arrange the same group as last time. They *all* must be ready; it will be on Sunday night."

Enzo nodded in reluctant acceptance. "I understand. I will try."

"You *will* do it!" commanded Massimino, and a strong wind blew wildly around the shop, causing the windows to shudder and the door to bang against its latch.

"Yes, yes, okay." Enzo's wide eyes met Massimino, his hands raised as if surrendering. "I will."

The wind slowed and then disappeared completely as Massimino felt a wave of exhaustion crash over him. He paused momentarily, taking deep, deliberate breaths to avoid exposing his present vulnerability.

"Good," he finally said. "The chapel is being prepared now; you must be ready, too."

"We will be, Master." Sofia had begun to sob, tears rolling down her full red cheeks. "Please, we don't mean no disrespect. The memories—they are just so...painful, even after all this time."

"Tonight, I will be dining with a guest in the castle. Please send your daughter...Caroline, and have her bring Luna with her," Massimino demanded.

Sofia stumbled over her words. "Master, Caroline is so tired—all the young women in the village are. You've been calling for them so much lately."

Massimino glared at her, his face filled with fury.

"Okay, okay," Sofia relented. "I'll make sure they are there."

Massimino's expression softened. "That's better." His eyes traversed Sofia's body, looking her up and down in contemplation before settling his attention on the scar across her left cheek he hadn't had the pleasure of fully studying until now. "You come, too."

Her eyes became wide with shock. "Me, sir?"

"Why do you seem so surprised?" he teased. "Have you forgotten the way?"

"No, it's just that...it's been a very long time." Her voice shook. "And I'm...married now, you know?" Sofia looked to her husband, crossing her arms over her plump breasts.

Massimino stepped up to the narrow counter, reached out, and grazed the exposed skin she had inadvertently pushed upward. Enzo opened his mouth as if to speak but the man could utter no words, only looking on as Massimino continued, fondling her as if she were a piece of the very meat she sold.

Sofia glanced from her husband to Massimino, losing herself in the intensity of his gaze as her body involuntarily responded to his touch. A gasp escaped her lips, but it was laced with something quite different than fear now.

"He does not get to decide," Massimino said, twisting a sensitive nipple through her silky dress. "I would have you on this very counter as your husband watched if I wished. Now, I have more pressing matters to attend to." He squeezed a little harder to make her wince. "You *will* be at the castle this evening. You may not be as...ripe, as you once were, but I believe you may still be of value to me."

Massimino ceased Sofia's torture, leaving her panting and unwillingly lustful as he looked at Enzo. "In any event, your husband will be busy this evening organizing the others in the group; he will have no time to miss you."

Enzo remained silent. There was a glint of rage in his deep-set eyes, but it disappeared as he bowed his head and replied, "We will do as you say."

"Good. Then I will be on my way." He turned to the entrance. "Do not disappoint me—either of you."

The bell clanged, and the door thumped closed behind him.

A level of fatigue he had not experienced for a very, very long time fell over him as he headed home. It forced him to walk slower than usual through the village before beginning on the stone trail that led up to the castle. The steep incline hindered him even further.

"Massimino?" came a haggard, frail voice from behind him.

An unnaturally old woman stood on the trail when he turned. Hunched over, her complexion was fair—pale, even—her hair thin

113

and white. Not much more than skin and bones, she had skeleton-like features

"You," Massimino said. "What do you want?"

"You look tired. And walking instead of soaring with your raven wings. What is the matter with you?"

"There is nothing wrong with me. Circumstances have been draining me lately, but this will soon come to an end once and for all."

"It is the heiress. You are using all of your energy to bring her here, yes?"

"And what if I am?" he replied gruffly, but Massimino knew she was not as easily intimidated as the rest of the villagers.

"I've heard your plans, Massimino," she croaked. "This is madness. You must not do this again."

"Nonsense, old woman. I now know what went wrong. Tell me, are you woefully incompetent, or did you intentionally deceive me? Either way, know that her torment—all the suffering she endured that night—it was all caused by *you*."

"What do you mean?" The old woman stepped back as Massimino approached, a hint of fear in her gray eyes.

"You know exactly what I mean. It seems your translation somehow managed to omit any reference to surrendering *willingly* to the ritual."

"I, I—" she stammered.

"Spare me your lies," Massimino snapped. "You are not the only one capable of learning ancient languages. I knew something was amiss, and yes, it may have taken some time—but I translated it myself. I have been using my...influence to ensure the heiress will be a *willing* participant this time around. This is why I am tired, as you say; she is powerful at resisting even though she does not realize she can. It requires much energy to reach this one, but I have done it in any case. And the strength of her power will only make this better for me once I...acquire all of it."

The old woman nodded. "That's why there is so much discontentment in the village. You are losing your hold."

"I am losing nothing," Massimino bellowed. "I will restore myself as I always do and complete the ritual, so I never have to feel this way again."

A sorrowful look fell over her face. "Please, Massimino. Will you release me?"

Massimino laughed. "Release you? After your betrayal?"

"And if I refuse you?"

Massimino stepped closer but this time the woman held her ground. "If you refuse me, I will extend this miserable life of yours even further, perhaps see to it that you remain an old wretched hag until the end of time itself. Do not test me."

"Massi—"

"Silence, and be gone," he interrupted. "I have no more time for this. You will do your part and that is all there is to it." He turned abruptly and continued his ascent.

What am I to do? The villagers, the congregation, Martin, the old woman, Emilia...I need to be stronger. I need Emilia's strength to break this damned curse—my freedom will not come if it all falls apart now.

Massimino felt the stone, gravel, and moss beneath each footstep with increasing awareness while gazing outward to the mountainous terrain in all directions. Fog and clouds hung heavily in the air, obscuring the features.

I need more, I must take all I can from one of the young ones this time and hope that it is enough to sustain me.

Chapter Sixteen

Emilia handed in her completed exam to Professor Jenkins, who was seated at the front of the lecture hall. "Enjoy your break," she mouthed with a warm smile and strolled out into the fresh air, confident she'd done well.

Relief swept over her, as it always did after an exam or assignment was done. Her preparation had paid off; she was glad her concentration hadn't been interrupted with thoughts about alluring mystery men doting on her then driving daggers through her heart on stone altars.

As she walked down the steps, she ran into Chelsea. She'd done her wispy blonde hair into a pair of space-buns atop her head, and she stuck her pencil into one of them. "Emmi, how are you?"

"Just finished my online journo exam—on my way home to finish packing. Amanda and I are leaving in a few hours—can you believe it?"

"I'm so excited for you! I can't wait to hear every foodie detail when you get back."

"I promise a full and complete report, as soon as I return!" Emilia joked. "So glad I ran into you Chels, listen, can I please ask a huge favor?"

Chelsea grinned, "Sure, what's up?"

"Well, Taylor—one of the girls in the freshmen group I tutor—she has her mid-term in Principles of Journalism tomorrow, and she was hoping I could cram with her tonight. I remember you totally aced that subject and I told her I'd see if you could help." Emilia tapped her fingers on the strap of her bag.

Chelsea shook her head and laughed, "You put the rest of us to shame Emmi, how do you always find time to do so much for everyone else?

I'll help her for sure, just message me Taylor's details and I'll sort it out…she'll be top of her class!"

"You're the best, thanks!"

"Don't even mention it. I'm just so glad you're finally getting closer to finding the answers *you've* been looking for. So jealous I can't come along too. *Hey*, I have to ask, did anything happen between you and Olly?"

Emilia felt her face flush. "Um…"

"Oh God, I knew it! I saw him this morning and he didn't tell me anything, but he was acting all smitten when your name came up. Now I see it written all over your face. Anyway, I want *all* the details, but I have to get to my exam." Chelsea adjusted her bag on her shoulder. "I must see you as soon as you get back to hear all about Europe—and Olly."

Emilia winked. "Sure, promise I'll tell you everything when I get back."

Chelsea gave Emilia a hug, squeezing her tightly. "Love you, Emmi. Safe travels! See you soon!"

"Love you too," Emilia said, hugging her friend goodbye. "Good luck on your exam and have a great break!"

It was mid-afternoon when Emilia entered their apartment again and Amanda bounded into the hallway from her room as soon as she stepped in the door.

"Hey! So, I've been looking into what's on in Paris while we're there and I've got some awesome ideas!"

Emilia cocked her head to one side and raised her eyebrows. "Yes, I'm fine and I think my exam went really well. Thanks for asking."

"Oh please." Amanda rolled her eyes. "Your exams always go well."

"It's not luck, you know," Emilia said. "I work hard and study. Anyway, Olly's going to be here soon so how about you tell me later. I really need to finish packing and get changed."

Amanda gave her a melodramatic sigh. "All right, do what you need to do. Oh, I checked the weather by the way; it's going to be pretty cold there so pack some warm clothes."

"Will do, thanks," Emilia replied as she headed for her room.

"And don't forget your passport…and the cable to charge your phone!"

"Thanks *Mom*, I won't!"

Emilia placed her phone on the dock beside her bed. She felt tired, so selected a playlist she hoped would perk her up. As the music played, Emilia stuffed suitable things into her suitcase for a week away in the cooler fall weather of Europe. Remembering that the combination of planes, trains, and automobiles meant it would be close to twenty-four hours until they reached their destination, she decided to take a shower.

"Knock, knock," Amanda called out as she waltzed into Emilia's room, "I borrowed this earlier but look, I remembered to bring it back this time."

Emilia rolled her eyes in an exaggerated motion but couldn't help laughing as she took the bottle of bodywash from Amanda and made a show of weighing it in her hand.

"And not even empty either!" Emilia joked.

"See, don't ever say I don't do anything for you! I'll leave you to it— hurry up!" Amanda grinned as she turned and left.

Emilia undressed and strolled into her en-suite bathroom, nodding her head in time with the music. While she turned on the faucets and waited for the water to heat up, she caught a glimpse of herself in the mirror.

Her eyes were drawn to a red blotch on her left shoulder. She grinned.

Oh Olly, that hickey! What are we, teenagers?

The room began to fill with steam as Emilia stepped inside and savored the hot water cascading over her face and body. Her supple breasts tingled, nipples hardening as she recalled her encounter with

Oliver. She closed her eyes and allowed herself to revel in the sensation. Everything felt heightened, as if she was aware of each water droplet trailing down her skin. The music was still audible over the stream and she let go, relaxing her mind and allowing the stress and angst of the past few days to wash away.

Mmm...this is exactly what I need.

As Emilia lathered herself with her favorite bodywash, inhaling the therapeutic, citrusy scent, her mind contemplated the dreams she'd had the past few nights.

Why do I behave that way in them? It's so strange. It feels like I love this complete stranger—that I'd do anything for him...I'm this aroused submissive, lusting for him, willing...no, wanting, to let him command me. It's so strong...so real, but it doesn't make sense.

And how do these feelings stay with me like this, even when I'm awake?

Emilia's inner musings were interrupted by the *ping* of a message playing through the speaker over the music.

Olly.

Even though she couldn't see the screen, she knew it was him. She finished up her shower, dried herself off, and went to check her phone.

Be there in 15!

She quickly messaged back, *Great! We'll be ready. Looking forward to seeing you.*

Emilia danced as she studied the contents of her wardrobe. Olly was picking her up and she wanted to make an impact. She turned an oversized black sweater into a chic dress, added a belt and topped it off with a pair of over-the-knee boots. Pulling her hair into a sleek ponytail, she grabbed some reflective shades and her large tote and looked at her work in the mirror.

Emilia applied some gloss to her lips and gave herself a satisfied grin.

Just then, another *ping* alerted her to her phone: *I'm downstairs. Need help with your bags?*

We're fine. Be down in a minute, she typed back.

Emilia stepped into the hallway, her wheeled suitcase in tow and tote over one shoulder.

Amanda was by the front door, cramming something into a side pocket of one of her two large suitcases. She glanced up at her sister and did a double-take "Oh, you look...great. We're going to get on an overnight flight to Vienna, right? You look like you're ready for a modeling gig."

Emilia bit her lip as she took in Amanda's graphic T-shirt and yoga pants. "I just wanted to look...good."

"Well, you do. But now I'm going to look like a slob next to you." Standing, she announced with a sigh, "I'm going to change."

"You look fine, and there's no time!" Emilia insisted. "Olly's downstairs already. What's all this stuff you've packed?" Emilia eyed the bulging luggage. "We're only going to be away for a week."

Amanda's face cycled through a few expressions—frustration and then deep thought—as she tried to come up with a way to stall long enough to remedy the situation. Finally, a look of admiration crossed her features as the likely reason for Emilia's fashion choice sprung to mind.

"You're dressed like that because Olly is picking us up." She gave her sister a sly smirk. "Oh geez, you're not really going to jump him in the car, are you?"

Emilia laughed as she stepped past Amanda. "Come on, let's go. We'll be late!" She offered to take one of her sister's suitcases to help speed up their departure.

They took to the elevator and when they were on the ground floor, the tone echoed off the lobby's marble walls. Oliver and Alfred stood chatting near the main entrance, but the sound drew their attention to the sisters. Emilia felt her heart beat a little faster as she anticipated seeing Oliver again and took a deep breath as they shuffled their suitcases out of the elevator. *Be calm.*

"Good afternoon, Miss Campbell and Miss Campbell," Alfred greeted in his professional yet friendly demeanor. "Let me help you with those bags."

"Thanks, Alfred," Amanda replied, tugging on one of her heavy suitcases.

"Emilia, you look amazing." Oliver walked toward her, their eyes locking. Under a beige aviator suede jacket, Oliver wore an untucked light-blue checkered button-down shirt and dark jeans.

"Hi, Olly," Emilia said before she could stare too long. "Thanks." A beaming smile crept onto her face.

Oliver slipped his arms around her waist while Emilia reached behind his neck. She closed her eyes as their lips met and felt a pulsating tingle sizzling through her body. She welcomed every sensation filling her— the masculine scent of his cologne, the feeling of his strong arms holding her to him, rough stubble contrasting with soft skin.

"Hi, Olly," Amanda sneered cheekily as she walked past the pair, the interruption breaking their kiss but not their embrace.

"Hey, Amanda," Oliver said, taking his eyes off Emilia to glance in her direction. "All set for your trip?"

"Yup, ready to go as soon as you two can tear yourselves away from each other," she quipped. "No need to hurry on my account though, if you need some extra time, I'd like to change my clothes."

Emilia giggled. Oliver looked puzzled.

"It's nothing," Emilia explained. "Come on, let's go."

Oliver placed his hand over Emilia's as she began to pull the suitcases, "Let me."

"Sure, thanks."

Emilia and Amanda watched the two gentlemen load their luggage into the back of Oliver's silver Range Rover.

"Where are you heading to and how long will you be away?" Alfred asked as the three got into the car.

"Emilia found out she's a princess and we're going to Europe to get her crown," Amanda joked. "We'll be back next week."

Alfred contemplated the response for a moment. "Well, I'm sure that makes sense somehow."

"Europe and back next week are the only parts to pay any attention to," added Emilia.

Alfred laughed.

"Oh, and Alfred, while we're away, would you mind checking in on Mrs. Davis every now and then, please? She doesn't really have anyone nearby so she'd love the company—and she might be coming down with something."

"Can do Miss Campbell," Alfred replied, his warm smile seemed filled with a sense of admiration.

"Thank you!" Emilia returned the smile with a nod.

"All right, I'll see you ladies next week then. Enjoy your trip."

The three shared a lively conversation on the way to the airport, Emilia and Amanda divulging to Oliver what they had learned about Zillah and Amanda's ideas for what to do in Paris after they were finished there. An accident on the highway meant they arrived at the airport uncomfortably close to their plane's departure.

"I don't think we'll have time for you to park and come in," Amanda said. "Is it all right if you just drop us off?"

"Of course, I understand," replied Oliver, even though he sounded disappointed.

When they reached the terminal, Oliver pulled into the drop-off zone and all three hopped out of the car. Oliver unloaded the suitcases onto the sidewalk before he and Emilia leaned into one another and kissed.

"I hope you have a really good trip and find the answers you're looking for," said Oliver, staring deeply into Emilia's eyes.

"Thanks, Olly. I hope so too. Oh, here...this is for you" Emilia slipped her tote around to her hip and reached inside. "I didn't have a chance to wrap it, but I think it's your size."

Olly laughed as Emilia handed him a new black T-shirt.

"Emmi, you didn't need to—"

"I know—but I wanted to anyway...I still don't know what came over me..."

Olly grinned and leaned in closer to Emilia. "Whatever it was, I liked it; I'd let you ruin all of my shirts for a repeat of that."

Emilia blushed and bit her lip.

"Hey," he held her hand as she backed away, not ready to let her go. "Will you let me know you made it there all right? Maybe even keep in touch while you're gone?"

Emilia smiled. "Of course. I'll miss you."

"Me too." Oliver smiled back before pulling her to him, kissing her much more passionately this time, his tongue inching into her mouth with longing as their last moments grew nearer. Emilia sensed herself melting into Oliver's body and didn't want the feeling to end.

"Come on, Emmi!" Amanda called, already towing her suitcases toward the entrance. "The plane's going to leave without us!"

She looked at him, suddenly torn. "I have to go."

He cupped her cheek and pressed his lips to her brow. "I know."

"I'll let you know when we get there, okay? See you next week."

They shared one last quick embrace and kiss before forcing herself to pull away and follow Amanda into the terminal. She turned back when she reached the door and was happy to see Oliver leaning against his car, waiting where she'd left him. Her heart liquefied as she waved. He smiled, returning the wave with a sexy wink.

The timing was tight, but with the help of an attentive gate agent and the priority security screening cards that accompanied their business class boarding passes, they made it to the plane with a few minutes to spare.

Onboard, Emilia and Amanda were greeted with champagne as they settled into their seats.

"Here's to a great trip and to finally getting some answers!" Emilia raised her glass to toast her sister.

"And to new romances!" Amanda smirked while clinking her glass against Emilia's. Then suddenly, Amanda gasped. "Did you tell Mom and Dad we're going away?"

"Oops, nope!" Emilia hadn't realized until now herself. "They're still out of contact I think, but I was going to email them; I just didn't have a chance. I'll do it now."

Emilia unlocked her phone just as one of the cabin attendants approached. "Cabin doors are closed and we're preparing to depart. Is that phone in flight mode?"

Emilia swiped and tapped her screen before smiling kindly up at the attendant. "It is now."

"Thank you, miss."

"Busted!" chuckled Amanda.

"Well, so much for that..."

"No biggie—like you said, they won't get it right away anyway—just send it when we land."

"Yeah." Emilia grinned as she put her phone away.

"Emmi, this is going to be so great," Amanda declared. "We're going to have a blast!"

"I know," she agreed. "I almost can't believe everything that's happened over the past few days. I'm so glad you're with me!"

As the engines roared and the plane accelerated down the runway, they grinned at each other, excited about the journey ahead. Amanda squeezed Emilia's hand as the plane took off into the evening sky.

Chapter Seventeen

T he main dining hall of the castle was spacious enough to easily accommodate the impressive sixty-seat, ornate table that dominated the room. It was made of oak and featured deeply carved dragons' heads with bared teeth, spanned wings and imposing paws. The greeting area comprised of two magnificent doors that reached almost to the top of the double-story ceiling. There was a huge fireplace on either end to warm the cavernous space and a passageway beside each which led via hidden corridors to the castle's kitchen. Opposite the entrance, tall narrow windows overlooked the lofty mountains beyond.

Affixed to the stone wall hung an imposing banner that displayed the Blagden family crest. Two swords crossed behind a shield with the letter "B" emblazoned in red. Amongst crimson filigree, two dragons faced each other behind the crest, a twelve-pointed star between them. The numerous tapestries almost completely covered the stone walls from which they hung.

Once a grand and lively space, the dining hall was now dusty and unkept. The tapestries had faded considerably from their original luster, some so vastly deteriorated that they now hung upside down, clinging only to their bottom hooks. Others dangled askew where a hook had failed, causing the tapestry to partially fold over itself. The crest, however, remained perfectly intact and proud; it appeared immune to the deterioration and neglect surrounding it.

Tonight, along with one of the fireplaces, several wall-mounted torches were lit. They burned brightly as their warmth radiated outward to where two seats nearest the flames were occupied.

Massimino sat at the head of the table with Thiess to his right. On display between them sat a large candelabra, its many candles illuminating the table and two faded gold dinner plates upon it. There were also a pair of wine goblets and a decanter, now only a quarter full of a succulent red wine.

Massimino took a sip, savoring the bold flavor and velvety texture. He watched Thiess absentmindedly push the uneaten remains of vegetables through the watery gravy beside a pile of well picked-over pheasant bones on his plate.

"Apologies, my friend," he said. "Times here are not what they once were."

A half smile formed on Thiess' age-speckled face and he set down his silverware. "It is fortunate I did not come for the food."

"The birds—they catch them in the forests around us," Massimino explained.

Thiess nodded. "Perhaps they should have been left there."

"Though this wine from the cellar is truly remarkable."

Thiess nodded again and reached for his goblet, taking a generous swig before looking to Massimino. "Ah, on that, I certainly agree."

"Then allow me to propose a toast." Massimino poured the remaining wine between their goblets then held his out toward Thiess'. "To nearing the end of this journey."

Thiess shifted in his seat before extending his goblet and touching it to Massimino's. "I welcome the end to this, and the reward you have promised."

Both men gulped the wine and Massimino watched as Thiess peered into his goblet. "I am weary, Massimino. It is getting late and we have more work to do tomorrow. Perhaps it is time to retire for the evening?"

Massimino smiled. "Perhaps you have a little energy left? I have arranged a surprise for you." Raising his hands slightly above his head, Massimino clapped twice.

A few moments later, Luna and Caroline returned, scuttling through the doorway beside the fireplace behind Massimino. Without speaking, they began to collect the dishes from the table with Luna beside Massimino and Caroline by Thiess. Both wore beige dresses made from a thin material that did little to protect any modesty they may have once had. On their feet were sandals nothing more than slave women in Roman times would have worn. This had been at Massimino's insistence; it was the only acceptable attire for a woman to wear while performing duties of any sort within the castle.

Thiess stared shamelessly at the women, at their bodies. He'd been doing so all evening as they had come and gone while serving.

A sly grin crept across Massimino's face as he observed Thiess undressing the young women with his eyes and savoring their beauty much as he had the wine. Luna's fair skin nearly blended into her garment, red tendrils cascading down freckled flesh as she maneuvered around the table. Caroline avoided eye contact most of the time, her dark brown curly hair a mixture of her parents while her large dark eyes mirrored her mother's—she also shared Sofia's voluptuous curves, but they were distributed in a more youthful, pleasing hourglass shape.

"This one here is Luna," Massimino reached out and rubbed her derriere as she bent slightly over the table, squeezing her soft flesh and causing her to inhale excitedly. Luna's body responded instantly to his touch. A deep red rushed to her cheeks; she was most likely unaccustomed to experiencing such a feeling with an audience present. "And her friend beside you is Caroline."

Massimino's actions had begun to stir something within him and Thiess looked on hungrily toward Caroline, gesturing toward her. "May I?"

"Of course, my friend."

Caroline wriggled with discomfort as Thiess forcefully ran his hand up the inside of her soft thigh before his fat fingers began poking aggressively in search of her entrance. Her eyes, like a frightened deer, pleading with Massimino as she opened her mouth to speak.

"Silence! You will do as I say," he instructed with a cold smile. "Now, be still and indulge my friend. He has traveled far and helped me greatly."

Beside him, Luna's body stiffened.

"Is this the surprise you mentioned?" panted Thiess as he continued to thrust his fingers inside Caroline.

"Ah, yes, of course." Massimino tapped Luna's rear in quick succession. "Luna, go and fetch Sofia. She came to the castle with you, no?"

Caroline tensed and looked to Luna desperately.

"Be calm," he commanded, snapping his head in her direction. "Do not even think about moving away. Sit on Martin's lap and get to know him a little better."

Thiess removed his hand from under Caroline's dress and pushed his chair back from the table, the scraping sound echoing softly. Thiess spread his legs as wide as he could against the armrests of the heavy wooden chair, making room for the girl.

Thiess took another gulp of wine, smirking like a hunter about to catch his prey. However, Caroline still hesitated.

"Now, Caroline." Massimino spoke calmly but firmly.

She stared down at the table as she tentatively sat on Thiess' lap. She'd barely rested all her weight on his thighs before his hand reached into her loose top and greedily groped at her breasts. Her eyes brimmed with tears as she looked up to Luna who was frozen, watching the scene unfolding before her.

Massimino patted her behind again, "Fetch Sofia."

"Ah...yes," she finally answered. "She is here. In the kitchen."

"Bring her here, quickly."

"All right." Luna gulped as she slowly backed away from the table. Her eyes were full of sorrow as she turned and ran, her sandals patting loudly against the floor. The sound gradually faded to silence as she left the room and continued through the corridor.

"These village folk," Massimino mused. "They are simple, I'm afraid." He swirled his wine and watched Caroline squirm on Thiess' lap as he continued to fumble with her breasts. He soon set about pulling down her dress, so it bunched around her waist as his other hand explored her backside.

"Simple perhaps, but certainly delightful." Thiess chuckled. "This reminds me of the only good memories I have of the last time I was here."

"It's amusing you should mention that," replied Massimino.

A gasp from the passageway drew their attention as Sofia entered, followed closely by Luna.

"Caroline, no!" Sofia cried as she ran to the table.

"Stop!" Massimino commanded as she reached them.

"Massimino, please," she begged. "We all understand about you and we do what you ask to serve you—to give you what you need from us—but not this. Not this man...not with Caroline." She had begun to sob, and Massimino found it as irritating as he had earlier. "Please, I beg you." Sofia raised her hand and gingerly caressed the scar on her face.

Thiess' eyes squinted then widened with recognition at the woman in the dim candlelight.

"Martin, I see you remember Sofia." Massimino grinned. "She certainly seems to remember you. Caroline is her daughter."

Distracted by this unexpected diversion, Thiess had stopped fondling Caroline's breasts, allowing his hand to rest on her leg. Caroline's cheeks flushed with embarrassment as she stared at the ground and sobbed much like her mother.

Thiess nodded slowly. "Yes, I remember Sofia..." Thiess swallowed heavily before continuing. "Why is she here Massimino, is there no end to your depravity?"

Massimino composed his response. "I simply want to ensure that my old, dear friend is rewarded for his efforts—and is incentivized to stay the course, as it were. I sense unease in you and do not wish for your conflicted thoughts to interfere with my plans. I believe Sofia was useful for you to work out some of your…frustration, with the circumstances last time, no?"

Thiess looked back to Sofia, his eyes fixing on her scar, "I do not know what came over me… I—"

"Perhaps it was simply your true nature shining through? In any event it matters not to me. Caroline, why don't you show my friend how welcome he is here…regardless of whatever darker urges he keeps suppressed."

Massimino waved his arm in a circular motion; a gust of wind encircled Caroline and Thiess, Caroline's naked flesh dotting with goosebumps. He smiled as he watched her expression change, the outward cooling effect was temporary and was followed by a familiar wave of heat and a deep, overwhelming arousal.

"I was angry then, what happened to the Blagden woman…what you did to her…what I helped you do to her…" Thiess frowned and shook his head.

Caroline looked up from the floor, glancing briefly at Luna and her mother before fixing her eyes on Massimino, a very different kind of pleading in her eyes this time.

"May I, Master?"

"But of course. I doubt I could stop you anyway."

Caroline turned to Thiess and, for the first time, looked him in his eyes as she lifted his hand and drew it up to her breast.

"Caroline, stop!" Sofia called out desperately, stepping toward the pair. "This man is evil! He will hurt you!"

"No," Massimino commanded.

"I am not evil…I just…" Thiess stammered.

Sofia turned to Luna, who wrapped her arms around her friend's mother to try and absolve her of the pain and helplessness.

Caroline only glanced at her before turning back to Thiess, moving to kiss him as she reached down and began slowly rubbing his hardness, involuntarily grinding herself against his leg.

Thiess pulled his head back as Caroline drew nearer.

"You are angry now too, Martin...release it, clear your mind," Massimino encouraged.

"No, stop." Thiess shoved the girl back. A look of confusion fell across her face as she tilted her head questioningly and slowed her efforts.

"No, don't hurt her!" Sofia sobbed.

"What is it, my friend?" Massimino asked with a cruel chuckle.

Thiess regarded Caroline for a few moments, seeing the desire in her eyes and actions.

"What happened then, it is not something I am proud of...I just couldn't control it."

As he spoke, the tension in Thiess' arms relaxed. Caroline seized the opportunity to once again bring herself closer to him, licking and biting his ear playfully to draw his affections and in turn satisfy her own burning need.

"Enough," Thiess growled, pushing Caroline away again.

"Please, Massimino, stop this." Sofia pleaded, tears streaming down her cheeks. "He is a monster, do not let him hurt my Caroline."

"What did you say?" Thiess shouted, his head snapped toward Sofia as his fists clenched, "I am no such thing!"

Massimino laughed. "Ah, there it is...the beast which rages within."

Massimino turned his attention to Sofia, "Surely you remember that stopping this is not so possible once it is begun. This is not a spell I can just turn off; she may be like this for some time—at least until she has been...satisfied."

Caroline looked to Thiess longingly and caressed her breasts. She was trying to seduce him, tempt him as she continued to grind herself against his thigh, the intensity of her arousal visibly building.

Thiess shook his head, attention on Massimino. "Why are you doing this? You are baiting me."

"Relax, my friend, you need not feel ashamed. It is best that you let go of some of this tension, this anger, before the heiress arrives," Massimino replied. "I have more options to tempt you; there is Caroline, of course, who you are already getting to know." He stood between Sofia and Luna. "Or these two are certainly delectable in their own ways."

"But Massi—" Luna began, a heartbroken look upon her face as her plea died in her throat.

"*Shh.*" Massimino held his finger to her lips. With a tug on the ties, Massimino unlaced her dress and allowed it to fall to the floor, pooling softly around her ankles.

"Please choose me," Caroline pouted.

"Be quiet now," Massimino scolded.

Caroline smiled and continued to absentmindedly rub Thiess through his pants as he gazed upon Luna.

The girl tried to cover herself but Massimino stilled Luna's delicate arms while staring into her eyes. "Do not be shy."

Luna allowed her arms to fall to her sides as Thiess' gaze roamed over her body.

"She certainly fucks well," Massimino said. "Even though she is only recently of age, I can attest to her talents. Or, perhaps more experience is what you seek, something...familiar?"

Massimino turned toward Sofia and ran his finger along her scar. "Do not move," he whispered as he removed her dress. Sofia shuddered, but knew better than to defy Massimino.

"Massimino, please...he is a monster, with you it feels good, with him it was horrible. Please," Sofia begged.

"Do not say such things about me!" Thiess thundered as he pushed Caroline away, knocking her against the table as he stood, his chest heaving, his face contorted in a scowl.

"Caroline!" Sofia wailed.

"Caroline, are you okay?" Luna's eyes were wide.

"She is fine." Massimino answered for her then turned back to Thiess, "The anger, let it out."

"Let it be me…please, if it must be one of us, I can't let him harm the young ones, I'll do it," Sofia whispered, head dropping as she squeezed her eyes closed.

She had resisted, and Thiess had overpowered her, forcing himself upon her several times during his last visit to Zillah. The disturbing nature of their coupling resulted in lasting mental and physical scars for Sofia. Although her body now showed some signs of aging, she was certainly still attractive. As the candlelight reflected tears flowing down her cheeks, Massimino watched as Thiess appeared to find her fear incredibly arousing.

Caroline was driven by the uncontrollable desire growing within, oblivious to the pain and torment being experienced around her. She sauntered over to Thiess and pressed herself against him while her hands roamed his tensed body.

"He wants *you*," Caroline said in an unnaturally lustful tone. "I can feel his…excitement."

"Is that right?" Massimino queried.

"Yes," Thiess replied curtly while staring at Sofia.

Massimino grinned. "Very well. It is decided then. She will be as your own for as long as you are here."

Sofia's eyes widened. "Massimino, please…" she cried, wrapping her arms behind his back, grabbing his shoulders and burying her face in the coarse fabric of the robe over his chest.

Massimino whispered into Sofia's ear as she clung to him. "The next time I give you or your husband a command, I expect I will not need to resort to threats for it to be followed." He shoved her away, "She is ready for you, Martin. Please take her elsewhere. I have...needs of my own tonight." Massimino directed his attention to Caroline. "Come to me."

Hypnotized, the girl obeyed his command, slinking toward Massimino.

With no bashfulness about his excitement on display, Thiess clenched and unclenched his fists, huffing as he made his way quickly to where the others stood. "Thank you," Thiess muttered before gripping Sofia by the hair and pulling her backward, away from Massimino, avoiding eye contact with him.

As Massimino's body became accessible, Caroline was insatiable in her efforts to intertwine her own with his.

Sofia's resistance, cries, and attempts to recover her dress were quickly subdued with a powerful blow across her face from Thiess. "I am no monster—it is just what this *place* does to me."

Luna cried out, trying to intervene and offer help to Sofia, who looked up at her longingly with tears pouring from her eyes and blood flowing from her lip. However, Massimino quickly grabbed Luna's arm, pulling her to his side.

Thiess proceeded to lead Sofia out of the dining hall through the main entrance; her stifled wails could still be heard echoing down the hallway long after they had left the room.

Caroline nuzzled into Massimino, longing to unite their bodies, while Luna continued to stare at the doorway. "Would you have *really* made me go with him?" she asked quietly.

Massimino stared at her but didn't reply until she turned to face him. "Of course. If you were what he wanted I would have gladly given you to him."

A pained expression fell across her face. "But...but...I don't mean anything to you?"

Massimino maintained a flat expression. "You have something that I need, for the time being. You are also fortunate that I am able to make it pleasurable for each of us while I take it from you. Right now, he is far more necessary for my plans than you are. Your body would be a small price to pay to safeguard his loyalty."

Luna was silent, staring blankly into the fire and looking as though she might burst into tears at any moment.

Massimino drew her closer and with his hand behind her head, guided her so she was facing him. "Do not burden yourself with these thoughts now."

As he filled Luna's body with warmth, she quickly abandoned any will to resist the intensity of the arousal washing over her. Now, both she and Caroline wanted nothing more than to surrender every part of themselves with passion and desire to their Master.

Chapter Eighteen

E milia and Amanda settled in for their overnight flight, eating their dinner and enjoying a glass of French Pinot Noir while watching a corny romantic comedy. After the meal service had been cleared away and the first movie ended, Emilia decided to get some sleep while Amanda wanted to watch one more.

Emilia held down the recline button as the motors buzzed and whirred beneath her until it had transformed into a flat bed. She spent a few minutes getting comfortable and arranging her pillow and blanket before sitting up and turning to Amanda. The cabin lights had been dimmed and her sister's face was awash in blue light from the screen, headphones over her ears.

Emilia tapped Amanda's arm and waited for her to glance over before wishing her goodnight.

Amanda didn't bother removing her headphones as she mouthed the same, too engrossed in her new movie.

Emilia lay back, pulled the blanket around her, and fell asleep easily to the drone of the engines carrying them onward through the dark night sky.

"Emilia…Emilia…" Massimino's distinctive voice danced in her ears.

Oh no, not again.

Emilia murmured contentedly as she rolled onto her back, stretching her arms out and feeling the soft satin sheets. It was warm, and she wondered if the crackling she heard was a fire.

Emilia opened her eyes warily, blinking a few times as she took in her surroundings.

Black satin sheets, amazing four-poster bed, incredible tapestries…geez it's hot in here. Where am I now?

"Hello, Emilia."

Massimino's voice drew her attention toward the foot of the bed where a now familiar figure stood. The elaborate, brightly burning fireplace at his back gave him a glowing, almost supernatural aura. He was dressed as usual in a simple black robe, his intense deep eyes studying her.

"Massimino." Emilia shifted to prop herself up, the top sheet gliding down to her waist.

Oh, of course I'm naked again, Emilia mused. *Why would I ever want to be dressed in my dreams these days?*

She was about to pull the sheet up to cover herself when she became distracted by the change in Massimino's expression, turning from a calm stillness to amusement.

Wait, can he hear what I'm thinking?

Massimino smiled. "When we are together this way, yes, I can."

Emilia pulled her legs up, closed her eyes, and cradled her face in her hands, resting her elbows on her knees.

Oh my God, what's going on with me? This just gets more and more weird every time.

Even with her eyes closed, she could hear and somehow feel Massimino walking around the bed, expectantly feeling the mattress dip as he sat down beside her. He placed his hand on her shoulder; it felt strong but soft and warm on her skin. She found herself inhaling his scent, clean but masculine, blending with the smell of burning logs.

This is all too real. It can't just be a dream, can it?

Emilia could feel Massimino grinning behind her. She removed her hands from her face and opened her eyes to look at him. The intensity in his gaze captivated and paralyzed her at the same time.

"No, this is not an ordinary dream, Emilia," he finally said. "Your body may not be here, yet, but you are. I have brought you here."

Emilia shook her head but didn't look away. "I...I don't understand. What do you mean?" she asked, breaking her stare to scan the space. "And where are we? This isn't the chapel."

He thought a moment. "It is difficult to understand. You have not been taught about the mystical realm or your place in it. What is happening here is beyond what your experience in the ordinary world can allow you to fully comprehend."

Emilia locked eyes with Massimino once more as she raised her brows. "Sure, well that answers...nothing at all."

Massimino laughed, and Emilia did, too. She was pleasantly surprised by the relaxed moment of intimacy they were sharing; a stark contrast to the intensity of their previous encounters. As bizarre as it still was, somehow, she began to feel more at ease.

Reaching out, Massimino caressed Emilia's hair, moving it away from her face and guiding it behind her ear. Emilia found herself unable to resist him. She leaned toward Massimino, who tilted his head, welcoming her lips to his and kissing her as Emilia felt a wave of pleasure sweep across her body.

His mouth possessed hers, and Emilia's tongue explored his as he coaxed it past her lips. A vision of her lying on the altar as Massimino held a dagger overhead flashed into Emilia's mind, causing her to pause and pull back from him slightly. She couldn't look at him and instead focused on the rippled satin.

How am I so drawn to this man? And why? I don't understand it.

"You are drawn to me because we are a part of each other's destiny," Massimino answered.

Emilia spoke aloud now. "A destiny where you stir a passion in me like no other lover one minute, and then plunge a dagger into my chest the next?"

Massimino was quiet, gazing over Emilia, indulging in her beauty as his eyes roamed across her face, her breasts and downward until the sheets bunched in her lap. She enjoyed watching him relishing her body and Emilia found herself wishing she were more exposed. There was an inexplicable urge to please him, and for him to desire her in return; it temporarily distracted her from the question she had posed.

"The ritual is difficult to understand," he finally said. "But it is necessary so that the...abilities and strength we each possess can become united. The passion is...an expression of the way I feel for you."

Emilia smiled shyly, flattered and satisfied by his response.

"What abilities and strength? You've said before that I'm not...ordinary?"

"It is unfortunate that you were taken away from here." He cupped her cheek and it warmed instantly so he let go. "If I had not found you, our union would not have been possible, and all of your gifts may have never been realized."

"What *gifts*? I don't even know where 'here' is, what do you mean by all of this?" Her brow wrinkled with confusion. "Please, Massimino. I want a real answer this time."

Massimino stared deeply into her eyes, causing the warmth to begin growing within, her body involuntarily shivering and writhing against the soft satin.

"All right, I will show you." He turned toward the large fireplace in the center of the room. "See how the flames naturally sway so erratically?"

Emilia felt the sensations within her body growing, her desire for Massimino increasing. She willed for it to slow down so she would not miss an opportunity for some answers. Her logical mind won the inner battle against her more lustful instincts as she sat up straight and looked to the fireplace. It only made her heated bare skin more sensitive as she watched the flames rising, falling, random and beautiful.

"I see the fire," she said. "Now what?"

"Watch."

Massimino raised his hand and waved back and forward. As he did so, the fire seemed to take on an order that matched the motions of Massimino's hand, the flames like music notes and he a conductor.

"How do you do that?" gasped Emilia, eyes wide and disbelieving.

Massimino stopped motioning with his hand and the flames returned to their haphazard state. "You try it now," he encouraged.

"Me?" Her breath caught in her throat. "But how?"

He gave her a tiny smirk. "It requires much focus to harness these abilities. It takes much time to learn and to practice. Let me help you." Massimino stood and offered his hand to Emilia. "Here, come with me."

She accepted; his touch felt electric as their energies connected, like sparks tingling through her body and stimulating all of her senses. Emilia inhaled deeply with want and Massimino smiled knowingly back at her.

"We will have time for that," he cooed, "but first, come."

Emilia kicked the sheet off and glanced around for a robe or cover up.

"You don't need anything," he said, stopping her. "You are perfect as you are."

Emilia smiled and stood confidently, feeling his rough robe scratching against her. "Why are *you* dressed?" she challenged.

"I need not be, if you would prefer it that way."

Accepting his invitation, Emilia untied and removed the rope around his waist. Massimino smiled as he pulled the robe over his head and tossed it toward the bed, Emilia's lips parted as she watched his broad shoulders and well-defined form glisten in the firelight.

"That seems fairer," she whispered as she sensually traced her fingers along the scar across his chest before pressing her body against his; the warmth within her that began earlier was now a blazing heat. She wrapped her arms around him as she craned her neck to kiss him. Massimino returned the gesture as Emilia moaned into his mouth, but it was over too soon.

"Shall we continue, or would you like to see some of what you are capable of?"

Emilia's rapid panting slowed to deep breaths as she subdued her lustful longing. "Yes, answers...please," she nodded.

"Then follow me." Massimino ushered her to the sprawling lounge area.

"Well, this looks interesting," she observed as they entered an area covered in plush, richly hued pillows and cushions.

"Many things happen here."

"I'm sure."

Massimino waved his hand and Emilia stared in astonishment as several of the pillows rearranged themselves so two sat opposite each other near the fire.

"Please, sit." Massimino gestured to the closer of the two pillows before seating himself on the other. They sat facing one another, the fireplace to their side.

Massimino reached out toward Emilia. "Here, hold my hands."

She obliged and allowed her fingers to intertwine with his.

"All right, now breathe. Deeply and slowly."

"You sound like my yoga instructor."

"Yoga?" Massimino replied as if amused by the word.

What on earth is going on here? I'm sitting in some massive old stone room with this guy who wants to sacrifice me so we can be united. There's a huge fire he can control with his mind—oh yeah, and we're both naked.

And then the guilt hit; *Olly. I feel like I'm cheating...it's just a dream,* she justified, unable to deny what Massimino had created within her.

Massimino laughed again. "Emilia, you need to concentrate."

"Okay," she said. "I'll breathe deeply and slowly."

Still feeling the desire growing within, Emilia focused her attention on doing as he'd instructed. Once the two had found a shared rhythm that seemed to agree with Massimino, he continued.

"Now, keep breathing that way and watch the flames. You do not need to wave your hand as I did—it is a habit, but not necessary. It all comes from within the mind. Perhaps even close your eyes and just imagine that the flames are swaying as you wish them to."

Emilia shut her eyes and visualized the flames dancing as they had for Massimino.

"Now look at the fire."

While not nearly as elegant as Massimino's display, there was certainly some flow to the movement. It lasted a few seconds before reverting to random flickering once more.

"Wait a minute," Emilia barely said. "Did I really do that? It wasn't the same as when you did it. Or were you doing it again?"

Massimino grinned. "Yes, you really did that. I only helped keep your mind focused. This is a skill you will need much practice to master. Over time, you will be able to do it yourself, and as your strength grows, you could make it appear more as I did."

"Whoa, cool! You seem to be able to control the wind," she remembered. "Can I do that, too?"

Massimino swirled his right hand and a blast of air circled the room as if a windstorm was in the chamber. The fire uncontrollably fluctuated as the gust swept around them for a few moments before ending as quickly as it had begun.

"Yes, like that," Emilia's eyes were wide with wonder.

"All right." He appeared pleased. "Hold my hands again and breathe as you did before."

Once their breathing again fell into a shared rhythm, Massimino instructed Emilia on how to visualize the wind performing as she commanded. As she did, a light breeze passed over both of their bodies and curled around them; the tickling sensation caused Emilia to open her eyes.

"Wow, this is unbelievable. What else can you do? What else can *I* do?"

"You have some very…useful abilities," he said, still holding her hands. "They have served your family well. Again, you would need to develop them and cultivate your strength for such gifts to be of any practical use. But with time, you could have some control over the lighter physical elements such as air and fire. You would have the power to experience the thoughts of others and even be able to…influence them."

Emilia wasn't sure how she felt about that. "You can read my mind and know what I'm thinking; can I do that to you?"

Yes. Massimino smiled slyly, though his lips hadn't moved.

"I just heard you, but you didn't speak?"

Come to me.

Emilia didn't need to be asked twice. She had exhausted every ounce of will to suppress the burning desire within her, and now she needed to unleash. Closing the distance between them, Emilia pushed Massimino backward into the pillows and climbed on top of him.

Emilia groaned as Massimino entered her and she rode him as he suckled her nipples, invading every corner of her flesh and bone. His hands made her body pulse with each touch and she was ravenous, losing count of how many times she had climaxed—it felt as though their bodies and minds had fused into one. Emilia wailed, and she could hear his satisfied groan as he thrust his hips into her. They carried on that way until they were both breathless and collapsed in a hot, sweaty pile, limbs intertwined.

As their breathing eventually slowed to a normal pace, the fire came back into focus.

"Will you teach me, Massimino?" Emilia asked.

"Teach you?" He stroked her hair as she lay against his chest.

"Will you teach me how to do the things you do?" she clarified. "I want to understand how it works, how to do these things myself...even if it is only in my dreams."

Massimino smiled as he considered the request. "There is much to learn—even within a dream, as you say. For now, accepting and surrendering yourself to the ritual is the most important thing."

Emilia stared into the fire for quite some time before it happened; she had slowed her breathing from its ragged, passion-induced state, and the flames began to swell and contract. They matched each inhale and exhale.

"Look, I think I'm doing it," she said, proud of herself. "Do you see?"

Massimino did not answer and Emilia could feel his body tensing behind her.

"What's the matter?"

"Nothing is the matter," he said softly. "Come, follow me—there is something else I want to show you." His voice seemed stern now, and his tone was more abrupt as he stood, pulling at Emilia's hand.

He led her past the bed, toward his desk, where Emilia stopped to marvel at the inscribed star pattern of jewels—diamonds at a glance—ornately set into the green marble. As she traced imaginary lines between the stars with her fingers, Massimino explained that the pattern was the constellation Corvus—Latin for "raven", which represented his aerie of brothers and sisters. It was his history—his heritage—and Emilia warmed at the notion that this mysterious, powerful stranger also longed to be reminded of his kinship.

After pausing for a few moments to study the pattern in greater detail, Massimino called her attention to one of the large windows which flung open with nothing more than a twist of his hand in the air. Emilia looked out in awe at the mountains in all directions and the brilliant stars overhead. To her right, a spectacular, nearly full moon hung low on the rocky horizon. On the left, the sky appeared a little lighter, the stars there beginning to disappear as if dawn would be breaking soon.

Massimino stood behind Emilia, embracing her naked body. He directed her attention to the lights dotted throughout the village below. Although detail was scarce in the pale light of early-dawn, clouds building on the horizon, Emilia could make out a narrow river in an inverted U shape from where she stood. There were also buildings perched along the riverbank. The area was mostly dark, though some scattered lights shone as if pixie dust had been sprinkled on them from above. The moonlight shimmered on the river, reflecting the ripples as the water flowed from a higher, unseen source in the snowcapped mountains, around and past the village, and onward along its journey back and forth to the bottom of the valley and eventually out to sea.

"It's beautiful," Emilia said. "Where is this place you've brought me?"

"It may look beautiful from up here, but it is not," his voice had taken on a hard edge. "If it were mine and someone offered me a single gold coin for it, I would accept."

"Surely you can't be serious, Massimino. You agreed to give me a real answer this time, remember? Where are we?"

Massimino turned Emilia around to face him and they embraced.

"My dear Emilia, this is Zillah, your home, and I believe you're almost here."

"…passengers and cabin crew please…seated with seatbelts firmly fastened…"

The verbiage pouring from the speaker overhead was loud and abrupt as the aircraft shook violently. It was descending as Emilia blinked her eyes open. She could hear screaming breaking through the fog of sleep; adult voices and children crying.

Amanda was straining against her seatbelt, grabbing at Emilia's arm. "Emilia, wake up! Emilia!"

The aircraft stopped convulsing and leveled out again; there was silence for a few moments before the speakers crackled to life and the

First Officer gave a brief report of their unexpected encounter with a pocket of turbulence.

Amanda leaned over to her sister. "Oh my God, that gave me a fright. Worst turbulence I've ever flown through. How did you manage to sleep for so long through all that?"

Emilia turned to her sister, not bothering to conceal how disturbed she was—but it wasn't because of the turbulence. "Amanda, what if…" She felt like a fool, but she forced out the words. "What if Massimino is in Zillah?"

Chapter Nineteen

Luna awoke with a shiver, cold and achy as she rolled from her side to her back against the hard, stone floor of the dining hall. She cringed as the pain and chill stabbed at her from the inside out. Opening her eyes, she peered toward the wooden rafters above her. The room was beginning to fill with the pale light of a cloudy day.

I need to get up, get warm.

She rotated her head to the side, gazing toward the fireplace. The fire was no longer lit, only a few orange glowing embers remained on the floor.

"Caroline, are you here?" Luna's voice was soft and croaky, her mouth dry.

After a few moments of silence, Luna got to her hands and knees just as she spotted her friend on the floor nearby.

"Caroline!" She stood and hobbled stiffly toward her. She was curled up in a ball, knees to her chest, her back facing outward as she huddled against the wall. Caroline mumbled something unintelligible and her body trembled.

As Luna reached her, she knew something was wrong. Caroline's dark brown hair was now mostly gray and her previously youthful skin now appeared pale and wrinkled.

"Caroline, are you all right?" Luna whispered as she placed her hand on her back. Her friend's skin felt cold and clammy, her breathing was irregular and strained.

"Oh, my goodness. Caroline, what has happened to you?"

"C-col-cold," she stuttered.

Luna turned and scanned the room for their clothes. Seeing the crumpled piles of fabric on the other side of the hall, she went and retrieved them. Suddenly, Luna froze with a pang of worry. She quickly recalled the prior evening's horrors and wondered what had happened to Sofia. Hanging her garment over the back of one of the dining chairs, she hoped Sofia would return soon to collect it.

Massimino, why?

Luna pulled her own dress over her head then laid Caroline's over her like a blanket. "Caroline, can you hear me?"

She nodded slightly and finally faced her. Luna wept uncontrollably at the sight of her friend; once glowing with youth and radiance, she now looked old and haggard.

"Oh, Caroline. Here, I will take you to the kitchen to get you warm and then I shall get you home to your bed."

Caroline just nodded, a tear rolling down her cheek.

Slowly, Luna helped Caroline dress, then assisted her as they made their way through the dark, cold passageways to the castle's kitchen. Caroline leaned on her the whole distance, unable to walk on her own.

As they neared, some light and welcomed heat spilled from the kitchen into the passageway, and a cheerful humming reached their ears.

"Mrs. Rossi, Mrs. Rossi!" Luna called. "Please help me!"

The humming stopped and a moment later the light coming from the entrance was blocked by the frame of a rather portly, older woman, her cheerful face quickly shifting to one of concern as she saw the two women.

"Oh my, what ever has happened?" asked Mrs. Rossi. "Who is that?"

"It's Caroline." Luna fought the urge to cry. "I don't know what's happened to her."

Mrs. Rossi supported Caroline's other side and guided them to a wooden seat by the fireplace.

"Oh deary, wait right here. I will be back in a moment," Mrs. Rossi muttered as she disappeared down another corridor.

Luna stood by her friend, gently stroking her hair and trying to bring her some comfort while she too enjoyed the warmth from the fire.

The kitchen was large, designed to adequately feed all who lived and worked within the castle as well as the numerous regular visitors hosted during its glory days. The ceilings were high stone arches, now blackened by years of accumulated soot and grime which clung to them. In the middle of the room sat a round, heavy wooden table with a dozen chairs surrounding it. Multiple wood-burning stoves and stone ovens occupied prominent spaces against the walls, along with two large pantry stores, and a cool room. There were three large sinks and a variety of different benches, many of which were unused these days. Spaces for pots, pans, and cooking utensils of every shape, size, and variety filled the walls. However, several hooks and holders were now empty, their counterpart having been lost or broken without replacement as times became difficult.

Mrs. Rossi returned holding a heavy, checkered blanket which she unfurled and draped over Caroline's shoulders before moving around to her front, where she crossed it over tightly. Caroline managed a meek smile as the cook fussed over her, and a sorrowful expression fell across Mrs. Rossi's face.

"I don't know what's happened to her," Luna said. "She was...normal last night, and now..."

Mrs. Rossi nodded. "I don't understand it myself, deary—but it's not the first time I've seen something like this, oh my." The legs of a wooden chair scraped across the stone as she pulled it away from the table and sat. She stared at Caroline shivering by the fire, her eyes closed.

Luna did the same and took a seat opposite the cook. "What do you mean? How?"

"That sorcerer in the tower, he's what," Mrs. Rossi said. "As for how, I haven't a clue."

Luna's shoulders slumped as she leaned to rest her arms on the table. "He was…different last night. I don't understand how someone could change so much."

'Different' didn't begin to convey how he had acted—what could have happened to her.

"You're young and new to Massimino's ways," Mrs. Rossi explained. "In my lifetime, I've seen things, heard things—awful things. There are some memories you cannot ever escape from."

"But he's always been so nice to me," Luna argued in a weak voice. "Being with him—it is…amazing."

Mrs. Rossi smiled wearily. "I once felt as you did. When I was young, he would ravage my body and I thought there could be no greater pleasure. I've never felt that way since, at least not in the physical sense—and that was…well I am almost old enough to be your grandmother, so…it's been a while."

Luna nodded. "That is how it has always been with me. Until last night."

"Yes, deary, he has been with every woman in the village," Mrs. Rossi spoke as if she were delivering facts, not stabbing her with each sharp truth. "That is just the way of things. Longer than anyone can remember, he has seemed to *need* us—or at least he needs something *from* us. For the most part, he makes us feel good and we have no real reason to complain. I know I always went eagerly when summoned. Then he leaves us alone when we're older, and we don't have as much to give him anymore. Perhaps that is why he never seems to get any older?"

Suddenly, the cook's eyes widened. "Tell me you don't always feel more than just a satisfied exhaustion after you've been with him."

Luna nodded. "It's true. I'm always *so* tired, drained—even more today than before."

"I see it on your face, deary." She offered Luna a slight smile, but there was no happiness behind the gesture. "It is—or was—the same for all of us. Usually, he just takes a small bit. We feel better again after some rest and a few days have passed."

Mrs. Rossi pointed to Caroline before continuing in a hushed voice, "Sometimes though, he wants—he *needs*—too much." Her eyes welled, a small sob escaping her lips. "The last time I saw something like this, I was around your mother's age. My daughter's best friend, Ruthie—God bless. It was dark times around here; there was some sort of ritual, but I was not involved, thank the heavens. Something went wrong and Ruthie was with him alone afterwards. He took everything she had." Mrs. Rossi closed her eyes and shook her head as tears streamed down her cheeks.

"Like what happened to Caroline?" Luna whispered.

"No, it was worse." Mrs. Rossi sniffled and blew into a handkerchief from her apron pocket. "She was *dead*; they found her down at the bottom of the tower, his tower. Oh, Ruthie...I saw her body, I'll never forget how she looked—the poor dear was broken and drained of life. Even worse than Caroline."

She dabbed at the tears, gazing at the ceiling as if it would make them stop. "You probably saved her life, Luna. If you had not been there last night to help satisfy his...hunger, Caroline may have ended up the same way."

The plop of a bubble in an oversized cast iron pot brought Mrs. Rossi back to the present moment. "Oh my, the oats."

Mrs. Rossi moved as quickly as her stout frame allowed, removing the pot from the heat and stirring in some water to stop them overcooking. After sampling some from the ladle, she set about serving up two generous bowls, placing one down in front of Luna along with a heavy spoon that landed with a clang.

"Here, eat. You need to regain your strength," Mrs. Rossi said before taking the other bowl and sitting by Caroline. "Here, poor girl. Please try to eat something." She spoke gently, bringing a small scoop to Caroline's lips.

Caroline half opened her eyes and mouth, allowing Mrs. Rossi to push the spoon and its contents inside. She chewed slowly, swallowed them down, and opened her mouth again.

"That's it, deary." Mrs. Rossi smiled encouragingly as she offered Caroline more oats.

"Is there anything we can do for her?" Luna asked between mouthfuls of her own breakfast; she was ravenous.

"I don't know..." Mrs. Rossi turned her head, staring out one of the windows that faced a decrepit garden. "Maybe. I heard stories, but I'm not sure. Do you know the old woman who lives alone on the outskirts of town, across the river?"

Luna nodded. "I have seen her in the town square sometimes—never spoken with her though, everyone says she is a witch or something. I dare not go near her."

The sound of stumbling footsteps coming from the kitchen's main entrance drew their attention.

Sofia looked frightful as she limped into the kitchen in a stained sheet she had wrapped around herself. Her left eye was bruised and there was a fresh cut across her cheek beneath it. A trail of dried blood and tears streaked down her face and neck, and her hair appeared as though it had been tangled in a storm.

"Caroline, Luna, are you all right?" Her voice sounded hoarse.

Mrs. Rossi stood quickly, "Sofia, what are you doing here? What has happened to you now? Oh, my."

She shuffled further into the room as fast as her pain would allow. "Caroline, Caroline!" she called, gasping in horror as she reached her daughter.

Caroline weakly lifted her arms and rested them on her mother's shoulders.

Luna stood to embrace Sofia. "It was Massimino—"

"How?" Her response was muffled as she sobbed into Caroline's blanket, her face even more swollen with fresh tears.

Mrs. Rossi could only shake her head solemnly.

"Bed," murmured Caroline, barely audible.

"You can take her to one of the rooms and she can rest," Mrs. Rossi offered.

"No, I want to get her as far away from here as possible," Sofia said. "I am taking her home. Thiess sent me away until tonight—says he's got business to attend and I should rest today, that monster. Here, Luna, will you help me?"

"That bastard," spat Mrs. Rossi. "He's as bad as Massimino."

"They're both evil," Sofia agreed emphatically. "We can't keep living like this."

The three began to hobble toward the kitchen door.

"Thanks, Mrs. Rossi," Sofia muttered. "I'll be back. Got no choice."

"Luna, deary, go to the old woman," Mrs. Rossi repeated, taking Luna's hands. "I don't know if she can help, but it is all I can think of."

Nodding, Luna wasn't any less terrified or uncertain as the women started down the rocky, steep path back to the village.

"Dark times..." Luna heard Mrs. Rossi say to herself as she closed the kitchen door behind them. "More dark times are coming."

Chapter Twenty

For the remainder of the flight, the girls enjoyed breakfast together and chatted more about the unusual dreams Emilia continued to have; she found herself holding back when it came to the more mystical elements she'd experienced though—they were just dreams, but the idea of talking about magic and powers seemed too ridiculous.

Amanda once again was able to provide logical explanations for her sister's runaway imagination and was certain that there was no chance at all of the man himself—Massimino—existing, let alone being in Zillah.

Both girls emerged from the plane looking fresher than might be expected after a tumultuous few days followed by an overnight flight. The impromptu vacation had them on a high and easily overshadowed any emotional fatigue and jetlag. They breezed through immigration and found themselves standing at the baggage carousel before it had even started to move, providing them both the perfect opportunity to power up their phones. After scanning her social media and reading a message from Oliver, Emilia tapped out an email to her parents:

Subject: Europe Trip

Mom & Dad,

Long story, will fill you in later. Amanda and I are heading to a village called Zillah in Slovakia for the break. Don't know many details yet but there may be some information about my birth parents there. Will keep in touch!

Hope you guys are having a great time on the cruise. Looking forward to some pictures!

Love you, Emmi

"All right, I emailed Mom and Dad. Nothing too much exciting going on, but I did get a really sweet message from Olly." Emilia gushed.

"Oh, so romantic!" Amanda batted her eyelashes and clasped her hands like a southern belle.

A buzzing sound and flashing lights preceded the clunking of the baggage carousel as it started to move.

"We're in Vienna!" Amanda declared; her face lit up as if she'd just remembered why they were in the airport to begin with. "Let's go and claim your magical—though most likely dilapidated—kingdom in the hills. Sans totally hunky, mind-blowing-sex-god-murderer, of course!"

Emilia rolled her eyes, slightly regretting having shared so many details from her dream but relieved she'd left out some of the stranger elements. Amanda pulled her in tightly, squeezing Emilia in a bear hug until the two began laughing.

"This is going to be great—oh, look," Amanda gestured to the carousel. "There's one of my bags!" She did a little dance on the spot.

With bags in tow, they passed through customs and headed into the Arrivals hall of Vienna International Airport.

"So, what's next? We take a train?" Amanda asked, falling behind with her two large suitcases.

"Actually, right now we need to find our driver who'll take us to the train station." Emilia spotted a man holding up a tablet with her name on it and waved to catch his attention. "There he is!"

They were greeted by the sound of humming traffic, intermittent wafts of jet fuel, and people talking in foreign languages as they exited the terminal. The air was cool and fresh—Emilia relished the breeze flowing through her sweater dress. Above, the sun shone brightly; its warmth felt exquisite as they walked the short distance to their car. The driver expertly loaded their luggage like pieces of a puzzle into a current model Mercedes sedan. As they climbed inside, the driver announced he would have them at the station in about forty-five minutes; their visit in Austria would be but a blink as they made their way from Vienna across the border into Slovakia, where they would board their train to Poprad.

"Okay, got it. I *thought* there was a train involved in this crazy journey!" Amanda giggled as she took in the sights through the window. "And then how far to Zillah?"

Emilia thumbed through the itinerary on her phone. "It says here, it's a couple of hours drive from Poprad to Zillah—there should be a rental car waiting for us at the train station. I remember Nancy mentioning that Jonathan wanted to make sure we had our own transportation for some reason."

"Wow, quite the quest we're on," Amanda said, scrolling through all the posts and updates she'd missed on the flight. "Why did your family have to build their kingdom so far away from everything? That's what I'd like to know."

In the rearview mirror, the driver raised a curious, bushy brow at Emilia, who smiled and shook her head to dismiss Amanda's comment. He smiled back and shrugged before focusing once more on the road ahead.

"This is a beautiful city," Amanda said. "It would be nice to spend some time here one day."

"Definitely!" Emilia agreed, watching her sister take in the historic buildings and bustling street scenes outside the windows. As they drove further out of the city, the mountains in the distance and the masses of plant life that naturally fringed the countryside towns were equally as spectacular.

The time passed quickly, and their driver occasionally drew the girls' attention to points of interest along the way.

"This is the UFO bridge." Emilia found the Austrian accent charming as the driver motioned to the cabled contraption that loomed over the road. "Not its official name of course, but this is how most visitors know it. There is a restaurant up the top, in the UFO part. The bridge takes us across the Danube—the other side is Slovakia. The train station is not much farther."

Shortly after crossing the bridge, they found themselves pulling into the station. The building was utilitarian, its exterior reminiscent of the country's socialist history in the second half of the twentieth century.

"Here we are," the driver informed them. "*Hlavná Stanica*; the Central Station in Bratislava."

The driver unloaded their bags and wished them a pleasant and safe trip.

Emilia and Amanda were among the first passengers to board, which was fortunate given they needed to find extra storage space for Amanda's luggage. They hoisted up the suitcases and staked out a set of four seats around a table.

They settled in and enjoyed the hustle and bustle surrounding them. Emilia watched as Amanda's attention was drawn to a group of college-aged men as they boarded; they strolled by with their backpacks and deliberately slowed to smile and make eyes at the beautiful women they saw sitting together. Amanda flashed a broad grin in response and twirled her wavy blonde hair between her fingers in shameless flirtation.

With a smirk, Emilia politely shook her head.

"Oh, come on, live a little!" Amanda defended herself. "You know, I don't really know what you and Olly are at this stage, but I think *technically* we're both single…and we're on vacation."

Emilia laughed. "Yeah, but between real, past, present, and imaginary, I feel like I've got more than enough men in my life right now."

"Well, when you put it that way…" Amanda giggled. "From what you've told me, I don't know any mere mortal who could compete with this Massimino you've dreamed up. I wish I could come up with a fantasy lover like that!"

"You want him? You can have him; he's making me crazy!" Emilia joked as she pulled her phone from her pocket and checked for new messages or calls.

"Anything else from Olly?" Amanda asked.

"Yeah, we've been chatting a bit since the car ride. All good back home. I haven't heard anything from Mom or Dad yet though. Have you?"

Amanda checked her phone. "Nothing here either, but I think they're still at sea so I wouldn't worry."

Emilia nodded and gazed out the window. With a low rumble, the train eased out of the station.

"I think I'm going to go see if there's a dining car," Amanda announced. "I need some water—and maybe I'll see those guys again." She suggestively raised her eyebrows. "Want me to get you anything?"

"Yeah, water would be great, thanks. And a coffee?"

"Sure thing!" Amanda slid out of the seat, contorting herself around the suitcase stashed under the table beside her. "Wish me luck!"

"You don't need it," assured Emilia.

Amanda winked. "True."

Chapter Twenty-One

"**L**una, what's wrong?"

She didn't stop to answer her mother. Instead, Luna bolted through the lobby of the old, maze-like building—the inn her parents owned—and disappeared through the squeaky door which led to the back-of-house areas and their family's living quarters. When she reached her room, she shut the door behind her and sank to the floor, clutching her knees to her chest.

What am I supposed to do? Can the old woman really help?

Luna felt the urge to cry, but something froze her tears. If she didn't act quickly, her friend might not survive.

Surely Massimino will help her if I ask him to? He cannot really be the monster Mrs. Rossi says he is, can he?

Lost in her thoughts, Luna jumped at the sound of knuckles rapping on her door.

"Luna, can I come in?" her mother pleaded through the barrier between them. "What is the matter?"

She was quiet for a few moments as she contemplated what to say.

Her mother knocked again. "Luna, please."

"It's all right, Mama," she choked out. "Something has happened to Caroline, but...I think..." Luna gulped around the lump in her throat, "I think I know how to help her."

"Have you eaten?"

"Yes, Mrs. Rossi gave me some breakfast. I am okay. I need to go back to the castle. To see Massimino."

"Again? So soon?" Even through the door, Luna could hear her mother's gasp. "You cannot."

"It's not like that," Luna assured her. "I just need to talk to him. *Please*, let me get ready. I promise to come and see you before I go back there."

Her mother's defeated, "All right," came before Luna heard her footsteps fade as she ambled along the well-worn carpet down the hallway.

I must get to Massimino right away.

The lukewarm shower did little to improve Luna's mood. Though her body no longer ached after having slept on a cold stone floor, she felt exhausted and had to will herself away from crawling into bed.

As she descended the stairs, her father called to her from the kitchen. "Luna, are you all right? What happened to Caroline? Your mama is worried."

Luna gave him a hug. "Papa, I am fine. I don't know what has happened to Caroline; I am going now to try and help her."

Her father's fair eyes searched her, but then he finally relented. "All right, I will see you later then?"

Her father kissed her gently on the forehead before she left.

Luna found her mother at the front desk, who hugged her tightly. Only a mother could sense a daughter's sadness.

"Oh, my Luna."

"I will be fine, but I need to help Caroline."

Her mother pretended to be preoccupied with the papers in front of her, fading red curls spilling over one shoulder. "What is wrong with her?"

"I do not know," Luna said. "I have never seen anything like it."

"I will try to stop in on her today." She looked up from her work, letting her glasses settle against her chest as she tucked them into her sweater. "Is Sofia with her? Does she know?"

Unable to answer, Luna shook her head and averted her eyes; the worn carpet seemed to have more and more bare spots.

"What is it?" her mother softly prompted.

"Sofia, she is not good either—"

"Sofia?" Her mother went rigid.

"It was Massimino's...guest. A man named Thiess." Luna cleared her throat. "He did terrible things to her—he hurt her, Mama."

Luna's mother's gaze simmered with hatred. "I remember him. Bad things happened the last time he was here, this cannot be good. Please, Luna, you must promise me that you will be careful."

"Yes, Mama, I promise. But I must go now." They shared one last embrace.

"Hello, anyone around?" came a man's voice from the dining room.

Luna looked at her mother, puzzled.

"We have some guests," she explained, expression tight with a forced smile. "And more are arriving tonight. I might need your help later—and tomorrow, too."

"Of course, Mama," Luna nodded.

"Hello?" the voice called again.

"I must go." Her face softened when she looked to Luna. "You look tired. Please do what you must and then come back and rest."

Luna made her way across the square and to the road leading up to the castle. She winced slightly as she began the steep incline but did not slow. As she neared the summit, two large, menacing birds flew uncomfortably close, squawking in her ear. She huddled her arms across her chest and cowered her head, watching them warily as they swooped past then drifted away. Although the day was predictably overcast, the dense forest bordering the town appeared alive as the wind blew between the tall pines. The village below somehow seemed less sad from this elevated perspective, the reality of its run-down state and troubled inhabitants obscured by the distance.

The main street was paved with cobblestones while alleyways and small lanes branched off in every direction. At its far end, the quaint town square was positioned close to the river and served as a meeting place for villagers to stop and chat as they went about their day. It was surrounded by densely-packed buildings and shops—the inn, owned by Luna's family, was a prominent feature, as was the church. Luna's eyes swept across the buildings—all built long ago, their construction styles varied; some stone, some brick, some with dark roofs, and others topped with shingles or tiles.

The butcher shop came into view and her thoughts returned to Caroline and the task at hand. Ignoring her exhaustion, she continued toward the castle. The compound had been built during a long period of growth and prosperity in Zillah. While the town was increasing in wealth and influence, the castle occupied the highest elevation and provided a strategic vantage point and clear visibility of anyone entering or leaving. By design, only a single roadway and bridge were built to gain access to the village, beyond the spectacular waterfall where the river dropped off dramatically to the base of the valley.

Protecting the perimeter were walls that formed a diamond-like shape; the western wall was built right down to the sheer cliff face on which the compound sat, providing a formidable barrier. A high tower at the northern tip afforded visibility along the river as well as the road to the village; it was attached to the main castle. Overlooking the valley below, a second tower—matching the first—was built at the southern tip. This one did not connect to the main part of the castle.

Everything was constructed from stone, with several smaller buildings like sheds, stables, and barracks dotted between. Most of these spaces were now unused and lay in an ever-worsening state of disrepair. The main entrance was located on the southeast side, facing the village.

When she eventually reached the top, Luna continued past the tall stone archway, the main opening in the wall surrounding the castle complex. Looking up as she often did at the sharp spikes of the metal gate, raised and held up by heavy chains overhead, Luna realized she had never seen it closed and wondered how long it had been since the gate had been lowered; if it could still move.

Once inside, Luna made her way to the kitchen entrance in search of Mrs. Rossi. She wanted to know more about the old woman before visiting Massimino. Outside the kitchen was a walled garden once used to grow vegetables and herbs. Now, it was overrun with weeds. Even those looked unhealthy, overgrown, and unruly as they sprawled onto the path and up the sides of the castle.

Let go, like most everything else, Luna pondered. *What was it that Mrs. Rossi said? 'Nothing good can grow when the sun never shines.'*

Luna opened the kitchen door, a bone-chilling scrape and screech announcing her arrival.

"Hello, Mrs. Rossi?" she called.

Receiving no reply nor seeing any sign of the cook, Luna hurried from the kitchen into the main hall, admiring the grandeur of a time long past. The arched main doors were Gothic style with large ring pull handles set in dragon's mouth rosettes. They were made of oak and opened to a double-spiral staircase that featured iron balustrades and intricately carved wooden bannisters. Tapestries of various shapes and detail hung along the walls, the brilliance of their color now faded. Luna pulled on the ring to open one of the heavy doors, heaving it closed behind her and continuing briskly down the steps.

The sprawling courtyard was once a spacious and welcoming common area with flower beds, slate roads, and pathways that connected the buildings within the castle grounds. The joy, laughter, and sense of community was non-existent these days; the paths were bumpy and unmaintained, and the lawns were mostly dead, save for a few scraggly tufts of grass that had somehow managed to find the resources they needed to survive.

In the center of the courtyard stood the bare branches of what was once a magnificent oak tree. It had done its utmost to live, the roots leaching whatever nutrients they were fortunate enough to meet.

The silence was broken by the rumble of a wheelbarrow being pushed over slate. Luna turned to see Franco, one of the younger men in the village who worked around the castle. His complexion reflected his Italian heritage and his thin yet toned build was the result of the strenuous tasks he was often responsible for.

"Franco!" she called, waving to him.

He stopped in his tracks, combing a hand through his dark hair. "Hello, Luna," Franco replied, his smile wide as he set the wheelbarrow down and ran to meet her.

Franco wrapped his strong arms around Luna's waist, lifting her easily from the ground and spinning her. She squealed with delight, the sound echoing off the stone surrounding them as she playfully batted at his arms and wriggled to get away.

"Put me down!"

Franco lowered Luna and they each stared longingly at the other. Luna could get lost in his deep brown eyes if she wasn't careful. Franco leaned in closer.

Nervously, Luna's gaze darted around the courtyard as she shoved Franco in the chest with her palms. "Not here," she whispered. "Someone will see."

"Maybe I don't care," responded Franco, challenging her.

"Well you should, you *know* how it must be. At least for now."

"Yes, okay," he relented, looking up toward the southern tower of the castle and frowning. Then a thought popped into his head and his grin returned once more. "Here, come with me."

Franco led Luna to a nearby workshop where he quickly opened the door and they both shuffled inside, pulling it closed and latching it behind them. A fire burned in the fireplace and the room smelled of sawdust and paint. On the main workbench were several items—a chair, a window shutter, and an end table—all broken but in some stage of repair. Tools lay scattered haphazardly around the space.

Before Luna had a chance to object, Franco caged her in against the door and pressed his lips to hers. Luna's attempts to resist quickly faded as the pleasant sensation of Franco's mouth and muscular torso beneath her hands overpowered any objections. Their breathing intensified, tongues intertwining and oxygen becoming shared. Franco slid his hands under Luna's top, eliciting a satisfying moan. She felt dizzy as his tongue trailed down her neck and his strong hands rubbed her nipples.

As she felt his hardness against her thigh, the reality of the situation compelled her to stop.

"Wait, wait," she protested. "We can't do this...not now."

"But no one can see us in here," Franco replied, moving his hand down her side and playfully squeezing her bottom.

"Stop it! Sometimes it feels like *he* can see everywhere."

Franco paused momentarily, then cocked his head to one side and moved in to kiss her again.

"We can't, Franco," Luna pleaded more sternly.

"Why not?" Franco's eyes were hopeful, but hers were filled with nothing but sadness.

"You know why not. I have to go and see him now—it's about Caroline, she's sick...or something."

Franco pulled away and stepped backward, a frustrated expression falling across his face.

"It's always *him*! Why do we have to live this way? It's not fair." Franco turned toward the workbench. "It's just not right that we have to hide like this."

Luna wrapped her arms around him from behind.

"Look, I have been thinking about it," Franco began in a hushed voice as he spun to look at her. "The time I spend hunting with my father and my uncles...I know the forest and the valley well now. What if I could find a way to leave, to find somewhere else away from this place? Would you come with me?"

She shook her head violently as she backed away once more. "No! You mustn't even say such things."

"But why—why can't we go? I *know* I can find a way out of the valley."

"Franco, you've heard the stories as well as I have. You know what has happened to anyone who has tried to leave."

"Maybe they are just stories," he scoffed. "They are meant to scare us into staying."

"They are *not* just stories. My aunt Nadia—my mama's sister—was one of them, I saw with my own eyes. Marched back through town for everyone to see and then taken up the hill..." Luna looked at the ground then back to Franco. "You know the stories too, they were never seen or heard from again—none of them."

The breath that escaped him was stricken with pain as surely as his expression. "I don't know what to do then," Franco shrugged, "I don't know."

Luna sighed, hugging him again. "We just have to wait. When I am older and Massimino no longer needs me, we can be together all the time."

Franco pulled back, forcing Luna to let go of him. "And in the meantime, you are just his plaything," he spat. "His to use however and whenever like all the other women trapped here."

"That's not fair!"

"Which part? Are you not his plaything?" His eyes narrowed as something occurred to him. "Or is it that you are not really trapped at all? Tell me, Luna, do you *like* being with him?"

She couldn't conceal the hurt Franco's words had caused, but there was some truth to what he was saying. Maybe that was what made it worse.

"I need to go now," she said. "I need to see Massimino about Caroline."

Franco's expression softened. "What...what is wrong with Caroline?"

"I don't know. Last night...it was different." Luna shook her head and closed her eyes as she thought back to what had happened. "Massimino...he...was different. He was not so kind—no, he was cruel." She fought back tears. "And his horrible guest, he hurt Sofia badly...terrible things. I can't—"

"What do you mean?" Franco interrupted.

"Caroline, this morning," Luna rasped. "She was an old woman somehow. It must have been Massimino—I need to go see him so he can help her."

"Don't you see, Luna?" Franco suddenly rushed forward. "This is what I am talking about. We need to leave here. We need to run—"

"Stop, please!" She could not let him continue. "Promise me you won't keep thinking about this. We cannot. I'll talk to Massimino. I'm sure he will help, okay?"

"But—"

"Stop!" Her voice was firm. "What are you doing today anyway?" Luna wanted to change the subject and part on better terms.

"Um..." Franco raked his hand through his black hair as he caught up to the new line of discussion. "We're working on the old chapel. *He* demanded it be cleaned up and made ready."

"The old chapel behind the castle?" Luna frowned.

"Yes."

"But no one ever goes there. What does it need to be ready for?"

"I have no idea." Franco shook his head. "I'm only doing what I've been told."

Luna bit her lip; there was nowhere else to go from here, but at least he wasn't angry for the moment. "All right, I must go. I'm sorry."

"Go," he insisted. "I'll see you soon."

Luna left the workshop and continued past the old stables toward the southern tower. When she reached it, she pushed open the heavy door and entered, passing piles of dusty items stacked and stored there as she made her way up the numerous flights of stairs. Luna heard voices as she neared Massimino's chamber.

Oh no, he's not alone, she realized. *Perhaps I should leave.*

After all, he had not summoned her, but she needed his help. She thought it best not to interrupt and decided to wait for an opportunity to enter.

The voices were muffled but Luna clearly recognized them both: Massimino and Thiess. She could hear broken parts of their conversation.

"...unable...update...email...connection...work here."

"Is better...less contact...outside world. Damage...tower. Must go...larger towns...down the mountain."

"Don't understand...live in this...village."

Curious, Luna inched her way further up the stairs so she could listen more intently.

"For me, it has been...necessity...villagers do not have a choice."

"I will have...fix...along with many things...you leave. Are you serious...leaving here?"

Luna continued tiptoeing up the stairs and their voices became clear.

"I have been here *hundreds* of years, my friend—hundreds of years too long. As soon as the ritual is complete, I will welcome with open arms the ability to leave this wretched place and never look back."

"And the Blagden girl will definitely agree to sign things over?"

"Do not worry. Even though she has not yet set foot here, I have already planted the seed as to how worthless this all is. Less than a single gold coin was what I told her. Once she arrives, the girl will see the appalling state of things and I'm sure will wish nothing more to do with it."

"Very well. I will travel down the mountain and obtain an update on the Blagden girl's—"

Sensing that Thiess would be leaving soon, Luna began to descend the staircase, not wanting to be seen. One of her feet slipped off the edge of a stair and landed with a thud, the noise catching both Massimino and Thiess' attention.

"Who is there? Show yourself at once," Massimino commanded, voice deep and loud.

Luna's heart raced; her chest felt tight.

"Luna? Do not make me come and find you."

Luna swallowed hard. *I cannot run. He'll find me and it will be worse.*

"Massimino? Yes, it is me." She did her best to conceal her fear as she started up the wooden steps.

Massimino watched inquisitively as Luna came towards him where he sat behind his desk, the vile old man across from him in an armchair. Their figures were visible through the fire as if they were rising from it.

"Luna," Massimino said. "I am surprised to see you again so soon. I thought you would be...recovering."

"I am tired, but..." Her eyes trailed to Thiess and back. "I had to come and see you. It is Caroline—something is wrong with her and she needs your help."

"Have you been here long?" Massimino asked, ignoring her plea.

"No...no." Luna was taken off guard. "I heard voices and...I did not want to interrupt. That is all."

Massimino stared at her intently, his expression blank as he sat at his desk, rocking gently. Thiess looked upon her as a wolf would a lamb, even licking his thin lips as he savored her naivety.

"Massimino, please, can you help Caroline?" Luna continued after a few moments of silence, doing her best to ignore Thiess' lewd stare.

"Come closer, Luna," Massimino cooed.

She obliged, feeling the heat from the fireplace sear her side as she passed.

"Martin, I believe you have work to do?" Massimino directed toward Thiess, his gaze shackled to Luna.

"Ah, yes." He scratched an age spot on his balding head as he stood. "I will get the update you have asked for and I must speak with the consultants today. I will be back later."

"Very good."

Thiess made his way to the stairs, glaring at Luna until he'd descended out of sight and his heavy footsteps faded to silence.

He caught her in his gaze. "Luna, you disappoint me."

"Massimino?"

"You come here to me, uninvited, asking for help, reeking of another man." His jaw set in a hard line. "What is it you expect me to do for you?"

"I...I thought—"

"You did not think at all. I am not here to help you—quite the opposite. You and everyone else in this village belong to me, and I will take whatever it is I need from you."

Luna followed Massimino's eyes to the pile of photos of Emilia stacked on his desk.

"Fear not, my precious Luna. The time has almost come for this arrangement to end." Massimino turned his attention to the path Thiess had recently taken to leave. "Though I cannot promise you that the new one will be any better for you."

"But please, there must be some—"

"Enough." His hand hovered in the air and she flinched. "It is only because I showed some restraint that she is alive at all. There is nothing I can do for Caroline. Now it is time for you to leave."

Luna stood still and silent; speechless, she was confused, but the distinct feeling of abandonment came over her. They had shared so many things—her body, her time, her dreams. Had she really meant nothing to him?

"Go." His voice brought her back to the moment. "I can feel my strength draining the longer this nonsense continues."

"Is there nothing I can say..." Luna licked her dry lips, "or do to persuade you? Please?"

Massimino stood and pointed to the staircase, the flames from the fire reflecting in his eyes. "Luna, go now. Before I lose my temper and you end up like Caroline—or worse."

Luna crossed her arms over her chest. "I would not let you hurt me as you did her."

Massimino's demeanor was suddenly calm as he gazed into the fire then back at her. "I think we both know if that was what I desired, then you would not only allow it, but you would likely beg me to do so. Now, be gone before I make that a reality."

She opened her mouth to speak, then abruptly turned and ran, the floorboards creaking beneath her.

Massimino sat back into his chair and listened to the sound of Luna scampering down the tower steps.

Two more days. Just stay the course for two more days.

He opened a hidden compartment within the central drawer of his desk and retrieved a tarnished gold medallion. Setting it down, he waved his hand over it. A woman's face appeared, hazily floating above the medallion like a hologram. She was beautiful, her ethereal glow like a drug for him. Massimino began to inhale deeply, feeling equal parts of pain and desire. Her skin was delicate—a pale canvas—and his eyes followed every outline. Her rosy cheeks complemented her angelic, sky blue eyes; Massimino took a moment to stare intensely into them, wishing he could drown there. Her plump, satin smooth lips smiled with purpose. Her soft, golden hair fell below her shoulders and he longed to tousle it, his mouth stinging with want as he recalled their most intimate moments when he had held her close, kissed her wildly, caressed her hair, and stared into her eyes. They exchanged a grin.

"I am close to avenging you, my love," Massimino whispered. "This time, I will be sure it is done right. Then I will defeat the one who took you from me and reclaim my place."

Chapter Twenty-Two

Luna slipped through the main gate of the castle, pausing to catch her breath; her heart was still erratic after her encounter with Massimino. As she gazed out across the valley, Luna caught sight of several small structures nestled within the woods on the far side of the river. She knew they had been abandoned long ago and were slowly being reclaimed by the surrounding forest, but there was one in particular that drew her attention. Luna could make out a cabin with a dark roof that blended in with the trees. It would have gone unnoticed, except for a steady plume of smoke rising from its chimney.

The old woman's home. I guess she's my only hope now.

As Luna walked the path back down to the village, total exhaustion consumed her, the events of the prior evening and her recent encounters with Massimino had drained her immensely. Luna staggered as she crossed the square, the village around her suddenly became hazy. Then, darkness.

Luna opened her eyes and blinked softly a few times as she stretched and nuzzled against the soft flannel sheets; she was comfortable and safe in her bed.

"Luna, are you all right, what happened?" her mother sat at the foot of her daughter's bed.

"Mama? What do you mean?" Luna's voice was groggy as she sat up, confused about why her mother had been watching her sleep.

"You collapsed in the square, Josephine came to tell us, and your father had to carry you back here."

"Oh my gosh—Caroline! I have to go to..." Luna gazed out her window and noticed the afternoon sky. "It is getting late."

"No, there is nothing you can do…I went to visit Sofia and Caroline…oh my, the torments we endure here."

"Is she, are they all right?"

"Sofia will mend, though who knows what terrors this evening will bring for her…Caroline does not awaken, no one knows what to do."

"Mama, I have to go…maybe there is one person who can help her, but I must go now. I am feeling okay…I'll rest some more later, I promise. I will be back soon." Luna remained tight-lipped about her plans for fear her mother would forbid the idea, and before she could protest, Luna kicked off the covers and got out of bed. She quickly grabbed her coat from the hook on the wall. and put it on over her long-sleeve black and white plaid pinafore dress.

"Luna, please, who do you think can help her? You are in no state to go anywhere yourself."

"I promise I will tell you, but I don't want to do this in the dark. I love you Mama; I will see you soon."

"Luna, please! Please stay…" Her mother's pleas went unheard and she watched helplessly as Luna ran from the room.

Luna bolted through the halls of the inn, down the stairs, out the door and into the street before following the road that led out of town. She continued past the turn-off for the mines and onward until she reached the abandoned mill.

The sound of gushing water became louder, echoing through the valley below as it spilled over the waterfall. The old mill had sat unused for a long time; Luna had never known it to be operational. Moss surrounded the lower areas and vines crept up the walls as if intending to strangle the structure; much of the wood had rotted away.

Luna took a worn path through the woods that appeared mostly unobstructed. It began closer to the village and sloped gently downhill. She could hear the babbling of the river growing louder, assuring her she was heading the right way. As Luna trekked on, she remembered vivid tales from her childhood about 'the old witch in the woods'. She swallowed the lump in her throat and kept going.

When she reached the river, Luna could only see the bridge and a small puff of smoke rising from the tree line. She knew the house was there, concealed by the wilderness lining the bank.

Taking a deep breath, Luna followed along the riverbank until she came to some stairs which led up to the mill in one direction or the bridge in the other. Ascending the stone steps with haste, she approached the bridge, which crossed over the river at a naturally narrower point before the waterfall. It flowed more rapidly there, and several rocks jutted out above the surface before the water disappeared over the edge.

The bridge had been built long ago, to allow mill workers access to their lodgings on the other side of the river. It was constructed of stone; the single, wide arch spanned the width of the river, supported by solid stone foundations on either side. Some of the railing closest to the waterfall had begun to crumble and fall away, but all things considered, it was stable and indeed a testament to the quality and skill of the masons who'd built it.

As Luna crossed, she looked first toward the waterfall, then back at the village. From this perspective, she could see homes—their windows, decks, and terraces offering lovely views of the river—though they were seldom used anymore. Luna noticed her family's inn with its wide footprint along the riverbank, rising three stories and standing out amongst most of the other buildings. The rest were typically narrower and two, or even one, story high.

She reached the other side and followed the barely discernable stone path into the forest. Before long, Luna emerged into a clearing. It was larger than it appeared from the castle, the view of the majestic mountains disappearing behind the tall trees.

There were several dilapidated cottages dotted around the area, and one set away from the others that appeared different. Light shone through the windows and smoke billowed softly from the chimney; it was occupied.

Luna was still for a few moments, almost forgetting to breathe as she swallowed hard and stared at the house. The hiss of the waterfall was still audible behind her. A bird squawking pierced the air, and she could feel her heart pounding in her chest as another lump formed in her throat and dried out her mouth.

What am I doing? I should not even be here. What if she really is a witch?

She was about to turn and run back to the village when she suddenly became frozen in place, unable to do anything but stare.

Luna watched as the brown door to the small, wooden cottage softly creaked open. A hunched figure emerged from the house and looked toward her. She was frail, one gnarled finger motioning, "Come, do not be afraid."

She had to squint to see the old woman's lips, cracked and wrinkled, moving, but the voice seemed as loud as if it were coming from within her own head.

"Please," said the woman, re-wrapping her long cardigan as if to conceal how she looked. "I will not hurt you. Come."

Luna was riddled with confusion; the strange voice again seemed to come from *within* her. The fear she had initially felt was now replaced with curiosity as the old, frail woman certainly did not appear to be a threat. Village life and her recent inexplicable experiences with Massimino had taught Luna that things were not always as they seemed, and she stepped cautiously toward the cottage.

"Please, come in." The woman spoke softly, offering a weak smile as she moved aside to allow Luna to enter. "It is all right," she assured her, sensing Luna's hesitation.

Luna returned the smile and went inside.

The ceiling was low, but the space felt warm and homely. A log fire crackled in the opposite corner, bathing the room in a comforting orange glow. Her eyes were drawn to the kitchen area where a variety of dried herbs hung from the walls, their bouquet filling the air and evoking an otherworldly sense. To the left was an open doorway leading into what Luna guessed was a bedroom. In the main room sat a reading chair surrounded by hundreds of books—on shelves, in bookcases, and piled on tables. There were so many books that one would be forgiven for thinking it was a library.

Near the kitchen was a round table with four seats. Two place settings had been laid out, complete with awaiting teacups and saucers, a freshly brewed kettle with steam still emerging from the spout, and a hand-painted dish with a few cookies.

"Hello, I'm…Luna." Her words were timid.

"Hello, Luna. I am Gerlinde. Come, sit down." The old woman pointed to one of the seats, "I had a feeling I might receive a visitor—such a rare event nowadays." Gerlinde gave a half smile as she poured tea for the two of them, her hands shaking slightly. "Cookie?"

"Thank you," replied Luna, placing one on the saucer beneath her teacup.

"I bake them myself," added Gerlinde, taking a bite and sitting down to join her. "So, how can I help you, dear girl? Why have you dared to visit the wicked witch in the woods?"

Luna blushed with embarrassment as she looked toward the fire.

"It's okay; I know what they say about me. Don't feel ashamed. I promise, I'm not nearly as bad as my reputation." Gerlinde chuckled under her breath, and Luna noticed her eyes were a sharp gray, appearing more youthful than the rest of her physical being; its former life had dimmed.

Luna took a sip of her tea. "It's my friend, Caroline. Something has happened to her."

Gerlinde slowly nodded, took another bite of her cookie, and washed it down with a gulp of tea. "Some*thing*, or some*one* has happened to her?"

"Yes, I think…Massimino…" Luna lowered her cup to her lap. "We were…with him, last night. She is only my age, but this morning she looked like—like she is very old and weak. Mrs. Rossi in the castle, she said you might know how to help her."

Gerlinde twisted her face into a grimace. "Massimino, why must you keep doing such things?" she sighed.

"So it *was* him, you know what he did then?" Luna let a spark of optimism into her voice. "Can you help her?"

All hope deflated when Gerlinde fixed her distinct eyes on Luna. "I am sorry, but no. To restore one, when they have been so completely...drained of their life, would require far more powerful magic than I am able to conjure. If I were able, I would have fixed myself."

"I don't understand. What do you mean, drained of their life?" Luna could feel her pulse quickening while at the same time her stomach plummeted with dread.

"It is a story that goes back over three centuries," Gerlinde said, returning her gaze to the tea in front of her but not drinking it. "Back to a time when this was a vibrant, beautiful village, sun filled the clear blue skies—nothing like the gloomy reality we know today. It was called the dark valley because of the color of the stone in the mountains, though these days, perhaps the name is even more fitting—for other reasons."

"I've heard stories of that time, too."

"Believe it or not, I was there." Gerlinde raised her eyebrows.

"But how? Please, I want to understand." Luna leaned closer.

She gave Luna something close to a shrug, but her arthritic bones made the gesture appear as though Gerlinde was heaving a sigh. "I can tell you what I know."

Luna settled back into her chair and took another sip of tea, listening intently.

"He never told me everything, but from what I've learned over the years, Massimino was once a very powerful sorcerer—even more so than now. Many centuries ago, there was a...conflict."

"Like a war?"

"No, no. More personal than that. It was between two men—over a woman. He has never uttered her name—at least never to me. The other man's name was Cassius; he was a sorcerer as well. By the end, Massimino had been almost completely stripped of his powers, and his life. A curse was forced upon him: he must seduce women and draw life from them in order to sustain his own."

Luna couldn't speak for several moments. "This means he is *hundreds* of years old—he has been in Zillah the entire time?"

Another hunched shrug. "I don't know how long he'd been alive before he came here, but he hasn't left since he arrived. He stays here and pillages the life from the young women of the village. He cannot allow for it to be any other way or he will die."

"But why...*here?*"

"That is one of my biggest regrets," Gerlinde whispered. "Mistakes."

"What do you mean?" Luna wished she hadn't been so naïve about Massimino and his feelings for her.

"I was a young woman here in the village; life was good, my family built the mill while my father and brothers ran it. I was very close with the young Blagden women, and...they recognized a spark of the mystic world in me too—they taught me, guided me—in these ways." She wiped away a tear before it could trickle down her cheek.

"Are you all right?" Luna was concerned.

"The Blagdens. They were wonderful people." She sniffled. "I was out in the forest one day, down in the valley searching for one wild herb or another, and I came across an injured man with a deep gash across his face. He was all but dead; grim and sickly—barely even breathing. I raced to get help, some of the men came with me and carried him back.

"The Blagdens sensed there was danger—a darkness, and ordered that he be removed from the village, but I knew he would not survive on his own. Instead, I hid him in a cave in the forest. I went to him with food, with water, but it didn't help him get well. He was not improving and continued to grow weaker. I still don't know how or why, but he looked at me—deep into me. Day after day, he would stare into me and something began to form—love? Passion? I cannot say.

"We were intimate together, I don't know how it was even possible in his state, but it happened and afterwards he was stronger somehow. He looked a little healthier, and it didn't make any sense to me at the time. I returned to him every day, as if I was raising him from the dead. He made me feel things I had never felt before. It was incredible…magical."

"It was Massimino?" Luna knew the answer.

"Yes." The old woman nodded.

"But then…" She wasn't sure how to ask. "What went wrong?"

"As his strength grew, so did his hunger," Gerlinde said, composed enough to drink her tea. "I think perhaps he did not realize this either—at least that's what I tell myself—but even though I was young, I became haggard and weak. My family and friends were all worried, but I never told them what was going on. Then one time, he was like a wild animal and I became much like you see me now.

"There was nothing more he could take from me, but now he was attractive and strong enough to go back to the village, where he began to charm the women there. He continued restoring himself, posing as a visiting merchant; no one realized what was happening. Eventually, he managed to win over the affections of one of the Blagden women. Once he had seduced her, he not only siphoned her life energy, but somehow absorbed her powers and abilities. This enabled him to rebuild himself as a sorcerer once more.

"Now, he could influence and control people's minds—bend them to his will. In no time, he all but ran the village. The locals started to get restless and unhappy with the situation. You see, he didn't have the strength to control that many people, but he still needed *some* in order to sustain himself."

Luna was stunned by Gerlinde's story. "How?"

"Well," she nodded to herself, "he closed the mines and the mill. Soon, money stopped flowing in. Many left of their own accord to seek work elsewhere, and when there were just enough people left that he could control, he tried to close the village off from the outside world."

"But why?" Luna was so confused.

"Cassius had left him for dead, so Massimino wanted to stop any news of his condition or whereabouts from reaching him. All these years, he has been fueled by vengeance—using this village as a haven until he is ready to seek out Cassius again and destroy him. Only a handful of people here are permitted to leave the village from time to time to run errands for Massimino, but when they do, their loved ones must remain behind—like hostages—to ensure they will return. He keeps the roads poorly maintained and the weather constantly miserable to stop outsiders from venturing here—at least in any significant numbers."

Gerlinde sighed, sipped her tea then took a deep breath before she went on.

"His strength has grown tremendously; he can manipulate the elements, and his ability to influence and read people's thoughts extends far and wide. His art of seduction, which took weeks to work on me, can now be accomplished in a matter of seconds."

Luna felt her cheeks heating as she thought about how a single glance from Massimino would make her feel; how he managed to embrace her with a breeze. "So, does that mean Caroline will end up like...you?"

"No. I hope for her sake that she does not." Gerlinde paused to place her empty cup in its saucer. "Massimino felt badly for what he had done to me—perhaps because he still had some semblance of a conscience then, I don't really know. At first, he couldn't find a way to make me how I was before, but he found a spell that would stave off my death and bind my own life to his own. He didn't realize that my body would remain so frail, so this life of mine has been a tortured existence. Normally, he will only take a small amount from each woman at a time. You feel tired after the seduction is over, but you recover, no?"

She waited for Luna's nod.

"Lately though, I sense he has been using a *lot* of energy on the heiress," Gerlinde said. "That is why this happened to your friend. He needed far too much—more than she had to give."

"Why are you here," Luna couldn't keep herself from asking, "alone and away from the village?"

"Massimino wouldn't allow me to leave with the others who had abandoned the village. Once the people here learned what I had done—that I had caused all of this—they would not permit me to stay and live amongst them. So, I am here. Forever punished for the choices I made, for falling in love, or lust, or whatever it was."

That didn't seem fair. "I can talk to my family and my friends for you."

"Thank you," Gerlinde glanced at her, "but no. Leave it be. I doubt it would make any difference."

"Caroline." Luna swallowed hard. "What will happen to her?"

Luna watched as the wrinkles around her mouth deepened. "She will die soon. There is likely not enough energy left within her body to sustain her life."

Tears caught in Luna's throat. "Can anyone help her?"

Gerlinde's lip twitched as she thought. "I don't think so—maybe there was a book, I don't know for sure, but Massimino had promised me if I helped him with a ritual, some time back, that he would cure me—that he'd found a way."

"But he didn't?"

"No. It was my own doing though, I'm sorry, that is too painful to talk about and it will not help your friend."

"But the book, it could, where is it?"

"When the ritual didn't work, Massimino was enraged, he suspected that I had betrayed him. He told me that he destroyed it, that there would be no way for me to be saved—and that I would suffer this existence for as long as he did. Even if he has not, you would need the ritual from the book and a powerful sorcerer to perform it, Massimino would never…"

"Did you betray him, how?"

"Enough now…"

Luna looked puzzled and studied Gerlinde for a few moments, the old woman slowly shaking her head, her hands trembling slightly in her lap.

"And what about the heiress? He has photographs of her."

"He believes she is the key to seeking his vengeance."

Luna didn't see how it all fit together. "Why?"

Gerlinde released a heavy, raspy sigh. "I am weary, Luna," she huffed. "So many memories…it's painful. I'm sorry about your friend. I truly am."

Luna gazed out the window. She knew darkness would fall soon and she didn't want to have to walk back through the woods alone when it did.

"I will go now and let you rest. Is there anything I can do for you? Bring to you?"

Gerlinde paused as if taken aback. It occurred to Luna it had been a while since anyone had cared to ask her such a question.

"When she arrives, the heiress," she finally said, "can you bring her to me? I wish to meet her. But do it quietly. I do not think Massimino would like it."

"Is it even possible to do something in the village without Massimino knowing?"

"He would like to have us believe that," Gerlinde said with a weak smirk, "but even he is not able to know *everything* at once. He must

decide where to pay attention and some of the magic I practice can..."
she squinted as she thought of how to explain, "conceal things if need
be. He will likely be none the wiser."

Chapter Twenty-Three

As Thiess rounded the last switchback up the winding road, he accelerated—letting the car work out some of the frustration he felt at having to make the arduous trek down the mountains and back up again in a single day, at Massimino's insistence. It was early afternoon, and the extra time he had to spend at the foot of the mountains searching for a cell phone signal meant he was late to speak with the consultants who, he had expected, would have completed their assessments by now.

As he passed the mill, Thiess spotted the road leading into the village ahead. His attention, however, was focused on looking out for the turnoff to his right which led toward the mines. Slowing, the lawyer eased his car onto the uneven, overgrown trail as it made a long arc rightward through the densely wooded forest.

He saw the mining consultants' truck parked near the second mine—shaft-B. Thiess pulled his car to a slow stop close by and began on foot toward the entrance.

"Hello? Hello?" he called as he approached.

He noticed that the chains and padlocks that had once secured access to the mine were open. "Hello? Are you down here?" Thiess called again, directly into the shaft.

"Hello…a minute," a muffled reply echoed up and out of the dark tunnel.

Thiess paced around the entrance; the gush of the waterfall could be heard in the distance and the smell of damp earth filled the misty air.

"Ah, Mr. Thiess. Hello," called Hanz as he emerged from the mine. He reached up to his hardhat and turned off the light.

Jakub, a local from the village, and Derrick, Hanz's protégé, followed shortly after. They were engaged in a conversation about tunnels and support, Derrick gesturing with his arms and hands in wild exaggeration as they walked.

"Hello, Hanz," Thiess greeted the large, middle-aged man. "What news do you have for me?"

"Well, there is some good news and some not so good news," replied Hanz, removing his hat and rubbing the back of his neck.

"Go on, please," Thiess wiped the sweat that had accumulated on his forehead during the drive up, "I am not so interested in games."

"Well, there is certainly gold in this area. It is very obvious in the first shaft and this one also."

"That is good to hear. So, what is the problem?" Thiess asked, nodding impatiently.

"The *condition* of the mines is very poor." Hanz switched his hard hat from one beefy, dirty hand to the other. "Very, very poor. It will take at least one more day, perhaps more to assess everything properly and provide a plan to restart production."

"This is frustrating." Thiess clenched and unclenched his fists, mind flashing to the prior evening when he had used them on Sofia. "Is there no way you can complete your work today as we agreed?"

"I am afraid not." Hanz had the sense to appear disappointed. "We only just began into this shaft here, and then there are the other two."

"Perhaps just one more," Thiess suggested. "The man who runs the village says the fourth is not accessible. I do not know the details."

"Yes, I understand. We are doing our best," Hanz replied. "There are many sections partially caved in and even some flooding—seems as though there has been some seepage from the river. While not uncommon, there is no way we could have known this ahead of time. It was a favor that we were able to squeeze this into the schedule, but even to study shaft-B and one more we will need *at least* another day. Perhaps two."

Thiess pondered the situation while gazing into the woods beyond the mine entrance.

"I spoke with our office earlier, good thing we travel with a satellite phone, the connection here, well, there is none," said Hanz. "Anyway, they advised that since we are here, we stay and finish. There will be some additional billing, yes, but if we are to go and then come back it could be at least a month or maybe two until that is possible."

Thiess contemplated how his arduous day of driving had been due to the lack of phone signal and ability to access his email but suppressed his bubbling rage and returned his focus to the bigger task at hand. Thiess looked toward Jakub, who was still engaged in a conversation of some technical variety with Derrick.

Thiess placed his hand on Hanz's shoulder. "Please, walk with me. This way."

He motioned Hanz away from the entrance and slowed his pace when he believed them to be out of ear shot. "Listen, there will be other parties arriving soon and it was important to me that this be finished before then. Nonetheless, I understand and appreciate your efforts to continue. We need to get this done and have a plan to re-open these mines as soon as possible. Do what you must. Please, if you must stay here longer, I implore your discretion—do not talk with anyone about what you are doing and what you find."

"All right, I understand," Hanz said, eyes darting to the mine. "We will work quickly and quietly then be on our way." He started in the direction of his colleague.

"Wait," Thiess blurted. "About the gold: how much?"

Hanz smiled, eyebrow raised. "Well, that *is* the million-dollar question, isn't it?"

"Hopefully *many* millions of dollars," Thiess interrupted.

"Yes," Hanz agreed with a laugh. "Before you get too carried away," he continued, "please be aware that substantial work will need to be done here. These mines have been abandoned a long time; there is extensive effort required to turn this into a modern mining operation." Hanz pointed down at the road. "And let's not forget about the infrastructure upgrades—big and small—that will be needed to get equipment up here and the materials out."

Thiess nodded in contemplation. "But you believe it would still be a profitable venture, even after all of that was put in place?"

"Absolutely, yes." Hanz glanced back at the others, who were still chatting. He stepped a little closer to Thiess, "I won't write this down—not at this stage—but the reality is that in today's dollars, there are hundreds of millions beneath our feet, just waiting to be pulled out of the ground."

"Incredible!" Thiess said, a half smile forming on his face as his mind wandered to the possibilities such a fortune might allow. "That is far more than I'd expected."

"Do you know why they ever stopped mining such rich ground?"

"I have no idea. I do not know the history, though I have an increasingly clear vision of its future—in part thanks to your answers here." Thiess grinned.

"About the fourth mine—shaft-D, as they call it: we are no strangers to assessing mines that are unstable. Are you certain you do not wish for us to investigate while we are here? It is best that we have a complete sense of what we are dealing with."

"I was only told it was unsafe, perhaps Jakub knows more."

Thiess and Hanz headed back to the others; Derrick was still talking, and Jakub seemed relieved at the interruption as the two men approached.

"Jakub, do you know why it is that Massimino says to stay away from the fourth mine?"

Jakub's expression fell flat, and his fair skin went pale. "Ah...um...it's not safe down there. I am not allowed to let anyone in."

"What do you mean, it's not safe?" Thiess pressed.

"Um..." Jakub looked like he was about to vomit. "I...I cannot. I'm not allowed."

"Hanz, perhaps you and your colleague can resume your work here," Thiess said, clapping Jakub on the shoulder. "We're going to talk about this some more."

Hanz nodded, appearing somewhat relieved to be released from what was turning into an uncomfortable conversation. "Come on, Derrick," Hanz said. "Let's get back to work."

The consultants returned their hardhats to their heads and activated the headlamps before heading back inside the mine.

Once they were gone, Thiess didn't feel the need to be professionally friendly. "I will be clear with you, Jakub: I don't trust what you're telling me. What are you hiding?"

He shook his head. "You'll need to speak with Massimino. I don't know what else to tell you."

Thiess paused, allowing some time for the frustration simmering within him to settle. "Jakub, Massimino is not here now, and I believe you know the answer. So, I am asking *you*. After the weekend, I will have a great deal more authority around here, so it is in your best interest to be forthcoming."

"I...I can't say," Jakub hesitated, looking at the ground to deliberately avoid making eye contact.

"Is it locked as these ones are? Do you have a key?"

"It is locked. I have a key."

"Then we will go there together now. Come along." Thiess started toward his car.

"But we—"

"You will come with me *now!*" Thiess ordered. "Do you have another light?"

Jakub nodded. He headed toward the mining consultants' vehicle and unclipped one of the flashlights from inside. He handed it to Thiess who tested it before proceeding to his car. "Come along, Jakub."

Reluctantly, he opened the passenger door and got inside.

"The mud; be careful," Thiess chastised as Jakub's boots stained the carpet of his otherwise pristine interior.

"I'm sorry, sir."

Thiess shook his head, started the engine, and drove farther down the bumpy, muddy access road to the mine shafts, continuing its wide arc through the forest. They passed the third mine, a worn sign which read 'Shaft-C' hanging crookedly from the gated entrance.

"Mr. Thiess, sir, I can't let you in there," Jakub repeated. "Massimino...he'll be furious about it, sir."

Thiess shifted in his seat. "You must understand one thing: in a few days' time, you won't be answering to Massimino anymore. You will be answering to *me*."

Jakub shrunk against the door. "Sir?"

"Massimino intends to leave this place after this weekend and I will be in charge after that happens." Satisfied he'd intimidated the man, Thiess relaxed and gave Jakub some room. "You had better learn how to start responding more truthfully to the things I ask of you."

Jakub stared silently out the windshield, pondering the information.

Thiess slowed the car as they rounded a corner and another mine entrance came into view. Shortly beyond the entrance, the road became a dead-end of dense forest, where he stopped and both men climbed out.

"Now, have you been in here before?" Thiess asked.

"Yes...yes, I have."

"What is so dangerous about it?" Thiess crossed his arms over his chest. "Why doesn't Massimino want the consultants to go in?"

"It's not the—" Jakub stopped himself and started again. "The mine is all right, no worse than the others anyway, it is what's inside that is the problem."

Jakub approached the sturdy metal gate blocking access to the mine and, after fumbling with his keys, unlocked and yanked it open. A loud, rusty screech sliced the air.

"Well, what is in here?" Thiess demanded.

Jakub stared at the ground and shook his head. Turning on his flashlight, he stepped into the mine, waving with his other hand for Thiess to follow.

Once his own flashlight was on, Thiess did so, keeping a short distance between him and Jakub.

It was damp and musty; the crunching of rocks beneath their feet was muffled by the moist earth walls surrounding them. The path sloped downward and turned slightly to the right as they walked. Wooden beams were set up periodically to shore up the tunnel and prevent it from collapsing. Silky cobwebs lit up as the flashlights swept over the space.

"What is it that's down here?" Thiess demanded again, crinkling his nose at the stale air and swatting at a cobweb which had entangled itself around the top of his head.

"Bit further...look out here." Jakub guided him, shining his light toward a section of wall that had fallen in, partially blocking their path.

Thiess looked back toward the shaft opening; they were now so far into the tunnel that the entrance was no longer visible. There was only darkness in both directions, and he began to feel quite uncomfortable.

"Suppose this is what you are here for, right?" Jakub called from further down the tunnel, shining his flashlight at the wall.

When Thiess caught up, his eyes were immediately drawn to the sparkle of gold embedded in the rocky mud surrounding them. He reached out and touched the precious metal, attempting to use his fingers to pluck it out.

"It must be broken. Need tools for that," advised Jakub.

"What is the problem in here?" Thiess asked, hand returning to his side. "Surely that little collapse isn't enough to prevent this mine from being surveyed?"

Thiess saw Jakub smirk in the darkness, and he once again felt uncomfortable. The gold-lined walls were unable to fully distract him from his unsettled feeling.

"No, that is not the problem. Follow me."

Thiess watched as Jakub set off again, his light bobbing away into the darkness before suddenly disappearing around a corner; an unpleasant stench consuming his awareness over the damp, stagnant air of the tunnel.

"Wait, I demand you tell me what is going on," yelled Thiess as he hustled to find where Jakub had vanished.

"Mind your step, sir," he called. "Wouldn't want to fall down that hole. No one gets back out of there." Jakub's flashlight pointed down toward a large shaft with a long vertical drop.

Thiess stepped carefully toward the opening, minding his footing as he neared the edge.

"This was once the main shaft down to the lower levels of the mine, that's why it is so much wider and deeper here," Jakub explained.

"And what is it now?" Thiess asked as he continued closer and closer.

"A tomb," came Jakub's solemn reply.

Thiess shone his light directly down the five or so stories the shaft descended. He gasped at the sight before him, recoiling slightly as he swept his light back and forth across the long, wide opening.

There were bodies upon bodies, mostly decomposed but some sickly hair and tattered clothing was still visible. The mass grave of sprawled human remains appeared to be several layers deep and, at quick glance, the styles of clothing and general condition made it appear that they had not all been deposited there at one time.

"Who are they?" Thiess stammered as he stepped back and looked to Jakub, his face dimly lit by the ambient glow in the confined space.

"These are the ones that tried to leave. Or they did wrong by Massimino. Hundreds—maybe more."

Suddenly, a deafening noise like a speeding freight train drew their attention and the men gazed uncertainly at one another.

"What's that—"

A violent gust of wind swept through the tunnel and encircled them.

Both men fought to brace themselves against the damp, muddy walls, clawing for the relative security of wooden beams and fearful of being swept into the shaft.

"It's him!" Jakub yelled over the thunderous gale.

"We must get out of here!" Thiess shouted over the near-deafening sound.

"Follow me! Hold onto the walls!" instructed Jakub, gripping a wooden support.

Jakub fought his way forward, turning his face sideways to shield it from the power of the wind and digging as best he could into the sides of the tunnel to prevent himself from being pulled back toward the shaft.

Thiess followed, and after a few harrowing minutes they had made their way back to the main tunnel that led to the entrance. Suddenly, the intensity of the gust strengthened, forcing them to the ground as they struggled to progress forward.

"Is there another way?" Thiess yelled.

"No, this is the only way."

The wind continued to howl, collecting soil, leaves, and other debris and hurling it around in a blustery vortex. Smaller stones pelted each of them and overhead, a loud *crack* rang out as one of the heavy wooden beams snapped.

Thiess looked up, following the source of the sound. He shone his flashlight into the darkness, pointing to where the noise had come from. Just then, a rogue object struck his outstretched hand. Thiess let out a screech, dropping his flashlight, which was swept into the wind as well. The beam of light jerked around the tunnel for a few moments before crashing against a wall and shattering.

Jakub's flashlight reached the source of the crack, illuminating the damaged beam above them; it appeared as though it could come crashing down at any moment.

Thiess wailed in agony as he clutched his injured hand to his chest. Two more loud cracks could be heard over the wind, both further toward the entrance.

"It's going to collapse!" Jakub cried as he crawled along the ground. "We have to get out of here!"

Thiess remained still for a few moments, the pain plunging him into shock.

"Come on! This way!" shouted Jakub, shining his flashlight at Thiess.

Thiess squinted at the bright beam of light. Pushing past his broken hand, he positioned himself into a crouch and hobbled up the tunnel again, gingerly limping and keeping his face down to avoid the airborne objects.

"We are almost there!" Jakub yelled.

Thiess saw the tunnel entrance ahead. Behind him, the creaking and crashing had caused a cloud of dust. He felt the ground rumble as the tunnel began to collapse, forcing him to stand and move one foot in front of the other, building to an awkward jog as he caught up to Jakub.

The pair groaned and gasped their way out of the entrance where they both collapsed, Thiess crying out once more as he tried clenching his hand. The two men lay on the cold, muddy ground; Thiess clutched at his chest with his left hand while holding his right above his face, squinting to assess his injuries.

"You...all right?" sighed Jakub.

"My chest...can't breathe...my hand...broken," Thiess wheezed.

The rumbling within the shaft softened and a brief silence fell over the area. Thiess rolled his head in the direction of the mine and saw an odd, bumpy depression in the ground where the tunnel used to be. The gate at the entrance was mangled on its side, the shrill craw of a raven overhead pierced the stillness.

Chapter Twenty-Four

The rattling of the train woke Amanda and she blinked a few times.

"Hey there, sleepy head. Enjoy your nap?" Emilia greeted her sister; she'd slept for quite a while.

Amanda grumbled in response.

"You're missing some spectacular scenery," Emilia prodded. "It's so beautiful!"

"Just give me a minute." Amanda yawned and enjoyed a deep stretch before sitting up.

"A little jetlagged?"

"Yeah, feels like it. I didn't really get much sleep on the flight—guess my body clock is all messed up. I'll be fine." Amanda looked out the window. "Wow, you're right! That's amazing!"

The rocky, ragged peaks of the snowcapped Tatra Mountains loomed nearby, while picturesque rolling pastures and bountiful farmland nestled itself between. Sprinkled amongst the lush landscape was the occasional town or village. Emilia was completely captivated by the stunning vistas and had found herself staring out the window in awe for most of their journey.

"Zillah is up there," Emilia said. "Somewhere in that mountain range."

"Really?" Amanda asked. "We're getting closer to where your family is from, then? How are you feeling about it?"

"A bit nervous. Who knows what the next few days will be like? I really hope it's not a dead end." Emilia winced at her choice of words as the scene from the altar flashed through her mind.

"Are you okay?"

"Yeah." She tried to shake it off without outwardly showing it. "Yeah, I'm fine. I'm trying not to have any expectations but…it's tough, you know, the anticipation?"

"Don't sweat it. You've got this, Emmi. And I've got your back no matter what we do or don't find out."

"Thanks, Amanda. I'm so glad we're doing this together." Her sister was an anchor in a foreign land.

"Me too!"

From the station, the girls loaded their luggage into their compact Mercedes Benz rental car.

As they drove along the main street on their way out of Poprad, Amanda motioned to a group of shops and restaurants. "When are you thinking we'll eat? Should we stop now?"

"Maybe," Emilia answered. "I'm not really too hungry yet. If we're only a couple hours away, do you think you can wait until we get there?"

"Sure, why not? Maybe the villagers will be preparing a feast for the arrival of their long-lost baroness!" joked Amanda.

"Oh, indeed," Emilia tried her best to sound regal.

"But no mysterious strangers named Massimino."

"Ah, yeah—" Emilia turned her full attention to the road and prayed Amanda couldn't see her cheeks flushing.

"Hold on," Amanda interrupted, and Emilia slowed the car. "You need to turn right up here." She pointed to an upcoming intersection, studying her phone as she read the directions.

"All right, looks like we're starting to head into the mountains."

196

"How stunning is all this!" Amanda said. "There's some dark clouds over there though, hope that's not where we're going." She motioned into the distance, where a blanket of fog hung low over the peaks.

"You know, I wasn't too worried about it until now—driving through these woods, it would be kind of nice if someone knew where we are. Imagine the headlines: 'Two American college students found in the mountainous woods of Slovakia eaten by—'"

"Now you need to turn left," Amanda instructed abruptly. "Yeah, these roads are starting to get a little more...off the beaten path. But I think you're being a little too dramatic there, Miss Journalist!"

Two and a half hours into what should have been a two-hour drive, Emilia began to question the reliability of Amanda's directions. The road had become muddy and uneven. It was riddled with potholes and felt as if they were driving out of the mountains again, rather than further in.

"I think we missed a turn back there," Amanda craned to look out the rear window.

"Just tell me where to go!" Emilia was frustrated they had gotten lost, and she didn't know where they were going now. "These roads are becoming more difficult, and I haven't seen a sign for ages."

The travel had begun to take a toll and the exhausted sisters began to snap at each other.

"I'm doing my best, Emmi!" Amanda defended herself, refreshing her screen again. "The map's not updating, and we lost cell signal a while ago."

Emilia braked but didn't park the car. She just needed a moment to think. "All right. I'm just going to keep driving along here a bit farther. Maybe we'll come across a sign or something that will help us figure out where the heck we are."

"Yeah, okay. It seems like Zillah is the only place in this direction— when I *could* see the map there was nothing else near it or past it," Amanda replied, keeping her eyes peeled out the window.

Emilia continued to drive for another five minutes or so but still hadn't found anything to help them figure out where they were or how to get to Zillah. "How about we turn around and just go back to that last little town we passed?" she suggested. "Maybe someone can give us directions?"

"That's probably the best thing," Amanda agreed. "This isn't a good place to be lost, and I'm sure we would have been there by now if we were on the right road. Let's go back."

Emilia slowed and turned the car, somewhat awkwardly on the narrow mountain road.

After what felt like an hour, the tiny homes came into view. When they'd first passed it, the sisters thought it was quaint. Now Emilia hoped there was at least one person in the area who could help them find their destination.

"There it is!" Amanda called. "That's the town we passed earlier."

"Any ideas where we should stop?" Emilia maneuvered the zippy Benz down a dirt path just wide enough for their tires. "I don't see too many people around."

Amanda sighed. "Probably because there's zero cell signal here." She checked her phone for what seemed like the zillionth time on the same stretch of road, then looked out the window again. "How about the tavern over there?" she suggested, pointing at a white building with a wooden shingled roof and a sign hanging at the entrance nearest the street.

Emilia pulled the car into the drive and parked in front of the tavern. There were a few other older-model cars scattered around the parking lot, but no people.

"Wow, I love the crisp mountain air." Emilia inhaled deeply, happy to be stretching her legs.

"I hope they have some delicious mountain food here; I'm starving," Amanda rolled her neck. "They'll just have to postpone the welcome festival for you."

The tavern had a rustic vibe, though it still felt warm and welcoming—at least at this time of day. A hockey match played on an overhead television toward the rear and the smell of beer hung in the air. A few locals sat around the horseshoe-shaped bar, talking and gesturing occasionally, hurling their discontentment at the game.

Upon hearing the door squeak open, the young bartender looked up at Emilia and Amanda, greeting them with a friendly smile—his day seemed suddenly brighter at the sight of them.

"Hello, welcome," he said. "My name is Tomas. Can I help you?"

Tomas was tall and lanky. He was dressed casually in jeans and a charcoal sweater, the sleeves bunched at his elbows.

"Hi, Tomas. I'm Amanda and this is my sister, Emilia. Yes, you can *definitely* help us." Amanda batted her eyelids in an obvious attempt to flirt with the barman. "We're lost and hungry," she pouted.

Tomas grinned, "This is no problem," he said. "You come, take a seat, and I fix everything!"

Emilia realized now that he had a rather thick accent, but it added to his charm. His light complexion was spotted with acne and his dark brown eyes complemented his oval-shaped face. His stubble needed a little upkeep, and his black hair was styled in a messy-bedhead kind of way.

Emilia and Amanda looked across to the empty dining area and opted for a seat at the bar.

"Now, drinks?" Tomas prompted.

Amanda looked to Emilia and shrugged, "Why not?"

"We're on vacation, right?" Emilia replied with a smile.

"How about some wine?" Amanda directed her deep brown eyes at Tomas. "What whites do you have?"

"Well that is easy. We have one." Tomas moved to a small fridge below the bar. "Here it is. From right here in Slovakia. They grow grapes down in the south. Fantastic." Tomas set two wine glasses on the bar, removed the cork from the bottle, and poured a generous amount in both. "Try it!"

The girls obliged, picking up their glasses and clinking them together.

"Thanks, Tomas. This isn't bad," teased Amanda with a cheeky smile.

Emilia nodded in agreement.

"Now, you said you need food," Tomas said. "Sandwiches and fries?"

"Any salads?" Amanda asked.

"What about club sandwiches and fries?" Tomas repeated. "You very far from tourist areas where things are more...cosmopolitan. Trust me, this is best choice." He shrugged with a friendly smile.

Emilia chuckled. "An order of club sandwiches and fries sounds perfect!"

"All right, I guess make that two," Amanda added.

"Great!" Tomas seemed relieved. "Let me tell cook and I be right back. Help you find your way to highway and tourist areas. Don't worry, you are not first to take wrong turn. Is easy to get back from here." He winked before disappearing into the kitchen via a door behind the bar.

"Wait till we tell him we're trying to go even *further* away from the tourist areas," Amanda smirked, raising her eyebrows and taking another sip of wine.

"Yeah, seems like we're definitely on the road less traveled—literally; we didn't see or pass a single car back there."

"I guess we're going to be arriving a little late then, huh? What are we supposed to be doing when we *do* eventually get there?" Amanda appeared to be more relaxed with alcohol in her hand and the promise of food on the way.

"Well, there is a lawyer we need to find," Emilia explained. "Martin Thiess."

"And he'll be the one who can *finally* tell us what this is all about?"

"I sure hope so," Emilia replied, taking a good gulp of her own wine.

Tomas returned and announced their lunch would soon be ready. "Tell me, where is it you trying to go? Poprad? The ski fields? I am thinking you are not hikers this late in season. You don't look like hikers." He flashed another grin that Amanda returned.

"Actually," Emilia said, "we've just come from Poprad. We're trying to find a village called Zillah."

"Zillah?" He scoffed. "Why on this planet do you want to go there? There are so many beautiful, *magnificent* places to visit around here. Zillah is not one of them." Tomas looked equal parts confused and horrified.

Amanda took it upon herself to set him straight. "Well, Emilia here—"

Emilia cut in by nudging her sister under the bar. "It seems that my family may be from Zillah, but I don't really know the details, we need to go there to find out."

"In Zillah, really?" Tomas didn't seem any less confused as he leaned on the bar. "Goodness. I have never been there, but I hear things. Is not a very…happy place. A lot of strange things have happened there—if you believe rumors. I don't know how much is real or not. They say a long time ago Zillah was jewel of the area, but something changed. Mines ran out of gold or something and everything fell apart. You *sure* you want to go there?"

"Well, it's not so much that we *want* to go there, Emilia kind of *needs* to."

"Well, I can show you where it is on map, then maybe when you are done there you can go to more beautiful places in my country!"

Emilia smiled. "Thank you."

"Hey," Amanda said, skillfully grazing his fingers as she reached in her pocket, "do you know why my phone won't work here?" She pulled out the device and showed him there was no service.

"Do not get me started." Tomas rolled his eyes. "Kills this town. Years ago, telephone company put up tower to cover here and all around, even probably as far as Zillah, but then freak storm and *boom!* —knocked down."

"And they never tried to fix it?" asked Amanda.

"Yes, of course. Many times. They come back and every time, after few days, *boom!* Something happens. They even tried different places to put it, but same thing. No one can explain. Doesn't make sense." Tomas shook his head. "Drives everybody crazy and then takes many months again to fix."

"So, no cell phone then?" Amanda resigned.

"If you need, we have phone here at bar," Tomas offered. "But to get signal, you need to go back close to one of the bigger towns or cities. Now, I go see if food is ready."

Amanda waited until the swinging door had closed behind him. "Oh my gosh, what *are* you getting us into, Emmi?"

Emilia tried to stay positive, but she'd be lying if she said she wasn't uncomfortable not being able to use their phones. "Let's just look on the bright side. Uh...we're in Europe together!"

"I'll drink to that!" Amanda replied, offering up her glass to toast.

Chapter Twenty-Five

As he lay on the damp ground, Thiess heard footsteps on the gravel. It was a slow, measured gait that contained no hint of reaction to the events that had just unfolded.

"Gentlemen! How fortunate you were able to exit the mine in time. I warned you that this one was unsafe; you should not have been here." Massimino stood over the two men, hands clasped behind his back, a placid expression on his face.

"Massimino!" Thiess moaned, still unable to catch his breath.

"Sir...sir..." Jakub stammered, scrambling to his feet. "I'm sorry, sir. Mr. Thiess, sir—"

"Dangerous places, mine shafts," Massimino said, resting his hands in front of him. "You are lucky to have made it out alive."

Thiess, chest still heaving, clumsily picked himself up from the ground, clutching his injured hand close to his body with the other, blood smearing his disheveled shirt. "Massimino, there are bodies. Did you—"

"I only see an abandoned collapsed mine, Martin," Massimino said. "I suggest you get your hand looked at by the doctor in the village. Do not disobey me again. The next time you may not find your way out."

Thiess recognized the coldness in Massimino's voice and knew without a doubt he had made all of this happen.

"You were able to get an update on the heiress?" Massimino asked with none of the same tone.

"Ah, um...yes," panted Thiess. "I received confirmation from the travel company that both women left on a train from Bratislava." He took a few moments to catch his breath. "They will then drive here from Poprad. Should be here later this afternoon."

Massimino glanced at Jakub, who quickly shifted his gaze to the ground. "I have wasted energy here. Send your sister, Hanna, to visit me in my tower."

"Yes...I will," Jakub nodded.

"Very good," Massimino said. "And Jakub, I trust this is a message that will not need to be repeated."

"Yes, of course, I'm sorry, sir—"

"Enough." He held up his hand, silencing the villager. Then without another word, Massimino turned and walked casually away.

Thiess pounded the door to the doctor's office before unsuccessfully attempting—again—to turn the locked handle. Exasperated, he paced up and down the street, looking for anyone or anything that might help break his present impasse.

Clicking noises followed by a squeak caused Thiess to glance toward the building. The door was now half-open with a reedy, middle-aged man poking his head out. He appeared groggy, rubbing his eyes before donning a pair of simple gold-rimmed spectacles.

"Doctor?" Thiess was past impatient.

"Yes, yes...I am Dr. Banik. Who are you?"

"My name is Martin Thiess." He neared the doorstep. "I've injured my hand."

"I don't recognize you. Where have you come from?" Dr. Banik warily observed him.

"I...I am working on a project for Massimino," Thiess decided on. "I need help, please."

"Oh? For Massimino?" The man's face filled with new life. "Of course, come in. Please pardon me. You caught me during my...nap."

Thiess entered the darkened office, picking up the distinct smell of alcohol on the good doctor's breath.

Great, one doctor in town and he's a drunk.

Dr. Banik flipped a series of switches near the door and the small reception room was suddenly awash in a harsh white light from the fluorescent bulbs overhead. Several flickered in a way that made the whole experience even more unsettling for Thiess.

"I'm afraid you'll have to excuse my receptionist. She has been here a little too long." Dr. Banik gestured to the life-sized model of a human skeleton that had been contorted into a chair behind the desk, which was stacked with piles of folders and scattered papers covered in a noticeable layer of dust.

"I am in a lot of pain, doctor," Thiess said, in no mood for jokes. "Please."

"Of course, come on through. This way." Dr. Banik guided Thiess down a hallway, flicking on another light as both men entered a cramped room. "In here. Please, take a seat on the bed."

The examination table was covered with faded blue vinyl, heavily worn and cracked in some areas; the speckled white floor tiles had been well-trodden and needed cleaning. Scattered old medical instruments lay across a bench—some deserving of a place in a medical history museum, and the original white walls were now a discolored yellow hue.

Maybe it is safer to go back down the mountain; could I drive myself there like this?

"Please, please, have a seat." Dr. Banik sensed Thiess' reluctance and urged him toward the table.

Thiess sat with a thud; the old foam padding having long lost any cushioning it may have once offered. Dr. Banik rattled over a stool and sat down in front of his patient. Thiess was again repulsed by the smell of alcohol and further agitated by the obvious tremor he felt in the doctor's hand as it held his, manipulating it somewhat painfully in different directions as he examined the injury.

"What happened to you?"

The chaotic scene from the mine flashed before Thiess, and he closed his eyes briefly as he relived it all. "I...I was in one of the mines. Something crashed into my hand."

"You didn't see what it was?" The doctor raised one unkempt eyebrow.

"No, it was dark, maybe it was a rock," Thiess replied, slowly shaking his head.

"All right, any other injuries?" asked Dr. Banik, looking over Thiess' dirty, torn clothing. "You have some scratches on your face."

"I had chest pain...when it happened, but I think that has settled down now. I am not worried about small scrapes, just my hand. What do you think the problem is?"

"I think there may be some broken bones. The hand has many of them," said the doctor, sliding the glasses off his nose and cleaning them on his shirt. When he breathed on the lenses, a foul odor wafted past Thiess. "I am embarrassed to say that our x-ray machine is...unreliable. We may need to take you down the mountain to a larger town with more facilities."

"I have some very important business that I must take care of here over the next couple of days," Thiess snapped. "Is there nothing you can do now?"

"I see." Dr. Banik rolled away, fumbling in drawers and cupboards. "In that case, I will do what I can here. Though when you've finished your business, I suggest you get this checked with an x-ray and—"

"Yes, yes," Thiess replied. "Actually, I will need to visit Poprad tomorrow and can go to the hospital there if it does not improve."

"Very well, it is in your *hands*." Dr. Banik smirked as he set about tending to the injury.

He cleaned and disinfected the deep gash, bandaging it tightly to maintain pressure on the wound and prevent movement. Despite a deep throbbing which continued to plague him, Thiess was satisfied.

"Thank you very much, doctor. Is there anything you can give me for the pain? It is…quite unpleasant and distracting."

Dr. Banik grinned.

"Ah, yes, of course. Do not worry, I have the good stuff. Wait here a minute." He winked at Thiess and headed further down the hall, leaving him with his thoughts.

Did Massimino really do this? The bodies; who were they? Things here are far worse than I realized. Christ, he almost killed me.

Through the wall, he heard more cupboards as the doctor opened and shut their doors; objects were being shifted around in the next room.

A few moments later, Dr. Banik returned. "Here you go. Take one of these with a glass of water when the pain is bothering you," he instructed as he handed Thiess a small orange bottle with no label.

Thiess eyed it warily.

"Be careful though," the doctor warned. "These are powerful—more powerful than the pain."

"I thank you for your help." Thiess stood from the table and Dr. Banik walked his patient back to the front of his office.

"I don't understand why they are not here yet," Thiess mumbled as he sat by Massimino's desk. "I received emails from the agent who arranged their travel and she confirmed that both women were taken to the train station in Bratislava this morning. The train departed on schedule and there was a car ready for them in Poprad, they should have been here hours ago."

"It is not a problem; I can feel that she is close now. I still do not understand why they did not just come with you," replied Massimino peering out the window behind his desk.

"It was the Americans; they are overly cautious," Thiess answered after an uncomfortable pause, holding his hand and grimacing.

Massimino didn't respond, instead gazing back down at the road leading into the village. He saw a figure walking toward the main square, red hair glinting ever so slightly as her silhouette passed beneath a streetlamp.

Luna, where have you been?

"Massimino, please, my hand," Thiess complained, interrupting his thoughts. "The pain is very uncomfortable. What happened this afternoon? Jakub said…did you…?"

"I have told you already, my friend," he said without glancing in his direction. "These things are best not discussed. I did warn you explicitly not to go there."

"You call me friend, and yet…" Thiess trailed off, holding up his hand and wincing.

Massimino slowly turned to face Thiess, amused at the anguish he observed. "Would you prefer I not refer to you as a friend?" Massimino asked coldly before staring back out the window.

A car had appeared in the distance, and Massimino smiled as he watched it round the final bend toward the village. "Ah, the heiress has arrived. Perhaps you should go now and meet them. I do not wish to make myself known to her yet—that should happen tomorrow, when the time is right. Tonight, I want to ensure she feels comfortable and safe. Go now. I wish you well in concluding your business with her. Please, for the time being, do not mention my name."

Thiess rose from his seat, saying nothing as he left. Massimino watched him impassively until his head had disappeared out of sight, then returned his gaze to the village below.

Chapter Twenty-Six

P
amela Campbell woke to the buzzing and dinging of her husband Brian's phone.

The sun had just broken over the horizon on a clear morning, illuminating the brilliant white and blue of the ship—*Ocean Explorer*—as she neared her destination through moderate seas en route back to Ushuaia, Argentina. One of the southernmost cities on the planet, it was the beginning and end of many Antarctic expeditions.

"I haven't missed that sound one bit!" Pamela said as she smiled up at Brian, who was propped up in bed beside her. His chest hair was still dark, sprinkled with gray and a few wrinkles. She still adored him as much as she had when they'd first met.

"It's music to my ears," Brian replied, reaching out to caress her golden hair as she lay on her side facing him.

"I guess it's true: all good things must come to an end."

"I figured we must be getting close enough to land again to get a regular signal. The Wi-Fi hasn't worked a single day we've been aboard and I kind of need to see what's been happening at the office." Brian frowned apologetically.

"It's fine; I understand. Anything from the girls?" Pamela rolled to her back and stretched.

"Ah..." began Brian as he scrolled through the long list of new messages that had queued up. "Yes, there's a few here—the most recent one is from Emmi, titled Europe Trip. Oh great, I guess they want to go away again," he joked.

"Tell them we haven't forgotten about the last one yet." Pamela shook her head against the pillow before looking back to Brian, his face suddenly distressed. "What's wrong, honey?"

When he didn't respond, she sat up. "What is it?"

Brian held up his hand, signaling for her to give him a minute as he put the phone to his ear for a few moments, listening.

"Her email said that they're...they're going to Zillah. I just tried to call her but, no answer—"

"What do you mean? *Zillah,* isn't that where—" her voice caught in her throat as she grabbed the phone from her husband.

"Yes."

Pamela read Emilia's email twice before Brian stood and opened the stateroom curtain, looking out to sea.

"Oh my God. What are we going to do?" Pamela asked, chewing her lip.

"I don't know," Brian answered without looking at her. "When I tried to call, it didn't even ring—just went straight to voicemail, like her phone is switched off. Here, let me try Amanda."

Pamela kneeled up on the bed and handed the device to Brian, who chose Amanda's number and held it to his ear.

"Same thing—straight to voicemail," he said, feeling the color draining from his face. "They might be on the plane already. I can't think of another reason both their phones are off." Brian was becoming more and more agitated as he reread the email. "She doesn't say exactly *when* they were leaving, just that they are going there for the break. God, how on earth is this even possible?"

"Maybe they're studying, sometimes they turn their phones off for that...?" Pamela tried her best to keep her voice even. "What if the same people who—"

"I know, I know," Brian interrupted, not wanting to hear the words he knew would follow. "Let me think for a minute."

Brian put on a bathrobe and stepped out onto the balcony, resting his hands on the railing as he stared across the ocean.

Pamela retrieved her phone from the bench in the dressing area and turned it on, checking to see if there were any other messages or information that might be helpful before joining her husband. She still wore her delicate night slip and cuddled up against Brian's back to shield herself from the cool breeze.

"I checked my phone too," she said. "There were a few other messages from the girls over the last week or so, but nothing else about Zillah or their plans."

Brian nodded. "I don't want to overreact. We don't really know what's going on, but given what happened last time, I just don't feel like we can take a chance. We can keep calling until we get through, but I think I need to go home and...make sure they're both safe." She heard him audibly swallow. "Perhaps it's time to let Emilia know the truth."

"I've always been afraid this day would come," Pamela admitted with a heavy sigh. "You're right, we need to go home and talk to Emilia."

"We're supposed to fly to Santiago today, we'll just skip our visit to Chile and go to Philadelphia—God I hope they're still there," Brian shared the same labored exhale. "I'll call the airline and see what we can do to change it. I'll try the girls again after that."

He briskly tapped out a message to both girls telling them not to pursue their travel plans—that Zillah was an unsafe place and to call as soon as they could.

Chapter Twenty-Seven

Emilia and Amanda devoured their lunch, then Tomas drew them a map with directions to Zillah. He wished them well and hoped to see them both again on their way back.

"Alrighty, take-two," Amanda joked as Emilia climbed behind the driver's seat.

"Should we go back down and find a signal so we can check our messages?"

"Oh...probably," Amanda was distracted by the clouds overhead. "But it's getting late and I don't know if we really want to end up driving along these narrow roads when it's dark. I think we should just keep going. We'll be lucky to get there by sunset at this rate."

"Yeah, okay," Emilia said, hoping to convince herself. They could call back home from the hotel when they reached Zillah even if their cell phones didn't work there. "I'm sure there's some way to call out from up there—hopefully they'll have a fast internet connection at the place we're staying."

Emilia pulled out of the parking lot and they began their journey into the mountains again.

"You know, if we didn't have to be in any particular place right now, this would be a gorgeous spot for a drive in the mountains, don't you think?" Emilia tried to lighten the mood, which had been steadily deteriorating as their exhaustion grew and the day wore on.

"Yeah, I suppose."

"Oh, come on, the forest is beautiful, and we don't seem to go more than a few minutes without passing some sort of breathtaking vista," Emilia replied, swerving to avoid another deep pothole.

"I just hope we get there soon," Amanda said. "These roads are really bad, and I don't want to be lost out here all night."

"Hey, you're the one navigating."

"Yeah, I'm navigating from a map on a bar napkin—wait." She held the drawing close to her face. "Slow down; that must be the pass into the valley he told us about. This is where we went wrong last time, don't miss it! Geez…why isn't there a sign?"

"I know, right? Okay, I've got it!" Emilia giggled, the car skidding a little as she turned the wheel hard to follow the uneven, windy road that passed between steep cliffs on either side.

"I'm sorry, Emmi," Amanda said after a while. "I'm just feeling tired and it's been almost a day since I showered. I feel kind of gross."

"Don't even worry about it," Emilia assured her. They were sisters; fighting was inevitable sometimes, and even more so when neither had slept in a warm bed or had a hot bath in over twenty-four hours.

"How are you doing so well?" Amanda asked. "You're all peppy, and you look great!"

Emilia shrugged as she steered the car out from the pass; fading daylight filtered through the windows. "Well, gee, thanks sis! Yeah, we're so close now, I just can't wait to get there and see what this is all about. After all these years of wondering, I never would have thought it would lead somewhere like this."

Amanda offered a tired smile and a nod. "I get it."

"What's next? I feel like it's been long enough that we need to look out for a river and bridge, right?"

"That sounds right." Amanda looked at the napkin again.

"And then we're almost there!" Emilia was more excited to reach their destination than ever.

"*Whoa*, who stole the sun?" said Amanda as she looked out into the valley. It was heavily misted and overcast; they could no longer see as far.

"Help me look out for the bridge," instructed Emilia, slowing the car to account for the low visibility.

"Yeah sure. It's kind of spooky here, huh?"

"Definitely. Maybe it will clear some as we start going back up again. I think I see it."

Ahead, Emilia could just make out the structure, which appeared rickety even from this distance.

Amanda squinted. "Ah, yeah. Is it just the fog, or do you think it's really as bad as it looks?"

"I'm sure it's...fine." Emilia was trying to reassure herself of that fact as well. "I'll go slowly."

Emilia drove carefully out onto the bridge. It creaked and moaned beneath them as they inched across. Amanda clutched her armrest and Emilia tightened her grip on the steering wheel. After a few nervous moments, both breathed a sigh of relief as they heard the stones crunch beneath the tires.

"I'm definitely glad we're not doing this in total darkness—though it's getting close," said Amanda.

"And up we go!" Emilia smiled at her sister as they trudged up the mountain.

"Eyes on the road!"

Emilia laughed and continued, focusing on the zig-zagging path through the forest. The fog cleared a bit as they ascended, but the drab skies remained.

"Come on, you can't tell me this isn't a little bit fun." Emilia giggled. "I feel like we're in a movie."

"All *right*," Amanda sighed. "This is pretty cool, I'll admit it."

Emilia slowed the car to a stop as they reached another corner. Before them was a gushing waterfall. "Look at that," she said, in awe of how it flowed in different directions from the basin below.

"Oh wow! That's magnificent!" Amanda agreed.

"Yeah, see? Things are getting better! Look, next to the waterfall: is that a building?"

"Um...yep," Amanda said. "We must be getting close!"

As they made their way around one more sharp turn, the twisting road straightened out ahead of them.

"Hooray, buildings! Zillah!" Emilia pointed excitedly.

"Just a few hours late," said Amanda, glancing down at the clock.

Emilia grew more relieved with each hint of civilization they passed. The streets were built of cobblestones, and they were a nice change from the muddy mountain. All the buildings were colorful but looked as though they had once been more vibrant; it had been a long time since they'd been painted. Leafless trees dotted the sidewalks, where she imagined people would gather if things weren't so gloomy.

"There's a kind of charm to it, even like this," Emilia finally said. "Do you think this is really where my parents were from?"

"I think we'll find out soon!" Amanda grinned, squeezing her sister's arm. "Where are we supposed to be going to anyway?"

"The booking is at Vitaj Inn. It is supposed to be in the center of town."

"And how are we supposed to meet up with this lawyer without phones?"

"I'm not sure." Emilia hadn't thought of that until now. "Let's get to the hotel first—before you start getting snarky again, and we'll figure it out from there."

"Perfect! I can shower!"

Emilia continued following the cobblestone street as it meandered back and forth, buildings on either side and laneways branching out sporadically along the way. Eventually, they reached the large, open square in the center of town.

Streetlamps glowed in both the park at the center and the street around it, though it appeared several lights were out, leaving patches of shadows. Buildings lined the square of all different shapes and sizes, some with signs hanging above the doors or over their front windows. It all conveyed a quaint style reminiscent of a medieval era long past. Lights shone from some of the windows that peppered the square, many still dark.

"That's it!" Emilia blurted, pointing to one of the larger buildings and the sign hanging in front of it which read *Vitaj Inn and Tavern*.

"Well, that wasn't so hard," replied Amanda.

There were plenty of available parking spaces and Emilia pulled the Mercedes into a spot just across from the inn. In stark contrast to the handful of older model vehicles parked around the square, there was one conspicuously new Audi on the opposite side.

They stretched their arms and legs and glanced around; the unmistakable smell of wood-burning fires filled the air. Emilia inhaled deeply; the combination of fresh mountain air, the scent of pine from the surrounding forest, and the smoky aroma was delightfully intoxicating. The chill in the air struck their skin and caused a tiny shiver up her back, but it wasn't unpleasant.

"Well, this is a pretty cute place to spend a few days, right?" declared Emilia with a wide smile.

"Yeah, definitely," Amanda agreed. "It's going to be a unique experience for sure..."

Emilia gazed upward; the dense clouds from earlier were now patchy, and stars had begun to shine. "Check it out. The sky is clearing! I bet the stars will be amazing up here, so far from city lights."

"Ah, yeah..." Amanda was distracted. "I'm sure the stars are cool and all but check *that* out." She pointed behind her sister.

Silhouetted against a dimming night sky and only sparsely lit, the structure looked as though it were a foreboding, shadowy ghost looming over the village; a mysterious castle amongst the scattered fog.

A shining light from a window at the top of the tower closest to them sent an inexplicable shiver through Emilia. Her body became stiff and she swallowed hard. "Um…wow."

"You all right?"

"Yeah, yeah…" She cleared her throat, reasoning her chill was from the air. "Gosh, that's really remarkable. Maybe we can go explore it in the daytime."

"Where do you suppose all the people are around here? So much for your welcome parade, it feels a bit like the village is deserted." Amanda scanned the shops for signs of life.

"No idea," replied Emilia as she glanced around the square. "Maybe they're just keeping warm inside somewhere. Let's get our stuff and sort out our room—"

Emilia stopped short when she saw the church. Though the exterior had been painted bright white, it was built from stone. It featured a pointed roof and spire which stood out amongst the surrounding buildings. Emilia was drawn into its shadow, but she couldn't move.

"What is it, Emmi?" Amanda asked. "The church? It looks kind of deserted, too."

Emilia gulped. No, it was just a building. It wasn't from her dream. That wasn't real.

"Yes," came her almost whispered reply as she moved toward it to look closer despite the darkness.

"Emmi, what is it?" Amanda pressed, following her sister.

"I'm…I'm not sure."

"Wait, this isn't the church from your wacky dreams, is it?"

"No," Emilia was quick to answer. "I mean, I don't think so. It's too big and I never really got to see it from the outside. It just made me think of it, that's all."

"Okay, good. That would have *completely* freaked me out." Amanda laughed, clutching her chest. "Maybe we can look in there tomorrow? You're sure though, right?"

Emilia slowly nodded. "Yeah, pretty certain, this one's much bigger than the one from my dreams. Let's go and check in."

"Great idea, then a shower and some dinner!"

"And hopefully find this lawyer, Martin Thiess."

As they dragged their suitcases, the impracticality of pulling heavy luggage over cobblestones soon became apparent. Emilia rolled her eyes as she helped Amanda to the inn with her larger suitcases first and planned to return to the car for hers. Their laughter rang out across the otherwise abandoned square as the girls bumped and bounced Amanda's clothing and beauty supplies into the inn.

The reception area was spacious, with two shabby sofas and a half-dozen older mismatched chairs and tables. Green wallpaper with gold flecks adorned the walls, many corners peeling, and a well-worn burgundy carpet with circular sun patterns covered the floor. The ceiling was high with ornate moldings embellishing the entire expanse. Several decorative iron chandeliers lit the space with a dim ambience, and oil paintings encased in antique golden frames appeared to be of the region, hanging on the walls between other overdone fittings and fixtures.

Centered at the rear of the room was an unattended reception desk with hallways leading to closed doors on either side of it; a baroque double staircase curved its way toward the mezzanine level and beyond.

Emilia and Amanda approached the desk, passing two arched entrances—on their left was a restaurant which looked to be unoccupied, and on the right was a bar, also with no patrons. The smell of stale cigar smoke permeated from the walls and furniture.

"Great, we've wound up in some spooky, empty village in the mountains," Amanda whispered.

"*Shh!*" Emilia turned to her. "There's a bell on the desk."

Emilia picked up the brass bell, ringing it twice before returning it to the counter. Amanda looked at her with wide eyes and an amused grin.

"Just a minute! I'll be right there!" called a woman's voice from a closed doorway beyond.

Suddenly, the door swung open with a squeak and a woman scurried out to meet the inn's newest guests.

"Hello, welcome to—" She stopped suddenly. "Oh, my goodness. You're...you look just like..." the woman stammered while Emilia and Amanda shared a confused glance.

"Hi there, I'm Emilia and this is my sister, Amanda. We have a reservation. Last name is Campbell."

"Emilia..." The woman settled a pair of glasses on her nose, fingers shaking. "Emilia *Campbell*. You're our visitor. Sorry, I thought you were—"

"Do I remind you of someone?"

"Never mind, I'm sorry." The woman threw her hands back as if to wave off her silliness. "So, you are staying here, not the castle? Your name is Campbell, you're not a Blagden?"

"Ah, yeah...that's what our travel agent had set up I believe? Yes, I might be related to the Blagdens; that's what I'm here to find out."

"Yes, yes." She flipped through the book in front of her and found what Emilia assumed was their information. "I have a booking for two; I just assumed it was tourists. Occasionally we do still get some around here."

"So, we're in the right place?" asked Amanda.

"Yes, of course." She smiled. "You just arrived here now?"

"Yes," Emilia answered. "We got a little lost in the mountains, but we finally made it!"

"Oh, I see. Well, *vitaj,* as we say in Slovakia. Welcome…welcome home." She seemed genuinely happy to have new visitors. "I am Pia. It's my pleasure to meet you."

"Well, thank you…I guess?" Emilia tried not to look as confused as she felt about the strange reaction. "I'm supposed to be meeting someone here. His name is Martin Thiess—he's a lawyer. Do you know where I can find him?"

Pia gave her a knowing nod though she looked displeased. "He is probably at the castle. If you wish, I can send someone up there to let him know you have arrived."

"Would it be possible to get to our room first and then we can track him down?" Amanda chimed in. "We've been traveling all day and I could *really* use a shower and some fresh clothes."

"Okay, that's not a problem. Let me get you a key." Pia turned to a board behind the desk where two-dozen metal keyrings hung from several rows of hooks. All but two rooms were unoccupied. Pia retrieved a key and handed it to Emilia. "Here you are. Room twenty is on the third floor; it is one of our nicest rooms and has two beds. I will call my husband to help you with your bags."

Pia opened the door behind her again and stuck her head through the opening, calling loudly to her husband. After a short wait, he burst through the doors, leaving them to swing and squeak behind him. He was tall and his kind face appeared eager to have customers.

"Marek, these are our guests, Emilia and Amanda," Pia said. "Please help them with the luggage, I've put them in room twenty."

"She is staying here?" Marek shot a puzzled look at Pia before looking at the girls, then back to his wife once more. He stepped closer to her and whispered in her ear.

"Campbell…Blagden…castle…reservation…Thiess," were the only words Emilia overheard clearly enough in the rather animated conversation between the duo that involved nodding, head shaking, hand gestures, and some shrugging.

"Is everything all right?" Amanda asked, her impatience growing despite the unusual conversation taking place. "I'd really like to get to our room if that's okay."

Pia and Marek stopped their chatter.

"Yes, I will take you now," replied Marek. "Please follow me." He was quite spindly, and it looked as though he felt the weight of the cases as he collected them but made a concerted effort for it not to appear so.

"Go ahead, Amanda," Emilia said. "I'll get my bag from the car and meet you up there."

"See you in a minute," she answered, following Marek to the staircase.

"Please, after you." He nodded for Amanda to go ahead of him. "When you get to the top of this set of stairs, there is another behind it. Take them all the way to the top."

Amanda began to bounce up the stairs, Marek shuffling behind her.

Emilia turned her attention back to the receptionist. "Ah, what you said before, it sounds like you recognize me. Who do you think I look like?"

Pia had pretended to go back to work in her book, but she seemed taken off guard by the question. "What? No, no. We've never met. But I can tell just by looking at you that you are a Blagden—the similarity is amazing."

"Really?" Emilia's skin tingled. "I've only just found out, but I believe I am—that's why I'm here. What can you tell me about them?"

"Well," Pia hesitated, but couldn't help but share some details, "the Blagdens built this whole village, the castle—everything. There are none left now though. Well, except for you..." Her voice trailed off.

"Please, go on."

Pia pressed her lips together. "Perhaps it's best if you speak with Mr. Thiess when we find him."

Emilia could have been blind and still know the woman was holding back. "Please, what do you know?"

"Nothing really. Mr. Thiess will be the one who can help you. I'm sorry." Her pleasant demeanor had changed to cool and professional.

Emilia sensed it was not worth pushing but wondered what else Pia might know. "I'm not sure I understand, but let's track down Martin Thiess as you say. I'm going to get the other bag from the car; I'll be back in a minute."

"Okay." Pia was back to smiling. "I will make sure we find him."

Chapter Twenty-Eight

Emilia headed back out into the cool night and across the empty street to where their car was parked. She retrieved her suitcase and was heading back across the square when a voice startled her.

"Miss Blagden—eh, Miss Campbell, is that you?"

Emilia turned to see a pudgy older man approaching her, slipping in and out of sight as he moved across the square between lit and unlit streetlamps. He was dressed in a disheveled tweed suit and she could make out a conspicuous bandage wrapped around his right hand.

"Miss Campbell, is it? I am Martin Thiess."

"Mr. Thiess! Hello. Yes, I'm Emilia." She smiled. She attempted to keep warm by crossing her hands over her chest and rubbing her arms while Thiess strode the rest of the distance to join her.

"Miss Campbell, I am unable to shake your hand," greeted Thiess, holding up his damaged limb for her inspection.

"Of course. Are you okay? And please, call me Emilia."

"Yes, yes, I…will be fine." He grinned; teeth yellowed with age. "Did you have difficulty getting to Zillah? We…ah, I was expecting you earlier."

"Well, actually, yes, we got a little lost in the mountains when our phones lost service."

"Ah, yes, that causes me much frustration. Just one of the many problems in this place. At least you are here now. There is much we need to discuss." Thiess waved his hand, motioning around the village.

The sound of a truck's diesel engine interrupted their conversation and they watched as the bouncing headlights bumped their way across the cobblestones toward the square.

"So, we should get you up to the castle," Thiess said. "There are two rooms prepared there. Where is your sister?"

"Oh. I guess we didn't realize that we were to stay at the castle. The travel agent booked us here at the inn."

"I see." His eyes darted to the building behind her and back to her face. "No matter. You do not need to stay here; it is better that you are up in the castle." He watched the truck as it drew closer.

Emilia looked past Thiess and up to the castle beyond. Its hard edges cut an imposing presence against the undulating mountains and the star-filled sky, even in the darkness.

"My sister is already in the room, likely in the shower by now. Perhaps we could just stay here for tonight and we can figure it out tomorrow? We've had a long day of traveling and it would be nice just to be settled for tonight."

Thiess was quiet a moment. "All right, I understand. Then you should go and put your things in your room and clean up if you wish. We can have dinner and discuss some important items that need your attention." Thiess' gaze wandered again to the truck as it parked in the square, then back to Emilia.

"That would be great," she agreed. "I'm really excited to talk with you about all of this, can you give me fifteen minutes? Maybe we could eat here at the inn? It looks like they have a restaurant."

"Ah...I have a better idea: there is an Italian restaurant across the square." Thiess turned toward the building with its synonymous green, white, and red lights framing the window. Two men hopped out of the truck, stealing his attention.

"Okay, we will see you there soon." Emilia looked curiously at the newcomers who appeared to recognize Thiess.

"Very good. You go now," replied Thiess, forcing a smile as he shooed her toward the inn's entrance.

Emilia, amused by the gesture, quickly collected her bag from the stone sidewalk and headed back inside. She had hoped to see Pia again, but there was no sign of her—or anyone else—at reception, in the restaurant, or at the bar. Emilia started up the stairs in search of their room, the wood beneath the carpet creaking as she ascended.

At the second-floor landing, the wallpaper pattern switched to a beige and gold striped design on the top half of the walls with wood paneling below it. The carpet continued down the corridors heading off to the sides, and there was a small mezzanine area with sitting chairs overlooking the lobby as the balcony wrapped around to continue up the stairs. Emilia placed her hand on the smooth, worn banister as she rounded the corner and continued up, hauling her suitcase before reaching the top of the stairs and finding their room.

She could hear the shower running as she entered.

The room was oversized, with gold embroidered curtains covering a door and window. There were two double beds, each with floral design bedspreads and matching pillows. The wallpaper was white with burgundy patterns, and there was a bygone-era sofa, along with a sitting chair and coffee table. The air smelled a little stuffy, indicating it was likely unoccupied most of the time.

"It's just me," she called.

"I figured it would be," Amanda replied from the bathroom down the hall. "There doesn't seem to be anyone else around." She sounded cranky as she turned off the water and pushed the shower curtain open with a rattle.

"What's up?" asked Emilia as Amanda emerged with a towel wrapped around her.

"So much for a hot shower," she griped. "It was barely warm. Ugh."

"The room is kind of cute," offered Emilia.

"If you like pre-vintage, I suppose. We may be the first people to stay here in years."

Emilia needed to get her sister's mind off their accommodations. "I found Martin Thiess—or he found me."

Amanda's eyes brightened. "Well that's good news. What did he say?"

"Not much yet. Apparently there was some mix-up though, he expected we'd be staying at the castle—can you believe it? We're going to meet him for dinner at the Italian restaurant in—well, probably ten minutes now, so let's hustle. I'm just going to change into something warmer for now; I'll shower when we get back tonight."

"What? The *castle?!* I mean, good call not making us move again tonight—but tomorrow? Yes, please! I'm telling you, you're totally royalty or something! Remember the way the woman downstairs reacted when she saw you?"

"Ugh, okay, enough of that—let's just get ready."

Emilia sifted through her suitcase and changed into a pair of black jeans and a white woolen sweater. She grabbed a light coat and flung it onto the bed before tapping at her phone a few times in search of a Wi-Fi access point, but her attempts were unsuccessful.

"I can't see any networks to connect to. Did you try?" Emilia asked.

"I tried before I got in the shower and none came up for me," Amanda said. "I wouldn't be surprised if there aren't any in this town at all—it's like we've gone back in time or something, Emmi!"

"We can ask at the front desk when we go downstairs again," said Emilia as she pulled the curtains open. The rollers squeaked but eventually slid across with some extra effort.

"Hey, can anyone see in here?" Amanda asked before removing her towel to get dressed.

"I don't think so. Doesn't look like there's any other buildings out there, just trees and mountains," observed Emilia, peering out the window. "When did you become shy anyway?"

After jiggling with the brittle handle, Emilia stepped out onto the stone terrace, closing the door most of the way behind her to keep the room warm.

The terrace featured a table and two matching chairs arranged around an iron firepit. A small pile of firewood laced with cobwebs was stacked neatly under the overhang by the door. Emilia looked up at the night sky, which was brilliantly filled with stars, and she paused, allowing her eyes to drink in the splendor of the moon as it rose behind the mountainous horizon. It appeared to be almost full, glowing a brilliant pale orange.

Emilia stepped to the edge of the terrace. The moonlight reflected off the flowing river below and made her think of the waterfall they'd seen earlier. Her eyes followed the river upstream until it appeared to curve around and out of sight. This rather distinctive feature drew Emilia back to the view from her dream on the plane. The view from the tower with Massimino.

No, it couldn't be.

She turned and faced the direction of the castle. From where she stood, it was blocked by the roof of the inn.

"So, what's out here?" Amanda's voice broke the otherwise peaceful evening as she stepped out of the doorway to join her.

She was dressed in dark wash skinny jeans, an off-the-shoulder batwing sleeved burgundy knit sweater, and tan knee-high stiletto boots. She had scrunched her hair with some product to accentuate her golden curls and her lips were painted with her favorite pinky-red.

"Just looking at the view," replied Emilia, startled after being lost in thought.

"Okay. It might be a place that time forgot, but the scenery sure is amazing!" Amanda laughed.

"Right?! I can see why my family chose here to build the village."

"Listen to you: *my family built the village!*" Amanda teased.

"Oh, Pia, the woman at the reception desk said..." Emilia shrugged, deciding it wasn't worth it. "Never mind. We should get going, are you ready?"

"Let's go." Amanda was already heading back into their room for her purse. "I can't wait to find out what this is all about!"

They grabbed their coats and headed down to the lobby. Pia was walking out of the restaurant and could barely stifle a giggle as they each ran down opposite staircases.

"I win!" Emilia announced in triumph as she reached the bottom.

"It's my heels!" Amanda protested.

"Oh, hello Pia," Emilia said, trying to compose herself. "We were just—"

"Never mind," replied Pia with a warm, genuine smile. "It's nice to hear happy sounds around here."

"Good news," continued Emilia. "I found Martin Thiess—we're going to meet him now."

"Ah, I'm very glad to hear," Pia said as she rounded her desk. "In that case, I wish you well for your meeting with that...man."

"Question for you," Amanda said, pausing in the lobby. "I couldn't find a Wi-Fi network to join in the room, is there a problem with the connection here?"

"Wi-Fi network?" Pia looked at her as if she had made up some new words. "I'm not sure what you mean."

"For the internet, emails, messages?"

"Oh, the internet!" Pia seemed to understand now. "I have heard something about this but I'm afraid we don't have that here in the village. You would have to go down the mountain to one of the bigger towns."

"This is going to be rough," replied Amanda, irritation obviously exacerbated by the difficulties they'd experienced with trying to connect since reaching the mountains.

"I can let you use our phone—it only works for local calls, we have the only one in the village, or maybe one more at the castle I think," offered Pia.

"Um, yeah, thank you...I'll keep that in mind," replied Amanda, forcing a smile.

"We'll be fine," Emilia said. "Thank you, Pia. We'll be back later."

Amanda was yet to be done with her list of issues. "Oh, by the way, I took a shower and the water was not so hot—are you able to check it?"

"I'm sorry, the equipment here is…older and not in such good condition." Pia looked embarrassed as she gave them an apologetic expression. "I will mention it to my husband, but it is unlikely that we can fix that."

"All right, I'll survive," sighed Amanda, "Bye for now." With a shrug, she followed Emilia toward the door.

The girls spotted three locals in the bar, while in the restaurant, at least one table was occupied by two men whose polo shirts and general manner suggested they weren't from around here. They were engaged in conversation, one of them quite animated, and each enjoying a beer. Emilia recognized them as the men who'd arrived in the truck earlier. The younger and more energetic of the two paused mid-sentence to watch as she and Amanda walked by.

Emilia grinned at her sister, who smiled and waved as they passed.

"Oh, Amanda!" Emilia shook her head.

"What? I'm just being friendly."

As they made their way across the square, they noticed a handful of people out and about in the village.

"Well it's good to know we're not the *only* ones here!" Amanda joked. The village, while certainly not bustling with life, was at least showing some signs of it.

"No internet, no hot water—Emmi, where are we? Is this what camping's like?" She shuddered. "So not for me!"

"Oh, you'll survive. It's just a few days. I would like to say hi to Olly though, and see if Mom and Dad have gotten back to us."

"Yeah, I'm glad our last few days will be in a big city, with fast internet and maybe even an enormous hot tub to soak in!"

Emilia felt an inexplicable need to defend this land where she'd never before set foot. "Come on. Sure, it may be a little behind on some things, but look around you. It's a gorgeous village, it just needs a bit of…maintenance."

Emilia grabbed Amanda's arm and hugged it lovingly, looking at her sister with wide eyes.

"Right, I see a little of the charm you're talking about but it's pretty rundown and *so* cutoff from the world." Then she finally relented. "Quite an experience, though."

They wandered around the storefronts and glanced into the windows; there was a bakery, a butcher, fresh produce market, a small grocery store, barber, doctor, apothecary, and a sign pointing the way to a coffee shop. Further ahead of them was a bar and another restaurant that looked to serve more traditional, local fare.

"I get the feeling that life here must be pretty tough," observed Emilia.

"Yeah, that's what I mean," Amanda agreed. "Several places are…well, closed and no longer in business. Some of the buildings are permanently boarded up, oh geez, that one looks like it burned down, and those that *are* still running look pretty…um…"

"They look like they're hanging on by a thread," Emilia completed Amanda's thought.

"Exactly. Maybe this lawyer knows more about why things are so grim."

"It's so far away from everything," Emilia pointed out. "The roads are really difficult to drive on and there doesn't seem to be much going on in the village."

"Sure, that all makes sense. So, if you *don't* turn out to be a baroness or a princess or whatever, since you love it so much, you can run for mayor and fix this place up! Vote Emilia!" she chanted.

"And why did I bring you along again?" Emilia rolled her eyes.

Chapter Twenty-Nine

Several bells jingled as Emilia and Amanda entered the restaurant, prompting a friendly-looking woman away from the kitchen to greet them. She was an attractive lady with a kind, round face and flushed cheeks; her curly brown hair was pulled back into a bun. She wore a full-length black skirt, thick tights, heavily worn black flats that needed a polish, and a crisp white frill-collared shirt.

The restaurant felt cozy and inviting; a fire burned on the wall to their right and the kitchen could be seen through a cutout in the rear of the space where an older gentleman was tossing pizza dough—he was no doubt responsible for the delicious aromas. A dozen or so tables were placed evenly around the room, topped with red and white checked tablecloths. Thiess sat alone at a table with three other empty seats while a younger couple occupied a table closer to the fireplace.

As the middle-aged woman made her way toward Emilia and Amanda, her eyes lit up with surprise but also recognition.

"My goodness me! The rumors, they are true," she gasped.

Emilia and Amanda looked at each other in confusion.

"You are the heiress, no? So beautiful, just like all the women in your family, just like your—" Her expression suddenly became sorrowful.

Emilia cocked her head to one side and was about to ask if she was all right, but they were interrupted.

"They are here to see me," Thiess stammered, quickly making his way over to them.

"Yes, yes. Of course, please…please…have a seat."

"Thank you." Emilia smiled at the woman as Thiess led the girls to his table.

Emilia noticed the man in the kitchen watching them intently, as was the young couple seated on the other side of the restaurant. They wore expressions of disbelief.

"Ah, Mr. Thiess, this is my sister, Amanda," Emilia smiled as she made the introduction.

"Nice to meet you, Mr. Thiess," said Amanda, offering her hand in greeting.

"Yes, yes; I am unable to shake at the moment," Thiess replied, holding up his hand.

"Oh my, what happened?"

"Ah, an…accident, earlier. It will heal. I have painkillers in the meantime." Thiess shrugged. "Please, sit."

The girls chose seats next to each other, opposite Thiess.

"Well, I suppose it is right to welcome you, officially, to Zillah," Thiess began.

"Thank you," Emilia replied. "And thank you for your generosity with the travel arrangements."

"What is done is done. I will work things out with Mr. Rothman in Philadelphia," said Thiess, looking as though he were suppressing an unpleasant thought.

The girls exchanged quick glances before the woman who had greeted them approached the table, introduced herself as Rose Venturi, and handed a single sheet menu to each of them.

Thiess asked for the veal without wasting time and forgetting the common courtesy of allowing ladies to order first. Amanda chose the pasta al pomodoro while Emilia went with lasagna. When Rose offered them the wine selection, the sisters agreed on a red she suggested. Thiess declined, gesticulating with his bandaged fingers and muttering something under his breath about not wanting to mix painkillers and alcohol.

Thiess waited until she had gone back to the kitchen to speak.

"Well, Miss Campbell—Emilia." He cleared his throat. "I do not wish to waste any time here. Quite simply, you are the last surviving heir in the Blagden line. As such, this now all belongs to you."

Both Emilia and Amanda straightened a little in their seats.

Knees wobbling beneath the table, Emilia asked, "Could you please be a little more specific?"

Thiess nodded and leaned back. "I mean the village, the castle, the farming land, the mountains surrounding it, and the valley below."

Everyone fell silent. Amanda slowly turned to look at Emilia, utter disbelief painted across her face. "Oh my God. I *was* right! You really *are* a baroness; do I need to bow or anything?"

Thiess snickered. "Actually, Emilia's relatives settled here from Germany and brought with them their customs. They held the titles of *Graf* for the man and *Grafin* for the woman. When translated, this would be equivalent to a count or a countess—which is a few steps up from a baron or a baroness in terms of nobility."

"So…you're telling me I'm a countess, then?" Emilia wished for that glass of red wine.

"Even though these days in the outside world, such rankings are mostly meaningless, your family continued to use their titles within this domain. We had to complete much research while seeking out possible heirs and finding you. Your ancestors in Germany were known by the name Scholz. When this land had been granted to them, it was called 'Blagden', which in German means 'The Dark Valley'. When they settled the area, they became known as Count and Countess Blagden—and the village was named Zillah."

Emilia nodded, unable to do much else. "We read about some of the history after speaking with Mr. Rothman. The village grew quickly and was successful for a long time but then they ran out of gold and it started to fall apart?"

Thiess stiffened in his seat, his expression indicating he was surprised by what she knew. "Yes…it was something like that. I cannot say for certain, as I was not here."

Just then, Rose approached the table carrying a tray with a hand-painted ceramic jug filled with wine, a clear pitcher of water, and glasses for all of them.

"Your food will be coming very soon." She nodded warmly, pouring the drinks and trying to remain unobtrusive.

"Thank you," said Emilia with a smile.

Rose touched Emilia gently on the arm. "It fills my heart with much joy and…and with sadness that you are here—"

"We have things we must discuss," barked Thiess, waving his uninjured hand in a shooing motion toward the waitress.

Emilia frowned and looked at Amanda, who raised her eyebrows in return before fixing her stare disapprovingly at Thiess, who was unapologetic about his behavior.

Amanda lifted her glass of wine and offered a toast to break the tension. "To my dear sister: Countess Blagden!"

Emilia's frown morphed into a smile as she clinked her glass against Amanda's. Thiess appeared disinterested, instead staring at the couple on the other side of the restaurant.

"Oh, not bad!" Amanda remarked after her first sip.

"I didn't know it was even *possible* to own a village." It sounded more like a question than a statement as Emilia set her wine glass on the table.

"Certainly, it is less common in the modern times," Thiess said, "though there are still circumstances, such as this, where for one reason or another it is the case. Here, it has been passed down without interruption along your family line for many, many generations. Your aunt—Katerina—then your uncle—Friedrich, passed away within a few days of each other almost a year ago. They had no children, and your parents would have been next in line. Their deaths leave only you: Emilia Blagden—born Emilia Meyer—presently known as Emilia Campbell."

234

"Wow." It left her as a breath, and she had to compose herself. Out of all the possibilities she'd been anticipating, this was not one of them. "I never even knew I had an aunt and uncle; my parents never spoke about any of this. This is *a lot* to take in right now." Emilia shook her head. "What can you tell me about my family?"

An uncomfortable expression fell across Thiess' face and he pressed his thumb and forefinger over his eyes, frowning slightly as he leaned back in his seat.

"And you thought we were coming here to pick up a set of pearls!" teased Amanda, attempting to lighten the situation.

"I'm afraid I do not know very much about your parents or your family, other than the lineage applicable to your claim." Thiess winced and looked uncomfortable as he nursed his injured hand, cradling it like a child.

Rose reappeared at the table, balancing two plates on one arm and carrying a third in her opposite hand; she set down each meal with precision.

"Mmm, this looks great!" Emilia complimented.

"Thank you. I am very glad you think so," Rose replied, clearly happy to have impressed her newest patrons.

"Mine too!" added Amanda.

"We do not require anything else; please leave us to our meal," Thiess demanded with an impatient growl.

Rose's face flushed and she glanced at Emilia before walking away, her shoulders slumped.

Emilia gave Thiess a stern look, but he was too busy with his plate to notice, clumsily cutting a piece of veal with his bandaged hand. She eyed Amanda, who obviously thought the same thing: Thiess was a complete jerk.

The sisters dug into their own food, commenting on how good it was and how the wine paired perfectly with what they'd chosen.

Thiess ignored their comments, instead continuing with his own agenda. "Now, however, is the part in which I must burst the bubble of this fairytale."

"What do you mean by that?" asked Amanda, looking intensely at Thiess.

"Well, unfortunately, this isn't a tale where the princess gets her castle and lives happily ever after," came his condescending reply. He hadn't looked up from his meal since it arrived.

"Countess," snipped Amanda, only a hint of her former humor remaining.

"What?" Thiess chewed a mouthful of food.

"You said she was a countess, not a princess," replied Amanda.

Thiess took his time swallowing, drinking his water. "Yes, countess, of course. Please forgive me; the pain in my hand, it seems to be getting worse."

Emilia wasn't convinced his injury was an adequate excuse for his attitude. "So, you were saying...about bursting the bubble," she prompted, staring Thiess down as she sipped her wine.

"Well, in this case, I am sad to say, that the kingdom is all but bankrupt." He didn't seem too devastated, stuffing his face again and using his bad hand no less. "The castle and the village are deteriorating; the condition of things becomes worse every day and the roads need to be rebuilt—as does the bridge down the valley. The businesses make no money so there is no income from rent and most of the villagers would leave at the first opportunity, but they're afraid for their...prospects in other places. Most of the land is unusable, the farmland no longer produces crops, then just mountains and valleys and, as you discovered today, very far from...everything. There is some money in your family's accounts, however only a fraction of what would be required to begin to improve things here. Even if everything *could* be repaired, since it is such a remote place, it is likely that it would simply begin to crumble again eventually."

"So...what is Emilia supposed to do then?" Amanda wanted to know.

Thiess looked down at his almost empty plate, assembling another mouthful. "Well, I may be your knight in shining armor, as it were."

Amanda took advantage of Thiess' distracted state to give Emilia an expression she could only describe as a silent scream, which made her stifle a laugh.

"The good news I have is that there is a company I represent, and they would be willing to take the village and the land and allow you to keep the monetary assets from the estate. That is almost two million euros."

"What!" blurted Amanda. "Two million euros isn't bad, Emmi. Better than a string of pearls! But that's a long way from bankrupt though, isn't it?"

Thiess snickered. "Believe me, the work that would have to take place around here would be *many* times that, and that is just to *begin* turning things around."

"And what would happen to the village?" Emilia asked. "The company would fix things?"

"Well, I believe plans are still fluid, as they say, but they are interested in developing some new infrastructure in the area; adding new roads and exploring new sources of revenue. I adore this village and all the people in it. I very much want to see this thing happen to them—I mean, the best thing *for* them." Thiess added a forced smile at the end then suddenly clutched his hand close to his chest. "This pain is unbearable. I can hardly stand it."

Thiess reached into his pocket and retrieved a small orange bottle, removed one pill, and swallowed it down with a gulp of water.

Emilia sat back and took another sip of wine, contemplating everything she'd just learned. "I feel like I need to think about all of this for a while."

"Time is not on our side, I am afraid," Thiess said, focusing on her for the first time since he'd received his meal. "Unless the estate is claimed by a verified heir before the one-year anniversary of your uncle's passing, everything will revert to the government. I imagine at that point, given the state of things here, they would encourage the villagers to relocate and merge it all into one of the surrounding national parks, allowing nature to take its course."

"And when is the deadline?"

"Tomorrow." Thiess' smile didn't seem the least bit apologetic. He really did see himself as a knight, rescuing the fair damsel. It only made Emilia distrust him more. "This matter must be resolved before midnight tomorrow. Practically speaking, tomorrow is Saturday and the registration office in Poprad is only open until noon—so it must be before that. I have prepared both sets of paperwork already—the first in which you claim your birthright to this godforsaken place, and the second in which you grant the title to the company, Graben Holdings."

"Wait," Emilia straightened, "a minute ago you told us you adore this village. Now it is a 'godforsaken place'?"

He blinked, seeming to realize himself. "The pain. It is the pain speaking." Thiess shook his head as if he didn't even believe the lie. "In any case, I cannot imagine that you wish to actually *live* here."

"Can't Emilia just claim the estate now and then we can work out the details on the second part later?" Amanda suggested. "You know, like after she's had more time to think through all of this? I mean, we just got here."

Emilia caught the clenching of his jaw; she didn't believe that was from the pain either.

"No, I am sorry to say that after Sunday she will not—I mean the company, their offer is only open until today or tomorrow at the latest. It must be concluded at the same time."

As Thiess gripped his hand, the sisters exchanged another skeptical glance.

"Perhaps you should get some rest, Mr. Thiess," Emilia finally said. "We can talk more about all of this tomorrow."

He appeared taken aback, ultimately forcing a smile. "But...all right. We will conclude these matters tomorrow. It is important that you sign the papers then—and early—so I may get them registered."

Thiess grimaced again, eyes darting between Emilia and Amanda a couple of times. "I am glad to have met you both. I will take care of things here; I will charge it to the estate. We will conclude these matters in the morning."

"Ah, well, I guess I'll thank myself later for my generosity tonight," jabbed Emilia; Amanda chuckled along while Thiess remained straight-faced. "Mr. Thiess, I hope you have a pleasant evening."

"Goodnight, Mr. Thiess," said Amanda.

"Mmph. Yes, goodnight," replied Thiess, nodding slightly.

As Emilia and Amanda made their way out, Rose hurried over to them. "How was everything? Did you enjoy your dinner?"

"Yes, everything was lovely. Thank you so much." Emilia smiled while Amanda nodded in agreement. "I hope we get to visit you again while we're here."

Without warning, Rose reached out and took Emilia's hands. "It is inevitable. The village is small, and this is your home. I am so very pleased to have met you tonight. Goodnight, Countess." Rose bowed her head and squeezed her fingers. "I pray that you may somehow be saved," she whispered, closing her eyes.

Emilia didn't know how to respond to such an odd comment, but her sister stepped in to put an end to the awkward situation. "Thank you, Rose. This was wonderful. Goodnight."

The bells jingled as Amanda pulled the door closed behind them and they began walking back to the inn. "Soooo—"

"Hold on a minute," said Emilia. "I just want to see something. Come with me."

Emilia tiptoed back to the Italian restaurant, stopping just before they were in front of it and peeking in the window. Amanda joined her, crouching down so she was next to Emilia.

As they watched, Thiess stood from the table. They could see his lips moving, but Emilia couldn't hear what he was saying. He was talking with Rose, who was facing him with her back toward the window. It appeared the conversation was escalating: the other couple looked on with concern and a man they assumed to be Rose's husband—wearing a chef's apron—had come out from the kitchen to stand beside his wife. Thiess appeared to be yelling now, waving his hands around. They could hear his voice, though they were still unable to make out the words. The shouting continued for a few volleys between the three before Thiess stormed toward the door, knocking over a chair in his path along the way.

"Oh, crap," whispered Amanda as she pulled Emilia away from the window.

They ran along the street and ducked into a narrow, darkened alley between two buildings. Thiess slammed the restaurant door behind him and stomped across the square. The sisters poked their heads around the corner to watch from the shadows as he thundered down the road, muttering something they could only partly make out.

"This place...burn...mine." Thiess spoke erratically as he disappeared along a path below the castle.

"Quick, let's get out of here before he comes back!" Amanda whispered.

"Yeah, good idea," Emilia replied.

They didn't speak until they were close to the inn again. "Well, he's certainly my top candidate for asshole of the year," scoffed Amanda, and Emilia burst out laughing.

"Oh my God. What a *horrible* man," Emilia agreed. "Seriously, what the heck?"

"Maybe it was just the pain talking?" Amanda offered.

"I don't think pain could turn a normal or kind person into that—and I don't trust him as far as I could throw him."

"Which isn't far," Amanda deadpanned. "But I agree. He's definitely up to something. Emmi, can we just stop for a second?" She halted her gait and Emilia waited for her. "Can you believe this? You've just inherited a *castle*, a whole village, and a couple *million* euros to boot—oh yeah, and you're a countess, too! Wait till I tell the girls! Even *I* can't believe I was right about this one—but I was!"

Emilia laughed along with her sister, shaking her head in disbelief as she looked around the village square.

"I can't even imagine what must be going through your head right now…are you as blown away by this as I am?" Amanda pressed.

"Yeah, of course I am!" Emilia shrieked. "But I…ah…" She felt conflicted; it was just difficult when it didn't feel right. "It's hard to believe—definitely mind-blowing for sure, but I feel kind of confused too…you know? I'm not sure what to think right now. I've had family here all this time—my mother had a sister and I never even knew. Do you think she knew about me? Why did they leave here? Why didn't they ever want to talk about it?" She had begun rattling off the questions rushing through her mind as they started back to the inn once more.

"So many questions to find answers to, Emmi. Maybe someone here knows something; we can ask around tomorrow."

"Good plan." Emilia let her mind wander as she took in the sights. "I *own* all of this, and I haven't even begun to know what's here—or up there." Emilia nodded toward the castle.

"Something tells me we're in for an exciting day tomorrow, but right now, we need a celebratory drink." Amanda grinned as she opened the door and entered the lobby of the inn.

"Yeah we do! I just need to use the bathroom—I'll head up to our room and come meet you at the bar, okay?"

"Perfect, I'll order the champagne, Countess!" Amanda wiggled her eyebrows. "Hey, since I'm your sister, do I get some sort of special title, too?"

"You'll always be special to me." Emilia winked. "Even if you *are* just a simple commoner!" she called as she raced up the stairs toward their room.

Pamela heard the beginning of Amanda's voicemail again and, frustrated, ended the call. She switched her phone to flight mode as their plane rolled away from the gate at Ushuaia.

"No answer on either of their phones again," sighed Pamela as she shared the obvious with Brian seated beside her.

"Let's stay positive. We don't even know if they've left yet," Brian reasoned. "We were lucky we could find a way to connect these flights to Philadelphia today. We'll be there tomorrow afternoon and we'll go straight to their apartment if we haven't been able to reach them by then."

"I hope they're still there," Pamela said, sliding up the shade on her window. "I really do."

"Me too. I checked the credit cards, they haven't bought any airline tickets...that's got to be a good sign" He patted Pamela's hand, "Surely they'll get our messages and call us back soon anyway."

Pamela squeezed Brian's hand. "I'm sure it will be fine. I'm just so scared for them both. From what you told me about what happened to Genevieve and Anton, those people there, they sounded like monsters."

Brian was quiet, squinting his eyes as a painful memory—one long buried—forced its way to the surface of his consciousness again.

"Let's not think about that for now," he said, shutting out the thoughts. "What happened to Genevieve and Anton was a long time ago, the girls will be all right."

Chapter Thirty

Amanda was glad to see the lights were still on in the bar. The long wooden surface ran along the left side of the space, all of its stools empty. To the right were booths, the faded, cracking green vinyl upholstery providing cushioning atop the seats surrounding dark wooden tables lined up against the front wall. Each booth had a window looking out toward the street and town square.

She waited near the bar entrance, looking out for someone who could help her get some drinks ordered. She could hear faint voices coming from one of the booths, though she could not see its occupants.

"...ever closed in the first place. I mean, you can see the gold just waiting to be mined. If the third is anything like the first two, there is an absolute *fortune* buried in there."

"I don't know, this whole place is so strange. I can't wait to be finished here...and that collapse today—what the hell happened? There is no geological instability we've observed."

"Do you suppose we'll be working on the project to re-open—"

"Hello, Miss Campbell. Can I help you?"

Marek's voice startled Amanda, and it caused an abrupt end to the conversation in the booth as its occupants craned their necks to see who may have overheard their discussion. Amanda recalled seeing them both earlier that evening in the restaurant at the inn.

"*Shh.* Mr. Thiess instructed us to keep what we're doing strictly confidential," one of the men whispered to the other, whose gaze lingered a few additional moments on Amanda. He smiled, and she returned the gesture and added a small, flirtatious wave.

Thiess? Amanda's thoughts whirred with curiosity.

"Miss Campbell?" Marek prompted once again, this time with a little impatience in his voice.

"Yes, I'm just waiting for my sister." Amanda snapped back to the present moment. "We were hoping to have a celebratory drink?"

"Ah, I am just closing up here." He spread his arms across the bar. "As you can see, it is not so busy."

"Is it ever busy around here?" asked Amanda with a friendly smirk.

"I am afraid not. Those days are long in the past."

"I see."

"Ordinarily, I would stay here as long as you and your sister would like, but unfortunately there is a...meeting with some of the villagers. I must go."

"A meeting *this* late?"

"It is not by my choice." Marek nodded. "Some things are best done under the cover of darkness," he whispered with a polite grin.

"Alrighty then," Amanda shrugged. "Do you have any champagne that we could take to our room perhaps?"

"Ah, yes! This I can help you with. One moment!" Marek lifted the hinged section of the bar top to allow access behind it. After some clanging, he retrieved an embellished silver ice bucket, filled it with ice, and nestled a bottle of Slovakian sparkling wine inside before placing it on the bar. "Two glasses?"

"Yes, please!"

Marek retrieved two dusty champagne glasses from overhead. Realizing their condition, he rinsed and dried them before setting them on the bar alongside the ice bucket.

"These are not called for so often." He spoke softly and with a slight chuckle. "This bottle has been in the refrigerator for a *long* time."

"I'm sure it will be wonderful. Please charge it to our room. Thank you, very much—and good luck with your meeting." Amanda winked.

"Thank you. Goodnight."

Carrying the bucket and glasses, Amanda made her way back to the lobby. Emilia was halfway down the final staircase when she entered.

"Change of plans?" Emilia asked.

"The bar is closing. Looks like we'll be celebrating in the room."

"Or how about on the terrace?" Emilia suggested. "It's a spectacular night!"

Pushing what she had overheard in the bar to the back of her mind, Amanda told herself she would bring it up tomorrow. Tonight, she wanted her sister to enjoy the part of her life she'd had no connection with prior to this evening. "Perfect, we can light that firepit!"

Emilia and Amanda sat out on the terrace in their coats warming themselves. The champagne chilled in the ice bucket on the table between them and was now half-empty. The warm orange glow from the fire lit the space and twinkled in their eyes while the mountains, valley, river, and village surrounding them were bathed in pale white moonlight.

"I feel like I've spent my whole life searching. Now I finally find my family and they are all gone… I'm the only one left," Emilia mused as she topped off her glass and stared out over the mountains and the twinkling stars.

"Yeah, so strange that there were never any links back to this place amongst your parents' things," Amanda added. "Or that your aunt and uncle never managed to find you. Maybe they had a falling out or something?"

"Maybe. I guess that makes as much sense as anything. This all just seems weird. We can't even call Mom and Dad to talk with them about it all—or Olly." Emilia was suddenly filled with longing at the thought of him. She wondered if he was thinking of her, waiting for her call. "I miss them all so much right now."

"Don't worry," Amanda assured her. "We'll see them soon and *I'm* here! We'll figure this all out."

"Thanks, Amanda. I love you. I think if you weren't here, I'd swear this was all just some crazy dream."

Amanda reached across and pinched her lightly on the arm. "Just making sure! Do you have any ideas about how to handle Thiess?"

The champagne tasted bitter at the mere mention of his name. "Ugh, Thiess. I don't even want to think about that awful man right now. I'd rather not sign everything over to this company he's representing, but what *am* I supposed to do with a village? Cute as it is here, there are all these problems. It's all worth less than a single gold coin." Emilia paused at the unnatural sound in her voice as she made that last comment. "I can see that he's not making that up—at least most of it. I'd like to know a bit more about this company though; who are they? What do they do? What do they want with Zillah? Why does it all have to happen so fast?"

"Yeah, I've been wondering some of that too, Emmi. I feel like he's hiding something, and we need to figure out what."

"I think the bubbles in this champagne are starting to go to my head," Emilia replied, setting down the glass and nearly missing the table. "Let's start fresh on this tomorrow."

"Ha! Such a lightweight," Amanda teased. "But yeah, good idea—it's been a huge day."

Emilia looked over to her sister and followed her eyes toward the fire. Despite all that she'd learned and everything she had yet to deal with, she felt immeasurably relaxed. Her mind flashed with recollections of her dream with Massimino, playing with fire and wind. Emilia consciously slowed her breathing, focusing on the flames as they danced before her.

She imagined the flames swirling upward and then back down, swaying back and forth.

"Ah, I think...I think I've had enough to drink. I'm starting to imagine the flames are...I don't know..." Amanda sat up in her seat.

"You can see this?" asked Emilia as she broke her concentration with the fire, and the flames returned to their natural flow.

"Yeah! Wait, you saw it too?" Amanda asked, looking confused.

"Yeah, um...I...yeah." Emilia squeezed her eyes shut in an attempt to clear her mind. "I think it's time for bed."

"Marek did say this champagne was old, maybe it's making us a little loopy? All right, I'll lead the way!" Amanda mused, giving Emilia a groggy smile.

"Actually, I'll be there in a minute," Emilia replied, watching the fire. "I just want to sit here a little longer."

"Okay, let me know if the fire starts...acting weird again," joked Amanda.

"Goodnight, sis. Thanks for everything!"

Amanda closed the terrace door and Emilia concentrated on the fire again. She quickly had control of the flames once more, conjuring streamer-like patterns she could direct at will.

Oh my God. Am I really doing this?

Emilia turned her attention away from the fire and it settled back to a normal flicker. Now she focused on her controlled breathing and the thought of wind whirling around her on the terrace. As she did so, a light gust tousled her hair and caused the flames in the firepit to waver. She barely registered the chill it created as it washed over her. Emilia surrendered to the fascination—and the power—of the moment.

Feeling more daring, she waved her hand around in a circular motion, imagining a stronger wind. Before she knew it, the air became a tornado-like funnel, extinguishing the fire. The force rattled the door before knocking the ice bucket to the ground with a clang and shattering the bottle against the stone floor, it's remaining contents fizzing in a puddle.

Emilia stopped suddenly, hair disheveled and breathing rapid as the door opened and Amanda stepped out.

"Careful, there's glass!" Emilia panted.

"Are you all right?" Amanda took in the scene from the doorway. "What happened?"

"I'm...I'm fine."

"Um, I think you should come inside now," said Amanda, looking around warily.

Emilia eyed the mess on the floor where the bottle lay broken but didn't move.

"We'll clean this up tomorrow," Amanda said. "Just come in, okay?"

Emilia rose shakily from her seat, walking on tiptoes to the door and into the room. Amanda pulled it closed firmly behind her and made sure it was locked before drawing the curtains.

In his chamber, atop his tower, Massimino stood by the windows behind his desk, overlooking the village below. He had just experienced a most unexpected feeling, and he stared down toward the source: the Vitaj Inn.

"Please...I...I *need...*" begged Vera, a shapely blonde beauty lying on the satin sheets of Massimino's palatial boudoir.

"You will take care of yourself," came his dismissive reply. "I will join you soon."

Vera pouted and grumbled briefly before closing her eyes and beginning to pleasure herself, first caressing her breasts and enticing her nipples, then sliding one hand down between her legs, bucking slightly against her own hand.

Massimino gazed out the window.

Emilia, how can this be? My lessons were so brief. How are you harnessing this power so quickly? Perhaps you are much more than I had expected or hoped.

He grinned with anticipation, lingering for a few more moments and wondering if there might be any more surprises. Eventually, Vera's moans grew louder and more fervent, drawing his attention back to the young woman in his chamber. Massimino flew to bed as if carried on the wind and landed atop her.

He hungered, and his hardness entered her; Vera's face brightened with delight. Her voluptuous breasts aroused, she moaned beneath him as their bodies writhed in unison and sweat glistened on each of them in the firelight. She shrieked in ecstasy as the first of what would be many climaxes that evening coursed through her body.

Chapter Thirty-One

One or two at a time, the villagers walked across the square and filed into the butcher shop. Enzo greeted each with a silent nod before directing them through the darkened store to an open doorway on the far side.

The narrow, rickety wooden staircase led down into a musty, damp basement. The rectangular space was lined with shelves along the far wall, filled with boxes overflowing with trinkets, equipment, and collectibles that were coated in dust and other loose items—older and recent—that had been discarded over many generations. A single overhead lightbulb in the center of the room cast a dim glow over the space.

A few other crates had been pushed against the perimeter of the room to create an open area in the middle in which a hodgepodge of chairs had been arranged in three rows.

When the last attendee, Gerlinde, arrived, Enzo closed and locked the door at the top of the stairs and descended into the basement. The murmur of conversations fell to silence as Enzo faced the group.

"I am sure you have all heard the rumors that an heiress has been found and that she is now here in the village," Enzo began.

All in the group nodded, their expressions somber.

"Massimino has asked—well, instructed—that I tell you all to be prepared for another ritual on the full moon this Sunday night. He also demanded that no one mention the ritual or speak of him—not even utter his name in the presence of the heiress—until after he has met with her."

Many shook their heads and disgruntled sounds filled the air.

"But I have met her," Rose called out. "She is beautiful and kind! She does not deserve this."

"How did he even find her? asked another. "She must have been born before her parents returned here, where has she been all this time?"

"That animal, Thiess; he is involved again," Enzo replied, pausing while he looked sadly upon Sofia in the front row. The damage to her face was clearly visible even in the low light. "My wife must return for more of his savagery once we finish here. Massimino has all but killed our beautiful daughter, Caroline…I fear this is all because I tried to resist him." Enzo's voice quivered. "Rose, I know what you say, and I am certain she does not deserve what will happen to her, but I do not see how we have any other choice."

"What if we were *all* to stand up to him—refuse to carry out the ritual? He needs us, no?" another villager contested, looking around the group to gauge support.

"Yes, it's true," Enzo said. "He needs our help to channel the energy for the ritual, but I believe that if we were to resist, we would wind up dead down the bottom of a mineshaft and he would find others to take our place."

"But surely he couldn't do this before Sunday?" Marek questioned.

"It is unlikely he would need to. The only requirements are that the ritual happens when the moon is full and it is aligned with the altar in the chapel, right?" Enzo directed his gaze at Gerlinde as he sought confirmation.

"It is true." The old woman nodded matter-of-factly. "This will happen again."

"He could simply imprison the heiress and wait until he is ready," Enzo theorized. "If the rumors are true, he has been around for *hundreds* of years. Waiting until the conditions are right again is surely of no great consequence to him. But it could mean the difference between life and death to us."

Many had taken to staring at the floor as reality settled around them.

"Look, we—all of us here—have not struggled as much as the others in the village," Enzo said. "We are able to own businesses and can visit the outside world on occasion. These…privileges have been granted by Massimino because of our loyalty and this is the price we must now pay for that."

"Go on, tell him," Marek whispered, nudging his wife.

"Is there something else to share, Pia?" Enzo asked.

"Yes." She spoke softly as she stood from her seat. "My daughter, Luna. She overheard Massimino say to Mr. Thiess that once the ritual is complete, he...he would be leaving, and Mr. Thiess would be taking over."

The group let out a collective gasp.

"Are you certain?"

"This cannot be..."

"Why? How?"

"I can't believe this! If he were to leave, we would be...we would be free!"

"Quiet! Quiet down, please! I was talking with Jakub earlier; he was in the mines with Mr. Thiess and a similar comment was made. I didn't believe it at first either, but now that another says the same thing, maybe it's true?"

The mood had become more positive and energetic at hearing this news, prompting several conversations.

"Please, please," Enzo called, raising his hands. "Everyone, settle down. If this is indeed true, then it doesn't matter how innocent the heiress is. She would be but a single sacrifice, necessary in order to free our village, free our children and ourselves of this...evil—of Massimino. We really had no choice anyway, but this may be a way for life to finally be better for us all."

Most of the group nodded their agreement, comforted by the opportunity of freedom. Rose shook her head silently, Sofia closed her eyes as a single tear streamed down her freshly cut cheek, and Gerlinde gazed from person to person.

"And what of the monster that is Martin Thiess?" Sofia stood and faced the group who became silent once more. "Are we just going to trade one demon ruling us for another? What does he want with us?"

"I heard Thiess is making plans to reopen the mines again," announced one of the villagers.

"The mines? That would mean money, which would mean jobs!" cried another. "And anyway, he is only a man; without Massimino to protect him, he would no longer be able to harm us—he would *need* us. If we have an opportunity to rid ourselves of Massimino, then we must take it."

The group again erupted into excited speculations.

Enzo looked sorrowfully at Sofia, knowing that he was about to do something he knew she would not understand.

"Quiet! Please! Listen...I don't like this, but I feel there is no other way forward for us here. We must do as Massimino demands. We must carry out the ritual."

After pulling their rented SUV into a tight parking space near Emilia and Amanda's apartment, Brian and Pamela hurried toward their building, the sky darkening and a chill in the air.

"Would you like a jacket out of the suitcase?" Brian offered as he saw Pamela shiver and huddle her arms across her chest.

"No, no—I just want to see the girls," replied Pamela continuing her stride toward the building.

Brian caught up and held the door for her and she managed a half smile at his chivalry. Brian took no offence—he knew she was anxious about the wellbeing of their daughters; he was, too.

"Good evening folks, can I help you?" Alfred looked up from behind his desk and smiled at the pair. "Oh, Mr. and Mrs. Campbell. How are the parents of my two favorite residents this brisk afternoon?"

"Nice to see you, Alfred—it's been a while." Brian extended his hand and Alfred shook it in return with a nod.

"Amanda and Emilia, are they here?" Pamela asked, her eyes pleading.

Alfred seemed surprised at the question.

"I'm sorry but you've missed them by a few days, let me see, when was it? Thursday, yes, Thursday afternoon they left here…heading to somewhere in Europe—they were very excited about it," Alfred said cheerily.

"Oh, Brian." Pamela's shoulders sank as she clutched onto Brian and buried her head in his chest.

"Is everything all right?" Alfred asked, concerned.

"What were you able to work out?" Pamela mumbled as she looked over to her husband, seeing him end the call on his Bluetooth headset as he drove along the New Jersey Turnpike toward their home in Short Hills.

Brian exhaled slowly before replying "Well, it's too late to go tonight, Susan checked all the options and the earliest we can leave is tomorrow."

"That means we won't get there until Monday—they left on *Thursday*, Brian. I've been trying to call, but their phones just go straight to voicemail. I wish I'd thought to check their social media sooner—Amanda posted a selfie at a train station on, I guess it was Friday morning over there, but nothing at all after that. I called a couple of their friends and nobody's heard from them since they first arrived in Slovakia. Brandon didn't know anything about the trip— apparently they broke up earlier in the week," Pamela sighed. "So much is going on—what if we're too late?"

"We can't think like that right now, Pam. We'll go home, I'll contact the embassy over there, and I'll see if I can find a police station in that area too—"

"You said the police were part of it last time!" Pamela barked.

Brian scratched his forehead. "We'll go and get some rest, keep trying to reach them, and fly out there tomorrow—I don't know that there is anything else we can do right now. We'll bring the letter from her parents and tell Emilia everything. No more secrets."

Pamela sighed, gazing at the darkened landscape out the window as they continued down the highway.

Chapter Thirty-Two

T he inn's restaurant was a mostly square room with windows facing toward the village square and twenty or so four-seat wooden tables and chairs arranged within it. The floors were dark hardwood, their once brilliant shine now scuffed by many years of wear and little upkeep. Burgundy cushions were tied to each of the seats and matching curtains adorned the windows, all drawn open to the sides and tied with sashes. Two squeaky, swinging doors led to and from the kitchen, and the walls were decorated with paintings from years long gone—paintings that depicted the village in better times; it's expansion, the mines, even one of the castle during its construction, as well as images of prior counts and countesses, and villagers.

Thiess plodded in carrying a leather document bag in his good hand. He walked directly to the table where the consultants sat.

"Good morning, Mr. Thiess," said Hanz.

Derrick, mouth full of omelet, nodded a greeting.

"Yes, good morning to you both," replied Thiess.

"Mr. Thiess, can I get you anything?" Pia asked meekly, peering down at the table as she spoke.

"No. Please ensure we are not disturbed. That is all." Thiess pulled out a seat and sat at the table. "Gentlemen, what news do you have for me this morning?"

"After we spoke last night," Hanz said, "I spent some time on a preliminary analysis of the ground scans and the other data we've been gathering, and, like we talked about yesterday," Hanz went on, "there is an abundance of valuable material in the ground here. We cannot figure out why these mines were shut down to begin with."

"Very good," said Thiess. "Their loss is my gain, I suppose. My main concern is how we go about getting it *out* of the ground."

"And that's where some of the challenges begin," Hanz explained. "The existing shafts are not in very good condition, so shoring them up, getting water out, and bringing everything up to modern safety standards is going to be a time-consuming and expensive undertaking." He paused so Thiess could absorb the information while he had a bite of omelet.

"I see. How much?" asked Thiess with raised eyebrows, voice flat.

"It is too soon to really estimate those costs, Mr. Thiess." Hanz shrugged. "It will certainly still be profitable, very profitable, but this is going to be a major project. With the castle and the village here, we cannot simply start clearing and digging big holes to get it out quickly and cheaply as they would in a new operation—well, relatively quickly and cheaply anyway."

"Wait, what do you mean?" Thiess snapped.

"I do not mean to complicate anything..." Hanz backpedaled. "I was simply pointing out that if the land was clear, it would be much less expensive and a lot faster to start digging into the ground and processing the earth. The tunneling that is necessary makes things more complicated. We just have to work around it—or under it, as the case is here."

Thiess' eyes widened. "Hanz, this village is a horrid place and it is already falling to pieces. I believe we would be doing the world a great service by removing it. Please, prepare your plans as you have just stated: to simply flatten the village, the castle—the entire forest if you must. I want the wealth removed from these mountains as efficiently and quickly as possible."

Hanz and Derrick looked perplexed, their gaze not on Thiess but behind him. He turned to see Pia stopped in her tracks, a horrified expression on her face.

"What do you want? I told you we were not to be disturbed," Thiess scolded.

"I...coffee." She gestured to Derrick. "He wanted more coffee."

"Then give him the coffee, quickly!" Thiess waved her on.

Pia began to pour, and though her hand trembled, she was able to complete her task without spilling any.

"I do not know how long you were standing there, but you are not to speak of anything you have heard here—not to anyone!" Thiess ordered. "I have Massimino's full support on this. Do you understand?" His anger turned into agony as the knuckles in his bad hand spasmed.

"I understand...I'm sorry," Pia timidly replied before hurrying back to the kitchen, the swinging door flapping a couple of times before settling closed.

"You see?" Thiess pointed in her direction. "This place—the people..." He shook his head as if he were doing them a favor, and perhaps he was. Putting a sick dog to sleep. "There is no future here other than what is buried beneath the surface."

Hanz and Derrick exchanged uneasy glances and ate to avoid having to respond immediately.

"Listen," Thiess continued, "this may seem harsh—I understand that—but the villagers here will have no choice in the matter. This will all belong to me and there is no value or benefit in keeping this sorrowful place."

"Are you sure the villagers feel the same way?" asked Derrick before taking a gulp of coffee.

Thiess snickered. "The reality here is a complicated one. I think most of these people would have left long ago if circumstances were different. This town is in ruins and it would take a monumental effort to restore or rebuild it, and for what reason? Zillah is but a relic from an era whose glory has long faded. Believe me, the villagers will be *far* better off when they have moved on and resettled elsewhere."

"But..." Derrick began, "surely you cannot make the choice for them? The woman just now, she was—"

"Yes," Thiess interjected, waving his hand dismissively. "In this case, I *can* make the choice and I *have*. Now, I have hired your company to provide a plan to reopen these mines, not to debate the future of this village. Please prepare that plan as I have requested."

"Yes, okay, Mr. Thiess. I understand," Hanz conceded. "I will prepare the plan." He gave Derrick a brief nod.

Derrick agreed. "I understand."

"Very good. I am glad that we are all on the same page, as they say. I imagine you have much work to do today?" asked Thiess in a more settled tone.

"Yes, we're going to try very hard to finish the field work in shaft-C today and then the rest of the analysis and planning can be completed offsite."

"All right then, gentlemen." Thiess stood. "I see that you have finished your meals. I would encourage you to please make haste; your extended presence here is already attracting some unwanted attention and unpleasantness from the locals."

Derrick protested, "But it was you who—"

Hanz placed his hand on Derrick's shoulder and he internalized his response. "We understand and will be on our way now. Good day," replied Hanz.

Chapter Thirty-Three

Emilia awoke to the sharp screech of curtain rings being pulled along the rusty rods followed by light streaming into the room.

"Good morning, sleepy head! I mean, good morning, Countess." Amanda giggled.

"Mmmmph, good morning," Emilia murmured through a yawn as she stretched and sat up in bed.

"Seems like you slept well."

"Yeah, right through." Emilia was surprised herself. "I was exhausted."

"I'm surveying your damage from last night," Amanda explained, looking out the window to where Emilia could see the broken bottle and upturned bucket, ice melted now. "What happened, Emmi? How'd you knock this over—bit too tipsy, perhaps?"

"Um, I don't—what time is it?" She wasn't ready to examine what had happened last night.

"It's just after seven. It's not so often I'm up before you!"

"I feel like a good night's sleep has been *long* overdue," Emilia replied.

"So, no weird dreams then?"

"Nope." Emilia shook her head in thought. "I don't remember any dreams at all—definitely none like the last few nights."

As Emilia sat up and pushed the covers back, Amanda giggled at her sister's choice of pink flannel pajamas covered in teddy bears and hearts. "Good thing Olly's not around to see this!"

"Oh, very funny," Emilia rolled her eyes. "They're my warmest set and super comfy."

Amanda grinned. "I guess yay to sleeping well *and* no bad dreams, then. I told you they'd pass. Now, what are we going to do today? I guess we'll have to speak with Thiess again and tell him your decision, and we've totally got to check this place out!"

"Yeah, all right. I'm going to take a shower and get dressed. Then let's go down and find some breakfast. After that we'll figure out a plan." Emilia released a sigh, still trying to rationalize everything that was happening.

Emilia and Amanda were just coming down the stairs when they spotted Thiess' balding head—he was sitting at a table near the front of the restaurant. Thiess looked toward the door and smiled as they entered.

"Good morning, ladies," he said as they reluctantly joined him—it was too late now to turn back; he'd spotted them. "I hope the day finds you well."

"Yes, thank you," Emilia replied. "I feel great—it must be the fresh mountain air!"

"I'd kill for a coffee right about now," Amanda muttered.

"Good, good. Your timing is excellent." Thiess ignored her comment. "We do still have some business to conclude today, and if I am to register the necessary items with the authorities in time, I will need to be on my way down the mountain as soon as possible. Please, this table is dirty, let's sit down over here and we can continue our discussion from last night." He picked up his case and guided the girls to the next table by the windows.

As Amanda sat down, she saw the two men she had overheard in the bar the night prior in the square.

"Mr. Thiess?" Amanda asked. "Those men out there getting into the truck: who are they?"

Emilia looked on curiously as she sat beside her.

"They are contractors doing some work here in the village. Nothing of interest," Thiess replied casually, clutching his hand again.

"What sort of work?" Amanda persisted.

"They are working at the mines actually. They arrived a few days ago and will be finished today."

"Are the mines operating?" Emilia asked.

"No, no. The mines were closed down and abandoned long before any of us were around," replied Thiess.

"So, what are those men doing there, then?" Amanda continued her line of questioning.

"Uh, some sort of safety and maintenance work," Thiess was quick to explain. "Nothing out of the ordinary—just part of the nightmare that is running and administering this failed village."

Thiess winced, reaching into his jacket pocket and retrieving his pill bottle. He opened it and took out a single pill before looking at the table and realizing there was no water.

"Hello, we need some service in here!" he called toward the kitchen. "Hello? Is anyone—" Thiess stopped as he saw the door from the kitchen swing open toward him.

A young girl with long red hair emerged but stopped in her tracks when she saw Thiess grinning lewdly at her.

"Ah, I remember you—Luna," Thiess said. "Come, come; I need water and my guests here are in search of food, yes?" He turned his attention to Emilia and Amanda.

"Yes, please! May we order some breakfast?" Emilia smiled at Luna.

The girl appeared startled as she approached their table but regained her composure by the time she was close enough for them to order.

"And some coffee would be great!" added Amanda.

"Well, don't just stand there," barked Thiess.

Emilia and Amanda stared crossly at Thiess and prepared to reprimand him.

"Water and coffee. Of course. I will be right back, I'm sorry," said Luna, nervously looking down at the floor before heading back toward the kitchen.

"Now then. Ah, where were we?" Thiess said as he retrieved his case from the floor. He unhooked the leather strap from the buckle and retrieved two bundles of paperwork. "It is most important that we get this in order right away—as I've said, the inheritance items where you claim the estate as the rightful heir must be lodged today or your claim will be forfeited. We must also complete the transfer documents or the company's offer will expire and you will be left with this place."

"Mr. Thiess, I think we need to talk about all of this some more," Emilia said confidently. "I don't feel comfortable proceeding with so little time to think this through and consider the options."

Thiess became tense, his face flushing red as he appeared to rein in his temper. His response was interrupted as the swinging door to the kitchen squeaked and Luna returned carrying a jug of water and a pot of coffee.

"No espresso machine?" Amanda joked.

"Oh, I'm so sorry," said Luna with a disheartened look.

"I'm just kidding," Amanda replied in a friendly manner which seemed to put Luna more at ease as she poured coffee into Amanda's cup.

"Forgive my sister." Emilia smiled at Luna as she reached for her cup. "You're not the first one who doesn't get her humor. I'll take some coffee too, please."

Amanda watched Thiess as Luna poured the coffee, his hungry gaze fixed firmly on her behind and appearing as if he was exercising some level of control by not groping her. Amanda caught Emilia's attention and with her eyes, directed her to Thiess. Emilia's mouth fell open at the display before her.

When Luna had finished, she smiled at Emilia before turning toward Thiess. Amanda noticed she avoided looking him in the face and that her hand trembled as she poured his water. Thiess grabbed the glass and gulped down a mouthful along with his pill.

"You mentioned you would like some breakfast?" Luna asked the girls.

"Yes, please! Do you have a menu?" Amanda asked.

"I'm sorry, but no...I can tell you that we have eggs and sausages—there are some cereals too." Luna shrugged with an apologetic look. "We just don't have that many people visit here and the food spoils if it doesn't get used. My mother makes very good eggs—or omelets. Oh, and there is oatmeal."

Amanda settled on scrambled eggs with sausages, while Emilia ordered an omelet. They both also asked for some orange juice.

"Yes, I am sure that is not a problem. I will bring these to you as soon as they are ready! Is there anything you would like?" Luna turned to Thiess, at first meeting his gaze and then averting her eyes.

"No, perhaps later though," Thiess replied with a callous grin. "You may be able to...assist me with something."

Luna visibly recoiled at his response.

"For now, leave us be." If he'd noticed her reaction, Thiess was unfazed. "We have important work to complete here."

Luna scampered off to the kitchen once more, not having to be told twice.

Thiess pushed the taller stack of documents toward Emilia, who flipped through them briefly before returning to the first page to begin reading.

"There is no need to read through it all," Thiess said after she'd digested no more than two paragraphs. "This set outlines your claim, the lineage we researched to support it, and a description of all the assets of the estate." He retrieved a pen from his case and removed the cap. "There are several signatures required; they have all been tagged for your convenience."

"Mr. Thiess, I am most certainly going to read and understand anything I'm going to sign, particularly for a matter as important and substantial as this." Emilia refused to be intimidated by him.

"But the timing is essential." She could tell he was finding it difficult to keep his voice even. "I had anticipated this being completed *yesterday,* so your delay has already set things back."

"Fear not, I am a fast study," Emilia replied flatly, returning her eyes to the paperwork and tapping her fingers on the table.

"Yes, she certainly is, and she doesn't miss anything either. Look, you're not going to win this one—Emmi actually read the entire Netflix agreement before we signed up," Amanda smirked.

"Very well," he sighed. "Suit yourself, but please be quick. This second set is for the transfer of the land title here to Graben Holdings—the cash assets will remain with you. It is a good deal I have been able to secure for you, and I trust you appreciate that."

Thiess' teeth clenched and Emilia wasn't certain it was from sliding another, shorter pile of papers across the table.

Emilia ignored him, continuing to read what was in front of her.

"I have to say, I do not understand this." Thiess hadn't been able to remain silent for more than a few seconds. "I am telling you what these documents say, and you just need to sign everything. Do you not trust me?"

Emilia sighed, calmly placing the papers down on the table and glancing at Amanda, who appeared to be stifling the urge to laugh. She looked back to Thiess, anger simmering in her eyes. Emilia heard the squeak of the kitchen door but didn't move her attention from Thiess, who returned her stare.

"Frankly, Mr. Thiess, I do not trust you at all." Emilia surprised herself at how strong she sounded, but she'd had enough of this man. "I have wanted to give you the benefit of the doubt—maybe your rudeness was a language barrier or because you are in pain, but I think you're probably just not a pleasant person. I find your attitude and behavior deplorable, and I will *not* be doing anything based on *your word*—least of all signing these documents. Now, if you would kindly stop interrupting me, I have some reading to do."

Thiess looked like she had socked him in the stomach, and a sheen of sweat had broken out on his wrinkled forehead. "But I—"

"I wouldn't say anything else right now if I were you," Amanda cautioned.

Luna had come from the kitchen and stood halfway between the door and their table, a glass of orange juice in each hand and looking as though she was fighting a smile.

"What are you looking at?" Thiess spat.

Luna averted her gaze to her scuffed shoes, but she didn't seem as scared anymore.

"I will return in one hour." Thiess stumbled out of his seat and stormed out the restaurant; they heard the lobby door slam a few moments later.

Luna slowly shook her head as she neared the table. "I do not believe anyone has ever spoken to him this way!"

"You seem afraid of him," Emilia said gently.

"He is a very bad man," she whispered, unable to meet her eyes. "He has done some awful things here."

Emilia wasn't as shocked as she should have been. "Like what?"

Luna looked around nervously, biting her lip before her attention snapped to the window. Emilia followed her gaze, where Thiess was heading up toward the castle. "It is not so safe for me to talk about it."

"Is everything all right?" Pia called, poking her head out of the kitchen. "I heard yelling."

"Yes, Mama." Luna smiled in her mother's direction. "I will explain." She turned to the girls again, seeming a little brighter. "I will bring you the food once it is ready."

Chapter Thirty-Four

Massimino grinned as he heard heavy puffing and footsteps ascending the final stairs to his tower—he already knew who was visiting him. "Is that my good friend Martin?"

"There is a problem." Thiess scurried across the wooden floor toward him, carrying his jacket; sweat visible in the armpits of his shirt.

The noise caused a young village girl in Massimino's bed to stir; she rolled over onto her back and sat up, her light brown curls draping down her back as the black satin sheet fell away from her body and exposed her breasts. Instead of attempting to cover up, she used her legs to smoothly kick off the covers until she was fully bare.

"Hello, I am Petra." She caressed her breasts, unable to control her desire. "Massimino did not say he would be inviting a friend."

Thiess peered at her for a few moments, and although Massimino saw that Thiess was having difficulty drawing his eyes from the spectacle, the pressing practical matters seemed to take priority as he moved past the woman. "Massimino, it is the Blagden girl, she does not wish to transfer the land, she does not trust me."

"I will *trust* you," moaned Petra, surprised that Thiess had ignored her advances. "Come over here and I will let you *transfer* anything you want." Her fingers crept between her legs.

"You'll have to excuse Petra." Massimino grinned. "I've planted the seed of desire in this one. . .it is now blossoming."

"I have no time for this now," Thiess grunted. "If we do not lodge the estate paperwork today, it will be forfeited to the government and I'll *never* be able to mine it."

"Please, be calm—"

"How can I be calm?" His beady eyes popped out. "You promised me, Massimino."

"I promised you that I would help influence her decisions in your favor, and there is no reason this cannot be as you wish, but you need to approach this in the right way."

"She is questioning things. What am I supposed to do? I don't understand this?"

"Martin, this one is not another village girl; she is not conditioned to submit. She is intelligent, strong-willed, and has a power all her own—though she may not fully realize it yet. You cannot just bully and deceive one such as her." He cocked his head to the side. "If you have been speaking to her at all like you are speaking to me now, then your efforts will most certainly end in disappointment."

"But—"

"I will do as I said and influence her to your way of thinking, but first she must fully trust and surrender herself to me. For this to work, you must also gain her trust—this is important. Now go. This is a vital day with much at stake for both of us."

Thiess was silent a moment, staring into the fire before he mumbled, "How did I get myself tangled up in such a situation?"

"My friend, it was *your* greed that led you here. Only a fool would expect that a path chosen for such a reason would be a pleasant one to travel. Now, if there is nothing more—and I hope there is not—please ask our guests to dinner in the castle this evening. Do not mention my name."

Thiess sighed, closed his eyes, and shook his head. When he opened them, he looked to Massimino, nodded that he understood, then left. He lingered only briefly to take in the sight of Petra pleasuring herself on Massimino's bed.

"Come to me…" Petra whined as Thiess trudged down the stairs.

"My beautiful Petra, you are indeed ready for me to take what I need from you," said Massimino. He stripped off his robe, his body glistening in the firelight as he climbed atop her shapely frame. She moaned with need at the sight of him, his hardness drawn to her as he stroked her hair and the side of her face before kissing her.

"Take all that you need," she whispered breathlessly as Massimino united with her, seizing every inch of her soul. She was his to do with as he pleased, and she wanted nothing more than to give herself completely to him.

Following their encounter, Massimino arose feeling as alive as he could ever remember; there was an otherworldly glow about him and a raging fire in his eyes. He was close. Close to realizing his long-sought goal. All he needed to achieve it was within his reach.

Massimino strode to the window overlooking the village, smiling as he gazed down upon it. His thoughts were locked firmly on Emilia: the key to his resurgence, his freedom, his vengeance.

"So, what does it all say?" Amanda asked, sipping from her fresh cup of coffee as Emilia placed the last page on top of the pile and shuffled them until they were all lined up.

"Well, it's pretty much what Thiess said," she answered. "The first document is my claim to the estate, and the second one transfers all the land, rights, and structures to Graben Holdings. There's one part that caught my attention for sure—even though I do get the money from the estate, it also says that if I die within the next year then the two million euros will go to this Graben Holdings company too, doesn't that seem a little odd?"

"What? That doesn't sound right...certainly not how this sort of thing would usually work. Does it say anything about who Graben Holdings is or what they will do with it?"

"No...nothing like that at all." Emilia shook her head and poured herself a glass of water.

Amanda's eyebrows drew together. "Apart from the weird money clause, could he be telling the truth, do you think?"

"Maybe." Emilia still wasn't quite convinced.

"He's definitely a jerk. Could he be an *honest* jerk?" Amanda laughed.

"Anything's possible I guess," Emilia said. "But the people around here seem genuinely scared of him. And Luna clearly thinks he's an awful person. Personally, my instincts tell me he's hiding things from us."

"Yeah, something is going on with him that's for sure, and nothing about it seems good." She wrapped her fingers around the mug like it would warm the chill Emilia knew her sister was feeling; there was still something about Thiess that wasn't right. "What do you think you'll do then? Oh, wait—time's up. Here he comes."

Out the window, they watched as Thiess strode across the square. His face was red with exertion and the scowl he wore appeared etched into the skin. The bells above the door chimed as he entered, wheezing as they heard him plod toward the booth.

"You're late," Amanda joked, and Emilia stifled a chuckle.

Thiess' face softened as he wiped some perspiration from his brow. "I feel that I may need to apologize. It may be that I have been...less friendly than you may be used to. I do not mean any offence. It is simply my way—the grumpy old man as it were. It is important that you feel as though you can trust me and perhaps my manner has...damaged that trust." He shrugged slightly with a smile that could have almost passed as genuine.

Emilia looked to Amanda momentarily, then back at Thiess. "I appreciate what you've said, and I hope that we can work together more positively going forward."

"I also hope for the same," Thiess replied as he sat down.

"I've read through all the documents," Emilia said. "I understand the timing of the estate paperwork and agree that it must be completed today. If you would be so kind as to pass me your pen, I will sign those now."

Emilia added her signature and initials to the necessary pages and passed them back to Thiess.

"Thank you." He sounded sincere—most likely because he was getting what he wanted. "And now for the second document?" Thiess prompted.

"With the transfer, I have some questions, so I'm not yet ready to sign this one." Emilia placed her hand atop the stack of pages. "I haven't even had a chance to look around the village to know what I would be signing away."

"It is a dying village," Thiess assured. "It would be more of a burden for you than anything else."

"That may be, but I'd like to understand," Emilia countered just as politely. "Who is the company? What do they want with the village? And why would the money go to the company if something were to happen to me?"

Thiess paused, looking out the window and carefully considering his response.

"The company is owned by private investors. They wish for their identities to remain confidential and I am authorized to act on their behalf to conclude this matter. As to what they want, there are several possibilities: improve the infrastructure, repair the buildings, I cannot say for certain. I believe the clause about the money is simply to keep the assets of the estate intact if some unfortunate event should befall you."

Emilia sat up straighter, the questions forming on their own and leaving her mouth without hesitation. "Why the urgency? I understand the estate acceptance must happen, but why is the transfer so urgent? No doubt this can be postponed for a few weeks while I explore my options here. Why does the estate need to be kept intact if I am the last Blagden? Surely it should go to my family or at the very least I could nominate someone in the village to inherit this money on behalf of the people here...or something? Maybe there's a better offer to be found?"

Thiess' eyes narrowed a fraction, but Emilia caught it all the same. "I can assure you, Miss Campbell, there will be no better offer. To anyone else in this world, Zillah is nothing but a forgotten, disintegrating relic. To put things bluntly, you are fortunate I was able to present this to you at all. Why, when all of the money in the estate is so generously included, could there be any hesitation to accept this very favorable proposition—all the good with none of the bad in this case? You are young and appear fit and healthy; this provision would only apply if you were to pass away soon, which, ordinarily, would be quite unlikely, so I think it does not warrant much attention." His smile was forced, and he appeared to be working hard to keep his demeanor calm. "A deadline such as this is a common business tactic. It is possible that they are considering other investments or projects and have set a deadline to avoid finding themselves in a perpetual state of waiting, missing other opportunities as a consequence." He inhaled sharply but kept it under his breath as he held his hand in his lap. Maybe he really was in pain.

"Who runs this village anyway?" Amanda spoke up. "Is there a mayor or something? Someone we can talk to about it?"

"Ah, as a matter of fact, yes." Thiess grinned; there was some food particle between his front teeth. "He is not a mayor, but more of an...administrator. He oversaw things for you family."

"Great, now we're getting somewhere!" Amanda seemed more awake now. "Who is he? I think we'd like to meet and talk with him. Right?"

"Yes, absolutely," Emilia agreed. "I'd like to see him now if possible."

"Of course." Thiess nodded, pleased with himself for some unknown reason. "I spoke with him today already. He would like to meet you tonight for dinner, at the castle."

"What? He can't make time for Emilia any sooner?" Amanda looked perplexed.

"Please, do not shoot the messenger," Thiess attempted a joke, raising his good arm above his head. "I am merely relaying his request. He is somewhat *particular*, but I am sure there is no offence intended."

"Well, all right." Amanda sat back in her chair. "It does seem a little odd though."

"Perhaps in our world, yes," Thiess replied. "Here in the village though...just one more reason I would suggest you unburden yourself of this place."

Emilia sat in thought, turning her head to look out the window. "Here's how I would like to proceed, Mr. Thiess." She could see the castle in the distance, amongst the mountains. "The estate paperwork must be lodged today, and you now have the signed documents. Please go ahead and file this. As for the transfer, please contact this mysterious company and its investors. Let them know I have not been provided with adequate time to consider their proposal and kindly request an extension."

Thiess' mouth hung open a second. "But Miss Blagden—Campbell— I think...I do not believe this will be possible. I strongly urge you to reconsider and not risk losing this opportunity."

"I understand and accept the risk, Mr. Thiess," she smirked, crossing her arms over her chest. "Please do as I have instructed."

"But—"

"Mr. Thiess," Emilia interrupted, "you said earlier you wished for our dealings to proceed in a more positive way and that you wanted to build trust. Doing as I have asked will go a long way toward achieving both of those." Emilia's tone was serious yet friendly.

The lawyer was silent, scratching at his goatee with his good hand.

"Mr. Thiess?" Amanda prompted.

"Very well," he finally answered. "I will do as you have asked. I must travel down the mountain and so it is possible I will not be back until this afternoon. I hope that during that time you will have a look around." He tilted his head in an attempt at an amiable gesture, but he twitched, making it look fake. "Please, visit anywhere you wish in the castle or the village. All of it is now yours." Thiess held up the signed paperwork for emphasis. "The villagers are merely tenants— though, as I've said, are generally unable to pay any rent. I trust you will see the benefit in accepting the offer. Oh, and I would warn against visiting the mines; they are in terrible condition and unstable—I can speak from personal experience when I had to visit with those maintenance workers yesterday, this place is a…death trap." Thiess raised his injured hand.

"That's all right," Amanda said, "I think our first stop should be the castle!"

"Very good." Thiess nodded. "I do hope you are not disappointed. As with everything around here, it is no longer as glorious as it once was. There are repairs needed almost everywhere you look." He stood, packed the paperwork into his case, and with a nod to Emilia and Amanda, left the restaurant.

"Well played, sis!" Amanda blurted as soon as the door shut behind him. She offered her coffee cup in a mock toast before drinking down the last of its contents.

Emilia let out a relieved breath. "I sure hope so. I don't trust him at all, but what if he's right? What exactly *am* I supposed to do with a village?"

"Yeah, I see that. Especially a village without internet and *so* far from everything."

Luna emerged from the kitchen not long after, only sticking her head out. "Is he gone?" she whispered.

"Yes, you just missed him," Amanda said.

She entered the dining room, carrying a fresh pot of coffee. "I do not like to be around him."

"I'm Emilia and this is my sister, Amanda."

"Yes, I know who you are." Luna smiled, filling each of their cups. "You are the heiress! It is an honor to meet you."

"Have you lived here long, Luna?" Emilia asked, cradling her cup with both hands and taking a sip.

"Yes, since I was born. It's the same for everyone here. In my lifetime I have not seen anyone new come—and nobody ever leaves." Her tone had taken on a hollow quality Emilia didn't understand.

"Really? *Never?*" questioned Amanda.

"No, this is just how it is here." Luna shrugged, clearing their dishes. "Not such a nice place, but it isn't terrible either. Most of the time, we have no choice."

"Do you know much about the history of the village—about the Blagdens?" Emilia was hopeful. "They are my family, but I don't know anything about them."

"I am sorry." Luna appeared genuinely disappointed. "I don't know so much about them; I did see the count in the village here sometimes but the countess, very rarely, only when I was young though. I think—from what people say—their lives were not happy. But if you do wish to learn more about them, I think I know someone who could tell you. There is an old woman who lives just outside the village. I could take you to her if you like. She told me she wanted to meet you anyway, and maybe she'll be able to help you."

Emilia's face warmed with a grin. "That would be really great!"

Luna gave her a shy smile. "I must help my family with some things around here this morning, but I can take you to her this afternoon if that is good for you."

"Of course, yes," Emilia answered, excited.

"Well, that's our afternoon sorted," Amanda said. "What are we up to this morning, Countess?"

Emilia rolled her eyes but couldn't hide her grin. "Come on, let's explore this village that I all of a sudden own! Who'd have thought it?"

"Now you're talking," Amanda said. "Let's go!"

Chapter Thirty-Five

The girls layered themselves with coats, scarves, and beanies then headed out into the street. The clouds had returned, making for a bleak day with light mist hovering in the surrounding mountains. They were both dressed in jeans, cashmere sweaters, and flat riding boots which proved a sensible choice to tackle the cobblestones.

"Hate to be a downer, but the daylight doesn't necessarily improve things around here," Amanda said. "Sort of just makes all the problems more visible."

Emilia sighed. "I *so* want to disagree with you—I *really* do—but you're kind of right."

As they crossed the street and headed to the park in the middle of the square, Emilia beheld her surroundings in search of the positive. "I love the architecture, though. The buildings are beautiful. It just seems like nobody's taking care of them. A coat of paint—or a few coats, some repairs, and this could be a stunning place."

She imagined the wood and stone structures as they might have once been; brightly painted, vibrant homes and buildings lining picturesque, tree-lined cobblestone streets—a quaint village nestled amongst the mountains.

"Yeah, I think maybe Thiess is right, I hate to say it, but the problem is that there's no money here, Emmi." Amanda's factual reply brought Emilia back to reality. "Everyone seems to be struggling. Look over there—those buildings are crumbling...and I'm sure the weather doesn't help either, it's so...bleh." She glanced up at the grim sky before pointing to a pair of old storefronts that sat side by side, falling in on themselves and half overgrown with vegetation.

"Wow, check out this fountain!" Emilia traipsed across the scraggly grass toward it, "The detail is incredible—at least on the parts still standing…" Through the murky green water, she saw several broken parts from the dragon statues, along with the central tower now laying submerged at the bottom. A frog croaked and leapt out, hopping away and startling both girls as they laughed.

The water had remained stagnant a long while and algae had overtaken most of it. The exterior was ornate; detailed curves and lines were etched into the stone, and Emilia couldn't help but touch.

Amanda peered over her shoulder. "Again, really neat, but it's kind of like everything else: needs some serious restoration. And, at the risk of agreeing with that awful man, two million ain't what it used to be…I'm sure Dad would cringe if he heard me say that," Amanda chuckled.

Emilia nodded, "But Thiess does have a point there—it would be nowhere near enough to fix all of this." Emilia sighed as she joined her sister, who was already moving on.

"Well, I'm guessing there's no visitor center around here, so probably no guided walking tour we can join," Amanda chuckled. "Where do you even start when you own a whole village?" Turning in place, she scanned their surroundings. "Hey, the church door is open a little. Did you still want to check that out?"

Emilia followed her gaze to the place of worship. After facing down the intimidating lawyer, she was ready to confront anything. "Yeah, sure. Let's go take a look."

"That's the spirit!" Amanda hollered as they set off across the square.

"Where do you suppose this administrator is?" Emilia mused as she looked around for signs of an official office. "It's kind of weird he didn't want to meet us right away, don't you think?"

"I'd agree with you under normal circumstances, really…and no offence to your village or anything, but *everything* seems kind of weird around here, so I'm not that surprised. Probably some lifelong bureaucrat making a powerplay—wants you to know things around here will be on *his* terms."

"Yeah, could be. I wonder what he gets up to all day. It's not like things are well *administrated.*" Emilia chuckled at the pun and received a comedic eyeroll from Amanda.

They crossed the road and walked up the middle of the wide stairs fanning downward from the main entrance to the church. The high arched entry contained two tall wooden doors, one of which was slightly ajar.

Their footsteps echoed off the cavernous space as they entered. It was quite dark and smelled of old wood with hints of incense and lavender. The natural light from the dreary day filtered through the stained-glass windows depicting saints and biblical stories. There were several dozen rows of pews on each side, and a central aisle between them.

A large altar was visible on a platform toward the front, and it was watched over by a dramatic wooden crucifix and sculpture of Jesus Christ. All the visible surfaces, including the floor, were covered in a thick layer of dust.

"Good news is this definitely isn't the one from my dreams," Emilia whispered, her voice carrying despite speaking softly.

"Hello!" Amanda called out, her voice ringing off the stones.

"Amanda, it's a church," Emilia scolded, covering her ears. She noticed footsteps and scuffs on the floor, some appearing to have been made more recently than others.

A shuffling sound ahead of them drew their attention forward. A darkened figure stood from one of the front pews and started toward them down the central aisle.

"Hello?" Emilia called. "Is it all right that we're in here?"

"Yes, of course," replied a friendly, familiar voice. "You are the countess now. You may be wherever you wish to be."

As the figure drew closer, they recognized it was the woman from the Italian restaurant, Rose.

"Good morning," Emilia greeted. "We saw the door was open and wanted to see inside."

"There have not been any priests here for a very long time, but I sneak in sometimes to pray." Rose smiled and took Emilia's hands in hers, squeezing them briefly. "I sense so much kindness and strength in you—so untouched by this place. But you still have their gifts. I can feel it."

Emilia wasn't sure how to respond. "Oh, uh, thank you."

"We were starting to look around the village and then head up to the castle. Where do you suggest we begin?" asked Amanda.

"Really? Then let me show you around," Rose offered. "I will be your guide."

"That would be wonderful, if you're sure?" replied Emilia.

"I would do *anything* for you, Countess." Rose grinned. "Please, come with me."

Rose pulled on her tattered coat and led Emilia and Amanda out of the church, stopping to pull the heavy door closed behind them. It scraped along the floor and shut with a bellowing thud.

"Come, we go up to the castle first. From there you can see the whole village and I can show you the home where your family has lived for many hundreds of years."

They descended the church steps, crossed the square, and began along the path that led up to the castle.

The crisp mountain air felt energizing. The girls enjoyed the picturesque scenes in every direction and the sound of the gravel crunching beneath their boots on the steep, upward climb. When they reached the top, the sheer scale of the castle was mind-blowing.

Amanda whistled. "Wow, that's a castle, all right!"

"It is impressive, yes?" Rose asked. "Imagine a time when this was one of the most beautiful places in the world."

"I *can* imagine," breathed Emilia, bewildered by the grandeur that towered over her.

"Turn around; you can see the village and down into the valley from here." Rose pointed in the direction they had come from.

The sisters shared a gasp as they took in the breathtaking vista surrounding them; densely wooded mountains, a spectacular deep valley, the quaint village hugged by the flowing river. From a distance, it appeared as if it were a scene painted by one of the Old Masters.

"It's spectacular! If only the sun would come out, it would be perfection!" said Amanda, her eyes darting back and forth, taking in the moment.

"The sun never shines around here," mumbled Rose, shaking her head before looking up to the southern tower.

Emilia thought it was an odd comment, but something else occurred to her, anxiety forming a lump in her stomach. "I feel like I've seen this before."

"How? When?" Amanda asked.

"Um...it was different somehow. It's day now but the shape of the river...and the village, it seems familiar. Perhaps in a dream..."

"Come now," urged Rose. "There is more to show you—this way." Her cheeks became flushed and she continued toward the castle's main gate.

"Wait, not one of *those* dreams?" Amanda asked as they tried to keep up with their guide.

"Yeah, I think so," sighed Emilia. "It was at night. Moonlight on the water and lights in the village, but the shape of the river is kind of distinctive."

As they came through a large stone archway, Rose announced, "This is the main gate to the castle. There are some other smaller entrances too, but this is the big one."

"No guards or knights?" Amanda joked.

"Not anymore. Not for a long time," Rose corrected herself. "People from the village are free to come and go as necessary. Some do work up here and some help in...in other ways. I used to spend much time up here when I was younger."

"You know, there were those pictures we flicked through on my phone when we were at the lounge the other night," Amanda went on, oblivious to Rose's stuttering. "Perhaps the view you're remembering was one of those?"

They both looked up at the raised metal gate overhead; the heavy chains holding it in place as they passed beneath.

"This here is the courtyard of the castle," Rose explained as they entered a patchy grass area overtaken by weeds. "A great many events big and small would have happened here over the years, mostly good but some—" She halted mid-sentence. "The village was not without some trouble in earlier days, but, in those times at least, your ancestors always prevailed."

Emilia found herself drawn to the top of the tower, gazing upon the closest window as if searching for something—some*one*—she felt should be there.

"Next thing you're going to tell me there are dungeons, too?" Amanda's voice drew Emilia from her thoughts.

Rose smiled. "Well, actually...yes. There *are* dungeons below the southern tower, and there are tunnels below the ground that connect most of the buildings together. But these things are not used so much anymore."

"Emmi, did you hear that?" Amanda nudged her shoulder. "Your castle has dungeons and secret passageways! Wait until we tell everyone back home about this!"

"Ah...yeah. Yes," she struggled to say. "This is all so much."

"Now let me take you through the main house," Rose beckoned, and Amanda followed. Emilia stood staring up toward the southern tower, something within her belly tingling; she couldn't look away.

"Emmi, let's go! Your kingdom awaits!" called Amanda from across the courtyard, the sound bouncing off the castle walls and around the open space.

Emilia broke her gaze and caught up with the others as they approached the main entrance.

The hefty iron handle creaked, and the heavy wooden door groaned its greeting as Rose pushed it open and the three entered the castle. The cavernous foyer felt warm, and the familiar dusty smell Emilia had come to associate with Zillah's old buildings was almost charming as it wafted past her nose and added to the atmosphere. Dust was visible in the air, the light flowing in through the windows catching and exposing the particles as they floated by.

Amanda spun around as they took it all in: the high vaulted ceiling, the carved dark wooden staircase, the banners, tapestries, and paintings decorating the walls. There were even a few sculptures positioned in recessed cutouts.

Even in the pale gray light the magnificence was hard to overlook.

"Your family was once capable of some extraordinary things, Countess," Rose said softly, gauging Emilia's impression.

"Please Rose, call me Emilia. I don't think I can get used to being called that."

"But, my Countess, I do not think I could get used to calling you anything else." She bit the inside of her lip. "I mean it with affection for you, as I am sure most of the villagers here will."

"I'd just go with it, Emmi," Amanda encouraged her. "Don't want to upset anyone, plus, it's kind of cool...just don't let it go to your head!"

The next couple of hours were spent exploring the castle. Rose guided them through the grand ballroom, solarium, reception rooms, kitchen, main dining room, and the many bedchambers. Rose shared stories that had been passed down to her, along with some of her more enjoyable experiences within the castle walls. Emilia ignored the unkempt condition, instead marveling at the beauty, ingenuity, and fine craftsmanship visible in all that her ancestors had built.

The girls were introduced to the cook—Mrs. Rossi, and two younger women from the village as they went about their chores. Emilia and Amanda found their work attire rather odd—flimsy, plain dresses made of almost sheer fabric—though neither girl seemed particularly unhappy or uncomfortable at their level of exposure.

"I guess customs here are a little different than we're used to," Amanda shrugged. "Who am I to judge, I suppose?" But...it is kind of strange...seems a bit...*wrong.*"

Emilia raised her eyebrows and nodded in agreement.

"And this was your late aunt's private chamber," Rose announced as they entered an area that was at least twice the size of their whole apartment back home.

The private chambers were on the eastern side of the castle, the windows framing three sides with views overlooking the mountains to the north, the waterfall and valley below it to the east, and the village to the south. The space was divided into several areas for sleeping, sitting, working, and bathing, and featured fireplaces and elegant furnishings.

"The maids have cleaned everything for you to stay, though you will find many of your aunt's things are still in here," Rose said. "I think they were expecting you last night."

"Ah, yes," Emilia admitted. "No one told me about this arrangement until we were already at the inn."

She shook her head. "Anyhow, you can stay at the castle tonight—it is where you belong after all." Rose gently touched Emilia's arm and told Amanda that of course she was welcome, too.

"Sweet, thanks!" Amanda grinned. "Hey, Emmi, we get to stay in *your* castle tonight. I hope it has hot water," she quipped.

"And it was just my aunt who stayed in here?" Emilia asked, ignoring Amanda's comment.

"Yes, most of the time, because of the...ah, I believe your uncle kept separate chambers."

"I never knew anything at all about them. What else can you tell me?"

"Well, we saw them only now and again. Your uncle would visit the village on occasion but, your aunt...not really, they say toward the end that she barely left her chamber. The terrible curse that befell your family, oh my..." Rose shook her head again, sadder this time.

"*Curse?*" Amanda blurted.

"Oh dear," Rose stammered, "I am speaking out of my place. Here, this is a photo of your Aunt Katerina when she was younger." She picked up a framed photograph from a table nearby and handed it to Emilia. The portrait was black and white, a stoic expression on a face not unlike her own.

"Amazing family resemblance, Emmi," said Amanda, looking over her shoulder.

"Yes, very much," Rose agreed. "All the women in your family were beautiful, and you, dear Countess, are no exception."

Emilia blushed as she set the frame back down.

"Hey, Emmi," said Amanda, picking up another photo from the table and handing it to her. "Check out this one—it looks like you when you were younger."

Within the frame, which featured an unusual design of unique symbols that almost appeared to glow, a young girl played at the beach. There was indeed a striking resemblance to Emilia when she was a child. "I think...I think this *is* me—"

"That is not possible," Rose interrupted.

"No, look, Amanda!" Emilia insisted. "It's the same swimsuit I'm wearing in that photo back home of my parents and me when we all went to the shore together as kids."

Amanda scrutinized the details. "Whoa, yeah. I think you're right— hey was that the day when that bratty kid knocked your sandcastle over and you got all mad about it, then a minute later there was a gust of wind and a random wave crashed into him and wrecked the sand fort he was building—remember that? He was stomping all around the beach and screaming, it was pretty funny..."

"Yeah, I *do* remember that." Emilia paused in contemplation.

I wonder how many times I've used these...abilities...without even knowing it.

She scanned the table filled with framed photographs, spotting a pair of faces she would recognize anywhere. "Look at this one. These are my parents! Rose, are these buildings here in the village?" Heart racing, she gestured to the background in the picture.

"Yes...this is in the village." Rose clamped a hand over her mouth, tightly closing her eyes.

"So, she *knew* about me?" Her chest suddenly felt weighted. "Why wouldn't she try to find me?"

"She...she wanted to *protect* you," Rose whispered, tears welling in her eyes.

"Protect me?" Emilia gaped up at her, unable to fathom what she meant. "From what?"

"I cannot speak of such things," Rose spoke rapidly, barely audible. "It is not safe—please, forgive me. I should not have shown you the photos, I did not realize—we must go. Here, please put these down." Rose's voice quivered and her hands shook as she returned the frames to the table.

"I don't understand. *Please* tell me," Emilia begged for answers.

"No, no," she mumbled. "I cannot say anything more. I am so sorry you have been drawn into all of this."

They continued their tour of the castle in silence, Emilia overcome with questions; she could feel the blood pulsing through her veins as she sensed there was more to be uncovered.

Amanda did her best to remain cheerful and inquisitive. "What's through here?" she asked as they passed by an opening off the central hallway.

Rose's eyes wandered up the large staircase. "They lead to the tower."

"Cool! Can we take a look? I'll bet the view is incredible from up there."

286

Rose sighed, "Bad spirits in this place, some not so good things have happened there."

"Like what?" Emilia was curious.

"Please, I do not want to talk about such things, not now—I will take you there but let us be quick."

Rose turned and started toward the staircase; her shoulders slumped. Emilia and Amanda exchanged confused glances as they followed behind.

The northern tower was attached to the back of the main castle and rose two levels higher. It was a wide square structure built from stone. The top level had a passageway all around the sides which was open to the air yet covered under the pitched roof.

"Between the hike up to the castle and now all these stairs, I definitely feel like I'm getting a workout on this trip!" Amanda puffed cheerfully as they reached the top, breaking the uncomfortable tension that had set over the group.

Rose guided them outside, each direction offering its own treasures. Mountains to the north and west, the valley to the east, and the castle complex itself as well as the village to the south. The river flowed from west to east around the town, and it was also possible to make out the top of the waterfall, misty spray rising from the bottom.

"What's that over there?" Amanda pointed to a dirt road curving around the mountain to the north of the castle.

"That is where the old mines are. They have been closed for a *long* time. No one from the village goes there anymore…" Rose trailed off.

There was a familiar-looking vehicle parked near what Emilia assumed was once a mine entrance.

"Those men, I do not know for sure—I only hear rumors—but they are here with Mr. Thiess," Rose said, looking distrustfully toward it.

"Yes, he told us they were doing some maintenance there." Amanda added.

Rose pursed her lips and nodded slowly.

"Come, over this side you can see the village and all of the castle." She led the way around the tower until they faced the village and the buildings within the castle walls below.

"From up here, the town looks like a nice place again," said Rose, smiling proudly as she gazed downward, her spirits lifting.

Emilia stared for a few moments at the top of the southern tower before something else caught her attention. Beyond the castle walls on the northwest side was a small building along with several objects that lined the hill beside it. A path led from a gate to the building. Emilia walked further around the tower to get a closer look.

Suddenly, a wave of fear crashed over her and she swallowed hard to clear the lump in her throat. Her eyes were wide, instinct telling her exactly what she was looking at. She glanced up toward the southern tower again, then back to the small building.

"What is it, Emmi?" Amanda saw her sister's frightened expression.

"Those graves are the resting places of many in your family. Your aunt and uncle, they are both buried there." Rose's voice was low.

"And the building?"

"Uh, it's…some old building—it is not used anymore."

"I-I'd like to go down and see it," said Emilia, doing her best to conceal her shock.

"Perhaps later?" Rose suggested. "There is nothing so interesting down there, and I was thinking that you would have lunch at my restaurant, yes? It would be my pleasure. Come, it is best we go back down now, anyway." She clasped her hands in front of her chest and smiled.

"I think that's a good idea, Emmi," Amanda said. "I'm ready to eat— that's for sure. Plus, it's getting on and we've still got some things to figure out before Mr. Thiess gets back."

Emilia noticed the slight scowl on Rose's face at the very mention of his name. "I'd *really* like to see the…building. Do you not want to show me?"

Rose let out a long sigh, gazing toward the mountains before returning to Emilia's questioning face. "I...I just cannot. There are—I have too many painful memories from that place, I would rather that I never have to go there again. I am sorry, but I must return to the village. Please come with me and I will feed you. And I would like you to meet...my husband, Nicolas."

Emilia glanced at Amanda, who gave her a shrug in return.

"All right, we'll go with you," Emilia relented, sensing Rose's discomfort was genuine. She lingered for a moment longer, staring at the structure and peering over the village again before following the others for the walk back to town.

Emilia noticed curious onlookers staring at her—perhaps for a little too long—as they strolled back into the main square with Rose.

"Last night, you and Mr. Thiess were arguing. What was that about?" asked Emilia as they passed the fountain, nearing the restaurant.

"Oh, never mind about that. He is not a very nice person." Rose waved dismissively as she spoke.

"Yes, I agree," Emilia nodded, "He doesn't seem very kind."

"Or courteous," Amanda added. "Or polite, or—"

"Please, Rose," Emilia persisted. "We saw him through the windows after we left the restaurant last night and he seemed very...agitated. What were you having a disagreement about?"

"He did not want to pay for dinner," Rose mumbled, staring at the ground.

"What?" Emilia felt her cheeks flush. "He told us he'd take care of it. Why didn't he want to pay?"

"He was saying he was a guest here; that he was going to be in charge soon, so we should look after him and treat him well. He has been here before, back when...many years ago. He was almost as unpleasant then, but he seems to have become grumpier with his age." Rose almost managed a giggle.

The girls looked at each other, their non-verbal cues each telling the other that a little more of the puzzle was falling into place.

"Okay. Thank you for telling me," Emilia said. "You know, our interactions with him have not been so great either. But don't worry, I will do everything I can to make sure he doesn't become a permanent fixture here—and *we'll* pay you for dinner."

Rose turned to her with a sad smile. "You are a kind and wonderful person. I only wish it was within your power. Thiess is unlikable, certainly, but he is far from the greatest darkness which overshadows this place." Rose turned and continued to the restaurant.

"What the fuck!" Amanda silently mouthed to Emilia and made a face that indicated she thought the situation was crazy.

Chapter Thirty-Six

The girls chatted away while they finished their lunch; they thanked Rose for showing them around the castle and headed back to the inn, where they waited for Luna in the lobby.

"So," said Amanda, all business-like as she leaned against the staircase. "I guess it is fairly obvious who the bad guy is in your fairytale here— trying to pass himself off as the knight in shining armor," Amanda scoffed. "What are we going to do about Mr. Thiess?"

"Yeah, thank goodness he's not pretending to be Prince Charming I suppose." Emilia chuckled and Amanda joined her.

"You know," Amanda continued, "from what Rose said, I wonder if he's involved with this mysterious Graben Holdings. Or maybe it's even just him? He's obviously got some plans for this place, but what?" She lowered her voice to a whisper. "And you know, I don't think I completely trust her either. It's pretty obvious Rose is holding something back."

"I know, I totally get that impression too," said Emilia, "but at least she seems kind."

"Yup. I agree, and I don't think Rose is who we really need to worry about. I was thinking, those two men in town, the ones working at the mines; I overheard them last night and I'm sure they mentioned Thiess' name as well as something about a lot of *gold.*" Amanda had begun to whisper even though there was no one else in sight.

"Are you serious?" Emilia shot her sister a curious look.

Amanda nodded. "What if he's trying to trick you, Emmi? What if this place *is* actually worth something?"

"I guess it's possible but look around. Does it *really* seem like they're sitting on a pile of gold? We'll have to figure out a way to know for sure. And even if there isn't anything in the mines, I still don't feel like I can unleash Thiess upon all these poor people—things seem bad enough here as it is."

Amanda thought for a moment. "I have an idea! The younger one— you know, the kind of cute one? He seemed a bit flirty, but the older guy doesn't want to let him talk. Perhaps if I can get him alone, we can find out some more?"

"Oh, Amanda..." Emilia giggled.

"*What?* I think it's a brilliant idea."

"Yeah, you're right. It is. How are you thinking to...isolate him?" Emilia winked.

"Well, I guess I just need to try and corner him here at the inn somehow." Amanda shrugged like it was simple. "Seems like this is where they're staying."

"Sounds easy enough, but what if he won't talk to you?"

"Not even an option!" replied Amanda just as Luna came in from the restaurant.

Her long hair had been braided into a crown around her head, creating a red halo, and her fair skin displayed many freckles before she donned her coat behind the front desk.

"Where are we going?" Amanda asked.

"Across the other side of the river. An old woman named Gerlinde lives there. She has been around for a *very* long time and seems to know a lot about the history here. If there is anyone who can tell the heiress about her family, it will be Gerlinde." Luna's tone was friendly, and Emilia got the impression she enjoyed being of service.

As they walked, Emilia eyed the houses and buildings along the main street. It was clear there was a lot of poverty with repairs of one kind or another needed in just about every direction.

"Do you know anything about the two men who are staying at the inn?" asked Amanda.

"Not much," Luna said. "I haven't really spoken with them. They have been here for a few days. I think they are leaving today—my mama said there will be no one staying at the inn tomorrow."

"Yeah, we'll need to pack and check out when we get back, too," said Emilia.

"Oh? But they took your things up to the castle already," replied Luna, looking confused.

"Well, that didn't take long!" Amanda blurted. "Not that I mind not having to pack again or anything, but it seems a little intrusive."

"Oh, I'm sure they were just being of assistance—we thought it was strange that you didn't stay there from the beginning, it is your home after all."

"Things here are just a little different than we're used to," Emilia said. "I'm sure it was meant to be a helpful gesture."

"We can take a shortcut down here." Luna led the way onto a small trail in the woods off the main road, leaves rustling beneath their feet.

"Cool! I can hear the river," said Emilia. "And the waterfall!"

"Yes, we are close now," Luna said. "The old mill is just up here a little way. There is a bridge to the other side, and Gerlinde lives not far from there."

The three continued along the lightly worn path through the woods until they reached a clearing and a cluster of cottages came into view.

"I feel like we're going hiking or something." Amanda chuckled.

Suddenly, movement at the far end of the clearing drew their attention. A cottage door opened, and an elderly woman hobbled out.

"That is Gerlinde, do not be frightened, I have spoken with her and she is kind," explained Luna.

Emilia and Amanda looked at each other curiously. What would prompt Luna to say such a thing— unless there was, perhaps, something to fear?

Gerlinde waited patiently as the three women joined her.

"You must be the heiress?" Gerlinde's voice belied her age, but her words and her eyes were sharp.

"Yes, hello. Um, I'm Emilia...and this is my sister Amanda," Emilia stammered as she looked upon the haggard woman before her.

"Hi." Amanda offered a stiff wave.

"Do you think you can find your way back to the village if I leave now?" Luna asked. "I need to go and check on my friend."

"I think we'll be fine. Thank you for bringing us here." Emilia smiled and Amanda nodded in agreement.

"Thank you, Luna," Gerlinde said, "for bringing her to me. How is Caroline?"

"She is still unwell; no better." Luna frowned. "I am going to see her now."

"I am sorry to hear this..." Gerlinde paused. "Okay, you go now. I have much to talk about with this one." She fixed her piercing eyes on Emilia.

"Yes, I understand," said Luna. As she set out across the clearing, she turned to the girls. "I will see you later—in the village or perhaps at the castle."

"Come now. Come inside," beckoned the old woman.

Emilia couldn't help but wonder about Luna's sick friend but Gerlinde's abrupt manner didn't allow any room to pursue it.

Within the cottage, the wood fire crackled and the smell of herbs created a cozy atmosphere.

"So, you don't know who you are—or more importantly, *what* you are. Am I correct?" Gerlinde probed, staring deeply into Emilia's eyes.

"Yes, I suppose. Mr. Thiess told me that I'm a countess—in Zillah at least." Emilia sensed something unusual about her but was unable to figure out what.

Amanda looked around the cottage with a slightly amused expression, alternating her attention between Emilia with Gerlinde and the eclectic decorations adorning the walls, shelves, benches, and tables. As she browsed the book titles, her demeanor appeared more concerned. Emilia followed her gaze and found that almost all of them related to mysticism, magical powers—some even appeared to be of a darker nature.

"Come, sit…" Gerlinde pointed to the small kitchen table, where a teapot, three teacups, and a plate with cookies awaited.

"Sure," replied Amanda in a hushed voice as she almost tiptoed her way to the table and sat down, eyeing Gerlinde warily.

The old woman poured some tea into each of their cups, the herbal aroma dancing around their noses. She offered the plate of cookies, Emilia biting into hers immediately while Amanda examined them for potential danger.

"This is delicious!" Emilia said.

"I baked these today, for you." Gerlinde smiled and the wrinkles on her face became more pronounced. "I am glad you like it; eat as many as you wish."

Amanda's distrust eased and she took her first bite as Gerlinde stared at Emilia for a few long moments.

"So, the lost daughter—the *last* daughter of the Blagden line—has returned. I did not expect this. Now, what questions do you have?" Gerlinde watched Emilia take a sip of tea and lifted her own cup to her lips.

Amanda looked to Emilia expectantly as she drank, the steam rising from her cup.

"Really, I'd like to know everything you can tell me," Emilia said. "My parents died when I was young and, although I've searched over the years since, I don't really know anything about my family at all."

Sadness filled Gerlinde's expression as she gazed at the fire, the sounds of crackling wood filling the brief void in conversation. "It was very unfortunate. Their loss still haunts the village to this day."

"So, they definitely were from here?" Emilia asked. "Genevieve and Anton—those were their names?"

"Yes. They were both born here and grew up in the village."

"Did you know them? Why did they leave?"

"I knew them both. Two very nice people; young and so much in love. Their romance was a difficult one in the beginning and they had to hide their affections. Your mother was a Blagden woman and of course there were responsibilities that came along with that, but your Aunt, being the older sister, well, she carried most of that burden. Your mother had a kind heart and was beloved by all in the village. Your father, he was a tailor...not an ideal match for a woman of nobility, and far too early in her life to settle down as far as...some here were concerned.

"But they persisted and found a way. When your mother became pregnant with you, they decided it was best for them to leave. This was not easy, but they managed to escape. They fled with you far away. Times were even darker when they disappeared."

"It seems that life here isn't so pleasant for anyone, I get it," Emilia admitted. "My aunt knew about me but never tried to find me. I wonder if she knew my parents died."

"Yes...of course she knew about your parents, and it caused her great pain. I knew your aunt—your *teta*, as we say here—very well. Although there were some...obstacles, and her poor health in later years, Katerina and I spent time together before she passed. Your parents and your *teta* wanted a different life for you—away from all the...difficulties of this place. Now that you're here in the flesh, all I can believe is that this...this is your destiny. We all tried to prevent it, but if you are here despite all of the efforts and sacrifices that were made, I believe what must be will be." Gerlinde shook her head slowly and stared into the fire once more.

"Don't you think you're being a bit too dramatic?" Amanda said defensively. "It's not *all* that bad. I mean sure, there's some work that needs to be done and we need to deal with Thiess, but you're making it seem a lot more intense than that."

"*Thiess?*" Gerlinde's steely eyes settled on Amanda.

"Martin Thiess, the shady lawyer; resident assho—I mean bad guy—around here?" Amanda replied.

"I see." The old woman sighed. "So, you have not yet learned of…I don't know that there is much more I can tell you without—" Gerlinde glared at Emilia as tears streamed down her cheeks. She turned to stare at the fire, sobbing softly. "Oh my, I am sorry. So very sorry. I cannot share anything more."

The girls were confused at her sudden emotional outburst. "Gerlinde, it's all right. There is nothing to be upset about. Please." Emilia knelt beside the old woman, trying to console her.

Gerlinde drew her trembling, frail hands upward to cover her face. Emilia rested a hand on her shoulder, trying to comfort her, and felt a strange tingling as she touched Gerlinde. She was about to back away when the old woman placed her own hand on top of Emilia's.

"There is nothing you can do. I am all right. Just so, so very…" Gerlinde squeezed her eyes shut even more tightly. "Wait, before you leave, there is something I must know." She released her hand and rose from her chair, eyes red and puffy as she faced Emilia and they both stood in front of the fireplace.

"Give me your hands." Wet streaks flickered prominently on her cheeks in the firelight as the old woman reached out, palms up, toward Emilia.

Emilia paused, took a deep breath, then let her hands sit atop Gerlinde's. The old woman immediately gripped Emilia's fingers and she needed to suppress the urge to pull back as Gerlinde tightened her hold and closed her eyes.

Emilia did the same and a strange sensation passed through her body—like pins and needles but more forceful. She quivered and pulled back slightly as a prickling shiver entered her right hand. It raced through every part of her body like a pinball in auto mode pinging to every vein. Then the sensation passed through her left hand, leaving a trail of goosebumps and a shudder in its wake.

Gerlinde abruptly released Emilia and her eyes shot open as she stepped back, breathing heavily. "It's strong in you. *Very* strong in you. This is most unexpected."

"Are you all right, Emmi? What just happened?" Amanda demanded answers.

"I'm...fine." Emilia wiggled her fingers as the strange feeling dissipated. "What was that? What did you do? *What* is strong in me?"

"I felt you, last night," Gerlinde said. "You were playing with your powers, no?"

"Um..." Emilia stammered. "What do you mean?" Suddenly self-conscious, she blushed. Emilia had never talked with anyone about her interesting encounters with wind and fire.

"Did you not summon the wind and make the fire dance?" Gerlinde raised her eyebrows suggestively. "You must have known—you are different from the others in your world. You see something happen in your mind first then it plays out before you—you sense thoughts and the presence of others just with intuition, no? None of this has been by chance."

"What on *earth* are you talking about?" Amanda exclaimed. "Emmi, this is getting weird. I think we should go."

"Of course," Gerlinde seemed to agree. "You may leave if you wish, I fear talking more about these things will cause trouble anyway." She glanced between the sisters. "Thank you for coming out here to see me." She shuffled to the door and opened it, waiting for them to exit.

"Um, thank you for your time, Gerlinde," Emilia awkwardly replied. "I really do appreciate you telling me about my family, at least a bit more about them...but I feel there is still a lot I'm missing. I don't even know what happened to my aunt and uncle?" Emilia shrugged as she stepped out of the cottage and into the forest.

"You are right, there is much more, but I'm unable...I only wish I could have done more to change the path you now find yourself taking," Gerlinde frowned.

"See? Now there's one more confusing thing to figure out." Emilia sighed. "I wish you would tell me what that means. I want to do everything I can to help the people who live here. I know Thiess is up to something and I am going to find a way to send him packing."

"I believe you would solve all of this if you could, but to alter this course now? This old mind can't even *begin* to imagine a way—not now that you are here. I'm sorry." With that, the old woman huddled back inside her cottage and closed the door.

Bewildered, the girls headed toward the river, making their way back to the village.

"WTF?" Amanda broke the silence. "So, I can't quite believe I'm saying this, but maybe the deal Thiess is offering is a good one. Take it and let's get out of here. This place is getting weirder and crazier with every new person we meet!"

"Yeah...maybe," Emilia replied. "All this cryptic talk bothers me so much—I *know* she knows so much more than she's telling us."

"Well, sure, Emmi. There's probably a lot she *knows*," Amanda made air quotes with her fingers, "but seriously, how much of that crazy shit do we really *need* to hear?"

"She wasn't *that* crazy, was she?"

"Emmi! What about 'feeling you' last night and blabbering on about 'your powers' and making the 'fire and wind dance', huh? And what the hell did she do when she was holding your hands? It looked like she was zapping you with electric shocks or something."

Emilia only shook her head, unable to answer that herself.

They walked in silence for a while. When they were halfway across the bridge, Emilia stopped to look back toward the village, then down to the waterfall and valley on the other side.

"What's up?" asked Amanda.

"Can I...can I tell you something without you thinking I'm going crazy, too?"

"Sure, what's on your mind?"

"Well, isn't that the big question right now?" joked Emilia.

Amanda laughed at her choice of words. "I'm glad you haven't lost your sense of humor! Go on, tell me."

Emilia paused. "You know, it doesn't matter. Maybe I just need to rest or something—let's keep going."

"Yeah, could be some jetlag making you feel a bit off—and don't get me started about Thiess and everything to deal with there, I can't even imagine what must be running around in your head right now." Amanda rubbed her shoulder and Emilia relaxed a fraction.

As they made their way back to town, the truck from the mines rumbled down the hill and turned toward the village.

"If they're leaving, it could be our last chance to find out what that asshole's plans are," Amanda said. "I'm going to go to the inn and see if I can talk with one of them. Why don't you go and have a rest—in your castle, Countess!" She tried her best posh voice as they continued walking along the cobblestone street.

"I still can't believe I have a castle!" blurted Emilia, giggling.

"Go on then," her sister encouraged. "I'll see what dirt I can dig up on our friend Thiess."

"I can come and help."

"You know, this may be better played solo." She winked. "Let me handle it and I'll meet you up there a little later."

"This poor guy's not going to know what hit him, is he?" Emilia asked.

Amanda grinned in that all-American girl-next-door way that would charm anyone with an ounce of testosterone. "Nope."

Chapter Thirty-Seven

Amanda strolled into the inn, searching the public areas for signs of the mining consultants. Nobody was around and the front desk was unattended; there were two missing keys.

Guess I've got a fifty-fifty chance of choosing the right one.

Amanda tiptoed up the stairs to the second floor, trying to avoid the creaky spots along the way. She made her way along the hallway to room twelve and paused for a moment to listen at the door.

Amanda could make out one side of a conversation, the voice sounding as if it were the older man talking about their plans to depart in hopes of being clear of the mountains before nightfall.

All right, let's try door number two.

She crept along the wall until she was standing outside the next room and listened carefully. There was shuffling, but no voice. Amanda suddenly became distracted by the sound of footsteps on the staircase. She felt her heart race—explaining why she was there was something she'd prefer to avoid.

Amanda knocked on the door as the footsteps from the staircase drew closer. Her chest tightened as she heard the click of the latch and the squeak of the turning handle. The footsteps on the staircase changed tone; they'd reached the landing now and were heading her way.

The younger consultant appeared startled, yet welcoming. He wore dark denim jeans and a belt, his chest was bare, and Amanda swallowed the lump in her throat as her adrenaline pulsed at the very sight of him. Before he had a chance to greet his unexpected visitor, Amanda smiled and pushed her way inside, locking lips with the German stranger and shutting the door behind her as she kissed him like an infatuated groupie getting her one shot with the front man of her favorite band.

He gladly obliged the advance, and Amanda continued her heated embrace. She hadn't expected to be so aroused and attracted to him; he had just showered and smelled of cologne, his strong frame enveloping her as they both moaned, realizing how much they craved release.

"I'm Amanda, by the way," she breathed as his tongue lunged into her mouth with fervor, his hand caressing her cheek sensually.

He chuckled. "Derrick," came his response in a heavy accent and he picked her up, wrapped her legs around him, and took her to bed.

They both lay on the bed, clothes strewn, hair tousled and breathing heavily after a carnal sprint that ended in both silencing their orgasms so as not to alert the boss next door.

"So," Derrick grinned as he turned to her, "that was fun. Now what can I do for you?"

Amanda giggled, propped herself up on her pillow, and lay on her side so she could see him. He was handsome; blond hair, azure eyes, full lips. Having previously only seen him from a distance, Amanda hadn't realized just how sexy he was. It was certainly not part of her plan to sleep with the guy, but now it was time to get back to business.

"Well…" She traced his abdomen with her fingertips. "I saw you the other night, and I saw your truck today at the mines. I was wondering…um, how long are you staying? What work are you doing? My sister and I are visiting for a few days and you didn't seem like you were from around here either…I was thinking maybe we could get a coffee. Or a drink?"

Derrick laughed, and Amanda's toes curled at the sight of a dimple on his left cheek. "This is a little bit backwards, no? I have bad news: we are just about to leave—I was packing my things when you, ah, came to visit me. We will be on our way down the mountain again before it gets dark." Derrick pointed to his bag that had been knocked off the bed during their tumble, its contents scattered on the floor.

"Oh," Amanda replied.

"Until right now, I was glad to be going home. It is a little…off, this place, you know?" Derrick whispered. "But you, well…I would have liked the opportunity to get to know you." He stroked Amanda's hair and kissed her once more before standing to get dressed.

"Anyway, I work for a company that operates mines all over the world." He tugged on a pair of pants. "It is a big company based in Germany. My division does consulting work, like planning to set up new mines or organizing geological studies to see if an area could be developed for one. It sounds boring I know, but I like it and I get to travel a lot. I started two years ago when I graduated from university."

"Doesn't sound boring at all," Amanda said. "Actually sounds pretty cool to me. But what does that have to do with Zillah? I read that the gold here ran out long ago."

"You know, I am not supposed to talk about what we are doing here." Derrick rubbed the back of his neck. "The man who hired us is very secretive and…" He didn't finish.

"Ooh, a top-secret mission; life and death. That sort of stuff?"

Derrick laughed. "Well, I am not a spy or anything. I think mainly he doesn't want the locals to know what he is doing—do you promise not to tell?" He pulled a tight-fitting white T-shirt over his head.

"Oh, of course." Amanda battered her brown eyes at him. "Cross my heart. I don't even know many locals."

"All right. It is very sad, but he is planning to flatten the village in order to reopen the mines; everyone here will have to leave their homes."

"Oh my." Amanda knew the guy was a bastard. "Why?"

"Greed." Derrick snickered. "Much less expensive and faster this way compared to fixing up and reopening the tunnels as they used to do it. It could still be done that way—would take longer and cost more, but still very profitable."

"But isn't all the gold gone?"

"No," he gasped. "That is the crazy thing: the mines have been abandoned for a very, very long time, but there is *so* much gold down there. It doesn't make any sense."

"When you say *a lot*, do you mean like millions of dollars?" Amanda twirled her hair.

Derrick paused before raising his eyebrows and replying in a hushed tone, "More like *hundreds* of millions."

"You've got to be kidding!" squeaked Amanda.

"Not kidding." He shook his head and grinned. "This is our job—my colleague has been doing this for many years and he is certain. I have seen gold down there with my own eyes!"

"Whoa," was all Amanda could say in return, turning and sitting up to look out the window.

"Please, you won't say anything to anyone living here or to my boss, will you?" he asked after a short time. "I am a talker, and you are a great lover; these things sometimes get me into trouble."

Amanda pulled the sheet across her chest and kneeled up to kiss Derrick, who stood at the edge of the bed. "Don't worry, your secret is safe—"

A loud knock interrupted them.

"Derrick? Are you still up here? We need to get going." Amanda recognized his older colleague's voice.

"Yes, almost," Derrick replied evenly. "I just need two more minutes."

"Okay. Please be quick, eh? I want to be sure we get down the mountain before it gets too late."

"Yes, Hanz. I will meet you in the lobby."

Derrick stuffed everything back into his bag and quickly scribbled his details onto a notepad by the desk. "I am sorry, but I must go. Will you—"

"Sure," Amanda winked, "let's keep in touch." She leaned in for a goodbye kiss.

Derrick scooped Amanda off the bed, kissing her gently before laying her naked body back down, grabbing his bag, and leaving.

Chapter Thirty-Eight

Emilia reached the top of the hill and entered the castle complex through the main gate. Crossing the courtyard, her attention was on the wall ahead; she needed to satisfy her curiosity about what she suspected lay beyond it. Between two of the buildings along the western wall was a passageway which led to an iron gate. Through the bars, Emilia spotted the building she'd seen from the north tower—it was a chapel and she felt her heart race; nervous anticipation set in as the reality of where she was and where she was heading became apparent. Emilia's senses heightened and she felt aware of things that would normally go unnoticed—the cold clack of the latch, the screech of the rusty hinges as she pulled the heavy gate open, the gravel as she stepped beyond the wall and onto the path that led to the chapel.

It was a winding route and the area seemed to have been tended to recently; the smell of cut grass lingered in the air, and even the path itself looked like it had been tidied and refreshed. A strong gust of wind blew by, causing Emilia to clutch her arms over her chest and squint a little as her hair flew around her face.

Emilia took in her surroundings: the encircling mountains seemed eerily familiar. The craw of a raven soaring overhead drew her eyes skyward as she continued on. When she reached the entrance to the chapel, the wooden doors were closed. She noticed two firepits—one on either side of the path, right where she expected them to be—each stacked with a fresh arrangement of firewood, ready to be lit.

Swallowing hard, Emilia gripped her chest as if to try and slow her rapidly beating heart while she fought the instinct to run back to the village, find Amanda, and get as far away from this place as possible. Instead, Emilia grasped the two large iron rings that served as handles and pushed.

With a groan, both doors opened. Emilia peered inside, not knowing what or whom she was looking for.

She felt relieved—and confusingly, disappointed—that there was no one there. Emilia stepped inside; the statues, pews, the charred beams across the roof, the floor, the altar, and even the musky scent were all exactly as they'd been when she'd visited in her dreams. There were differences too: the space was bathed in the pale light filtering through the windows, creating a cold, gloomy feeling. Many candles had been meticulously arranged around the space, yet they were not lit.

How is this even possible?

"Hello?" Emilia called, a muffled echo the only response.

She kept going, every detail serving as a reminder she'd been there before. Emilia ascended the steps and found herself standing at the altar. She felt the rough, cold stone as she brushed her hand over it.

Oh my God. Even the stains are here.

Emilia looked toward the back wall of the chapel. Behind the altar, below the windows framing the mountains and dreary clouds, were the same daggers she'd seen in her dreams.

The dagger he used to kill me.

"Hello, Emilia."

She froze in place for an instant, body overcome with a tingling force as the unmistakable voice rang in her ears. Emilia spun toward the entrance.

He stood just inside, wearing a black robe with his hands clasped at his waist. His eyes expressed elation while his lips conveyed a confident smile—an almost cunning smirk. Emilia knew his blue eyes, his square jaw and neatly trimmed beard. She knew him anywhere.

"Massi...Massimino."

"Welcome home." He started at a measured pace toward the altar.

Emilia swallowed hard; her hands shook ever so slightly as adrenaline coursed through her body. She opened her mouth to speak but no sound came.

"Why so apprehensive, my dear Emilia?" He regarded her from a short distance. "Do you not remember all the pleasant moments we've shared?"

"I…" Emilia steadied herself against the altar behind her, glancing at the daggers and then Massimino again. "I…uh."

"Do not fear," he said, expression becoming softer. "It is not time for that right now."

"But…you're just a dream." Emilia's breathing was shallow as uncertainty engulfed her mind.

Massimino ascended the steps to the altar and stood directly in front of Emilia, close enough that their bodies slightly touched. He gently caressed her cheek before brushing hair behind her ear, inhaling as he did so; smiling.

"How I have longed for this moment," Massimino whispered as his intense gaze caught hers.

"Me too," she whispered breathlessly, realizing just how true that was. "Is this real?"

Massimino shifted, now pressed firmly against Emilia and sandwiching her between the hard stone and the warmth of his body. His earthy scent was like a drug as she pressed her hand against his chest, needing to feel him. She'd already been conditioned to become aroused by this man, and Emilia worried it wouldn't take much to give in to him.

His nose grazed Emilia's. "It has all been real—in some way—but if you are asking if we both are now physically in the same time and space together, then the answer is yes."

Emilia closed her eyes and opened her mouth, tilting her head slightly and moving closer. Massimino responded in kind, and they embraced while sharing a kiss. It deepened into something much more as her fingers crawled up his back, into his hair. Massimino encircled her waist, inching up her jacket and the sweater underneath. They finally broke apart, both panting heavily; Emilia could feel his breath on her forehead.

"I can't understand why I feel this way," she gasped. "I don't even know you."

Massimino smirked. "Emilia, we are each other's destiny, and we know each other better than many others ever will. You already know this to be true. Embrace it and surrender yourself to this, freely and completely. These feelings within you are good, are they not?"

"I *feel* it so deeply," she whispered like it was a secret. "Everything you say burns in me—and yes, it *does* feel good. It just doesn't make any sense."

"Not everything in this world makes sense, my Emilia." His voice vibrated through her. "Surrender yourself to this; you know deep within that it must be this way."

"Please help me make sense of it all. I need you to do that, Massimino. These dreams, this past week has all been so...unbelievable. You must help me understand what it is you want and *why...*" She was determined not to cry as she glanced behind her. "Why should I be okay with what you...do to me on this very altar?"

Massimino paused, looking to the daggers then out the window above them. "You are starting now to learn of your abilities, who you really are, and who your family was. You come from a long line of women able to bend the world to their will."

"You mean the wind and fire?" she asked. "I've been practicing what you showed me, and the old woman in the woods was telling me some things about my powers, too."

Massimino's eyes widened. "The old woman in the woods? She has spoken with you?" His relaxed tone gave way to a snappy response and he appeared alarmed.

"Yes. She told me more about my family."

"And what did she say about me?"

"Well, nothing...she didn't even mention you," Emilia replied.

"Is that so?" His head tilted, stroking Emilia's cheek, contemplating her.

"Please Massimino, tell me more about the dreams." She wouldn't let him distract her.

Massimino grinned. "The ritual I have shared with you is a way for us to connect—deeply. To merge our powers, our abilities; to strengthen us so we can be a part of each other forever." He cupped her chin and leaned into her, swiping his tongue across her lips and sending her into a frenzy.

Though her body tingled, her sex throbbed, and she felt as though she would bend to any request he bestowed upon her, Emilia pushed past her desire in the quest for answers.

"But...you stab me with a dagger—*that* dagger." She pointed to the weapons on the wall before staring at Massimino. "Do I die?"

He looked toward the daggers then the altar. "The ritual is a complex one. You must trust me—it is what is necessary and what is best," he answered quietly.

"Massimino, that doesn't answer my question at all." She sighed.

He turned back to Emilia and stroked her face, gazing intently into her eyes. Emilia felt a warm sensation flood through her body, calming and peaceful, erasing any will she might have felt to resist or protest.

"Emilia, do you trust me?"

Emilia swallowed hard. "Yes."

"Emilia, will you surrender yourself willingly to me when the time comes?"

Her lips quivered slightly. "I...I don't know. I don't think—"

Massimino leaned down, and Emilia closed her eyes as they kissed tenderly at first, then with increasing passion as Emilia set the pace. Breath ragged, Massimino broke their kiss and drew away, eliciting a disappointed moan from Emilia, who opened her eyes only to plead with them.

"Come now, it will be dark soon. Let us prepare for dinner." He took her hand and gently pulled her with him toward the chapel's entrance.

"It's still cloudy," she observed as they walked back along the winding path, gazing up to the sky. "The stars and the moon were spectacular last night—if it stays like this though, we won't be able to see them."

"The days are gray here, but at night the stars always shine." Massimino stopped walking and let go of Emilia's hand.

He stood still with his eyes closed, concentrating on something she couldn't guess. "Look up," Massimino instructed as he remained still.

To her astonishment, Emilia watched as the clouds were swept from the skies, dispersing beyond the valley. In their place was a perfectly clear expanse with a handful of faint twinkling stars that were already visible in the fading light.

"How...did you...? Can I do that, too?" Emilia's eyes were wide with wonder as she looked to Massimino, who was smiling back at her. "Please teach me all of this. I can't believe it's all real!"

"Slow down." He grinned, amused at first. Then it became a wicked smirk and Emilia had to revert her gaze to the sky. "Of course. I would love to teach you all I know, but it begins with the ritual."

"That can't be the *only* way. You were showing me the other night in that dream—you know, one of the...fun ones," Emilia retorted. "I'm a great student. Look: I've even been practicing."

Raising and rotating her hand for effect, she conjured up a brisk wind which encircled the pair, drawing them close.

Massimino's eyes opened a little wider with surprise. "I am impressed, Emilia. So much progress so quickly, and without anyone mentoring you in these ways. But you need to remember, these tricks with the wind are *easy* compared to the far more complex abilities—entering another's mind, particularly over a great distance, for example."

As they came upon the castle courtyard, Emilia found the area was now illuminated with torches, casting long, erratic shadows.

"Will you teach me, *please?*" Emilia begged playfully as they approached the center.

Massimino halted as they reached the point where their paths would diverge; Emilia stopped as well, looking at him expectantly.

"My Emilia, the answer to your question is the ritual," Massimino cooed. "By merging our souls together, the outcome of what we can accomplish could be limitless. I am afraid I must now part from you temporarily. I have some business to attend, but we will dine together in the main hall."

"But I'm supposed to be having dinner with the town administrator tonight—the lawyer, Martin Thiess, arranged it."

Massimino chuckled. "I control everything around here. It was I who instructed Martin to invite you to dinner."

Emilia laughed, trying to conceal her cheeks blushing. "Oh, of course...I should have realized."

"Go now and prepare. I have arranged for a gift to be delivered to your chambers, and for your sister also. I will see you again soon."

The thought of parting ways left a sinking feeling in the pit of Emilia's belly. Why did she feel so connected to him? Was it because he knew about her family and could give her more answers about her past? Was it the incredible way he made her body pulse with lust? Perhaps it was the power he displayed, the way he could control the elements at his will. Maybe he would teach her how to master powers of her very own. He felt like a magnet she couldn't pull away from and she found herself wrapping her arms around his neck, closing her eyes, and eagerly kissing him.

"I'll go to my chamber..." Emilia breathed the words into his mouth, "...but only if you join me." In that moment, there was nothing he could not take from her—not even her very life—that would quell her desire to have him inside her in every possible way.

Massimino grinned. He responded without words as he grabbed Emilia by the hand and led her toward the castle. Faster and faster they moved, Emilia struggling to keep up as the stairs, the halls, even the world around blurred into nothingness as the excitement, anticipation and primal passion burned within her.

With nothing more than a swift wave of his hand, the doors to Emilia's chamber burst open, his pace not slowing until they reached the bedroom. He released her hand and turned to face her; chest heaving as she softly panted.

"This is real, you're real...this is really going to happen..."

"Yes," Massimino's eyes shone as if he'd just been told the world was his and his alone. He smiled. "Come to me, Emilia."

Eagerly advancing toward Massimino as if she had no free will of her own, Emilia pulled off her jacket and flung it away. The pair embraced and leaned into each other, enraptured in an intensely passionate kiss. As their lips locked and tongues explored each other's mouths a swirl of wind encircled them both, lifting them from the ground and carrying them through the air toward the bed.

Emilia couldn't help but giggle at the unique sensation; their clothes flew free from their bodies mid-air before they landed gently atop her mattress.

"No, wait," Emilia protested playfully, "Let me see if I can do that." Emilia fought the fiery heat within her and concentrated as Massimino watched her curiously. A sudden burst of wind, surprising them both, lifted the pair from the bed and spun them so Emilia was now on top as they crashed back onto the bed.

Emilia laughed, her body bouncing as her hair swished, tickling Massimino's face; surprise melting into a smile as he let out a deep chuckle of his own.

"Hmmm, I guess I'll need to practice that move," she giggled, "For now, I don't mind being on top."

Before Massimino could respond Emilia straddled him, and pushed downward, gasping as she slowly felt all of him inside her, the sensation overwhelming as her body began to buck and writhe, driven by lust and pure carnal instinct. Emilia moaned, their bodies so rhythmic, fingers entwined, so desperately in need to be with the other. *Inside* the other. He slammed her, grunting as a wild beast would as it devoured its prey until they climaxed together, panting feverishly, the heat of Massimino's orgasm pulsating within her.

Emilia crashed into Massimino's chest, feeling the sweaty sheen of their skin touching as she locked her lips with his, her body, still working on instinct, continued to slowly grind her hips on him.

"Massimino…that was incredible." Emilia panted as another wave of ecstasy washed over her body causing her to shudder.

Emilia rolled to her side, inhaling sharply; emptiness remained as he withdrew, though she still felt his essence within her. She allowed her head to sink into the soft feathery pillow and rolled over to look at him.

Usually a picture of composure in her dreams, Massimino appeared uncharacteristically disheveled, his hair mussed, his chest rising and falling rapidly. Emilia could somehow feel how fast his heart was beating though she was not touching him.

"Yes…that was…it has been a very long time since…I have experienced that level of…intensity…" Massimino turned away from Emilia, gazing toward the windows, the moon visible in the darkening sky beyond them.

Emilia propped herself up, her elbow on the pillow, resting her head against her hand while caressing Massimino's chest with the other, feeling his hair between her fingers and lightly digging her nails into his skin.

"Mmm, I want more of this with you Massimino," Emilia purred. "Maybe we can wait a while on this whole ritual thing…?"

Massimino sighed as he turned to face her, his expression flat. "I wish we could, but the road that has led us here offers no possibility to turn back now."

Emilia searched him, her lips parting in a playful smile.

"I must go, there are things I must…tend to." Massimino moved to the edge of the bed and stood, Emilia's hand falling onto the mattress.

With a swirl of wind Massimino's robe flew across the room to his outstretched hand, he deftly donned it, tying the rope as he turned back to Emilia.

"I will see you at dinner—do not forget to look in your dressing room."

Emilia blinked in confusion at the sight of Massimino disappearing; a window popped open. A moment later, a raven's craw pierced her ears and a blur of black feathers took the form of a bird. It gazed at her with pitch-black eyes before it jumped from the window ledge and soared through the air until it was gone.

Whoa.

In a palatial four-poster bed, entangled in the bedding with pillows too numerous to count, and covers pulled in every which direction, Emilia grinned and clenched her toes into the smooth sheets. The scent of lavender filled the room though it's calming qualities did little to soothe her; she felt fire inside—flames burning like those in the fireplace opposite where she lay.

Oh my God, this is real…all of it!

Chapter Thirty-Nine

"**E**mmi!" Amanda shouted.

Emilia opened her eyes and they immediately darted around the room. She was naked, and her sex still throbbed from her encounter with Massimino. The sheets were burgundy silk and the fireplace was roaring with purpose. Massimino was gone. She was in a palatial bed in her aunt's chamber in the castle.

Standing, she grabbed a silk robe from the edge of the bed and called back to her sister, "Yeah?"

Amanda burst in. "Oh my God. You're *never* going to believe this."

"Believe what?" Emilia asked impatiently, frustrated by the abrupt return to practical matters following the intense satisfaction of her afternoon tryst.

Amanda stepped closer and hissed, "Thiess. He's lying to you!"

"What do you—"

"The mines are *full* of gold—*hundreds* of millions. He's working on a plan to demolish the town and reopen the mines; that's why he's trying to trick you into signing it all over so quickly. Wouldn't surprise me if this mysterious company is his own, or at least some made-up company that belongs to his friends. Either way, he's up to no damn good."

"No way." Emilia was astonished. "How did you find all of that out?"

Amanda relayed the details of her afternoon session with one of the consultants named Derrick; they agreed to confront Thiess over dinner.

Candles had been lit on elaborate candelabras all around Emilia's chamber, and the two fireplaces blazed ambiently, creating a warm atmosphere.

"Wow, look at this place!" Amanda said. She glanced at Emilia, covering up in her black silk robe. "So, how was your afternoon? You look...relaxed. Got some rest? What happened to the bed, more sleep rage?"

Emilia rubbed her fingers along the robe, admiring it before her eyes wandered to an open wardrobe where an elegant, one-shoulder, hand-sewn red satin gown hung.

"It's beautiful!" Emilia gasped, as she removed the dress from the hanger and held it in front of her. "What do you think?"

Amanda looked puzzled. "Spectacular, Emmi. Is it one of your aunt's? She had good taste! Maybe you could wear it in Paris...not so appropriate to meet with Thiess and the town administrator in something this sexy, is it?"

Emilia looked at Amanda, eyes wide as she bit her lip. "I have some news too..."

"Oh?"

"I, um...met Massimino this afternoon." Emilia gazed at her sister, speaking quickly before she could react. "He's real and he's here—and we're having dinner with him tonight; he told me there would be a surprise in my room, and this must be it. He said there'd be one for you, too!"

"Wait, *what?* Forget about dresses—did you say you *met* Massimino? He's *real?*" Amanda stared at her sister like she had sprouted another limb.

"This afternoon, when you went to the inn, I went to the building we saw from the tower, the one Rose didn't want to take us to...it's a chapel—the one from my dreams, and...Massimino was there."

Amanda shook her head as she sat on the bed. "Emilia, you're *seriously* freaking me out right now. How can you be so calm about all of this?

You remember what happens in your dreams, right? He's some sort of crazed murderer."

"No, no, it's so not like that," Emilia defended him immediately. "He's...he loves me. Ugh, I know it sounds strange—everything here is—but somehow, on some level, I think I was kind of expecting he would be here. I think I've been searching for him, subconsciously or something..." Amanda didn't look any less concerned. "I'm sorry, I know none of this makes any sense."

"Well that's the understatement of the year," Amanda retorted in a fierce whisper. "And what the hell do you mean he *loves you*? You don't even *know* him. And the nightmares—what if he's really like *that*?"

"I don't understand it myself," Emilia sighed. "The dreams, this place, Massimino...everything feels so surreal."

Amanda took a deep breath. "Okay, let's sit down for a minute." She guided Emilia by the hand to an antique sofa facing one of the fireplaces. "All right, so you're not dreaming. I'm here too and can vouch for that."

"Yeah, okay."

"Are you sure you didn't just lie down for a nap this afternoon and have another dream about Massimino?"

"No. I went straight to the chapel after I came back up here." She was sure of it. "When I got there, it was different than in the dreams— pale and gray—but everything else was the same. Even the...daggers. I was looking around and then Massimino turned up."

"Did he try to hurt you?" she asked.

"No, nothing like that. We just talked—well, at first anyway." Her face heated. "We kissed too. And he showed me some...magic. God, I want him, Amanda. Like, I *really* want him—we made love and it was...incredible, I can't describe it. It's this crazy powerful attraction, but it's somehow deeper than that, too. He says it's our destiny to be together and I kind of believe him—I feel it too. When I think about all the trouble I've had opening up to other guys, you know, and how things never seem to work out? It's the opposite with Massimino, I want to give him...*everything.*"

"Um...all right." Amanda tried to remain impartial to her sister's seemingly child-like emotions. "And what about Olly?"

"Oh, Olly!" Emilia clutched her chest as if to tame the emotions stirring inside her; with Massimino no longer a figment of her imagination, Oliver hadn't entered her mind. "He's great...I really do like him, but this feeling with Massimino is something else. It's like a fire in me, burning and multiplied by a thousand or something."

"Whoa, Emmi." Amanda's concerned eyes searched her sister. "I've never seen you like this. Sure sounds...interesting, especially considering you just met the man *today*—the same one you've been dreaming about." She seemed to be saying it all out loud to convince herself. "Wait, what do you mean by *magic*, exactly?"

"I've been wanting to tell you...it seemed too bizarre though, and I just didn't know how to say it." Emilia was willing to divulge everything now that Massimino was real and she wasn't crazy. "It started in one of the dreams—but I can do it here, too. Remember the fire the other night and the broken bottle? Well, I did that."

"Emmi, what do you mean?" Amanda wrapped her arms around her middle. "I'm really getting worried. Did that old woman do something to you? It was bizarre what happened in her cottage—maybe that's it?"

"No, no...she just knows the truth; I was controlling the fire," she explained. "And I made the wind knock the bottle off the table."

Amanda stared blankly at her. "Can you hear yourself? What *are* you talking about? I think maybe the lack of sleep or the stress of everything going on is catching up with you or something. What you're saying just doesn't make *any* sense." Amanda embraced her sister as if trying to squeeze the rationality back into her.

"I know, I totally get how this all must sound," Emilia added. "I can hardly believe it either...but—" Her gaze wandered to the flames in front of them. "Okay, watch this. Look at the fire in the fireplace."

Closing her eyes, Emilia slowed her breathing as she concentrated on one section of the logs. Opening her palms, she lifted her right hand and waved it back and forth, creating a gentle sway amongst the flames. Amanda released her arms from around her sister, blinking as she watched Emilia control the flow of the fire.

"No way," Amanda whispered, spellbound by the motion. "Okay, Miss Magician, show me how you stop it."

Emilia ceased moving her hand, holding it still in front of her for a few moments as the flames stood on end, awaiting their next command. She dropped her hand and the fire returned to its random rhythm.

"Holy shit! So, I'm starting to feel even more freaked out now." Emilia could feel her sister shaking, struggling to hide it. "What's going on?"

"Honestly, I'm freaking myself out, but it *is* real. Watch, I can do it again—and I'm getting better and better at it, too." Once more, Emilia directed the flames, mesmerizing Amanda in the process before demonstrating her ability to summon and control the wind inside the closed chambers.

"*Whoa.* This is next level." Amanda stammered. "I...I don't even know what to say. Could we both be dreaming here?" She appeared rattled by the experience.

"I don't think so. Massimino said these abilities have been in my family forever and that with some practice, I could improve even more *and* learn other magic, too. He said the way to understand it all faster is to complete the ritual—the one that happened in the dreams."

Amanda froze, eyes wide. "The one where he kills you? With the dagger? In the chapel?"

"Yeah."

"Well that doesn't make any sense, does it?"

"No. But none of this does. I need to talk to him more about it, I guess. Plus, I think Gerlinde knows more than she's letting on. I could try talking to her again, too."

Amanda sighed and slumped into the sofa. Finally, she sat up, straightened herself, and looked into Emilia's eyes. "I don't know what to tell you. As if the past few days haven't been…unbelievable enough, now you're saying Massimino is real and he's coming to dinner tonight and that you have some sort of magical powers, too?"

Emilia nodded slowly.

"Then I want to meet him. There's nothing else to say right now." Amanda threw her hands in the air, obviously frazzled. "This is just…I don't even know what this is."

"Okay." Emilia felt butterflies flapping around inside her. "He said he'd be there, and I'm kind of excited for you to meet him!"

"All right…" Amanda reluctantly agreed. "Let's see where this all leads, I suppose. But no daggers or churches tonight. Promise?"

Emilia giggled as she ran her hand over the red silk of the stunning fitted gown she'd laid on the arm of the couch. "Okay, promise. I know I wasn't wearing *this* dress in my dreams, so it should be safe." She winked.

"Oh, Emmi, what *have* you gotten us into? This was supposed to be a chill trip to Europe to claim some family heirlooms," quipped Amanda, shaking her head at the strange place and unbelievable circumstances they'd found themselves in.

The entrance to the main dining hall was dramatically lit by candles and elaborate candelabras. Tea lights were speckled across the mantel and even the torches mounted on the walls had been set ablaze. Light spilled across the floor in front of the large, open double doors and the sound of a piano playing classical music grew louder as the girls approached.

Emilia had finished dressing in the gown Massimino had provided; it was a plunging v-neckline with an open back, and the rich red satin fabric felt sensual; it contrasted spectacularly with her fair skin. Emilia had found some spectacular jewelry in her aunt's dresser and decided on a cascading diamond leaf pattern necklace to complete her look.

She felt like royalty. As she'd suspected, Amanda found an equally elegant gown in her room—it was emerald, with a sweetheart neckline and a mermaid silhouette saturated with sequins that glimmered in the candlelight. She had gotten ready in record time.

As they entered the room, Emilia spotted Massimino and the lawyer; both men stood from the impressively long table to greet them. Massimino had dressed in a dark, impeccably tailored vintage suit, while Thiess appeared rather crinkled in the same tweed jacket and pants he'd been in since meeting with the girls earlier in the day.

Massimino smiled, making his way over. "My goodness." He took her hands. "It is quite possible you are the most beautiful woman to have ever walked these halls."

Emilia had no time to acknowledge the compliment as Massimino swept her into his arms, pulling her close and kissing her. His tongue invaded her mouth and she was shocked at how easily she yielded to him—in front of her sister and in public, no less. She also allowed his hand to travel to her behind, squeezing her firm flesh through the fabric.

When she finally surfaced, Emilia spotted Amanda over his shoulder; she looked stunned at such an open display.

"I'm sorry." Massimino grinned as he took a step back, eyes never leaving Emilia's. "I could not help myself."

Emilia inhaled sharply, face as red as her dress for more than one reason. "No...it's fine," was all she could manage.

Torn between the heat he had stirred within her and what was decent, Emilia backed away so he could greet her sister.

"And you must be Amanda." Massimino turned his attention to her, taking Amanda's hand and drawing it to his mouth, where he kissed it tenderly.

"Yes, I'm Amanda." Emilia couldn't recall her sister's voice ever being so squeaky. "And you are the mysterious Massimino I've been hearing *so* much about."

"Indeed, I am." Massimino smirked.

"Nice suit." Amanda remarked, composing herself as she appraised her sister's mysterious suitor.

"Why thank you…tailoring such as this is a dying art, I'm afraid."

Everyone went quiet for a moment, before Amanda broke the silence with her humor.

"So, he *does* exist." Amanda leaned toward Emilia, who smiled back at her, biting her bottom lip. "And he's hot," she added in a loud whisper.

Massimino laughed before returning to Emilia. Hand on the small of her back, he guided her toward the end of the table.

The dining hall was opulent and befitting of the rest of the castle. More torches were lit along all the walls, bathing the space in an orange-yellow hue, while roaring fires burned in the mammoth fireplaces at each end. Glowing candles attached to several candelabra chandeliers hung from heavy chains above the table, and a solo pianist sat playing a grand piano in the corner at the opposite end of where they were heading.

"Hello again, Emilia, Amanda," Thiess greeted as they approached. "I trust your day was pleasant and you were able to explore the village?"

"Yes, Mr. Thiess," answered Emilia with a displeased expression, biting her tongue to hold back all she wanted to say to the lawyer. "We learned a *lot* today. Zillah is a very interesting place—all sorts of hidden treasures to uncover, it seems."

"Very good, very good." Thiess didn't appear to be listening, or maybe he was too concerned with his hand; while it looked to have been redressed with fresh bandages, the man still appeared to be experiencing an uncomfortable level of pain. "I'm sure you could see there is not so much potential for a happy future here."

Emilia could swear she saw Massimino smiling at his discomfort while he treated the limb like it was a bubble about to burst.

"Here." Thiess handed a large folder of paperwork to Emilia. "I have done as you asked and congratulate you as the full, registered, and rightful owner of all you see—a crumbling village and decrepit castle surrounded by mountains that deem it difficult to access and impossible to even make a phone call—otherwise known as Zillah! My trip down the mountain today was successful, and this is your confirmation of that."

"I thank you very much, Mr. Thiess." Emilia took the folder but didn't bother opening it, sensing that at least that part of Thiess' comment was truthful.

"I...ah..." Thiess went on, mouth distorted in a scowl that could have been from pain or frustration. "I was also able to speak with the representatives from Graben Holdings." He grimaced again, letting out half a grunt. "They understand you would like more time to consider their offer and have graciously agreed to allow you to respond by tomorrow. It is as far as I could push the deadline, I'm afraid." This time, Thiess didn't bother hiding his anguish, jaw clenched and squeezing his eyes shut for a moment. "I do hope this can be suitable for you and that we can finalize this matter." He was unable to stifle an audible gasp, muscles going rigid at what Emilia assumed was another wave of pain.

"Martin, my friend," Massimino said, taking command of the conversation with his soft words. "Please, you are going to hurt yourself badly if you continue. I suggest we let this matter go for now."

Thiess opened his mouth to protest but instead plastered on a false smile. Reaching into his pocket, he retrieved a couple of pills and washed them down with his glass of wine.

"Tonight, we must celebrate the return of the heiress, Emilia, to her home," Massimino announced, clapping twice.

A young woman with black hair and pale skin appeared from the hallway that led to the kitchen. As they had seen on others who worked in the castle, the girl wore a plain dress made of sheer fabric. She seemed envious as she looked to them, then scuttled to Massimino's side.

"Yes, Master," she whispered.

Emilia and Amanda glanced at each other; eyebrows raised at the unexpected greeting.

"Emilia, your family still has some exceptional vintages in the cellar." Massimino had barely taken his eyes off her since she'd entered the room. "Might I suggest a champagne toast?"

Emilia nodded. "That sounds perfect. Yes please."

"Ilsa, our lost heiress has returned." He didn't glance at the young woman. "Please fetch a bottle of champagne from the cellar at once, and another of this red wine as well."

"Of course, I will be right back." Ilsa nodded and bowed to him as she turned and left the room. Emilia spotted the ties along the back of her dress, which could easily be undone and didn't seem practical.

"Massimino," she said, "The way the young women are dressed within the castle. Why so...*revealing?*"

"We are blessed with some beautiful young women in the village, and that beauty should be celebrated, not hidden." Massimino shrugged with an unapologetic smile. "That is my belief anyway. Besides, they enjoy it as well. Their attire in the castle also helps to facilitate the *special* relationship I share with them."

"Oh...really?" replied Emilia, feeling a pang of jealously stream through her.

"It sounds like one big sexual harassment lawsuit waiting to happen if you ask me," added Amanda, unamused.

"I assure you that all of the women are quite willing in their participation," Massimino said to her, no change in tone or expression. "It is a pleasurable experience for all involved. Please, Emilia," he turned to her. "You should not feel jealousy—none can hold a candle to you." Massimino smiled knowingly. "It is a custom here in the village, and one that I appreciate may be difficult for someone raised elsewhere to understand. It is the way it has been for a very long time and one of the reasons we make efforts to limit interactions with outsiders."

"Well, you're correct in saying it is very difficult to understand," Amanda wasn't satisfied with his answer. "Things like this are certainly not acceptable where we come from. Right, Emmi?"

Emilia did not speak; she just nodded her head in agreement.

"So, Amanda," Massimino decided to change the subject and Emilia felt better already. "Apart from these matters, what do you think of our humble village? I dare venture that it is quite a bit different than you're used to in many ways."

"Ah, yeah, that would be putting it mildly." Emilia shot her a look and when her sister next spoke, she was less sarcastic. "Emilia and I spent some time today with a lovely woman, Rose, who showed us around the village and the castle. I'm sure it was a lovely place once; why has it been so neglected? Aren't you responsible for running the town? Why haven't you done anything about it?"

"Amanda!" Emilia scolded, embarrassed that she was asking him such probing questions when they'd just met. Then again, she reasoned as her face flushed, she'd done a lot more with Massimino in a much shorter amount of time.

"No, Emilia. It is all right," Massimino calmly replied with a dismissive hand gesture. "It is a good question your sister asks. I am sure she is simply looking out for you."

He grinned warmly at her then turned back to Amanda.

"I came to this valley a very long time ago. Almost since my arrival, I have helped Emilia's family—the Blagdens—look after the village. The condition of things is neither accident nor incompetence, I can assure you. Privacy and seclusion have been preferable in lieu of more public interaction with the outside world." Massimino gave her a slight shrug. "The state of things here has been a result of that preference, thereby also perpetuating it."

"This is why you would be very wise to rid yourself of this massive liability," added Thiess. "To restore it would be a tremendous financial burden."

"Uh-huh," Amanda said, not bothering to stifle her attitude toward him. "How do you two know each other anyway?"

"I have known Martin for many years now," Massimino said. "Since he was a much younger man."

"Massimino here does not seem to have aged a single day from when I first met him," Thiess interjected. "It makes no sense at all to me!"

"My good friend Martin is quite the resourceful man. He assists me in circumstances where I must interact with the outside world. Our relationship began some time ago—he helped me acquire a rare and sought-after book. Since then he has also aided me in procuring even more precious things…and people—such as finding you, Emilia." Massimino took her hand.

Ilsa returned carrying a tray with the champagne and wine bottles along with four glasses. She proceeded to pour and hand out the drinks.

"Thank you, Ilsa," Massimino said as she waited by his side. "Now, please tell Mrs. Rossi that we are ready for our meal."

Once the young woman had disappeared back into the kitchen, Massimino raised his glass. "Allow me to propose a toast to the return of our long-lost heiress! This is a most joyous occasion. To Emilia!"

All four clinked glasses and proceeded to sip their champagne.

Chapter Forty

For the second consecutive night, a steady stream of villagers filed into the butcher shop and down to the basement. As the last of the group took their seats, Enzo made sure to lock the door before descending the creaky stairs.

"I appreciate you coming again tonight," he said once he was at the front of the room. "I know we weren't expecting to meet again until the ritual tomorrow, but Pia has some information that is very alarming, and I thought you should all hear it."

Pia stood from her seat and looked around the room; everyone stared curiously back at her, save for one or two villagers, whose body language suggested they'd rather be elsewhere.

Pia informed the group that she'd overheard Thiess talking with the mining men and that he planned to demolish the village—that everyone would have to leave.

The room was suddenly a flurry of urgent conversation.

"Why would he do that?" asked one villager over the noise. "It doesn't make any sense."

The room fell quiet again, everyone listening intently for an answer.

"It's something about the mining being easier and cheaper that way," Pia went on. "He wants the gold that's still in the mines—and he hates this village and all of us."

"Are you sure? Can he even do that?" called another villager.

"What I've heard is that he's been pressuring the heiress to sign over the village to him before the ritual," said Enzo. "If she does that, he'll be the owner. He could do anything he wants."

"Can't we just stop her from signing it over?" suggested another villager. "The ritual is tomorrow night; we'd only have to delay it for a day."

"She's the last Blagden, who knows what would happen to our village then? We could be forced to leave anyway."

There was silence for a few moments, then Enzo replied, "I don't know what would happen in that situation, but I think the bigger problem would be Massimino. What I understand is that he promised the village to Mr. Thiess for his help in finding the heiress and bringing her here. I think he'd be very upset if we were to interfere with those plans—we could all pay dearly."

"We'll just have to stop him," a villager demanded. "We'll refuse to leave."

"Or maybe it's time we left anyway," another suggested. "I would've left and taken my family long ago if we'd been allowed."

The group's reactions varied, some agreeing and some vehemently opposed to being forced to leave their homes and businesses.

"Maybe there is another way." Gerlinde stood from her seat and although she spoke softly, her voice carried a weight that brought the room to a hush. She had been waiting patiently to bring up her idea.

"What other way?" asked Enzo.

"The heiress."

"What about her?" called one of the villagers.

"Her powers, her abilities—they are stronger than I ever felt in her family before. She doesn't know what she is doing with them or how to control them, but if we can help her—"

"Her family has been enslaved by Massimino for so many generations," interrupted a woman from the center of the group. "If what you say is possible, why have none of the others ever done so? Massimino is far stronger than they have ever been. You can't tell me that this heiress is stronger than he is."

"It is true that Massimino is stronger," Gerlinde allowed, back hunched in a permanent stoop. "Far stronger than she—"

"Then *how* could she defeat him?" the woman insisted. "We all know the things he is capable of."

"The ritual is the key," Gerlinde explained. "For it to work, he—they *both*—will need to open themselves up and let down any resistance to each other. I know everyone here will remember what results when that does not happen."

A regretful murmur of agreement spread across the group.

"In that vulnerable state, it *may* be possible," Gerlinde said, leaning on the chair in front of her for support. "If she is indeed strong enough, she may be able to end his life."

Every heart in the room skipped a beat at the mere possibility of an end to the sorcerer's reign.

"But she must be under his spell by now," someone pointed out. "Even if this could work, how can we be sure she will agree to it?"

"I'll need to help her." Gerlinde's sharp eyes addressed the villagers. "I know that her strength has been draining Massimino of late, even still this will not be easy, but perhaps it is possible. I am willing to do all I can to help right this wrong."

"And let us not forget that Thiess has no power of his own," a man said. "Once Massimino has left, what is to stop us from simply making him *disappear*? He wouldn't be the first to go down a mine around here and never come back out."

"But the heiress." Rose stood and scanned the room. "Surely, if there is a chance we can save her, we must take it? Besides, if we kill Mr. Thiess, we don't know what will happen to our village. The best option is to help Emilia."

"If we help her and she fails, Massimino will kill us all and he will *never* leave this place. Thiess may be bad, but he is a man and we can work something out with him," suggested one villager.

"My heart tells me to help the heiress," said another. "That is the best outcome for all of us. I have not met her, but if Pia and Rose say she is kind, I trust and believe them. And if she was not under the control of Massimino, maybe she would do good here and our lives could improve."

"But Massimino is just too powerful for this to work—if we try that and fail, it will be a disaster."

The crowd burst into a string of loud chatter which made it difficult for anyone to concentrate or hear. Gerlinde gave her aching ankles a break and sat down, deciding to wait out the noise.

"*Quiet! Quiet!*" called Enzo from the front of the room.

The boisterous conversations became intermittent whispers.

"I would also like to help the young heiress," Enzo continued, "but we have to face reality here; I can't see how one so young, so inexperienced could defeat a force such as Massimino. I believe we must do whatever we can to rid ourselves of him, and this may be our *only* chance so we must take it. We can work out whatever new problems may arise, but they can't be worse than this one."

They pondered the options before them in muffled silence.

"I truly believe this is possible and that the young heiress can defeat him." Gerlinde stood again, hands gripping the chair. "She is strong, and I think that her inexperience may be an asset in this fight. The other members of her family were controlled by Massimino and under his influence since they were young. She hasn't suffered this. Yes, he does have *some* hold over her, but I can help her to break free from this and teach her what she must know. This *can* be possible."

"Let us not forget, old woman," a villager from the front said, craning her neck in her seat to face Gerlinde, "that it was *your* past follies that caused this mess in the first place. I have a difficult time trusting your ideas. I think we must do what is practical; wishing our way out of it will not—*cannot*—work."

"Please, please, everyone," Enzo called for order once again. "We will talk around in circles all night at this rate. We know the options available to us and we all understand the benefits and risks of each. I think the only way we can proceed is to vote. By show of hands, who believes that helping the heiress is the best way?"

The room was mostly still, but Gerlinde and Rose raised their hands.

"All right," said Enzo. "And those who believe we should help Massimino complete the ritual?"

Some looked toward Enzo while others peered around the room, but eventually the remaining ten hands were all raised—including his.

"Very well." Enzo's expression was grim. "The decision is overwhelmingly in favor of carrying out the ritual. Rose, Gerlinde, I'm sorry. I think I speak for many here when I say I wish this could be your way, but the risk and the price of failure is just too high. I need to be sure you will both do your part and support the group's decision."

Together, they solemnly nodded, Rose also mouthing *'yes'* before her head slumped, and she stared at her feet.

"Please, go home now and get some rest," Enzo said, bringing the meeting to a close. "I am afraid tomorrow will be a dark and difficult day. We must be prepared and at the chapel before midnight. Goodnight to you all."

The group stood and left the basement without uttering a word, many avoiding eye contact as they shuffled past the chairs, up the creaking stairs, and out into the night.

As the villagers dispersed in different directions around the square, Gerlinde followed Rose as she headed back to her restaurant.

"Rose, I must speak with you," she hissed, scuffling up behind her and clutching her arm with her frail, bony hands.

Rose appeared startled as she turned to face Gerlinde. "Ah yes, what is it?"

There was no time to waste. Tightening her fingers around the woman's coat, Gerlinde said, "I need you to help me."

"Please, let go of me…" She swatted her hand away, but the request seemed to outweigh Rose's fear. "What do you need help with?"

"We must try and save the heiress. *Please*, I can't do this alone."

"But what can we do?" Rose's eyebrows drew together. "We have already agreed to help in the ritual. The rest of the group will not be swayed—perhaps one or two, but most are too scared and will never budge."

"They won't have to," Gerlinde explained, "and I'm not suggesting that we don't fulfill our obligations. I just want to find a way to give the heiress a chance."

"What are you saying?" Rose had lowered her voice.

"I must speak with the heiress, but I can't go to the castle." She glanced upward at the hulking structure. "He would never permit it. But you can go—will you go there tomorrow? I need you to bring her to me. To my cottage."

Rose looked anxiously around the square; Gerlinde saw there were a few people around in the sparsely lit area and none seemed to be paying them any attention. "I…I don't know…"

Gerlinde persisted. "I know you want to save her too—this may be the only way."

"I…" Rose gulped. "I will think about it. You must go now, before someone sees."

Rose turned back toward her restaurant and Gerlinde limped her way across the square, beginning the long, dark trek back to her cottage in the woods.

Chapter Forty-One

T he conversation in the castle's dining hall turned to more general chatter about the village and some of its residents before Mrs. Rossi—wearing a plain brown dress, apron and hair pulled into a bun—appeared with Ilsa carrying trays filled with food, which they placed on the table. They thanked and excused the two women before enjoying their meal: local roasted goat with herb stuffing, green beans, roasted potatoes, pan carrots, and a red wine au jus.

During dinner, Emilia and Amanda talked about their lives in America while Massimino shared some interesting historical facts about Zillah, and then somehow, they landed on the topic of magic.

Massimino demonstrated his power of the flames around the room, performing quite an enchanting display. Amanda, however, sensed this playful exhibition was something to fear.

Emilia's desire for Massimino seemingly grew with each word he spoke, and Amanda began to feel this was not an altogether natural attraction. As impossible as it would have seemed to her a few days earlier, the only logical explanation was that her sister was being manipulated by Massimino—under his spell.

Following a toxic cocktail of alcohol and uncontrolled doses of pain killers, the conversation took a dramatic turn when Thiess, appearing increasingly inebriated, raised the topic of transferring the title of the village again.

"I do not understand your reluctance to accept the offer," he grumbled. "Surely by now you have realized that keeping this place is not an option. Will you sign the transfer paperwork tonight—or at least in the morning so I may leave tomorrow to advise the company and they may commence their work?" Thiess' words were somewhat slurred, his demeanor aggressive.

"Martin, my friend, please." Massimino frowned. "Now is not the time for such discussions."

"This matter should have been completed by now, Massimino." Thiess' voice had taken on a hard edge. "You know as well as I do that this needs to be done before tomorrow or else—"

"Or else what, Mr. Thiess?" Emilia's tone exuded frustration and Amanda was happy she was sticking up for herself. "Why is this so urgent? You still haven't been able to answer this simple question. At least not in a way that makes any sense. If I am stuck with a worthless village—as you claim—what does that matter to you?"

"Massimino, are you going to do something here?" Thiess spat, almost yelling.

"Martin, please calm down and be patient." Massimino fixed him with his intense blue eyes, but he remained cordial. "This is neither the time nor the way to your goal."

"And exactly what goal is that, Mr. Thiess?" Amanda snapped, then directed her focus on Massimino. "And what's your part in this, oh mysterious one?"

Massimino glanced at Thiess somewhat pitifully before returning his gaze to Amanda and responding with a somewhat exaggerated shrug.

"I...I...only want to make sure that the village is...safe and..." Thiess stopped, grasping at his hand again. Reaching into his jacket and retrieving two more pills from the container, he swallowed them with a gulp of wine.

Emilia laughed and Amanda couldn't help but join her.

"Mr. Thiess," Emilia went on, "as I understand it, you plan to demolish the entire village in order to mine the enormous quantity of gold buried in these mountains."

Thiess appeared visibly shaken by the revelation and in his inebriated state, knocked over his wine goblet as he reached to pick it up—which in turn only caused him to become more frazzled. Clumsily righting the goblet on the table and refilling it from the decanter, the deep burgundy liquid continued to flow across the table, shimmering in the candlelight.

Thiess took a sip of wine followed by another as he fought to compose himself.

"I do not know what you are talking about," Thiess barked, jaw clenched. "Where did you hear such things?"

"Ladies, please, excuse us for a few moments." Massimino smiled rather awkwardly as he stood and made his way toward Thiess, placing his hand on the agitated man's shoulder. "Martin, please, get up and come with me."

"Why should I come with you?" he slurred. "Everything you've done to me...you almost killed me."

Massimino cocked his head. "Please, my friend, you are not thinking clearly. Let us speak privately."

"Get your hands off me," Thiess grumbled, pushing his chair back and stumbling to his feet. "What? What bidding are you going to command me to do now? Where is my reward, Massimino? She will not sign the papers!" He stuck a grimy finger in Emilia's direction.

Massimino placed his hand on Thiess' back and guided him away to the far end of the room, toward the pianist who was still playing soft classical music—it was completely unbefitting the scene currently unfolding.

"This is getting weird, Emmi, even for Zillah." Amanda's eyes darted between her sister and the two men. "And if I'm being completely honest, I don't feel safe," she whispered.

"I'm sure Massimino will sort it out," she replied, not looking nearly as worried as she should have been. "I wish he would just send that awful man away—especially now that we know what he's up to."

The girls could hear fragments of a rather fiercely whispered conversation, but they were unable to make out the details.

"Martin, please," Massimino hissed. "If you keep going like this, there is *no possibility* of you getting what you want."

The man's face was red, lips stained from the bottle of wine he'd had to himself. "You promised me. I found you the girl and I have brought her here to you. You must do as you've said and give me the village!"

"Lower your voice," Massimino whispered, but there was no mistaking his command. "The village is not mine to give you; it belongs to the heiress. I have tried many times now to help you convince her, but you do not listen."

"I know what you are capable of, Massimino," Thiess growled. "You wave your hand and raise the wind; women fuck you with a glance; you need to force her to do this."

He shook his head. "Ahh, Martin, it is not quite so simple. I cannot take control of her and make her behave as I decide. All I can do is *influence* behavior, choices, and over time guide someone in a direction which can be beneficial to me. Over a *long* time, as with the women in the village, I have conditioned them to be very agreeable and subservient—it is what they are used to; it is all they have known."

"What do I care about this?" Thiess scoffed, "The women of the village are of no concern to me. I need you to make that Blagden girl do this."

"I am trying to explain what is possible and what is not." Massimino crossed his arms; it was like talking to a greedy child. "Emilia is another story altogether. Our time together has been very limited, and I have had to work incredibly hard over these past days to create an emotional connection from nothing so she may be agreeable to what must come. I cannot simply threaten her, or these efforts will surely unravel and fail.

"Nonetheless, I have done *much* to help further your cause, but you must realize that some of this effort must come from you for this to work. Instead, everything you seem to do has sabotaged it. I do not understand."

"Sabotaged?" Thiess slurred. "Nonsense. I have done nothing wrong." He whimpered as his injured hand grazed the fireplace.

"Martin, I cautioned you not to move so quickly with opening the mines. The consequence of those men being here has potentially defeated your effort. I advised you to form a good relationship with Emilia and yet you have not done so—you continue to deceive her. Look at you with that hand. Still, you have not made the connection that your lies only intensify the suffering you feel."

This appeared to grab the lawyer's attention. "Wh...what do you mean?"

"After you demonstrated your deceit in visiting that mine, I crafted your future deceptions to be more obvious, and even despite the pain, you continue to lie and deceive with frightening frequency. You must change your ways. I assure you there is no possibility to get what you desire if you do not."

Rage engulfed Thiess' face as the implications of what he was hearing reached his inebriated consciousness and his abhorrent instincts wrestled his better judgment for control.

"Who...who are you to say and do such things?" Thiess yelled, the sound piercing the length of the stone hall.

Emilia and Amanda jolted at the outburst—as did the pianist, who looked up for a few moments; still playing albeit with a few missed notes.

"Martin, calm yourself and quiet down," Massimino replied in a measured tone.

"I will *not* be quiet!" he roared. "I have done *everything* you have asked. And instead of giving me what you promised, you lecture me. You try to *kill* me. You use magic to play tricks and cause me pain. You call me a liar!"

"Enough." Massimino's calm was diminishing. "I insist you stop this at once."

"You want honesty? Is that right? Then why don't you tell her?" Thiess nodded toward Emilia. "Go on now, tell her about her parents. Tell her how you killed them. Tell her what you plan to do to her tomorrow—"

Suddenly, Emilia rushed toward Thiess. Her sister stood as well, trying to take her hand and stop her.

As the pianist continued to play, Thiess' tirade was cut off by a loud, forceful wind which crashed through the dining hall, rattling the banners and tapestries. Several objects fell to the floor as the fiery torches wavered and the pianist finally abandoned his post, scrambling toward the entrance.

"Emilia, wait! We need to get out of here!" Amanda yelled, desperately trying to be heard over the howling of the wind.

Massimino watched as Emilia turned back, silky dark hair billowing around her. "I have to find out what—"

The wind intensified further, extinguishing all the torches and candles.

Chapter Forty-Two

B *ang! Bang! Bang!*

"Emilia! Are you in there?" Amanda called as she pushed and pulled, one hand on each of the handles of the double doors leading to Emilia's chambers. No matter how hard she shook and rattled them, the heavy lock would not yield. "Emilia!"

Stepping back, she studied the furnishings and décor around the hall—searching for something that might assist in prying open the doors. The pale light of an overcast day filtered in through the windows, casting soft shadows over the hanging tapestries, vases and statues.

Amanda could see no way to make use of any of the items, so she tried once more to rouse anyone who might be inside before heading back down the hallway in search of someone or some*thing* that could help. Uncertain of where to commence her search, Amanda started toward the dining room: the last place she had seen her sister. She shuddered at the memory of last night as if the wind had never left her bones.

Not having encountered anyone along the way, Amanda approached the doors to the dining hall with caution. They were unevenly ajar and as she reached them, she quietly stepped to the gap between and peeked inside.

Scanning the length of the room but seeing no one, Amanda pushed the closest door a little further open, the heavy hinges letting out a dull groan as she stepped inside.

The room looked as if a storm had thundered through it; most of the fittings that had been hanging from the walls were strewn around, and the few that still held on clung by tattered threads. Chairs were tipped and upended—some even smashed.

"Amanda, is that you?"

She jumped as the voice behind her broke the silence and she turned to face the entrance. "Oh, Rose," she breathed, recognizing her friendly face. "You startled me."

"Oh my, what happened here?" she asked, surveying the mess.

"Last night, Massimino and Mr. Thiess, they—"

"Oh no, I see he has revealed himself to you—and in a frightfully dramatic way, no less. Please, say no more. Where is Emilia? I need to speak with her, it is important."

"I don't know. I haven't seen her since last night—when this happened." Amanda fought tears. "I think she's in her room, but it's locked and she won't answer. I can't get in. I was looking for someone who can help me get to her. Do you have any ideas?"

"All right," Rose said, bringing Amanda into her arms the way a mother would. "It's all right. We'll find Mrs. Rossi. She will know how to open the door. Come with me; we must be quick." She took Amanda's hand and led her into the kitchen.

They found the cook, leaning over a pot and stirring. She appeared as if she'd never left the stove, still in her plain dress and apron with tired eyes. After explaining the situation, she led them to the laundry and housekeeping area of the castle, where piles of old, discolored linen as well as cleaning supplies filled the dusty space. Mrs. Rossi unlocked a small cupboard fixed to the wall to reveal many iron rings with even more keys hanging from them.

"The one we need is not here," she muttered, shaking her head and pointing to an empty hook.

"Could it be one of these other ones, just in the wrong place?" Amanda asked, flipping a few of the other rings with her fingers.

"No deary, I'm afraid not," answered Mrs. Rossi. "That key is distinct, and the one in here is the only like it—apart from the one *he* has. I can't say when it would have gone missing. The chamber has not been locked since the last countess passed."

"We must get in there, and *quickly*," pleaded Rose.

"What do you want me to do, break the door down with my rolling pin?"

"Of course not. It's just that..." Rose trailed off.

"You know, I saw Franco around here earlier," Mrs. Rossi said. "He's probably out in the yard somewhere, or in his shed—just be sure to knock first. That Luna's been visiting him lately; never know what you'll walk in on." She raised her eyebrows. "I can't believe Massimino hasn't discovered the pair. Perhaps he is slipping."

"Or is too preoccupied with other problems," mumbled Rose as they made their way out to the courtyard.

When they reached the shed, they heard some muffled voices and shuffling inside. Amanda moved to the window, but the thick layers of dirt masked whatever lay beyond. After a few moments, the door opened a crack, just enough for a young man to poke his face out.

"Mrs. Venturi, what are you doing here?" His dark features were pleasant to look at, but Amanda didn't care about him—or anything else—right now. "And who is this?" He nodded toward her.

"Hi, I'm Amanda. I'm guessing you're Franco. We need your help right away!"

"What does she mean, Mrs. Venturi?" he asked, still not stepping outside. "Why are you here?"

"The new countess, Emilia," Rose replied, "is locked in her chamber and the key is missing. We need your help to open the door."

"But, I cannot..." He appeared distracted; his gaze unable to stay in one place too long. "Does Massimino know about this?"

"No," Rose said flatly. "It is very important we get to the countess. Her life may depend on it."

"If he finds out I helped you, who knows what he will do?" Franco visibly recoiled. "No, I am sorry...I just cannot. I need to get back to...to...work now. Please leave." He began to push the door closed.

"And how much trouble will you be in if Massimino finds out about your guest?" snapped Amanda, wedging her foot between the door and preventing him from latching it.

"What..." Franco's eyes widened, "what guest?" Franco replied nervously.

"Hello, Luna!" Rose called into the shed.

The unexpected greeting caused Franco to ease up on the door momentarily, which allowed Amanda to push it further open and step inside.

"Hello," Luna replied quietly, divulging her hiding place as she stood from behind a table in the middle of the room.

"Look, Franco," Amanda said. "I don't care what you two are up to in here and I don't want to cause any trouble, but I *really* need to get those doors open and get to my sister. Please, will you come with us?" It was a question, but her tone implied more of a friendly yet firm demand.

Franco paused, questioning Rose with his eyes.

"It is the right thing to do," she said. "Please, we do not have much time. It is already almost midday."

"I think I need to go with them," Franco didn't look away from Amanda, finally seeming to realize how badly they needed his assistance, "I will see you again soon." He grinned at Luna, taking her in as if she weren't wearing her revealing work dress.

"I understand." Luna turned to Amanda and Rose. "You must promise not to tell anyone. Massimino will be very mad if he finds out I was here."

Rose nodded.

"All right, you go. I will get some things together and meet you at the Countess' chamber," instructed Franco as he collected a bag from a nearby workbench and searched the scattered instruments for what he believed he might need for the task.

Franco spent a few minutes examining the lock before retrieving a small pick tool from his bag and setting to work. All the while, Amanda pounded on the door, pressing her ear against the wood for any sign of her sister.

Thirty minutes later, there had been no progress.

"This is impossible!" Franco tossed his tools to the ground. "This should not be so difficult. Perhaps it is that the lock is old or…I don't know, but it does not seem we will be able to get inside this way."

"But we really need to get in there," Amanda pleaded, as she anxiously tugged on the pull strings of her 'UPenn' hoodie.

"And fast. We must get to her soon," Rose added.

Franco sighed and stood up, taking hold of both handles and pushing and pulling to try and force the doors open, but it was no use. "Wait here," he said when he gave up on that approach. "I will be right back."

After a few minutes of waiting in silence, Rose turned to look out one of the hall windows and Amanda leaned against the wall, sliding down until she was seated on the floor. Dropping her face to her knees, Amanda wrapped her arms around her head.

What the fuck is going on? What else can I do? How do we get out of here?

The sound of Franco's footsteps caused Rose to turn toward him and Amanda lifted her head, weakly smiling when she caught sight of the sledgehammer in his fist. Climbing to her feet, she waited beside Rose at a safe distance.

"If this does not work, I have no more ideas," Franco announced as he raised the hammer above his head.

There was a loud *ding!* as the head of the sledgehammer struck one of the handles and the sound of splintering wood surrounded it. Franco stepped back after the first strike and examined the result. "Now perhaps we are getting somewhere," he grinned.

"I think you're right! Keep going!" Amanda urged him on.

Franco continued the assault on the door and after successive strikes, both handles had finally yielded and fallen to the floor. A few more blows and they were free to open.

Franco wiped the sweat from his forehead as he admired his destructive handiwork.

"Thank you, Franco!" Amanda rejoiced as she flew through the doors and entered the chamber.

Amanda raced through the rooms, seeing no sign of her sister. She reached the bedchamber and there, lying in the middle of the bed in the same red dress she had worn the prior evening, was Emilia.

"Emilia, wake up! Emmi!" Amanda called to her sister as she rushed to the bed.

"Oh my, is she all right? Why does she not wake?" Rose queried aloud, hurrying into the room.

"I don't know," Amanda cried. "Emmi, please wake up!"

Amanda leaned over the bed to get a better look and check her pulse. Emilia's chest rose and fell, eyes eerily still beneath their lids.

"She's breathing, but I don't know how to wake her." Amanda gently shook Emilia by the shoulders. "Emmi! Emmi! It's me, Amanda. Wake up!"

"It is Massimino," said Rose flatly. "He must have cast some sort of spell on her. I do not know what to do." A tear ran down her cheek.

"Where is Massimino?" Amanda turned to her, enraged at the man who had done this. "I want to go and see him *right* now!"

"He..." Rose backed up. "He...will be in his tower, but you cannot go there. He will hurt you, or even kill you, if you confront him."

"I can't just leave Emilia like this! I have to find out what's going on. I need to wake her up and get her out of here as soon as possible."

"I know...but I fear he will not allow it." Rose couldn't meet her gaze.

"Can you just help me carry her to our car? We'll get her to a hospital—or is there a doctor in the village?" Amanda fired questions while pulling Emilia toward the edge of the mattress.

"The doctor in the village is a drunk and I do not think he could help us with this anyway." Rose shook her head.

"We have to do something. Let's get her to the car."

"No, no," Rose said, stopping Amanda and resting Emilia's head on one of the many pillows. "If we move her away from him and she is still under his spell, there is no telling what may happen to her. We must find another way." Rose's eyes widened. "The old woman," she whispered. "I was coming to find your sister to take her to Gerlinde; it is very important that they speak today. You wait with the countess in case she wakes, and I will fetch Gerlinde instead. I will return as fast as I can."

"I don't know." Amanda didn't want to involve any more magic. "Can we trust her? What can she do?"

"Honestly, I do not know if she can do anything at all," Rose admitted. "But she is the only idea I have—it is far too dangerous to confront Massimino. Especially today, and he will never allow you to take her from the village."

"Why? What's so special about today?"

"Now is not the time." Rose made her way to the cracked doorframe. "First, we need to help the countess. Wait here with her and I will be back as soon as I can, okay?"

"Dammit! This is ridiculous," growled Amanda. "None of this makes any sense and all I know is that Emilia is sick or in danger or both. I have to help her!"

"I understand this is difficult," said Rose calmly, "but she is in more danger than you realize. That is why we must find Gerlinde; she is our only chance."

Amanda's eyes welled with anger-filled tears; her jaw clenched. "I need you to tell me truthfully, Rose. Does this have anything to do with the dreams Emilia has been having? Massimino was doing some sort of ritual in them—he killed her with a dagger on an altar. Is that what this is all about?" She stood in front of Rose and stared into her eyes.

"Yes. That is exactly what this is about," Rose answered stoically, grabbing Amanda's hands and squeezing them tightly. "And that is why we must act quickly. Massimino is preparing for the ritual tonight; I must go now if we are to have any hope of changing the course of things."

Amanda felt numb as she looked down at her sister. "All right," she sighed. "I don't know what else to do. Please come back as soon as you can."

"Hello? Anyone in here?" a cheerful voice called as they entered Emilia's chambers.

"Who are you? What do you want?" Amanda shouted warily as she rose from the bed.

"Calm down, dear." The woman eyed the broken doors before stepping inside. "It's me, Mrs. Rossi. Rose asked me to bring some breakfast. Here, deary…see?" Mrs. Rossi held up the tray before her as Amanda came closer.

"Oh." Amanda felt foolish for yelling, but she needed to protect her sister. "Um…Emilia can't eat anything. We can't wake her up. Rose went to get Gerlinde; she thinks she can help, but I just don't know what to do." Amanda looked back toward Emilia lying on the bed. She appeared so peaceful when their circumstances were anything but.

"It's all right." Mrs. Rossi set the tray on the table between the sofa and fireplace. "Massimino…why does he do such things? They say Zillah was once beautiful and prosperous, but all I've ever known is a world ruled by him—and that has not been much of a life."

"I don't understand," Amanda said under her breath. "The things he is capable of…how is any of it possible? Where I'm from this stuff is only real in movies. Now we're in the middle of a living nightmare."

Mrs. Rossi set about pouring a cup of tea from the kettle she'd brought. "All the best stories are borne from something real, aren't they? I don't know the details about who or what he is, or how he came to be here, only the realities."

"Why don't you just leave? Everyone seems miserable here, but you all stay."

"Don't have much of a choice, deary. He will not allow anyone to leave."

"What do you mean?" Amanda asked. "He keeps the whole village here—against their will?" She neared the table, glancing at her slumbering sister.

Mrs. Rossi gave a quick nod.

The tray contained two bowls of oats with sugar, oven-baked bread that had been toasted, and some freshly squeezed juice.

"Please, deary, eat something," Mrs. Rossi urged. "This is going to be a big day, and you will need all the energy you can get."

"Thank you. I'm famished, but I feel bad about eating while Emilia is like this."

"Nonsense. You need to eat; I would tell your sister the same thing if it were you in that bed. Please do not let this go to waste."

The pair sat at the table and while Amanda ate, they talked more about the village, its residents, and of course Massimino. Mrs. Rossi could not elaborate about the chapel or the ritual, conceding only to hearing rumors over the years but knowing nothing of such things herself.

Chapter Forty-Three

Hustling toward the cottage, Rose was short of breath as she finally entered the overgrown clearing on the opposite side of the river. Fear consumed her; the ever-present knowledge of the consequences she'd suffer if discovered filling her mind.

She reached out to knock on the old woman's door, but it opened before her knuckles made contact.

"Why are you here alone?" came Gerlinde's abrupt greeting. "Where is the heiress?"

"Massimino has done something to her. She is in the castle, but we cannot wake her. Please, you must come and help."

"Come inside." The old woman ushered Rose into her cottage. "I cannot go to the castle. If Massimino finds out, I fail to imagine what torturous revenge he would seek for my disobedience." She hung her head as she closed the door with a thud.

"You *must!* There is no way we can bring her to you—her condition does not allow it. Her sister is with her now—she wants to escape. I did not know what else to do but come to you."

"Escape?" Gerlinde's smile held no humor. "If only it were that simple. They should never have come here in the first place. Now, I am afraid there is no way out for her other than ending Massimino's reign here."

"There must be something you can do," Rose pleaded.

The old woman stared into the flames of her fireplace in search of inspiration. "We would need to make sure Massimino is distracted for me to get into the castle. If he is paying any attention at all, he will sense me approaching."

"Some sort of diversion in the village perhaps? Something to draw him away from his perch in the tower?"

"There is very little that distracts that man...especially on a day such as this. All he will care about today is preparing for the ritual tonight. Perhaps if you had a fresh group of young, willing women hidden somewhere," Gerlinde mocked, gazing back at the fire.

Rose took a deep breath. "What if...*I* was to go to him? To keep him occupied, while you help the countess."

Gerlinde shrugged. "You may not be as old as me, but you are no spring chicken either. What makes you think he'll be interested? It has to have been quite some time since you were summoned to the tower, no? Besides, you'd be lucky to survive. He's already drained one of the young girls to near death this week. You may never come back out again."

"It has been a very long time, but perhaps..." Rose refused to think about it too deeply. "It's all I can think of. If I do it, are you sure you can help Emilia and save her from the ritual?"

Gerlinde didn't look away from the hearth, flames reflecting in her brazen eyes. "I wish I could be sure. If Massimino's attention is elsewhere, I should be able to awaken her. What happens tonight will ultimately be up to her; all I can do is give her the tools I know and set her on the path—but with so little time..."

"We must try, risks or no risks. He cannot harm me too much anyway; he needs me for the ritual. If I can help save her—even if it is just to give her a *chance* against him—I will do it."

"Very well, if you are willing, then I will do all I can." Gerlinde stood and hobbled to a set of shelves by the fireplace.

After searching for several minutes, she sighed in frustration before heading to her bedroom. Some rummaging followed, then she returned holding a small, tarnished silver pendant.

"Here, take this. I don't know if it will work but it is said to be able to mask your thoughts, or at least cloud them from one such as Massimino—so long as he does not look into you too deeply."

Rose held out her palm and noticed the twelve-pointed star design on the oval-shaped pendant as Gerlinde deposited the delicate chain into her hand.

"Put it on," Gerlinde instructed, before guiding Rose back toward the door. "You should leave now; I hope for both our sakes that this works."

As Rose reached the main gate, she glanced at Emilia's section of the castle before turning her focus toward the southern tower, peering up with a mixture of fear and dread.

Knowing Massimino would be wary of her visit, Rose had to do all she could to conceal her feelings. A few calming breaths were the best she could manage as she entered the doorway at the base of the tower. She had to be convincing; several lives were now in her hands, and there was no turning back. Rose gripped the pendant around her neck and said a silent prayer as she ascended the stairs.

"Is that the charming Rose climbing to the top of my tower after many years away?" Massimino's voice greeted her as she ascended the final flight of stairs, heart hammering and breathing shallow.

"Yes," Rose said meekly. Fighting her fear, she clenched her fists and began again, this time more confidently. "Yes, it is me. How did you know?"

"It is difficult to keep secrets from me around here, my beautiful Rose," he replied calmly. "You know that as well as anyone." Massimino stood beside the fireplace with his hands clasped at his waist, dressed in his black robe.

"Yes, I do know that." Rose forced a smile which she hoped appeared genuine. Her eyes wandered to the bed, where one of the young women from the village was sleeping; her mussy black hair and a half exposed back made it difficult to tell who it was. Rose was amazed at how familiar it all felt even though it had been such a long time since her last visit. The warmth of the fire seeped into her skin, and all too soon her body began to betray her thoughts and feelings toward this man as she felt a pulsing need growing within her.

"To what do I owe this pleasure, Rose?" Massimino stared intently into her eyes, circling her like prey. "I trust everything is well in the village and the group is preparing for the ritual tonight?"

"Yes, Master," she said without hesitation. "The village is fine, and our group has met. Some are unhappy, but all have agreed to participate as you have instructed."

"Some are unhappy?" He cocked his head to one side as he took her in. "Help me understand this. Are you one of them? Is that why you are here?"

"No, Master, not at all." She somehow managed to make her voice ring with conviction. "I believe the memories of the last ritual were firmly etched in the minds of all those present, but I would not worry. It is simply…unbelievable to some that another…opportunity like this has been possible. When it is time, all have pledged to do what you have asked."

"I see. Then I pose my question again: why are you here, Rose?" Massimino's tone and demeanor had not changed.

"I…I thought…I, ah…" She swallowed and started again. "I know today is a very big day for you and I know how important it is for everything to go well, especially after what happened last time. I, I would like to…be of service and I know that perhaps the younger women from the village do not have much more they can give to you." Rose paused to look toward the young woman lying in bed, her bare, pale skin contrasting against the smooth black satin.

Massimino's eyes followed Rose's gaze and he gave her a wry smile. "Rose, are you really offering what I think you are? You must have missed me."

She felt a long-forgotten, yet pleasant warmth stirring between her legs as his sea-blue eyes met hers. The welcome feeling continued to spread and created new sensations throughout her body; inside her. It was a hunger that would only be sated in one way. As Rose found herself becoming more and more aware of the heat from the fireplace, it felt almost unbearable as she gazed back at Massimino—a man she feared, reviled, and hated on so many levels. However, right now the only emotion she was aware of was a smoldering desire to be with him—to please him.

Rose reached behind her back, fumbling to unclasp the buttons of her old, faded dress. She suddenly regretted not changing into something more appropriate, more enticing, but it was short-lived. She smiled mischievously at Massimino as she slipped off her shoes and let go of the dress, allowing it to fall to the wooden floor in a rumpled heap around her feet. Rose's nipples hardened as her clothing fell away, overly sensitive under his watchful stare.

Inhaling, Rose forced herself to stand as upright as possible, pushing her shoulders back and thrusting her chest forward. She licked her lips as she watched Massimino with an intensity that rivaled his own. "Yes, Master. I believe I have missed you. Will you have me again?"

Massimino took a few moments to appraise Rose's body, walking around her as if she were a statue on display. "You have aged well, my beautiful Rose. I am glad you have come to me today." Massimino stepped toward her.

The pair met before the fireplace, and he finally enveloped her in his arms. Rose reveled in the sensations inward and outward, finding herself intoxicated by the feel of him, his scent, and even the roughness of his robe; it filled a yearning within she hadn't realized existed before now.

Rose tugged at the rope, untying and then flicking it playfully away. They worked together to raise the robe over his head, discarding it on the floor. As Rose came closer to Massimino, she savored the feeling of their naked bodies together, skin to skin, and allowed herself to surrender completely to him.

Chapter Forty-Four

A dark figure stood in the broken doorway, wheezing and hobbling into Emilia's chambers.

"Hello?" Amanda called, standing up and ready to attack.

Mrs. Rossi looked toward the entrance and held up a hand to calm her.

"Hello? It's Mrs. Rossi—I'm here with the countess' sister. Rose told us she was going to fetch you, and we've been waiting." She stood from the table and headed for the entrance. "The countess, she has still not awakened...under some sort of spell, we think."

"That's why I've come," Gerlinde replied, her voice frail, breathing strained.

Amanda joined them at the entrance. Though Emilia's situation continued to weigh heavily on her, she did feel better with food in her stomach and a little more perspective about Zillah from Mrs. Rossi— who looked on as Gerlinde hobbled into the room, shocked by her appearance.

"Oh my. So, it is true..." Mrs. Rossi whispered. "The rumors about you. You're as old as they say. You are a witch?" She seemed to immediately regret speaking such thoughts aloud.

Gerlinde peered scornfully at Mrs. Rossi then turned her attention to Amanda. "Where is the heiress? Take me to her."

"This way. She's in here." Amanda led Gerlinde back to the bedchamber where Emilia lay helplessly asleep.

"Ah, I need to be getting back to the kitchen," Mrs. Rossi said abruptly. "If you need anything else, just fetch me. Pull this cord over here." She pointed out a decorative golden rope hanging in a corner just outside the bedroom that had gone unnoticed until now. "It will ring a bell downstairs, and someone can come up right away."

Mrs. Rossi was obviously uncomfortable around Gerlinde, so Amanda smiled gratefully despite not wanting to be left alone with this old woman. "All right..."

Gerlinde got right to the point before the cook had made it to the stairs. "How long has she been like this?"

"I don't know exactly," Amanda answered, recounting what she could of the events leading up to this.

"Definitely the work of Massimino, this is." Gerlinde scanned Emilia with her gray gaze; it reminded Amanda of the sky, the mood that hung over this place. "He is preparing for a ritual tonight—must be trying to keep her from going anywhere until then. It is very important that I speak with her. There are things she must know." Gerlinde sighed and subtly shook her head. How I wish I had told her more yesterday. I must try to weaken his influence over her, to break their connection and bring her back so she can understand things as they truly are."

"Okay." Amanda tried to sound calm and failed. "How do we wake her? What can I do to help?"

"For the moment, just stand back. I must try to reach her."

Amanda stepped away from the bed and observed as the old woman sat down beside Emilia. She took Emilia's hands, closed her eyes, and stayed completely still.

As silence fell over the chamber, Amanda shifted her gaze to Emilia; her eyelids remained closed as movement began beneath them—their rhythm seemed to become synchronized with the old woman's. Then, their breathing pattern harmonized, and Amanda felt goose bumps rising on her skin. The air crackled as if electrified, and the fine hair on her arms stood up.

Amanda looked on, powerless to know whether the old woman was helping or hurting her sister. She eventually grew impatient, her mind conjuring the worst scenarios she could imagine as time ticked on. "Gerlinde, what's happening?"

The old woman made no attempt to respond, continuing as if she hadn't heard the question. Amanda paced the room, unable to warm up. "Gerlinde, can you hear me?"

Still, there was no answer. Amanda glanced at the tall grandfather clock in the sitting area; more than twenty minutes had passed since Gerlinde had begun.

Emilia's eye movement suddenly intensified, and her breathing was more erratic.

Oh God, what do I do? Is she hurting her?

Amanda glanced at Gerlinde once more and saw a tear trickle down her wrinkly cheek. "Emilia!" she cried to her sister, desperately hoping she could somehow hear.

"Please tell me what's happening—I'm scared," Amanda begged.

Gerlinde didn't reply, she simply continued her vigil over Emilia.

"Emilia!" Amanda sobbed. "Emilia...please—"

Gerlinde sensed a chill on her shriveled skin. As she opened her eyes to a darkened world, she was aware that her body did not ache, and she was no longer hunched; she felt weightless. A heavy fog hung in the air, clouding her vision in every direction. The spicy scent of anise permeated the atmosphere and seemed unusual yet strangely befitting of this unnatural, otherworldly place.

"Countess? Countess?" Gerlinde's voice was calm as she called out into the murky blackness.

The thick air swirled as Gerlinde took a few steps forward while attempting to sense her way through the obscurity; leaves rustled and twigs snapped against the damp earth beneath her feet as she meandered on.

"Countess, where are you?"

There was still no reply, though the eerie silence was broken by the sound of unseen branches creaking in the wind overhead. Gerlinde held out her hands, cupping them before her as she closed her eyes. Suddenly, a burst of orange light illuminated the darkness and she allowed her eyelids to open, squinting at the brightness as a fiery orb levitated from her hands and hovered in the sky above her, bobbing slightly as the ball of fire churned.

The orb's glow lit up the thick fog, through the haze she could make out the ghostly trunks and limbs of nearby trees; hefty, ancient pines.

"I must find the Blagden girl," Gerlinde spoke to the orb.

Responding to her command, the orb brightened momentarily then began to spin, rising higher in the air until it disappeared into the fog, leaving Gerlinde in darkness once more.

Gerlinde scanned the space around her but found nothing. She waited in silence and blackness. After several minutes, the area brightened as the fiery orb returned, beaming with greater intensity and prompting Gerlinde to follow as it moved slowly through the forest.

The orb slowed when it reached a rocky mountain, then came to a complete stop above a path leading upward. The fog wavered as a gust of wind blew past, rustling her hair and prickling her skin as an unnerving howl rang out through the trees.

Gerlinde nodded to the orb and it began to move again; she followed as the uneven, rocky path snaked its way up and into the mountainous terrain.

As she neared the top, the orb slowed; bright flashes of lightning pierced the starless black sky and illuminated the fog-shrouded forest below. Booming rolls of thunder closely followed and seemed to rattle the foreboding landscape.

The thunder reverberated through her body, and the sensation compelled Gerlinde to make haste. She continued to the top where the orb was waiting above an entrance to a cave. She saw light and felt warm air spilling from the opening as she approached.

Gerlinde stepped inside, her gaze immediately drawn to the fire burning brightly in the middle of the cozy space. Emilia lay beyond it, dressed in a red satin gown atop an arrangement of soft blankets and plush cushions. The cave felt alluring: safe, warm, and inviting. It had been quite some time since Gerlinde recalled such feelings; a lover's embrace—his embrace.

Gerlinde made her way to Emilia, who was lying on her side, body curled toward the fire and a gentle, contented expression on her face.

"Awaken," Gerlinde whispered. The fire cracked as she spoke, reacting to her words.

Emilia's eyes flickered open, and the flames sparked in their emerald brilliance.

"Gerlinde?" Emilia's voice was soft and peaceful.

"It is important that you come with me. We do not have much time." Gerlinde spoke with focused intention.

A lazy smile formed on Emilia's lips as she purred and stretched before sitting up. "No, I'm not going anywhere—this is where I belong. He will summon me soon, and I must be ready for him."

"But you must come with me—away from this place—so I may help you see things as they truly are."

"Gerlinde, everything is fine...I've never felt this way before. It's...wonderful—magical. All is as it should be."

Several bolts of lightning streaked across the sky beyond the cave entrance and an ominous boom followed shortly after.

"I need you to look within yourself," Gerlinde persisted. "You must find your own strength and your own will...I can only begin to imagine the draw you feel to this place, but it is not real. You are in grave danger."

"It seems to me the danger is out there." Emilia cast her gaze toward the cave entrance and the sinister darkness in the distance. "In here,

I'm...safe. I have found my destiny, and I will leave only when he calls for me," she cooed.

"This is his deception; he intends to kill you—"

Gerlinde was cut short by another spectacular bolt of lightning followed by more thunder.

"Gerlinde, what's happening?" a familiar voice reverberated around the cave.

Emilia appeared to search for her sister. "Was that—"

"There is much I must tell you," Gerlinde interrupted, "but this place will not permit it—we will be discovered. The only way is for you to come with me."

"That doesn't make sense," Emilia argued. "I feel nothing but care and comfort and...love. Why would you come here and say such things?"

Gerlinde paused, staring into the fire. "The only way this can work is for you to seek out enough truth within yourself to break free of this illusion. Away from here, I can tell you all you have longed to know—and all you wish to understand—about your life and your parents."

"My...parents?" Emilia frowned as she trailed off.

"Yes, your sister Amanda. She said there was some confrontation last night and Massimino's truth was revealed. Please, do you remember?"

Emilia was silent as she watched the flames; their flowing natural state transformed into an orderly stillness as a breeze whistled around the cave.

"Yes, you remember?" Gerlinde pressed.

"My parents...Thiess...he said—"

A brilliant chain of lightning blanketed the sky, each bolt seeming larger and more spectacular than the last and matched by the increasing intensity of the ensuing thunder.

"But it can't be..." Emilia shook her head. "The way I feel—I have longed to find this my whole life, and now I finally have..." She stopped short and sat straighter, arms around her middle. "I can't leave." Emilia's expression belayed her inner conflict.

Gerlinde remained stoic. "This is not real. I promise you, there are truths you must know and preparations we must make if we are to save you and your sister from him."

"Gerlinde, can you hear me?" Amanda's distressed cry was filled with worry and fear, causing Emilia to clutch her hand to her chest.

"Amanda?" Emilia whispered. "Is she in danger?"

"Yes, you both are—"

"What danger, and what truths? This all sounds so cryptic—tell me what it is you know. I don't understand."

"Your parents—" Gerlinde's words were muted by the increasing force of the elements as they appeared to be moving closer and continued to escalate. Both Gerlinde and Emilia shuddered as thunder shook the mountaintop, causing dust and small stones to cascade around them.

"I cannot tell you now," Gerlinde said. "The emotion such a revelation could stir in you would most certainly bring him here, and if that happened, we would have no chance. We must leave this place while his focus is elsewhere. You must look inside yourself. You can feel the truth...you know the truth; your will is strong enough to overcome this." Gerlinde sighed as a tear rolled down her cheek.

"Emilia!" Amanda's voice rang out around them.

"Amanda?" Emilia called as yet another deafening round of thunder and lightning crashed. "Where is my sister?"

"She is out there, where we must go." Gerlinde hurried back to the entrance of the cave, turning to Emilia and encouraging her to follow. "You cannot help her if you stay here. Come with me."

Emilia closed her eyes and clenched her fists. She screamed and the fire roared, the tips of the flames reaching the cave ceiling as a gust whirled within the space. Emilia appeared shocked at the display, and as quickly as it had sprung up, the elements settled once more.

"But I don't want to leave," Emilia murmured.

Gerlinde's eyes widened, fearful that the intensity of Emilia's reactions would be sensed by Massimino and certainly draw dire consequences.

"You must stay calm. Search within yourself—you know what is right; you are stronger than this place," she repeated.

Another bolt of lightning struck, illuminating a sky filled with menacing clouds.

"You can save her and yourself, but the only way is to let go of this place...this fantasy."

Emilia fixed her gaze on Gerlinde as she stood and started toward the cave entrance, each step filled with trepidation. Gerlinde could feel the sensations clawing at Emilia as if they were her own—love, safety, euphoria—all calling and beckoning her to stay.

"How can it be right to leave this?" Emilia's voice had become watery as she halted. "It's the world of my dreams. Massimino...I am his whole world, and he is everything I could have ever wanted." She took a step toward the blankets and pillows.

"It is an illusion," Gerlinde said. "It is a lie. The truth you seek, the safety you need for you and your sister, they are this way."

Emilia paused, eyes darting between the serene warmth of the fire and Gerlinde. "It's strange...I sense on some level that you're right...but I don't know if I can will myself to go with you."

Gerlinde was solemn as she considered how she could overcome the power of Massimino's spell.

"Please tell me what's happening—I'm scared." Amanda's distressed voice echoed around the cave again, as if pleading from afar.

"Amanda?" Emilia gasped; the firelight and shadows dancing across her face only served to highlight her anguish.

"She needs you," Gerlinde whispered.

"I believe you," she replied. "I hear it in her voice. I love her so much…I can't let anything happen to her." Emilia took a few more reluctant steps toward the entrance.

Another flash of lightning streamed across the sky and the thunder raged around them. Gerlinde saw Emilia swallow hard as she reached the opening.

"Yes, come, that's it," she encouraged. "You know in your heart what he offers you is not real, and while the road we must now embark on will not be pleasant, it is the only way."

"Emilia! Emilia…please—" Amanda continued to cry out for her sister.

"And Amanda?"

"She will certainly not survive this if you do not return."

Gerlinde sensed the conflict within Emilia, her resolve faltering as the allure of this place coaxed her back.

Emilia gazed out into the darkness, her hair twisting in the wind and her gown billowing around her legs. She gathered the fabric and crossed her arms over her chest, bracing herself against the chill for some time and staring into the black nothingness before turning back to the comfort of her cave.

Chapter Forty-Five

"P lease—" Amanda froze as Gerlinde opened her eyes. She let go of Emilia's hands, placing them gently at her sides as she gazed at her placid face.

A breath of air inflated Emilia's lungs and her eyes popped open.

"Emmi!" Amanda cried. "Oh, God, Emmi! Are you all right?"

Emilia blinked a few times before sitting herself up. "Amanda...? What happened?" She stared down at her red gown, wrinkled from sleep. "Is this a dream? Where...?"

"Shh, just be still," instructed Gerlinde; her voice sounded hollow and fatigued. "Be calm and take a little time to become reoriented."

Amanda sat on the bed beside Emilia and embraced her tightly; Emilia hugged her back.

"Oh, Emmi. I was so worried about you. Are you okay?"

Confusion fell across Emilia's face "What do you mean?"

"You've been here, asleep...under some kind of spell since last night," Amanda replied, sounding exasperated.

"I don't know..." Emilia bit her full bottom lip. "The last thing I remember is the dining room, Massimino...and Thiess."

"We need to get out of here!" Amanda jumped from the bed and began to pace. "This is crazy—we have to go as soon as you can get up."

"What?" Emilia's throat sounded raw. "Where's Massimino? What happened last night?"

Amanda answered, "Massimino and Thiess were having a fight or something and then—"

"But what were they fighting about?" she asked. "I remember Thiess saying that Massimino killed my parents—did you hear that too, or was it a dream?"

"Yeah, Emmi. I heard that." Amanda nodded, not understanding what it meant herself. "He was drunk or something. It's not possible, right? How would Massimino have been in Upstate New York and responsible for your parents' car accident?" Amanda stopped herself, knowing her sister was most likely overwhelmed. "Anyway, I think you need to eat something. Then we need to get you dressed and we're gone. We can keep talking about all of this on our way out of here, okay?"

Amanda hurried to the table where the tray from Mrs. Rossi had been left. She offered a cold bowl of porridge and a glass of juice to Emilia.

"Thanks, I'm thirsty." After several large gulps, she handed the glass back to Amanda and took the bowl in its place. She stirred the spoon around; it had become thick and lumpy.

"Eat up and be quick about it," instructed Amanda. "Where did they put all your stuff? We can leave our clothes—just need to find our passports. We need to go."

Gerlinde had wandered over to one of the windows which overlooked the road in and out of town as well as the waterfall and valley. "I am afraid you won't be able to leave."

"You can't keep us here!" snapped Amanda.

Gerlinde turned from the window, a hint of amusement on her wrinkly face. "My dear, if it were up to me, you would have never come at all. Only the Gods know how I—along with your parents— tried to make sure you never knew this place existed."

"Then what do you mean by saying we can't leave?" Amanda softened her tone slightly, though she remained guarded and suspicious.

"What do you know about my parents?" Emilia asked with wide eyes. "You're holding something back from me; I could feel it yesterday—"

"Please, one question at a time." Gerlinde interrupted. "I promise to tell you all I know. I wish to help you survive this." She looked from Emilia to Amanda. "Massimino is the one who will harm you—your sister as well, if she stands in his way. By virtue of who you are and the powers you possess, you are more valuable to him than anything else in this world."

"Then we've got to get out of here," Amanda protested. "Right now."

Gerlinde sighed. "You would be lucky to make it past the castle gates. Massimino is a very powerful sorcerer. He has ruled this village and pillaged the gifts of the Blagden family for centuries. The only reason we are even able to speak now is because Rose is...distracting him. It can only last for so long, and then his attention will return to your sister, keeping an eye on her as he finalizes preparations for tonight's ritual."

"But—"

"Amanda, I believe her." Emilia touched her sister's arm before turning to the old woman. "Gerlinde, what are you proposing we do?"

She appeared at least a little relieved. "I need time to create a protected place here in the castle that will let us talk and make plans away from Massimino's awareness. I don't think it would be safe to move you to my cottage right now." She seemed to take in Emilia's disheveled gown and Amanda's sweatpants and unbrushed hair. "You both should make yourselves ready for the day then meet me downstairs— you will know the way. I will be ready then."

"All right, Gerlinde," replied Emilia, ignoring Amanda's reluctance. "We'll do as you ask."

Gerlinde nodded in acknowledgement before collecting her bag and hobbling out of the chambers and down the hallway.

"Emmi, what's wrong with you?" Amanda said as soon as she was gone. "We need to leave. You saw what happened last night—and you've got no idea what I've had to go through this morning! I honestly didn't know if you'd ever wake up, and now all this talk about rituals?"

"I hear what you're saying." Emilia was unnaturally at ease—or maybe there was only room for one of them to freak out now. "But I need to figure out what's going on. There's more to all of this and like it or not, I'm part of it somehow."

Amanda struggled to remain calm, lest her sister disregard the urgency of the situation. "Emmi, these people want to kill you—and possibly me. We're up in the mountains, miles from anywhere, with no way of calling for help. You want to know things? Well, I know things: Mrs. Rossi told me some horrid stories about Massimino and how he hurts and imprisons people—he kills people. I feel like he's got some sort of spell over you, so you think he's something incredible, but he's not. He's a very bad guy, Emmi. You need to wake up!"

Emilia took a measured breath. "Okay, I agree this is all beyond crazy, but I don't think it will take long to hear Gerlinde out. I feel a lot clearer about things now, I can't explain it, but can we go see her first and then make a final decision about it all? Plus, what if she's right and Massimino will try to hurt us if we leave? You saw what happened last night."

"Ugh, I wish I'd dragged you down to the car and driven us out of here while you were sleeping," groaned Amanda, shaking her head.

Emilia smiled and hugged her sister, who stood with hands by her sides until she let go.

"Well, that probably would have been a good idea an hour ago, or maybe it would have been as Gerlinde said and he would have stopped you anyway—and maybe even hurt you." Emilia shrugged. "Either way, here we are; I'm awake, I actually feel pretty good, and I'd really, really like you to come with me to talk with Gerlinde, so…please?" She tried to soften her sister's resistance.

"Oh, hell…all right!" She sighed dramatically. "I'll give you ten minutes, but only if we leave straight after we're done. Got it?"

The girls sprang into action, showering, changing, and gathering only what they needed ahead of their planned departure. They hurried along the hallway and down the main staircase in search of Gerlinde.

"This place needs an information kiosk with a map, like at the mall," Amanda huffed, her irritation and fear for their safety continuing to spill over.

"We'll find her—I feel like she's this way." Emilia gave her a disarming smile, and Amanda could see how much her sister appreciated her support, even if it was given reluctantly.

They found Gerlinde chanting something indecipherable while scurrying around a dusty room that was decorated in an eclectic style. Burgundy and silver seemed to be the pallet; heavy velvet curtains had been drawn and four lavish sofas with metal details set into the wooden frames formed a rectangle in the center, where there was a sizeable dark oak coffee table. Medieval artwork and statues, including tarnished knight's armor and paintings, adorned the walls and surfaces. A single fireplace was the only source of light and cast a shadowy atmosphere over the space.

Gerlinde was busy placing short candles, evenly set, around the perimeter of the room with fronds of some sort of herbal bouquet between them. She barely looked up from her work as they entered. "Sit down. I am almost ready to begin."

The sisters glanced at each other; Emilia appeared curious while Amanda tried to plead with her eyes that her concerns had not diminished at all.

Emilia grabbed Amanda's hand and pulled her toward the sofas. Gerlinde lit the candles and the musky air was soon replaced with the aroma of pine and oakmoss; marjoram and mint. Though not unpleasant, the smell was somewhat overpowering.

Once satisfied with her efforts, Gerlinde pulled the heavy doors closed and turned the key to lock them.

"Did any of the dreams where you died look anything like this?" Amanda whispered, inching a little closer to Emilia.

Her sister searched her surroundings then stared Amanda in the eye. "No, nothing like this."

"I guess that's something…but it doesn't make me feel a whole lot better."

Gerlinde approached the sofas through the growing haze and sat down opposite them. "These conditions are not so ideal, but Massimino sees and knows a great many things. This arrangement is necessary to prevent being discovered. We don't have long; he will no doubt grow suspicious when he tries to find you and is unable."

"Please, I want to know everything you can tell me," Emilia said. "My parents, Massimino, the village…what's going on here?"

"And how do we get out?" added Amanda.

Emilia nudged her leg and she understood the cue to back off.

As Gerlinde shared the story of Massimino's fall from grace, his arrival in Zillah, and her role in how the village's history came to pass, Emilia and Amanda sat in shock and disbelief. Amanda could see the pain on her sister's face. Hearing that her family had been enslaved by Massimino for centuries as he slowly and deliberately bled them of their power was horrifying. Knowing he was also oppressing generation after generation of village women to preserve and restore himself must have only added to the insult.

"But…how can all of this be?" Emilia's voice was hardly audible. "The Massimino who visited me in my dreams was…he was kind and the…the pleasure I felt with him was like nothing I've ever experienced."

"He is a master of seduction," explained Gerlinde. "What you feel when you are with him is real, but he cannot be trusted. He only does these things to make getting what he wants—what he needs from you—a little easier. The less resistance you offer, the more readily he can take from you. Do you see?"

"And Emmi, don't forget the part where he kills you with a dagger," Amanda added, softening the blow by holding her hand.

Gerlinde nodded. "Tonight, as the full moon rises above the mountains, Massimino plans to complete a ritual in which he will sacrifice you in order to acquire your powers and strength."

"But why?" Amanda asked. "You said he stole the powers from Emilia's ancestors, but they lived for a long time, right? Why is he doing this anyway? He's already very powerful."

"Yes, Massimino can slowly, over time, draw these things from others and accumulate them within himself," Gerlinde explained. "However, when done that way, he is only able to take a small portion of what they have—and even this takes a long time."

Settling into the musty cushion, the old woman sighed as if deep in thought.

"You must understand that Massimino is not all he seems," she went on. "Yes, he is powerful, but there are others from that world who are even more so, and a very long time ago, one of them placed a curse on him. He must continue to take life energy from others—like the women in the village—in order to maintain his own existence."

"So, he uses the ritual to take Emilia's powers and she dies in the process?" Amanda asked as her sister fell silent.

"Yes. Massimino studies magic in all its forms—particularly the dark arts. Some years ago, he came across an obscure ritual whereby the powers of one may be transferred to another, completely and fully, in their most pure and raw form. The ritual—if he were to complete it with one such as yourself—would allow him to acquire all that you are. He is convinced that not only would this return him to his full strength as he was before he arrived here, but he believes he will then somehow be able to break the curse he carries."

"But...until a few days ago I didn't even know I had these powers," Emilia spoke up. "I honestly don't care if I have them. Can I just give them to him? I mean, without having to die?"

"I have never heard of anything like that," Gerlinde said. "As I understand this world, because one's powers are so entwined with their being, it would not be possible for the physical self to survive once separated from the mystical. If Massimino knew of a way, I'm sure your ancestors would have done as you are suggesting—to rid themselves and this place of him. This is an obscure ritual; I have never encountered another like it. Typically, an elder who is perhaps close to death might use it to allow their essence to be transferred to a younger protégé—but even that is uncommon."

Gerlinde took a deep breath, preparing to tell them what could perhaps be the worst of it, and Amanda squeezed her sister's hand.

"For the ritual to work, both participants must be completely willing. This is why he has spent so much of his own energy on you; to create this artificial sense of trust and the desire to please him. He shows you the ritual so it is familiar, and then he dangles the prospects of love and passion in front of you to convince the mind that this idea of emotional bliss is everything you desire—worth dying for. This lack of willingness, a fierce resistance in its place, is why it was a horrible disaster last time—"

"What?" Emilia interrupted. "He's done this before? Did he kill my aunt?"

Gerlinde shifted in her seat. "No...at least not directly. Their tale adds another link in the chain of tragedy that has become your family's legacy since Massimino arrived in the village."

The sisters sat silently, waiting for her to continue.

"Although I didn't witness it myself," Gerlinde said, "I have no reason to doubt what I heard. I know directly how distraught the Countess was over your mother's death, and how horribly Massimino had treated your aunt after that. She was not right in the head: she threw herself from the top of the tower in the north. They say your uncle suffered a heart attack upon hearing the news and did not survive. It is possible Massimino had something to do with that."

"Oh my God," Emilia blurted, aghast.

"Perhaps it's not so bad," Gerlinde offered. "At least they're now at peace and no longer subject to his evil ways."

"Then who was it?" Amanda piped in, the urgency to leave temporarily overtaken by her curiosity. "Who did he do this ritual with before?"

"Please, tell me the truth," Emilia said, fiddling with the fabric of her sweater. "Did this have something to do with my parents? Last night Thiess said…"

Amanda looked at Emilia, feeling a pang of fear growing within her.

Gerlinde glanced toward the fire then around the room, examining the haze which still hung in the air. "Of everything I need to tell you today, this will be the most difficult for you to hear. What do you know of your parents' deaths?"

"They…they died in a car accident when I was young. In America. Was Massimino there?" Emilia was hungry for answers.

"No, he has never left Zillah since he arrived here." Gerlinde shook her head, white hair a curtain across her face. "I believe what you were told about them and how they passed is not what actually happened."

"Why would that be?" Amanda asked. "What do you think happened?"

"Do not fault those who have told you otherwise. Their intention, I am sure, was to protect you from the dark truth—to keep you from this place." Amanda could tell Gerlinde was fighting back a sob. "This is not what I think, but what I know. I was here for it all but…I couldn't stop it."

"Stop what?" Emilia pressed.

Gerlinde sighed heavily. "As I told you, your mother and father escaped this place when they discovered she was pregnant with you. It was not easy, but we managed to hide her pregnancy. Your aunt agreed to stay behind and help keep Massimino distracted. On that day— and for several following it—we worked together to sever his growing connection with your mother and to conceal your parents from Massimino's attention so they could leave the valley and travel beyond his awareness."

"Yes," Emilia breathed. "Please, go on."

"Massimino was enraged and it took a long time for him to settle again. It was most difficult for your aunt—he needed her and what she was—so Massimino couldn't kill her, but he certainly tortured her for helping your parents. With the other women it was at least an enjoyable experience—as you know. For your aunt, it became the opposite and...she became quite mad."

"See, Emmi?" Amanda said. "We need to get out of here. This place is messed up and you're in real danger."

"Okay." Finally, Emilia relented, seeing things as they really were. "But please, let me hear what Gerlinde has to say first."

Gerlinde took a deep breath to steady herself. "During this time, Massimino uncovered the ritual and set about finding a way to use it. Since he had already been draining her powers for some time, your aunt would have been less than...suitable. He needed another Blagden woman whose powers and abilities had not been corrupted. None of us knew where your mother and father fled to—for your own protection. Massimino could not take from us knowledge that we didn't have."

She leaned towards them a fraction. "You see, your aunt and mother were able to remain in contact through their powers; they could communicate across distances since they shared such a bond. Massimino found a way to use this contact and track their location to some extent—despite the great distance—and then got that lawyer involved. It was he who ultimately found your parents before convincing your mother to return."

"Could that have been the trip they took?" Emilia looked at Amanda, tears welling in her eyes.

"They probably didn't tell you where they were really going—again, to protect you," Gerlinde surmised. "Their biggest motivation for leaving in the first place was to make sure you wouldn't ever become entangled in this mess. When they arrived, Massimino imprisoned your father in the dungeons and started preparing for the ritual."

"Oh my God." A single tear sprung free, rolling down Emilia's cheek. "I...just can't believe all of this."

"The ritual had been written in an ancient language and Massimino was not able to decipher it all himself," Gerlinde went on, gaze returning to the fire. "He turned to me, as I had dabbled in such ancient texts in the past. The ritual also called for a congregation of twelve to bear witness and to focus the energies of the exchange. Massimino selected eleven loyal villagers to join with me and I taught them the steps and incantations necessary."

Gerlinde clenched her jaw as though she found it difficult to continue.

"I wanted to find a way to prevent all of this—so badly. I wanted to save your mother and...perhaps even redeem myself for the mistakes I had made. I thought I'd found a way; the ritual dictated that both parties needed to completely surrender themselves willingly to what would happen—each open and vulnerable with no resistance. I thought if I didn't include these elements in the translation then the ritual simply would not work and Massimino would give up."

"So, what happened?" Emilia leaned forward, sitting right on the edge of the sofa. "She didn't come home." Emilia swallowed the lump in her throat. "Oh my God, are you saying she didn't die? Is she still alive somewhere—my father, too?"

Gerlinde couldn't meet her eyes, tears glistening on her face in the firelight as she shook her head. "No, no. They're both dead. The ritual wasn't working, and your mother fought it—fought him—with all she had. It was horrible...horrible." Her voice broke and she paused. "Massimino forced some of the congregation to hold her arms and legs down on the altar; she used every ounce of her energy to resist him. Wind howled around that small space, the flames of the candles engulphed the walls and ceiling...it was as if we were in hell. Your mother had a strong will—that is for certain—and she resisted fiercely, but she was no match for Massimino. In the end, she writhed and screamed until she was hoarse, her body bruised and bloodied on the altar."

Tears flowed down Emilia's cheeks as the horrific details were revealed. Amanda hugged her sister but couldn't help sobbing herself.

"Most of those present could no longer bring themselves to look on," Gerlinde continued. "Several of us even pleaded with him to stop, but it was no use. In a state of anger and confusion, Massimino plunged the dagger into her chest anyway. She drew one final gasp before she collapsed, lifeless; her head rolled and her eyes—despite their green brilliance having faded—pierced those of us who hadn't the good enough sense to flee already."

Gerlinde swallowed hard, determined to finish. "Those memories will haunt me until I am finally able to die—should that day ever come to release me from all this. Neither of them—not your mother and not your father—revealed that you even existed; how he came upon that knowledge, I don't know. I believe only your aunt and myself knew your mother was pregnant when she left here, and I promise you I never spoke a word about it."

"I-I...how..." Emilia was overcome with emotion and Amanda was helpless, only able to hold her close.

"I didn't tell you this to sadden you," Gerlinde said, "but I feel it's the only way for you to fully understand who and what it is you are up against."

"Emmi, listen to me," Amanda said calmly. "We need to go now, okay?" Grabbing her hand, she attempted to pull her sister from the sofa.

Emilia resisted Amanda's efforts and pulled until she sat back down. "And my father, what about him?"

Gerlinde shook her head again. "Late the next day, some hunters found his body at the bottom of the cliff to the west of the castle; his throat had been slit. Only Massimino would have done that."

Emilia let out another sob as more tears streamed down her face. She turned to Amanda. "So, who did we bury—back home...? I remember the funeral."

"Once word arrived that someone was coming to search for your parents, Massimino gave orders to make it appear as though there was a car accident at the bottom of the valley," Gerlinde explained. "Since your parents had a life beyond the village, Massimino was concerned that their deaths—unlike all the others—might expose him and all that was happening here."

"A car accident?" Emilia exclaimed, every muscle going rigid. "My mother was tortured, and they were both murdered."

"No doubt Massimino used his influence to conceal the truth or simply threatened anyone who may have worked contrary to him." Gerlinde let out a soft, ragged sigh. "A man did come looking—an outsider; I don't know who it was. Or why, or what happened to your parents' bodies after he had claimed them. I'm sorry, I have told you all I know about that."

"But Mom and Dad," Amanda finally said, "they arranged everything for the funeral. They told us about the car accident in New York. How can any of this be true?"

"Believe me," Gerlinde said. "It would have been far easier for me to tell you a lie now and to pretend that none of it happened. I have nothing to gain by deceiving you—in your heart you know there is no deception here—use your gift, and you will sense the truth in my words."

"I trust her, Amanda," Emilia conceded. "I know it's hard for you to understand, but it all makes sense now. Everything Massimino has said and done since that very first dream—he's been trying to make me want to do this, and it was working."

"All right." Amanda's voice trembled. "Whether it's true or not, Gerlinde, please...can you help us escape? We need to get out of Zillah or Massimino will kill Emilia." She'd become shrill by the end of the sentence and had to stop to clear her throat and regain her composure.

Gerlinde shook her head again. "I'm the last person in the world who would risk yet another mistake...if I knew of a way, I would help you flee. It just isn't possible for you to leave—especially today. Massimino will be more vigilant than ever and the whole village is loyal to him—or at least fearful of him."

"Then what are we supposed to do?" Amanda asked.

For the longest time, all three of them stared into the fire, unable to utter a single word.

Chapter Forty-Six

Massimino rose from the bed and glanced back at Rose. She shifted at the disturbance, nuzzling her head against the soft satin; her eyelids fluttered, and her skin shone with perspiration as her body worked to quell the fire he'd created within her. Ilsa remained still and undisturbed; her breathing calm.

I must have worn her out if she was able to stay asleep through that, he smirked.

Massimino's naked form strode to the windows facing toward the castle, his mind focused. His expression quickly changed from intense concentration to discontent.

"Where is the heiress?" he murmured under his breath.

The sound of a pleasurable moan escaped Rose's lips as she stretched in the bed, drawing Massimino's attention once more.

"You," he thundered. "Why did you come here? What have you done?"

Rose's eyes sprung open, Massimino sensing her fear as the flames in the fireplace intensified along with his fury.

Rose opened her mouth as if to speak but no words came, it appeared she lacked the strength to form a response or defend herself.

"Where is the heiress?" he roared. "I demand you tell me." Massimino paced toward the bed; toward Rose.

Once more Rose attempted to speak but seemed to be paralyzed.

As the flames billowed from the fireplace, Massimino rolled his hand in a scooping motion and caused a gust of wind to lift Rose's limp body from the bed as though she were a ragdoll. A look of panic fell across Rose's face as the wind constricted her body; no scream escaped her lips, no limbs moved in protest—until the wind subsided and she fell in a heap upon the bed.

The crash of Rose's body as she landed on the mattress startled Ilsa, who awoke and let out a squeal.

"Silence! Go back to the village," Massimino instructed, waving his hand dismissively before he reached for his robe and threw it over his head. He tied the rope around his waist as he charged down the spiral staircase. When he reached the bottom and entered the courtyard, he saw Franco crossing the space ahead of him.

"Franco!" he called out, startling the young man.

"Massimino...yes? What is it?" Franco replied, changing direction and heading toward him. They met in the courtyard, near the oak tree.

"One of the women from the village—Rose—is in my tower," Massimino explained. "I need you to make sure she is taken to the dungeons and kept locked up until tonight. This is very important; I cannot afford for her to cause any more trouble today."

"Of course, sir. Is everything all right? You seem—"

"I am fine," Massimino said, no time to talk. "Do as I have asked. And if you see the heiress or her sister, do not allow them to leave. Do you understand?" He didn't wait for a reply before storming off.

As Massimino neared the castle, he paused and closed his eyes, again concentrating on each room. Shaking his head in disbelief, he quickly made his way up the stairs, not bothering to close the door behind him as he climbed another set of steps to Emilia's chambers.

He wouldn't let his anger get the best of him yet, but when he saw the shattered double doors he broke into a run and rushed to the bed.

She was gone.

"Whoever did this will pay," Massimino muttered through gritted teeth.

As he turned to leave, he noticed the tray and remains of the food sitting on the table. Furious, he hurried downstairs.

Mrs. Rossi was clearing up some dishes and humming a tune as Massimino entered the kitchen. "Where is the heiress? Who let her out?"

"What?" The woman jumped at his voice. "What do you mean, Master?"

"Did you not make breakfast for her this morning?"

"I…I…was up there, yes, with her sister Amanda—lovely woman. I do not know how she broke the door; I guess she wanted to get to her sister is all."

"I am not concerned about the door. I want to know where the heiress is."

"What, is she not in her bed?" The cook's eyebrows rose on her sweaty forehead as she added ingredients to some steaming water. "When I saw her up there, she was dead to the world—they were worried as can be that the heiress would not wake up. I left some food up there in case she did, but that is all. I have not seen her anywhere down here, sir—I swear to you. Dead to the world."

"Who is *they*?" Massimino demanded.

"Um…uh…" She stopped what she was doing. "Amanda. Her sister Amanda was with her up there."

"And who else?" He was growing more impatient by the second.

"I don't know…it was the sister, Amanda. We chatted for a few minutes. The heiress was asleep the whole time."

A light breeze began to blow around the kitchen and the fires in the stove and oven wavered. Massimino's eyes locked onto Mrs. Rossi's. "I don't believe you. This is your *last* chance—answer truthfully." The intensity of the wind increased.

Mrs. Rossi gasped and tried to back away but bumped into a chair behind her, stumbling a little before balancing herself.

"Oh, my. I…I'm sorry, sir." That was more like it; Massimino preferred it when people were afraid of him. "The witch, Gerlinde was

378

up there, sir—she scares me, that one. I left as soon as she arrived. I should have said something, Master. I—I don't know why I didn't."

The wind subsided and the flames settled back to normal.

Of course, the only place in the village I cannot see. Old woman, you will regret this meddling.

"I cannot afford to waste my strength dealing with you now, but rest assured I will in good time." Massimino stormed out without giving her an opportunity to reply.

Once outside, he took a few running steps before leaping into the air. As he did so, he transformed into a raven, its shiny feathers black as night. Massimino soared high above the village, circling overhead for a few moments before setting his sights on the group of cottages across the river and diving for them. As the magnificent bird reached a height a few feet from the ground, it spread its wings wide and pulled back, so its talons pointed downward. At that moment, Massimino reappeared once more, landing on his feet. He paused momentarily, silently studying the cottage before him, the one he knew belonged to Gerlinde.

He paced around the cottage, shouting threats, "I demand you come out at once, you cannot hide the heiress from me."

Time passed without any response or sign of acquiescence.

"Come out *now* or I'll tear your pitiful cottage apart!"

As daylight faded, Massimino's patience drew thin. Waving his hand in a circular motion, a force of wind pounded against the door until it yielded to the assault and flung open, the sound of items crashing and breaking inside could be heard as the wind dissipated and Massimino entered. He searched the space, prepared for an ambush in an area his senses were unable to penetrate.

There was no retaliation, and rage consumed him as he realized the cottage was empty.

Where is she? I must find her; the time is almost upon us.

Airborne once more, a mangled cottage in his wake, Massimino felt his anger intensify as his search for Emilia continued. Now, circling overhead as the sky grew darker and the evening settled in, the raven scanned the forest and the valley below, the village streets and the castle's courtyard; sharp eyes seeking out its prey.

Suddenly, a small slither of light coming from the front of the castle drew the bird's attention. His curiosity grew when only a few moments later the light disappeared; after making another pass, he gently descended, reemerging as Massimino on the main steps of the castle.

Chapter Forty-Seven

For the better part of the afternoon and into the evening, Amanda watched her sister practice her newfound powers. Emilia had strengthened her gifts; the elements bent to her will, and she was even able to lift Amanda as well as other objects with her mind alone. However, Amanda would rather flee before Emilia needed to use these powers. What they were up against was far greater than half a day's worth of learning. Her frustration grew as her efforts to rally an escape continued to be rebuffed; she was now very anxious to leave.

"Emmi, you've made incredible progress," she said after Emilia had set her back on the ground, "but if we're to believe Gerlinde, Massimino has been building his strength and honing his powers for *hundreds* of years—maybe more." She tried to sound supportive. "You were there last night; you saw what happened. I know I sound like a broken record, but we really need to go."

Gerlinde pulled back the velvet curtains, peering out briefly to gauge the hour, a slither of light from the room escaping momentarily, before she quickly closed them and turned away from the window.

"Ordinarily, you would be no match for Massimino. Even if you practiced every day of your natural life, it is unlikely that you could ever defeat him."

"Um…was that supposed to be a pep-talk?" Amanda quipped.

For the slightest moment, Amanda thought she could see a hint of a smile form on the old woman's face, but it quickly disappeared and returned to a scowl.

"What we have in our favor," she said, "what we must take advantage of, is Massimino's vulnerability during the ritual. For it to work, he must open himself up, surrender completely to *you*—each of you to the other without any guard or reservation."

"But what if he enters my mind, he makes me feel things—do things that I wouldn't normally do or feel?" Emilia only paused to take a breath. "Won't he know I'm going to do something before I do it?"

"Yes, this is the last and perhaps most important thing I must show you today; all our lessons so far have been building to this," Gerlinde answered. "I must teach you how to prevent him from knowing your thoughts. And not only that, but how you can mislead him to believe you are thinking something you are not."

"Wait, wait, wait!" Hands on her hips, Amanda shook her head in disbelief. "Emmi, you can't seriously be thinking about going through with this. I still can't even believe this magic is a real thing—or whatever it is that's going on here. How are you thinking this is going to work: you roll up to the ritual, pretend you're happy to sacrifice yourself, and then knock him over with a breeze? It's crazy! There's no way this is a good idea. If you go to the ritual, he's going to end up killing you, just like you've seen in your dreams—or worse, like he did to your mother...I'm sorry, I didn't mean to sound so...we need to get you out of here, Emmi!"

"Countess, please." Gerlinde ignored Amanda's rant. "Massimino is no doubt searching for you—we don't have much more time; I must impart this knowledge now." She held out her elderly hands, "Give me your hands, and I will share with you as much as I can."

Emilia did as she asked, and the force Gerlinde used to latch on was startling to both sisters. Gasping, she closed her eyes involuntarily.

Amanda looked on, sensing their last chance to escape ahead of the ritual had probably come and gone. She watched cautiously, thinking how bizarre such a scene would have seemed a few days ago; her fear continued to build, and now panic began to simmer along with it.

Amanda's gaze was broken by the sound of banging; the doors in the sitting room were rattling. "I think we've got company."

She saw Gerlinde frown, but her eyes remained closed, her grip on Emilia unchanged. Emilia shook as if the intensity of what had been happening suddenly increased.

The noise had stopped, but the rattling became a rumbling echo. The doors continued to hold up against whatever force was behind it, but that didn't make Amanda any less terrified. Gerlinde grimaced, and Emilia was now making audible moans as if she were in pain as well.

The old woman's eyes opened suddenly, and she released her hold on Emilia before turning directly to the doorway as the pounding intensified.

Emilia blinked a few times, seemingly dazed. However, her sister looked much more alive than Amanda had remembered seeing her in the last few weeks.

"I don't know if I was able to impart all I hoped to," Gerlinde panted. "I had to push so fast—I had no choice. The lock will not hold for long and I do not have the strength to keep the doors closed, not against his force; Massimino has found us. You must go. He can't know what we have been planning, and he must believe that you shall participate—voluntarily—in the ritual." The chaos of crashing and banging grew and Gerlinde had to raise her voice. "He must not suspect!"

"Emilia, come on. Let's get out of here," Amanda shouted as she grabbed Emilia by the arm and started pulling her toward the window.

Emilia followed somewhat reluctantly, turning back several times to Gerlinde. "Amanda, we have to help her. We can't just run."

"You heard her, Emmi." Amanda wasn't going to be delayed further; they'd already lingered in this hellhole too long. "She wants us to go."

"But—"

The doors burst into flames and a heavy, dark smoke streamed in. The fire blazed with an unnatural intensity and Gerlinde appeared to be faltering, becoming clumsier by the minute. Unsure of what to do, Amanda crouched to hide behind one of the long sofas, pulling Emilia with her.

"Amanda, I need you to go and get help," her sister urged. "I can't leave her—please…go and find some people in the village who will help us and bring them back here. We need to finish this."

"No way." Amanda couldn't believe what she was hearing. "You're coming with me right now, and we are getting the fuck out of this place."

"We have to," Emilia called over the fire and wind. "If we run now, he won't let us get far. I have to fight him, Amanda—it's the only way. Who knows what he'll do to Gerlinde, I can't leave her alone with him, but I don't know if I can beat him either—so I need you to go and find help...*please!*"

Amanda opened her mouth to reply but the crunch of the wood around the locks gave way, stealing the opportunity from her.

Massimino stood amongst the fiery opening. "Old woman, what do you possibly hope to achieve with all of this? You really think you can teach this young one, so new to this world, how to resist me?" he bellowed, striding into the room. "Why do you insist on being such a thorn in my side? You will most certainly pay—where is she?"

"Gerlinde is right," Emilia whispered, moving closer beside Amanda. "We can't run, we can't escape him; he will hunt us down—this is our only chance. Please, I'm begging you...I will distract him. I need you to go and get help! Go, please!" Emilia insisted. "I have to stay and do what I can. This is my home. I love you."

Chapter Forty-Eight

"What have you told her, Gerlinde?" Massimino bellowed, as windy gusts sent books, teacups, and other trinkets tearing through the air. "Have you been filling her head with lies and poisoning her against me? You couldn't just leave well enough alone, you meddling witch? Tell me, what new mess have you created that I must now clean up?"

"She has told me the truth, Massimino!" Emilia screamed as she stood from behind the sofa and hurried to Gerlinde's side. She could only pray Amanda did as she asked.

"Countess, why are you still here?" Gerlinde looked grief-stricken that Emilia had not gotten away.

"You see, old woman?" he replied in a smug tone. "You cannot change things. She is drawn to me, and nothing you say will change that."

He gazed into Emilia's eyes and her feet carried her closer to him. His deep stare locked with hers and she felt him, once again, stirring the space between her legs. Previously, his magic would have rendered her powerless to the arousal, ready to submit to him if it meant he would quell it. Though Emilia felt the sensations rising, she found she was able to suppress them—at least to some extent—so the effect was dulled.

"No, Massimino," Emilia said. "Gerlinde has told me the truth. The truth about who you are, the truth about what you have done to this village—to my family—for centuries. The truth about what you did to *my parents*. There is no way I will help you. You can forget about killing me in your ritual to steal my powers—oh yes, I know about all of *that*, too."

Emilia whipped her hand around several times and turned the air into a churning gust, followed by a surge in the dwindling flames around the door.

'No!" Gerlinde's voice rung out in alarm. "It won't be possible for you to defeat him, not like this, you must try and get out of here—"

"What is the matter, old woman?" Massimino chuckled as he spoke. "Something not going to plan, again? You senseless fool—"

He was cut off as a shot of wind as strong as a jet engine drove him backward out of the room; the sound of some unseen piece of furniture crushing under his body could be heard from the hallway.

"You were saying?" Emilia boasted with a smile.

But Gerlinde was somber, "Countess, you must run. Get out of here before he returns—he won't trust you now. I don't know what we could possibly do…not now that this has happened—"

Emilia was confused. Why was Gerlinde so discouraged? Then, the sound of a deep, evil laugh preceded Massimino's return to the sitting room.

"My dear Emilia…you disappoint me so." He fixed his robe and then his hair. "The memories we've created these past few days, the passions we've shared…all the lengths I went to so it might at least be an enjoyable experience for you as I took what I needed. Now though, I see where I stand. I will need to approach this a very different way," Massimino growled.

Emilia adopted an offensive stance, preparing to strike Massimino again—with even more force if she could manage it. Massimino stood perfectly still and stared directly at her.

It began as a twinge of pain in her temple but quickly grew in intensity as it spread throughout her body, throbbing through every inch of muscle and bone.

"Fight it, Countess! Fight it!" called Gerlinde.

Emilia heard her words, but the meaning didn't reach her, the agony engulphed her like flames.

"You can stop this!" Gerlinde persisted. "You must fight it!"

Massimino remained silent, a neutral expression on his face as he continued to gaze upon Emilia, now on her knees, both hands holding her head as she sank and coiled further and further against the floor. Emilia felt an unusual awareness grow within her. As she fought against the pain and began to filter some of what Gerlinde had shared with her that afternoon, Emilia visualized Massimino's assault as an invasion within her and strained against it. Gathering all the power she could, Emilia pushed back and for a few moments, the pressure on her head lessened.

"That's it!" Gerlinde encouraged. "Fight it! Push him out!"

With a casual sweep of his hand, Massimino toppled Gerlinde; a burst of wind sending her head crashing against an end table, his focus never leaving Emilia. Even with her eyes closed Emilia could sense what had happened and she heard the old woman cry out.

Emilia strained to repel Massimino, rising from the floor into a crouch before she stood, opening her eyes and staring back toward him. She hoped the rage she felt inside reflected in her eyes.

"I won't let you...do this!" Emilia screamed through another wave of pain, like needles pricking her bloodstream.

It was no use; there was no shock or disappointment in Massimino's expression. Instead, the wicked sorcerer's mouth morphed into a broad smile.

"Silly young woman, you are certainly far stronger and have learned faster than I thought possible," he cooed. "But I have been doing this for a great deal longer. You think the old woman can teach you a few tricks and that is all it will take to stop me?" Massimino sighed. "Emilia, I believed you to be wiser than this. Now enough of this nonsense." He sounded equal parts amused and condescending.

Massimino swooped his hand downward then up; wind blustered through the room and knocked Emilia onto her back. Distracted by the sudden assault, Emilia's resistance gave way and abruptly, a new, far more powerful wave of fire pulsed through her veins. She lost consciousness; it was her mind's only available response to protect herself.

Massimino stood over Emilia as she lay on the ground, completely still apart from her breathing, which was slowing to a normal rhythm. As he gazed down upon her, Massimino shook his head before looking across to where Gerlinde was attempting to push herself up from the floor, blood flowing down her face from a large gash on her right temple.

"Look at what you have done, old fool." He spoke softly, but the fire in his voice made her flinch. "Do you forget where your treachery and deception led us in the past? Do you want to see this beautiful young woman tortured as her mother was? Why would you do this?"

Franco appeared in the doorway; black hair tousled like he had been running. "Oh, Massimino...I...I heard the commotion and saw the flames." He panted slightly as he took in the scene with wide eyes. "Everything all right?"

Massimino didn't look away from Gerlinde as she struggled. "It will be. There is still time to right this wrong. I must get the heiress to the chapel..." he glanced at Emilia, peacefully slumbering. "Where is her sister?"

"I saw someone jump from the window, Master," Franco answered and Massimino faced him, suddenly interested in what he had to say. "Ran toward the village."

"Go to the village and gather a few people to help you," he ordered. "I want you to find the sister and bring her to me."

"Ah...okay. I can do that, sir," Franco didn't appear pleased with the request, but Massimino didn't have time—nor did he care—to hold the boy's hand.

"Go now." Massimino waved him away, bringing his focus back to the other woman at his feet. "And as for you..."

Gerlinde looked at Massimino as she patted her temple, blood on her fingers.

"That scratch will be the least of your problems if you do not let go of this fantasy that you can stop me," Massimino bellowed. "You *will* help me to complete this ritual tonight."

"Do your worst." The old woman clenched her jaw, defiant even as he towered over her. "No one else can take my place—you know that. You threaten to make me live for an eternity? So be it, I have endured this long. But I will not help you to kill her!"

"Then consider this," Massimino sneered. "If the ritual fails again, I will ensure that what happened last time pales in comparison to what I will do before this night is through. This young woman's blood will be on *your* hands, and you will suffer for it every day of your long and miserable life." He let that sink in, smirking as her defiance faltered. "But if you play your role and the ritual is performed with success, this young woman will die a noble death. Her essence may live on within me—perhaps she will even return some light back into my own tortured soul. And when I am free from my curse, I will release you; then you may finally succumb to the ages as you so wish." Massimino spoke calmly, confident that he had left Gerlinde no option to disagree.

Tears filled the old woman's eyes as she glanced at Emilia lying motionless on the floor.

"Good," barked Massimino, knowing her mind had changed. "The hour draws near, and I must get Emilia to the chapel. Tell me you will do as I have said."

Gerlinde leaned against a shelf for support, hanging her head in defeat. "I will complete the ritual, but please—I beg you—release me immediately after. I won't be able to go on with the guilt."

Massimino didn't reply as he stooped down and hoisted Emilia over his shoulder. Heading past the charred, still-smoldering doorway, he stepped outside.

Chapter Forty-Nine

Without looking around, Emilia knew exactly where she was. She felt the flat, rough stone beneath her; she smelled the musky air mingling with the enticing scent of Massimino standing over her.

"Emilia...Emilia, my love," he whispered, rubbing her shoulder. "Wake now." His grinning face greeted her. "There you are. It is almost time."

"The chapel...?" Emilia tried to sit herself up, but she could only lean on her elbows. "Was I dreaming?"

Massimino stroked her cheek, staring longingly into her eyes. "Perhaps. I do hope they were pleasant dreams. Now, my love, the congregation has assembled, the moon is rising. Are you ready, Emilia?" His tender touch sent electric sparks through her body. "It is important that I know you are ready to surrender yourself in every way to me—completely and without reservation."

As Massimino caressed her, Emilia felt her attraction growing, an arousal brewing within her. She glanced through the chapel windows to see the most spectacular moon she could remember, amongst the stars filling the sky, it was awash with a reddish tinge as it hung just above the mountains.

"I was worried you would not awaken in time, but now we can complete our union tonight. Tell me, is this where you want to be and what you want?" Massimino's voice was gentle and reassuring.

"I...um..." Emilia replied, uncertain as she turned her head and saw a dozen robed figures arranged in a semi-circle at the base of the sanctuary. The chapel was aglow with candlelight, forming majestic patterns on the walls and ceiling—familiar, alluring, terrifying. The chapel doors were closed, preventing her from seeing outside.

A trickle of memories flowed into her consciousness, disparate and disjointed; not enough to form a complete recollection.

"Am I dreaming now, Massimino? Was I dreaming those terrible things? My parents..." She frowned as her gaze settled on him. "Did you?"

"My love, I do not know what you speak of," he murmured, closing the limited space between them. "You are safe with me. Remember, this is what you want—this is what *we* want, together." Massimino spoke calmly, staring into her eyes while his hand wandered downward, cupping and teasing her breast and enlisting pleasure as a distraction. A wave of arousal coursed through to her inner soul.

Emilia sighed and bit her lip, unable to answer to the contrary. "This is what I want," she found herself responding though it felt as if someone else had taken control of her words.

"Yes, Emilia, that is right." Massimino smiled wryly, and a look of hunger flashed in his eyes.

A pang of fear cut through the heat rising within her. "Wait, you must tell me the truth." She was almost breathless as she became more uncomfortable and worked to suppress the sensations.

As Massimino spoke, Emilia turned her attention to the robed figures, their faces obscured by their hoods. She studied each, searching, seeking. As her eyes wandered from one to the next, a figure in the center moved, raising what appeared to be a haggard female hand to shift the hood a little, revealing an equally haggard face with a large, gaping gash on her forehead and dried blood on her face.

Gerlinde. She's hurt. What happened?

For a few moments, the old woman gazed intently at Emilia before returning the hood over her head, hands clasped in front of her. As Massimino followed her gaze, Emilia fixed him with a deep stare; the memories came flooding back, overpowering Massimino's attempts to manipulate her thoughts.

Emilia pushed Massimino back from his position hovering over her and jumped down, standing beside the altar to face him.

"Oh, Emilia." His voice softened with a sigh. "I have tried to make this a pleasant experience, but you insist on making that an impossibility."

Emilia let out a laugh at his audacity. "Pleasant? You consider killing me and stealing my powers a *pleasant* experience? I think you've been hiding in this village, up in your tower with your harem of lustful women, for far too long. You've lost touch with reality, if you ever knew it to begin with."

"Your strength and intellect work against you in this situation, I'm afraid." He shook his head. "Why couldn't you just embrace the feelings I worked so hard to create in you and surrender yourself?"

"You can forget all about this." Emilia ran her hands across the stains on the altar. "You killed my mother right here. The realization hit her at once, and it was like they had died all over again. "I promise you, there will be no more of my family's blood spilled. I am going to be the end of you."

The dazzling array of candles surrounding the chapel undulated with each inflection of her voice; her anger made it effortless to control them.

Massimino's features became stern with tension. "My dearest Emilia, your threats and boldness will only make this victory more fulfilling. You will most certainly submit yourself to me before this night is through." Then he grinned, calling, "Bring me the sister!"

A rattle and creaking could be heard as the heavy wooden doors of the chapel swung open. The firepits, path, and skyline outside were identical to Emilia's dreams, but this time two scraggily villagers wrestled with Amanda, dragging her against her will into the chapel.

Massimino's attention remained firmly on Emilia, a broad smile forming on his face as he savored her reaction.

"You let her go right now!" Emilia screamed as a gust of wind blew past the altar.

"Or what? It seems you have remembered everything else, but are you forgetting how our last encounter ended in the castle? I am far more powerful than you, Emilia." Massimino paused, fire blazing in his eyes. "If you do not surrender and submit yourself freely to this ritual, I will kill your sister also."

Rage simmered within Emilia, but she did remember what had happened earlier. She would not risk harm coming to Amanda.

"Bring her to me," Massimino demanded.

The two villagers battled a wriggling and squirming Amanda as the robed congregation parted to allow them through and re-formed when they had passed.

Amanda's cheeks were streaked with tears, she had a bruise growing on her left eye, and her clothes were torn and dirty. She had been gagged with a tattered piece of cloth and her hands were bound behind her back with rope.

Emilia wanted to reach out and free her sister. "What have they done to you?"

"She is fine, I assure you," Massimino answered. "She was a little difficult during her capture, but I have given word that she is not to be harmed any further, so long as you cooperate."

Emilia rushed toward Amanda and the villagers instinctively moved to stop her, but Massimino waved them off and they stood down. Emilia pulled the gag from Amanda's mouth and wrapped her arms around her sister, squeezing tightly.

"I'm so sorry," Emilia sobbed. "I'm so sorry I got you involved in all of this."

"Emmi, you can't do what they say," Amanda shook her head rapidly. "You just can't—"

"Enough!" Massimino cut her off, drawing the attention of all present as he strode to the back of the sanctuary and retrieved one of the ceremonial daggers from the wall. "It is time you choose if one of you survives this night, Emilia. And you must do so now." Massimino glanced over his shoulder and Emilia could see the moon nearing the top of the center window.

"How can I trust you won't kill her anyway?" Emilia protested.

"Emilia, you can't do this!" Amanda cried, gripping her arms.

"My dear Emilia," Massimino sighed. "Whether you trust me is of no relevance. You have no other choice." He touched the tip of the dagger to Amanda's neck before gently, almost seductively, trailing it downward, across her chest, the razor-sharp blade beginning to cut through her top.

Emilia watched the dagger move and felt her heartbeat increasing as she recalled the dream where she had surrendered herself on the altar.

Massimino didn't take his eyes off Emilia as he continued his little dagger tease. "The time is—"

"All right, I'll do it—" yelled Emilia, "but you must take her out of here." Her instructions were somber; she accepted what needed to be done as she fixed Massimino with a cold stare. "I want her protected from this."

Amanda's knuckles turned white as she grasped at her. "Emilia, no! Please, stop! Don't do this!"

"Silence! Remove her at once," Massimino thundered, waving his hand toward the entrance.

The two figures who had escorted her sister in tore her away from Emilia, ignoring her protests.

"I love you," Emilia mouthed to Amanda as she was dragged away.

The congregation again parted to allow passage and Amanda kicked and screamed, crying and pleading for Emilia to stop as she was dragged from the chapel. Her pleas became muffled once the doors were closed again. Then everything was silent.

They must have gagged her again. Assholes. If they've hurt her…

Focus, I need to focus now.

Emilia felt short of breath and could feel her heart pounding wildly, her pulse seeming to echo within her head as adrenaline raced through her.

Oh my God, this is it. I'm actually going to have to go through with this. Fuck!

Massimino stood over Emilia, staring deeply into her eyes as he studied her. "The ritual will not work unless you willingly partake. It is critical that you know this—if you are deceiving me, I will kill both of you. Do you understand?" His demeanor had calmed now, his voice too smooth for what he was saying.

Think...focus...I need to calm my mind. I need to convince him that I'm willing to do this or he'll hurt—kill—Amanda. Of course I'm willing to go through with this if it means saving my sister...I'd do anything.

Emilia swallowed hard. "I understand." She turned to stare out the window and saw the moon just about at its peak. She then glanced down at the remaining dagger, its shiny gold and silver glinting in the candlelight. "Let me remove any doubt you have right now about my commitment, and my willingness..."

She slipped from his gaze and sauntered over to the wall to remove the second dagger. Another surge of adrenaline flowed through her as she felt the weight of the weapon.

This is heavier than I expected—cold, hard, smooth...these designs; they're beautiful, or at least they would be if I weren't about to...can something be beautiful and awful at the same time?

Focus, focus...I need to focus.

He needs to know I want this. How did I feel when I was with him, in my dreams, in his tower, in my chambers—I would have said yes to anything he wanted then; longing, desire, lust...love. I need to feel all that again, now. He needs to feel me feeling that way again; Gerlinde showed me how.

Emilia felt her hand tremble. Her heart was beating so fast she couldn't be sure it wouldn't burst through her chest right then and there. She felt dizzy, and a lump formed in her throat, but she summoned her composure.

All right, breathe in...

Emilia forced a slow and steady inhale through her nose.

Breathe out...

Emilia closed her eyes and slowly and purposefully exhaled through her mouth, repeating the process over again while allowing the emotions she'd felt with Massimino to flood her thoughts.

"Are you stalling? We do not have much time—do I need to have your sister brought back in here?" Massimino spoke, his tone resolute.

"No, no...I'm just...here," she swallowed hard, "let me show you how much I want this, how willing I am...I believe this is what happens next," Emilia said, looking Massimino in the eye as she came to stand in front of the altar.

As Massimino looked on, Emilia lifted the dagger to her neck and began to slowly, sensually, cut open her white linen robe. She felt the air on her skin as the slit grew and when the opening was wide enough, she pulled it apart at the chest and let it fall to the floor, bunching around her feet.

"Now it's your turn, Massimino." Emilia panted slightly as she kept her eyes locked on him, consciously breathing in and out at her measured pace.

At first, he appeared confused by her change of heart, but ultimately, he stepped before Emilia. She held her dagger near his chest, about to cut his robe from him. "Perhaps it is better if I do this." He halted her movements before turning to the figures. "Begin—the moon is in place! And let me be clear: I do not care if this chapel bursts into flames or the ground opens beneath us. You are not to stop until the ritual is complete."

The congregation began to chant the same eerie tones Emilia recalled from her dreams.

These sounds. Were they the last my mother ever heard? Will they be the last thing I ever hear?

Though fleeting, the thought was more than powerful enough to energize Emilia, forcing her mind back to the moment and galvanizing her against what was to come. "I do want this Massimino—yes, for

Amanda, but for me too. The feelings you've stirred since you found me, they're still within," Emilia placed her hand on her chest, "I can't help but feel them...do you feel them too?"

Massimino gazed upon Emilia as her eyes filled with lust, he studied her, staring intently as if probing to the very depths of her soul.

"I do," Massimino murmured as he pulled his robe over his head, tossing it to the floor beside him. She set the dagger on the altar with a *clink* before placing both palms on the rough stone surface and lifting herself backward until she sat, her naked chest heaving, legs hanging over the edge, crossed at the thighs. Massimino stepped directly in front of her, never breaking his gaze, eyes locked firmly on Emilia's, his expression conveying a cautious excitement.

Oh, fuck—this is really happening. Breathe. Emilia swallowed hard; she could feel her head spinning as the ultimate moment drew closer.

"Now I lie down on the altar." Emilia spoke softly, staring intimately into his eyes. "There is nothing I want more than this, Massimino."

To her shock, a tear rolled down his cheek.

"It must be now, Massimino," Gerlinde's shrill voice broke the silence and he looked out the window; the moon was blood red and exactly centered above them. The chorus grew in intensity.

Now? Oh my God, this can't be real...but it is. Stay in the moment, there is no other way to save Amanda—to end this.

Massimino drew his dagger and swiped down and across his chest, cutting a fresh gash. Blood dripped from the wound along roughly the same path as his scar.

The candlelight illuminated the blood, the crimson liquid seeping slowly from the sorcerer's chest.

Oh fuck, oh—

"This may cause you pain—I am sorry," breathed Massimino as he placed the dagger in position, delivering a cut across her chest to match his own. Emilia let out a gasp as the cold, sharp blade pierced her skin.

"Emilia, please say these words after me," Massimino whispered into her ear, eyes glassy with more unshed tears.

Emilia breathed heavily, forcing a small smile and nod.

Massimino spoke first. "From the dying to the living."

"From the dying to the living," repeated Emilia.

"I open myself completely."

"I open myself completely."

"Let all that is within."

"Let all that is within."

"Go forward within the other." Massimino's eyes were fireballs as he finished his decree.

How many of these lines are there, how will I know when...

Emilia did her best to subdue her fear. "Go forward within the other."

The chanting reached a crescendo, almost deafening as it filled the small space.

Massimino locked his eyes on Emilia once again as he took the dagger handle in both hands, this time lifting it high above his head, the blade pointing directly toward Emilia's chest.

The air surrounding the pair became electrified, sparking around them.

"What's happening?" Emilia gasped.

"*Yes*, it is working!" Massimino cried, gazing down at Emilia with wonderment. "I am sorry. I wish there was another way."

The static-filled air became a whirlwind, extinguishing many of the candles. The chanting continued unchanged as Massimino prepared to thrust his blade downward.

This is it. Emilia's hand trembled as she moved it, but it quickly became steadfast, as if understanding the importance of its task. Suddenly Massimino let out a scream over the chaos and stared down at the source of his anguish.

Tightening her grip on the dagger now wedged in Massimino's chest, Emilia pulled herself up and narrowed her eyes. "You are *not* sorry and there *is* another way! This is for my parents," she whispered harshly. Through clenched teeth, she continued the upward thrust with her dagger, feeling it scrape against his ribs as it pierced his heart deeper and deeper. She felt the warmth of his blood flowing over her hand before dripping to the ground.

Massimino gasped, but she was not finished. "For my family...for everyone in this village..." Emilia fought against the pressure of his bodyweight as it pressed into her. A glint of reflected candlelight drew her attention to the weapon he still held above her. Emilia's hair whipped wildly in the wind and she screamed to make her voice heard over it, "The people you've hurt and tortured and killed—this is for all of them." With all that remained of her strength, Emilia grabbed hold of Massimino's arm, squeezing tightly as he resisted, finally forcing his hand to relent.

"*Aargh, Emilia!*" Massimino growled as blood continued to spill from his wound. No longer able to keep a grip on his weapon, it fell from his hand, clipping the far side of the altar before rattling to a stop on the marble floor. As each drop of precious liquid flowed from his body, his once powerful glow seemed to fade away, along with his very life.

Is it done? A sense of fear washed over Emilia. *Oh God, what if that didn't work? Could someone that powerful really have become so vulnerable?*

Emilia felt the resistance in Massimino's arm falter as more of his bodyweight pressed downward against the dagger she still clutched; its blade buried in his chest.

As quickly as it arrived, Emilia's fear ceased. Replaced with a sense of calm, a wave of tranquility crashed over her and she lay back against the rough stone surface of the altar; her eyes growing heavy, her mind and body surrendering to the strange sensations encircling her.

Is Massimino doing this? Is he still—

The forceful wind continued to roar, its pace increasing as it swirled wildly, the candlelight dimming as wick after wick was extinguished.

Emilia released the dagger, unable to continue supporting Massimino's weight. With his body slumped over her, the wind ceased, and a white light filled with golden sparks suddenly enveloped them both. She inhaled deeply and felt her body tense and shudder uncontrollably as an unknown force surrounded her. It felt powerful, this soul-like presence she now owned and controlled. It wanted to be one with her, cloaking Emilia in a cocoon of warmth until it finally appeared to permeate her physical being.

Chapter Fifty

Emilia opened her eyes, staring up at the chapel ceiling as light streamed through the windows. Though she immediately knew where she was, it didn't feel like it ever had before; now it seemed calm and bright, safe—as though a darkness had lifted. She turned her head and saw Rose and Amanda rushing toward her, and not far behind them was Gerlinde, rising from a makeshift bed on one of the pews. All three were still dressed as they had been the night before, appearing exhausted and bearing wounds and injuries of their own.

All had blankets wrapped around them; Emilia could tell she was naked underneath hers, the rough stone of the altar prickling her skin as she moved.

"Emmi, you're awake!" Amanda leaned closer to hug her. "You passed out and we couldn't wake you—Gerlinde insisted that we not move you, so we stayed here all night."

"Ouch!" Emilia said softly.

"Oh, sorry. Are you in pain?" Tears filled Amanda's eyes.

"Yeah, um..." She wasn't quite sure how she felt. "I feel fine—great, actually. My chest stings a bit, though." Emilia lifted the blanket, searching for the cause of the discomfort. It stuck to the dried blood smeared there. "Oh, so it wasn't a dream."

"No, dear Countess," Rose said. "It is a *miracle*. I cannot believe you are alive and you—" She couldn't meet Emilia's eyes or finish her sentence.

Wrapping the blanket around herself to shield against the cold morning air, Emilia sat upright. "What?"

Emilia followed Rose's gaze to the floor; Massimino's body lay naked in a heap, where it had fallen from the altar.

"You killed him," Rose whispered. "Never in my wildest dreams did I imagine you could have done so, at least not like this. You are brave beyond belief. You have rid this world of a terrible evil."

Emilia felt herself tremble with shock, the gritty reality of the prior evening lay cold and lifeless on the floor beside her. "I, I used what you taught me, Gerlinde. I was able to distract him the way he had often done with me. I kept his attention away from my inner thoughts and I was able to make him feel what I wanted him to." A shiver ran up her spine as recollections of what had happened flashed before her eyes and she huddled further under the blanket. "I was so scared he'd see through me though, but I suppose it...worked."

"Indeed. You have learned a great deal and I think, perhaps, he was so fixated on getting his way that he only saw what he wanted to see. His desire for revenge and his anger, these made him vulnerable while your focus and determination, and your love—for your sister and your family—made you strong." The old woman nodded, her sharp eyes scanning Emilia curiously.

"Why are you looking at me like that?"

"How do you feel?" she asked, studying her as if she were some strange creature. "How do you *really* feel?"

"You look like you've just come back from a day at the spa!" Amanda joked.

"Oh, very funny. I wish I could say the same for you," Emilia jabbed back.

"Yeah, I probably look like I've been attacked by a mob of villagers, forced to watch my sister surrender herself to some mad sorcerer, and then barely slept on some hard church pew while worried sick you'd never wake up again. Meanwhile, you've been through something a whole lot crazier and somehow look perfect!" Amanda shook her head in bewilderment.

"How do you feel *inside* though?" Gerlinde persisted.

"Really, I feel...amazing." That didn't begin to encompass how she felt. Strong, empowered, awakened—none seemed adequate. "I'm sure

402

given everything that's happened I should feel terrible, but it's really the opposite. I feel like I could run a marathon or climb a mountain."

"Impossible..." muttered Gerlinde, shaking her head.

"What's impossible? It's how I feel."

"Quickly, give me your hands," snapped Gerlinde, thrusting her bony fingers toward Emilia.

This time Emilia was ready for the claw-like grip as she reached out her hands; the old woman closed her eyes. Emilia felt the tingle flowing through her body, familiar with the sensation now and making no effort to shy away from it. As the feeling subsided, Gerlinde's eyes shot open and she shook her head in disbelief.

"What is it?" Emilia pressed.

"Tell me, what do you remember as the ritual was happening? After you stabbed Massimino?"

Emilia recalled the look of fire in his eyes; then shock before the life faded from him. How his eyes rolled back, and she felt him collapse into her.

"Yes, and then?" Gerlinde asked, still not satisfied.

Rose and Amanda curiously looked on.

"Um...what else?" Emilia pondered the events on the altar. "Oh, there was a lot of wind—and golden sparks—almost like stars, but they were popping all around the chapel. Then there was a tremendous white light—it was bright...warm, and I thought I might be dying, but, it didn't really feel like that. It was unlike anything else I've ever experienced—super intense but...peaceful too. I'm sure that makes no sense at all," Emilia shook her head at the recollection. That's the last thing I remember."

"Perhaps it was Massimino dying?" Amanda offered.

"Yes, in a way..." Gerlinde hesitated, "I—I think that the ritual completed last night. When I touched you just now, I could feel that the energy within you is so much stronger than it was before. I could feel *him*—Massimino. At least some part of him is within you. I don't know what any of this means or what may come of it, but I believe your life is never going to be the same again."

Emilia was stunned, unable to speak. Her sister didn't appear to have that issue.

"Whoa, wait a minute," Amanda blurted. "You're saying that instead of Massimino taking Emilia's powers, she now has all of his?"

Everyone fell silent, turning to Gerlinde for answers.

"Essentially, yes," sighed the old woman, plopping down on the bench with a grunt. "Though I have no real experience with this," she cleared her throat, "it will likely take some time for the full effects to be known. To absorb such strength and immense power from one such as Massimino—and with so little experience in these ways—I fear your body and your mind will have a difficult time assimilating all of this within your being."

"What? I didn't mean for this to happen—I didn't want his powers. I just thought I had no choice but to k—" Emilia gulped, "kill him—while he was vulnerable, like you said." Emilia couldn't believe what she was hearing. Massimino was dead, body on the ground. She had been willing to sacrifice her life to save Amanda's. Surrendering to the ritual, to Massimino, for the sake of her sister was maybe enough to make this all possible. "But I really do feel fine. Better than fine. In fact, I don't remember ever feeling so good!"

"That is heartening to hear," Gerlinde said with caution. "I certainly hope it continues this way for you."

"And if not, you will help me, right?" Emilia asked with a smile. "I'm sure we can figure this out together."

"I am not the one to help you with this journey," Gerlinde answered. "And, with Massimino dead, the spell he placed upon me will be lifted and this frail body may finally succumb to the ages that have ravaged it. It's unlikely I will survive to see the end of this day."

Emilia's heart dropped. As she watched Amanda and Rose's reactions, she could tell Amanda felt the same. Rose looked on neutrally; she understood the way of things.

"No, you mustn't be sad for me," Gerlinde said with a kind smile. "I have survived far beyond what nature should have permitted, and I have wished for this a very long time. The only thing I can offer you is a name: Cassius. Massimino spoke of him many times early on, but I don't know if he would be a friend or foe. I caution you to be wary, but I believe him to be of Massimino's world and, as such, may be able to provide you some answers."

"I can't believe this is goodbye—you've helped me so much." Emilia clutched her chest, wishing circumstances could be different. "Is there anything I can do for you?"

"You have released me. There is nothing more I could want for; I only hope that you don't come to hate me should this become too much for you to bear. I must go back to my cottage now." Gerlinde grasped her hand and kissed it as a tear streamed down her cheek.

Emilia, Amanda, and Rose watched silently as the old woman shuffled her way out of the chapel and along the path until she was out of sight.

"Countess, there is something I have wanted to tell you..." Rose spoke softly, clasping her hands at her chest. "He forbid me to, but now..." Her eyes welled with tears as she glanced back around the chapel then to Emilia once more.

"Rose, what's the matter, please...tell me." Emilia encouraged.

Rose smiled, taking Emilia's hand as a gentle tear ran down her cheek "It is about your father, Anton." Rose closed her eyes to slow the stream of tears now flowing from them. "He, he was my brother."

"Oh my gosh, Rose...*really*? I'm so sorry..." Emilia was stunned at the news as she realized Rose too had lost so much in all that had happened. Then it hit her. "Wait, so that means you're my aunt? And Nicolas is my uncle?"

Rose could only nod as she gripped her chin, doing her best to smile as she shed more tears.

"Amanda, I've got an aunt and uncle—I have family here!" Emilia exclaimed, overcome with joy.

Rose and Emilia embraced around their thick, heavy blankets; holding each other tight, they both understood the significance of all that had been sacrificed, won and lost, for such a remarkable family reunion to now even be possible.

"Come now." Rose tugged on Emilia's hand, guiding her down from the altar. "We must get you cleaned up and fed."

As they emerged from the chapel and into the morning light, the three stopped to watch the sun rising over the mountains beyond the castle and the village. Rose began to cry once more, and Emilia understood the reason: the reign of Massimino had ended. The darkness, the gray, dull, cloudy era had been replaced with a bright, sunny new beginning.

THE END

Epilogue

E milia stood alone in her chambers, gazing upon herself in one of the tall mirrors as she shrugged off the blanket. The fresh cut snaked its way across her chest, and she ran her fingertip gently along it.

As if what happened last night wasn't unforgettable enough, I've got this wicked souvenir, too.

The reality hit her like a sledgehammer: the mess of dried blood on her skin was partly hers, but mostly Massimino's.

Emilia...Emilia.

Emilia tensed. She thought she'd heard Massimino's voice calling to her, but it was a distant echo.

Quickly reassuring herself that this could only be her imagination, Emilia shook her head and went to take a shower. As she watched the blood wash across the grey stones before it disappeared down the drain, she studied the wound on her chest. Although it stung as water rained over it, Emilia was impressed that it already appeared to be healing.

Freshly showered and dressed herself, Amanda came bounding into her sister's chambers as Emilia was drying off, wrapping a towel around her.

"You still doing all right, sis?" Amanda asked.

"Yeah, I guess so. I mean, what am I supposed to think about all this?" Emilia wiped water droplets from her face. "I really do feel great, which I suppose is good; there's going to be a lot to do around here now."

"Totally!" Amanda agreed. "I was wondering what you were thinking about doing with the village. I don't know about you, but I'm starving.

Can we chat about it over breakfast?" She smiled as though she couldn't be happier to be alive—even more relieved that her sister was okay.

"Yeah, of course." Emilia rummaged through her suitcase and pulled out a champagne silk cami, dark denim skinny jeans and a low-cut, white V-neck sweater. "Just let me get dressed," she called as she strode toward the bathroom.

Emilia soon emerged looking and feeling like a goddess. Her silky hair fell past her shoulders, accentuating her cleavage, her lips shimmered with gloss and her green eyes shone like emeralds.

"Wow, you're glowing, Emmi." Amanda cooed.

Emilia smiled. "Thanks. Yeah, crazy I know, but I feel pretty amazing right now—kind of fierce or something—but in a good way; I feel like I could do anything!"

"Then go with it," Amanda agreed. "It's totally working!"

Emilia and Amanda were eating breakfast in the kitchen and recounting the extraordinary details from the prior evening's events. Mrs. Rossi and two of the young women working at the castle were listening intently when there was a knock on the back door and a group of villagers were invited inside.

Rose was the leader, guiding them in to stand around the countess. Some were fearful after the stories they had heard about the ritual and Massimino's collapse; others were perplexed at the beautiful weather, none having ever experienced a clear, sunny day in Zillah. Those involved in capturing Amanda, including Franco came to express their deepest regrets and asked for forgiveness, explaining they felt they had no choice but to obey Massimino. After apologies were made and accepted, and Emilia had satisfied their curiosities, all were converted and asked if she could visit the village and help set everyone's mind at ease. Emilia agreed to visit the town square that afternoon.

As the group was leaving, Franco stayed behind with his father, Domenic, and asked to speak with Emilia about some sensitive items.

While they strolled around the courtyard, they first discussed what to do with Massimino's body, which remained in the chapel. Domenic advised that Massimino commonly threw villagers' bodies into the mines as a convenient way to make them disappear and suggested the same may be fitting for him; but Emilia felt strangely opposed to this idea.

Despite being told it was reserved for Blagden family members only, Emilia insisted that Massimino be buried by the cemetery. Confused, yet not wanting to deny the countess' wishes, Franco and Domenic agreed. She also told them of the Corvus constellation engraved in his desk—and asked for the raven symbol to mark his grave.

The second matter of business was the prisoner, Thiess; Massimino had locked him in the dungeon following their confrontation at dinner. Domenic explained that Thiess had been injured quite seriously, and when he and Franco went to check on him, they discovered his lifeless body lying on the cold stone floor of his cell.

Emilia asked that they work to determine who his family was and organize for the body to be returned to them. Domenic protested, arguing that it would bring undue attention to the village and raise questions that could be difficult to answer. Emilia explained that she would handle any such queries. After all, Massimino had killed Thiess, and she had killed Massimino in self-defense. The times of secrecy and seclusion were an unfortunate part of Zillah's history, but she declared they would not be a part of its future.

Emilia wandered arm-in-arm with Amanda around the castle compound, then suddenly looked up toward the southern tower, feeling drawn to it on some subconscious level.

"That's where Massimino lived?" Amanda asked.

Emilia nodded as she continued her upward gaze.

"I know we'll probably have to go up there and look through his things at some point, but not now," Amanda said. "Let's get down to the village and see who's turned out to see their new countess, the heroine who vanquished the evil sorcerer that tormented them for, geez—hundreds of years—Emmi, you're literally a hero!"

Emilia couldn't help but laugh and playfully nudged her sister as they walked to the main gate.

"Seriously though, what are you going to do?" Amanda asked.

"I really don't know yet", Emilia shrugged, "I feel like I need to make everything right somehow. This is my family's village; who else can do it? And I'm so sorry—please don't hate me," Emilia gripped Amanda's arm, "but we'll probably have to postpone our trip to Paris."

"Oh please, don't even mention it…this is way cooler—and we can go to Paris any time. Especially since you've got your very own castle in Europe now!" Amanda practically squealed. "Have you thought about college, though—and what about Olly and our parents?"

"Yeah…I guess we'll need to go down the mountain or see if there is any way around here to reach Mom and Dad—and Olly. I really miss them." Her stomach fluttered at the mere thought. "Hey, maybe they can come here and spend a little time while we sort this out? I'm going to need all the help I can get! I don't think college will be that big of a deal; I've only got a few credits left and I'm sure something can be worked out. You're in the same boat, right? I don't want to do this without you."

Amanda grinned. "Emmi, you know I'm with you. How many people get to say they have a badass sister with magical powers—and by the way, they own a village and a castle on a mountaintop. Oh, and mines filled with gold!" She stifled a laugh at her own joke and then became more serious. "No matter what, if you need me, I'm here. Plus, this is really a beautiful place when the sun's shining like this. Just don't go turning all evil and crazy or anything. Gotta say, what Gerlinde said was a bit spooky, don't you think?"

"Yeah, kind of." Emilia agreed, but she felt she owed her sister the truth. "I'm not really sure how to describe it, but…I can feel something going on inside me. I don't think it's bad or anything, but it's different for sure."

"I definitely never thought I'd find myself having to deal with this sort of thing, so just talk to me about what's happening with you Emmi.

We can work on finding answers—we'll have to figure out how to reach that Cassius guy Gerlinde talked about, right?"

Emilia appreciated Amanda's determination to work through this new mystical and magical world she'd found herself a part of; a world that had been unimaginable only a few days earlier.

As they turned the final bend into the village, Emilia and Amanda were greeted by a carnival-like atmosphere. It seemed the entire population had gathered at the town square, adults engaged in lively conversation and children playing together while basking in their first experience of sunshine. The mood was charged, and everyone was thrilled to catch a glimpse of Emilia as she strode down the mountain.

When the pair reached the base of the hill, a crowd had formed with many people eager to introduce themselves, thank Emilia for what she'd done, and welcome her to the town. It felt surreal, and Emilia was gracious as they waded through the mass of people.

She suddenly spotted a familiar face coming toward her and smiled in Rose's direction.

"Countess, please, the stairs of the church," she said. "If you climb to the top, everyone will be able to see you."

"Um, all right!" Emilia called over the noise and made her way to the church with Amanda following.

"I'm going to wait down here—you're the one they want to see," Amanda said before giving her a bear-hug at the bottom of the steps. "Go get 'em!"

"And I thought last night was tough. Seems like it was just the beginning—I really can't stand public speaking!" Emilia joked back as she began climbing the stairs.

When she reached the top, Emilia paused. She couldn't imagine anything that could wipe the smile off her face as she looked out at the crowd. They had fallen silent, waiting for her to speak.

"A week ago," she began, "I didn't know who I *really* was or where I had come from. These past few days, I feel like I've lived another whole lifetime and, in the process, discovered myself, this magnificent place, and all of you."

The crowd cheered and called out words of encouragement.

"I have to be honest," Emilia went on. "I don't know what I'm doing when it comes to running a village, or mines—or living in a castle."

The crowd erupted in laughter.

"But while I may need help from many of you to do it, I can promise that I *will* restore my family's legacy here. I will do my best to make right all the wrongs that you have endured. Zillah was once a jewel, and together we can make it shine again!"

The cheers and applause continued, and Emilia looked at Amanda, who was beaming and holding up both thumbs.

Emilia's attention was drawn to a silver SUV doing its best to navigate around the crowds of people, eventually parking to the side of the road before the square. Both front doors opened, and Emilia recognized its occupants immediately.

"Mom? Dad?" She called down to her sister, "Amanda, Mom and Dad are here!" Emilia screeched as she hurriedly descended the stairs and pulled Amanda by the hand in their direction.

The afternoon was spent showing Brian and Pamela around the village. They recounted their extraordinary tale, which the Campbells still couldn't quite believe even as they saw Emilia demonstrate what she'd learned before their eyes. As the day drew to an end, the Campbells were shown to a spacious guestroom at the castle and they made plans to have dinner at Rose and Nicolas' restaurant in the village.

While Amanda and her parents were settling in and freshening up, Emilia slipped quietly away and ventured down the hill. She traveled through the festive village, stopping to meet and chat with villagers as she went, before making her way across the bridge and through the woods.

Emilia could see Gerlinde sitting on a bench outside her cottage. She stared toward the sunset as the fiery orb neared the mountains.

"Countess, what are you doing here?" she asked without looking away.

"I wanted to check on you," Emilia replied. As she came closer, she could tell the cottage was damaged—it appeared to have been ripped apart by a storm. "What happened here?"

"I believe Massimino came here looking for us last night. He must have destroyed my cottage in anger when he didn't find you," Gerlinde sighed. "It is of no consequence now; I will not be needing for anything in there anymore."

Emilia sat down on the bench beside the old woman, wrapping her arm around her.

"I have one favor to ask you, Countess."

"Anything!"

"I would like to be buried on the top of that mountain over there, so I shall always be where the sun sets."

"Yes, of course," Emilia agreed; it was the least she could do. "Absolutely."

Gerlinde rested against Emilia and seemed to relax.

"You must promise me too, that you will seek out someone to help you at the first sign of any trouble."

Her eyebrows drew together. "What sort of trouble?"

"After a ritual such as this, his body may be dead, but a part of him can go on within you. You must be on guard against that, and it will not be easy to do—he was powerful and determined. You may be changed by this in ways we cannot even realize, ways that may not be apparent for some time. I am sorry. My plan was never for things to end this way."

Emilia swallowed hard, knowing deeply what she was hearing to be true. "Please don't apologize. I know your intentions were good."

"This cannot be undone in any event. You will have to seek out a way to balance this within yourself." Gerlinde's breathing was shallow and Emilia wondered if the time was near. "There will likely be many changes ahead for you. Some will be good; others...challenging."

"I can't say I understand, but maybe I'm not supposed to right now."

"You are strong, Countess." Gerlinde looked at her for the first time since she sat, squeezing her hand with cold fingers. "And you come from a noble line. I believe you have what is necessary to turn this into something good. Just remember to keep your guard up."

"Thank you—I will." Emilia smiled warmly and squeezed Gerlinde's hand.

The pair sat in silence until the sun disappeared behind the mountain. As the last glimmer vanished, Emilia felt the old woman take her last breath.

Emilia, Amanda, and their parents settled around a table by the fireplace at the restaurant. After they ordered their meals, Brian pulled a letter from his jacket pocket and slid it across the table toward Emilia. The feel and color of the paper indicated it was old, on the front of the envelope were the handwritten words: 'Brian and Pamela'.

"Emilia, I want you to know that we never, ever wanted to deceive you," her father started.

"We didn't know what to do, honey," her mother added. "We found this letter in your parents' house—we went there after they didn't come back as planned. After that, your father—Brian—came here to Zillah to look for them."

"Wait, you've been here before?" Emilia asked, perplexed.

"Yes, I found your parents, but they were already dead." He stared at the table. "The officials said it was a car accident, but I saw the bodies; it was obvious they had been murdered."

"Yes, I know," Emilia muttered. "I know what really happened."

"I arranged for them to be brought home so they could be buried, and between the way they died and this letter, we didn't want you to be in any danger so we—" Her father didn't continue, instead looking out the window where the villagers were still celebrating.

"We asked Dan to help and together, we made up the story about the car crash and he put together a police report." Pam spoke softly. "We only wanted to protect you—we honestly thought they might hurt you too if you knew about this place, so we kept quiet all these years. We didn't expect that our silence would also put you in danger."

Emilia opened the envelope and read the letter.

> *Brian and Pamela,*
>
> *Anton and I must travel to our homeland, a village called Zillah in Slovakia. We went to great lengths to escape there and it is only because my sister's life is in danger that we are forced to return. There is a chance that we will not come back. If that is the case, you will no doubt find this letter.*
>
> *If you are reading this, I ask that you do whatever you can to keep this knowledge from Emilia. We risked much to ensure she could grow up away from that place and live a normal life, unburdened by the world that exists there. She is special, and dark ones will stop at nothing to draw her in if they find out about her.*
>
> *Please let her know that she is loved more than anything, and please continue to give her that love in the future.*
>
> *Genevieve and Anton.*

Tears welled in Emilia's eyes. After reading it a second time, she folded the letter back up, returned it to the envelope, and placed it on the table.

"I understand completely," she said, voice strained. "You did everything right. I can't thank you enough for taking me in, raising me, and loving me the way that you have." Emilia smiled through the tears at her surrogate parents.

The rest of the evening was much happier as they talked about ways to restore and revitalize the village. Brian and Pamela gladly offered to help and made plans to enlist their connections from various industries to assist in the effort.

As they were preparing to leave the restaurant, Emilia asked Rose if there was a way to contact the outside world from the village. She found herself missing Olly immensely and didn't want to wait to travel down in search of a signal. Rose let her know that Massimino had been the only one who could make phone calls beyond the village, and she believed that he had a phone in his tower.

The group thanked Rose and Nicolas for the delicious meal, and Emilia and Amanda hugged Rose in gratitude for everything else she had done to help them. When they stepped out into the square, the atmosphere was intoxicating. For Emilia, seeing joy and celebration in a place that had been heavy with sadness and fear only a couple of days before was a welcome change.

After Emilia said her goodnights, explaining that she really wanted to speak with Olly and was going to go to the tower to call him, the trek up the hill to the castle felt wonderful. Amanda had been a little wary and offered to go as well, but Emilia assured her that she would be fine and would return soon to sleep.

The light that usually glowed from the windows in the tower was absent for the first time in a long time. As she walked, Emilia gazed over the courtyard, the old buildings shimmering by torchlight, taking on a new beauty as she felt herself relax. Although there was much work to be done, there was no immediate threat or mystery to solve.

Upon reaching the doorway at the base of the tower, Emilia clasped the iron ring with one hand and pushed against the weathered door with the other. There was no lock, just the solid click of the latch as she turned the handle and stared into the dark.

In the doorway, there was an unlit torch protruding from the wall. Emilia searched for some way to light it before she had another idea.

Emilia closed her eyes, visualizing it burning. She saw the unmistakable burst of orange and felt subtle heat as she opened her eyes, shaking her head in wonderment at what she had just done.

Emilia began her way up the creaky stairs, lighting torches with the power of her mind as she went. By the time she reached the top, a playful snap of the fingers was all it took to add glowing firelight along her route.

The room was dimly lit by the pale blue of the moon shining through one of the tall windows. Emilia stepped toward the large stone fireplace, and with a dramatic upward motion of both her arms, ignited the wood before standing back.

Shadows danced on every surface while Emilia wandered around, perplexed by the strange feeling of comfort—of belonging—that the space inspired.

Emilia made her way to the desk and gazed down at the intricacy of the engravings on the surface, touching the highest star with the tip of her finger before tracing the invisible path that connected each star to the next. Emilia glanced at the old-fashioned phone before strolling past the desk to look out the windows.

The sky overhead was clear and the incredible beauty of the moon floating above the mountaintops, its light reflecting off the river below, made Emilia's heart soar with pride. These were her roots; after years of wondering, she had found them. The village was still much more alive than usual, though as it grew later the festivities were winding down. Somehow, Emilia could sense the locals looking up toward the tower, a conditioned fear of the light unexpectedly piercing the darkness once more.

Emilia settled into the plush chair behind the desk and picked up the heavy handset. She commenced the long process of dialing international codes and Oliver's number on the old dial of the rotary phone.

After a few rings, he answered and the two shared a long and at times animated conversation. Oliver wondered if Emilia was playing some sort of trick on him when she shared the story of her travels thus far;

it sounded like a tale of a great adventure at first, though by the end, he was enthralled with what had unfolded. Emilia broke the news that she might need to stay in Zillah for some time and was warmed by Oliver's promise to visit as soon as possible. He also insisted his family's resources were at her disposal to help bring the mines back online and rebuild the village.

They both confessed how much they missed each other and longed to be reunited. The where didn't matter, they just wanted to see each other again. Emilia described the village and couldn't wait to show him the hidden, fascinating world she'd inherited.

After setting the receiver down, Emilia leaned back in the chair. The room now felt hot as the fire continued to burn in the hearth. She removed her sweater and draped it over the armrest. Glancing around, Emilia noticed the collection of books arranged on shelves behind her. She planned to go through Massimino's things over the coming days as she worked to understand and restore the village. For now, she let that go.

Emilia stood, unusually comfortable in the heat. Pulled by an unknown force, she found herself drawn toward the bed. She gently ran her hand along the closest post and examined the intricate carvings as her fingertips traced over them. She contemplated the black satin sheets as memories of her encounters with Massimino flooded her mind. Reaching down, she caressed the soft fabric, which released a familiar tingle and warmth within her.

Just as she thought she should go back to the castle, a gentle breeze played with her hair.

Emilia...our bed. The whispered words washed over her like a puff of air.

The arousal within her grew, suppressing any fear or urge to flee.

With one hand still on the sheets, savoring their texture, Emilia caressed her breasts with the other, her fingers skimming the smooth fabric before slipping beneath her top; a thin silk strap sliding off her shoulder. Closing her eyes, she let go of any will to resist the pleasurable sensations enveloping her.

"Hello? Countess? What...?"

Emilia's eyes sprung open as she spun toward the staircase, immediately recognizing Luna who appeared shocked, her eyes fixed on Emilia.

"I'm sorry. I saw the light coming from the window and came to see if perhaps he was—" Luna was quiet as she came closer. "I, I can feel *him* here. He always had such an effect on me, and I feel it now, as when he would summon me."

Emilia simply nodded, gazing into the fire as if waiting for Massimino to appear. "I don't know how to explain it, but I feel it, too."

Even though there was still distance between them, Emilia could feel Luna; her pulse was racing, heat gathering inside of her and a pang of uncertainty as to how she could settle this need without Massimino. Emilia looked back at Luna, the two women staring sensually at each other's bodies.

"You are looking at me in that way. The same way he did. Are you...?" Luna's voice trembled slightly as she took a few steps toward Emilia.

Moving to the corner of the bed, flames glowed in Emilia's eyes as they remained locked with Luna's. She gripped the bedpost with one hand while tearing away at the delicate silk straps of her top with the other, allowing it to fall to the floor.

"My dear Luna, come to me."

SO, WHAT DID YOU THINK?

A humble request—

I really hope you enjoyed reading *Valley of Secrets*. Reviews are incredibly valuable, especially to independent authors, and I would be most grateful if you could take a few moments to share your thoughts on this book by writing a review. I'd appreciate it so much.

Visit www.amazon.com/author/morganknight to get started.

KEEP IN TOUCH

Where will *The Last Heiress'* journey take her next?

Secrets will continue to unravel, more power will be unleashed, and new, darker passions will be ignited.

Sign up to receive the latest updates about *The Last Heiress* series—and you'll be sure to never miss a moment.

Visit www.morganknightauthor.com today!

Facebook @morganknightauthor | **Twitter** @mknightauthor
Instagram morganknightauthor

COMING SOON

The Last Heiress Series

Book 2 - The Demon Within

As Emilia struggles with the ramifications of the ritual, and works to understand her powers, she is unaware that other unknown forces are out to destroy her. When a handsome visitor arrives in Zillah, Emilia is immediately drawn to him as he educates her about the world of sorcery she's found herself caught up in—but can he be trusted?

ABOUT THE AUTHOR

Morgan Knight is a reformed techie who discovered a passion for writing a little later in life. Morgan loves being entertained and enthralled by words and ideas that spark the imagination, and transport readers to other worlds.

These days you'll be hard-pressed to find Morgan without an e-reader close by. Hiking, sailing, taking long walks—especially by the sea, listening to music, tackling 1000-piece puzzles, savoring velvety red wines and devouring anything smothered in Buffalo Sauce are among Morgan's favorite guilty pleasures.

Morgan confesses to having developed a serious case of the travel bug. Visiting authentic, old, and romantic places around the world helps Morgan draw inspiration for writing novels.

Morgan Knight is married with two children and lives in sunny Queensland, Australia.

www.MorganKnightAuthor.com

CPSIA information can be obtained
at www.ICGtesting.com
Printed in the USA
LVHW031143250121
677402LV00022B/740/J